# SOMETHING FISHY

"You said you would wear the bodice!"

"I'm playing a mermaid! It looked unnatural."

"But we agreed—"

Konstanze shrugged. "What use was it? They would have thought they were seeing my real chest whether I wore the bodice or not."

"But I knew the truth, and you couldn't have known I wouldn't." He knelt down beside her, a new suspicion forming. "Or did you mean for me to?"

"For God's sake, Tom, you think awfully high of yourself! I thought I was too far away to be seen, that's all there is to it. The bodice drags against the water. I wanted to see how fast I could swim without the fins. It had nothing to do with you!"

Her words were fierce, but her throat and cheeks were red with embarrassment. "You swam along this entire section of coast on your back," he said. "Wherever we were, you must have known I would see and know you weren't wearing the bodice."

She met his eyes, glaring. "I wasn't thinking of that. I was enjoying myself, that's all."

"That's not all," he said softly, some instinct telling him that she was bending the truth, that she *had* been aware he would see her and know the difference. "If you want my attention, you don't have to put yourself on display to get it."

"You're insufferable!"

"And you're a bad liar." He touched her cheek with his fingertips. She held still as he trailed them down to her lips, lightly brushing their full curves. They parted and then her wide eyes met his, uncertainty and hunger in their depths. He felt the gentle warmth of her breath on his skin, and she leaned toward him. He pulled her into his arms and kissed her.

# the Mermaid of Penperro

# LISA CACH

LOVE SPELL  NEW YORK CITY

A LOVE SPELL BOOK®

April 2001

Published by

Dorchester Publishing Co., Inc.
276 Fifth Avenue
New York, NY 10001

ISBN 0-505-52437-6

The name "Love Spell" and its logo are trademarks of Dorchester Publishing Co., Inc.

Printed in the United States of America.

Visit us on the web at www.dorchesterpub.com.

*To Aunt Eva,*
*who always swam with us to Big Rock*

# the Mermaid of Penperro

# Chapter One

"Konstanze, my darling, I have something new for us to try," Bugg whispered heavily into her ear, and laid a book in her lap. Her elderly husband was standing behind her, bending low over her shoulder as she sat on the sofa in her sitting room, a coal fire burning in the grate before her. His whisper carried the stench of rotting teeth and brandy. His clothes smelled of tobacco, stale sweat, and sour hints of urine. A shudder ran across her shoulders and up her neck.

She reluctantly opened the front cover of the book, finding the name of Edmund Quarles inscribed there in a shaky hand. Mr. Quarles was a good friend of her husband—perhaps his only friend—as well as his solicitor. The two of them had been drinking and con-

11

spiring for hours, huddled together in the dark, dreary drawing room downstairs.

"I was wondering what the two of you had been discussing," Konstanze lied, wishing he had stayed downstairs with Quarles and left her alone with her private thoughts. She had been busy imagining herself a princess on a South Sea island, her dark red-brown hair dressed in fragrant tropical flowers, her body clad in a wrap of bright cloth. In her daydream she lived in a palace made of palm, the dried fronds rustling in the warm breeze as she sat and looked out over the turquoise water. Dark, half-naked men knelt at her feet, offering pink and yellow fruit from wooden platters. . . .

"Look inside," Bugg urged.

She gave a little sigh and fanned the pages of the book, then stopped at the first illustration, her attention suddenly focusing. A woman lay on her side on a bed, her hands and feet trussed, her chemise pulled up to expose her naked thighs and hips. Her face wore what was supposed to be an expression of fear and distress, but looked rather more like a bad case of colic. Behind her a dark-faced man with bulging eyes, fully clothed including wig and tricorn hat, had his arm pulled back and ready to strike, a bundle of twigs clenched in his fist.

Bugg's breathing grew heavy in her ear, his warm, foul breath moistening her skin. "The idea stirs me," he said. "Does it stir you, Konstanze? Does it heat your blood as it does mine?"

Surely he could not be serious? She turned to the next picture, this one of the same bound, naked woman crouching down, her bare buttocks in the air. The dark-faced man leered, a cat-o'-nine-tails dangling from his grip.

"I have a riding crop I can use," her husband said, his voice shaking with excitement.

"John, I do not think I wish to try this," she said quietly.

"Are you frightened?" he asked, his eagerness showing.

"I do not wish to be bound and beaten."

" 'Tis only a game. 'Tis only play." He reached down her chest, cupping her breast in his palm, then pinching the nipple, hard, between his fingers.

"John, stop it!" she protested, and shoved his hand away.

"Are you excited?"

"No!"

There was a moment of tense silence; then she felt the sudden change in his mood. "You could try it once, to please me," he said, his tone going harsh, and suddenly he wrapped his arm around her neck, his elbow beneath her chin, painfully jerking her head up. "For me, Konstanze, darling?" he said into her ear. "Your dear husband? You can do that much, I am thinking, for the man who saved your tender young self from the poorhouse."

She held perfectly still, her eyes wide, her breath coming in shallow gasps. John Bugg's fits of rage came only rarely, and only when he had been drinking, but he was dangerous while he was in one. It had been many months since his last fit, but at that time he had shoved her against a wall, pinning her there with his hands around her throat. She had been frightened he would choke the life from her, but he had released her without doing further harm. She had wondered since if the next time she would escape so lightly.

"I want you to go into our room and disrobe down to your chemise. I want you to let down your lovely hair. I want you to find me something from which to make bindings for your pretty hands and feet. I'll fetch the crop myself, my darling. I will do that much for you," he said, and stuck his tongue in her ear.

Konstanze squeezed shut her eyes and nodded against the arm around her throat.

"No, not like that! Stupid girl, can't you do anything right?" Bugg complained, and swung his riding crop at her.

"I'm trying my best," Konstanze protested even as she rolled away from the crop, its leather tip striking the coverlet instead of her thigh. He was too drunk to match her reflexes, and she could not control the instinct to avoid his blows. Her hands were tied together in a strip of linen attached to the bedstead, although so poorly knotted that she could have released them with a few twists of her wrists. Her fear of him had been subsumed by a horrid sense of humiliation at being trussed naked to the bed, like a disobedient animal, and part of her watched as if from a distance as she shamed herself further by trying to accede to his wishes.

"You're supposed to hold still!"

"It's very difficult, John." She'd like to see *him* hold still for the crop!

14

"And you're supposed to moan."

"Ohhhh . . ." she tried, thinking of the illustration of the woman with colic. She pulled from memory the last time she had suffered severe indigestion, after eating a meat pie that had gone bad. "Ohhhh . . ."

"Wait until I hit you! You can't moan just lying there unharmed. What's the point?"

"I'm sorry. I'll try to wait until the proper moment."

"Stick out your rump, like in the picture."

She rolled to her side, pulling her knees up and arching her back. The bedroom air was cold on her buttocks, and for an absurd moment she felt like a toddler about to have her bum wiped.

The whistle of the crop through the air came again, and again she avoided its bite, pulling in her buttocks just before the leather would have struck her.

"God damn you, Konstanze!" Bugg lifted the crop again and again, but each time she heard the whistle and moved out of the way.

"Ohhh, ohhhhhh," she moaned, in the hope that perhaps he might think he had struck her. "Ohhh." She pictured moldy bread on her plate, waiting to be eaten. Bruised and rotten pears. Meat gone gray, with an iridescent sheen of green.

"Just . . . hold . . . still . . ." Bugg ground out, his breath coming in pants now as he kept swinging.

"Ohhhh . . ."

Suddenly Bugg was on the bed and on top of her, pulling at her hands until they came free of the linen strip; then he took her by the arm and dragged her off.

"John, I'm sorry! I'm trying my best!"

"Do I have to show you how to do everything?" He

15

slapped the handle of the crop into her hand, then flung himself facedown onto the mattress, his legs hanging off the side.

Konstanze frowned at the crop in her hand, then at her husband's bare and hairy buttocks with their loose, grayish white skin. He looked like a plucked goose.

"Hit me!"

"Who, me?"

"Do you see anyone else? You think I want Quarles to come do it?"

"I can't strike you," she said.

"You can and you will. I'm showing you how this is done."

She stood barefoot and naked, her hair around her shoulders and brushing the small of her back. For a moment she felt fragile and exposed, her flesh sensitive to the drafts of the room, to the worn carpet beneath her soles.

She looked at Bugg. The crop felt firm and warm in her hand. His buttocks awaited.

"Why are you taking so long? Brainless girl, I should have left you to the Paris whorehouses, although even they wouldn't want the likes of you. Can't do the simplest thing—"

Her fist tightened on the handle of the crop, and a bitter stream of long-suppressed anger seeped up from within her heart. With a rage and a strength she had not known she possessed, she pulled back her arm and whipped the crop against that plucked goose's butt.

Bugg screamed.

The crop whistled again and again as Bugg struggled to escape its strokes, obscenities pouring from his mouth. She got him on the back, on the thigh, and when he turned around she got him right across the groin. She couldn't stop herself, even as she saw the fury in his eyes. He shouted at her, but she could not hear the words, her own senses overwhelmed by the thrill of the crop in her hand. With each stroke she felt her breasts jiggle, her buttocks jolt, and each movement was a confirmation of her physicality, of the power of her own body. She was Boadicea, barebreasted warrior queen of Britain! She was mighty, and she would destroy the enemy!

"On your knees, dog!" she ordered, whacking him across the crown of his liver-spotted head. The blow caught him off balance, and he fell off the edge of the bed to all fours on the carpet. Possessed by the madness of power, she swung a leg over his back and sat astride him, and with the crop gave him a hard smack on his haunches. "Trot, dog!" She gripped a fistful of his hair, jerking hard, and gave him another whack on the rump with the crop.

Bugg roared in fury and threw her off to the side, pinning her leg beneath him and then using his superior weight to keep her on the floor as he crawled atop her. He wrenched the crop from her hand, and Konstanze felt her power drain away with it, the spirit of Boadicea fading into the air. She looked up into the eyes of her husband, and knew fear beyond anything she had felt before. What she had just inflicted upon him would be nothing compared to what he was about to do to her.

\* . \* . \*

17

She lay on her belly, naked, her tears long since stopped, her eyes staring at the candle that burned low on the bedstand. The odious Bugg snored beside her on the mattress, each breath an insult, a reminder that she belonged to the vile creature. There was a hot, tight ball of emotion in her chest that made it difficult to breathe. It was grief and rage, coming together to coat her heart in black hatred for her husband.

She had been married to John Bugg for two years, since her mother, an opera singer in Paris, begged on her deathbed that Konstanze marry the man and secure for herself a stable, respectable future. Bugg had been paying their bills for two months by then, and had seemed a generous, gentle man, thoroughly devoted to her. Becoming his wife and returning to England had seemed preferable to being penniless on the streets of Paris, especially as the war with England showed every sign of starting up again.

Bugg's demeanor had changed, though, almost as soon as her mother was buried and his ring was upon Konstanze's finger. He had gone from the generous, well-groomed, avuncular man she had first known to the filthy, drunken, controlling beast in bed with her now.

She didn't know why he had changed, but the first inkling of trouble had come on their wedding night. Something had gone wrong, although she did not know precisely what. Bugg had put his hands all over her, grunting and muttering words she could not understand as he rubbed his hips up against her loins and her buttocks. For painful minutes he'd shoved his hand between her legs and handled her roughly, hurting her in places she hadn't known she could be hurt. She had bitten her lip and shut her eyes, tears leaking out the sides, and waited for it all to be over.

And then he had stopped, cursing, flinging the sheet over her and leaving their bedroom. He had returned only when thoroughly drunk, and promptly fallen asleep while she lay awake beside him, empty and confused, feeling a failure as a wife. She had expected no pleasure from their joining, and had received none. She had thought, though, that the man was supposed to derive some manner of enjoyment from the encounter, and it did not look as if her husband had done so. Neither was she at all certain just what part of his activity had constituted the consummation of their marriage, although she had the throbbing remnants of pain to confirm that she was virgin no longer.

She had felt a faint stirring resentment toward her mother. The woman had been so obsessed with protecting Konstanze from all that was unladylike that she had never discussed what went on in the marriage bed. She had rushed Konstanze away when any of her theater friends began to gossip on the topic, and Konstanze herself, sensing her mother's wishes, had refrained from asking questions despite her natural curiosity.

The morning after the disastrous wedding night she had gathered her courage and asked Bugg if she had displeased him somehow, if in her ignorance she had done something wrong. He told her to shut her mouth.

She had not asked again.

The candle on the bedstand guttered and went out. Konstanze was cold but did not pull the sheet over herself, for the discomfort fit her mood. The chill on her flesh seemed one more thing for which she could blame Bugg. He could at least have covered her when he was finished. He would be sorry if she perished of a lung disease, for he would never be so fortunate as to fool another young woman into becoming his wife. She imagined his weeping distress as she lay in bed, her skin translucent with approaching death, her gray eyes sunken into purple shadows.

She wrinkled her nose and switched the image from herself to Bugg lying in the sickbed, his face turned skeletal from wasting illness, raw red sores on his skin. Much better. She would nurse him as if a devoted wife, bathing his forehead with a damp cloth while subdued visitors whispered in awe of her saintlike patience and goodness. She would sing soothing melodies to her dying husband, and a handsome young man come to pay his respects would stand in the hall and listen, unwilling to interrupt her angelic song.

Bugg snorted and rolled onto his side, then held his breath for a moment. She winced, knowing what was coming. A moment later he broke wind and breathed out a sigh of contentment. The man was as revolting as a hog, and just as healthy.

Two years of marriage played through her mind. The first year was a blur of grief as she mourned for her mother, paying little attention to the state of her marriage. After that, the memories were mostly of her feelings of revulsion for and a growing fear of her husband—and of his son, John Bugg II, who when he was at home leered and panted after her, varying his amorous attentions only with spiteful remarks that came from his jealousy of her position in his father's heart. She supposed Bugg II was afraid that his father would spend his fortune on her. He needn't have worried. The old man, now that he had Konstanze, was as possessive of his coin as he was of her person.

When the emotions of grief and revulsion had not been present, there was nothing of the two years to remember. She had passed her time in daydreams, creating worlds of her own in which to escape, much as she had when she'd been younger and unhappy, with no way to alter her circumstances. She had not even the heart to sing, which had once been the joy of her life. She did so now only when Bugg demanded a performance.

In their bed at night, Bugg's attentions had come with less and less frequency, and it had grown increasingly easy to ignore her husband's fumbling hands and muttered curses. She had closed her eyes and imagined she was on a ship bound for India, the waves slapping at the hull, or that she was onstage in Vienna, singing for the nobility as her mother once had.

For two years she had been all but absent from her life, living in her head except for those too-real moments of fear and revulsion.

This was not how Mama would have wanted her to live, and it had not been her intention in asking Konstanze to marry Bugg. And this was not how she, Konstanze, wanted to live. She was twenty-four years old, and her life was slipping through her fingers, pouring away for the pleasure of a dirty old man with a mean heart. Konstanze did not like what she was becoming, and she did not want to live a life of hatred and violence such as she had experienced tonight.

She slid off the bed and drew her wrapper around her chilled body, cautious of the welts Bugg's crop had raised on her skin. She lit a fresh candle from the embers in the hearth and slipped into her sitting room, easing the door shut behind her.

In the drawer of her secretary, hidden beneath the blank stationery, she found the key and deed to the cottage in Cornwall, secreted there months ago, and examined repeatedly. The solicitor who'd delivered them, Mr. Rumbelow, had by chance come to the house when Bugg was out of town on business. He'd said it had taken a hired agent over a year and a half to track her down as the last surviving heir of Robert Penrose, her maternal great-uncle. That she had been tracked down at all was owing only to the perseverance of the will's executor, a Mr. Thomas Trewella of Penperro, Cornwall.

Penperro was the small fishing village near which her great-uncle had lived. Konstanze had spent the first ten years of her life living with her grandparents in Mousehole, Cornwall, and remembered visiting her great-uncle on two occasions only. Both times they had gone by sea, for Cornwall was inaccessible by land, the roads few and rough and aswarm with highway robbers. People here in "civilized" Kent thought Cornwall to be the end of the earth, nearly as remote as the jungles of deepest, darkest Africa.

It was that very inaccessibility that interested her now. Bugg knew nothing of her Cornish ancestors, and had known both her mother and her only by the name of her deceased French father, Crécy. She could slip away to Cornwall and take up residence in this cottage, and if she were careful—very, very careful—perhaps he would be unable to track her down and haul her back to Bugg House.

The idea of running away had been with her since the solicitor's visit, but fear had held her back. With Bugg, foul as he might be, she had security. She had lived and traveled with her mother for six years, more than long enough to know how precarious was the life of a single woman who had only herself upon whom to rely, even a woman with her mother's talent. A woman could not blithely sally forth into the world as could a man, confident of finding work and of being able to preserve his physical safety. Konstanze knew she often had her head in the clouds, but she was not ignorant of practicalities, or of the dangers of leaving Bugg's protection.

She forced herself to remember Bugg sitting atop of her on the floor, beating her with the crop, his breathing growing loud and heavy with excitement.

There came a time when the dangers of the unknown were preferable to the miseries of the familiar. She would not give John Bugg one more year of her life.

# Chapter Two

*Near Penperro, Cornwall*

"Look at it, Hilde! Just look at it! It's perfect," Konstanze said to her middle-aged maid as the driver of the wagon pulled to a stop in front of a gray stone cottage. It was a stark rectangle on the slope of a bare green hill, with no landscaping to soften its features. The only ornamentation was a small porch, no more than a foot deep, whose thin walls were formed of gnarled sticks of driftwood fitted close together.

*"Wunderbar,"* Hilde grumped. "It looks cold," she said in German, her native language. She had been lady's maid to Konstanze's mother Mary—or Marguerite, as she'd called herself—all through her years on the stages of Europe, beginning with her first performance in Vienna. Hilde knew a little English, enough to shop and to tell other servants what to do,

but otherwise she stuck stubbornly to German.

"I know it is not much compared to Bugg House," Konstanze replied in German, "but it has its advantages."

"*Nicht* Buggs."

"A fine feature indeed, you must agree."

As the driver unloaded their trunks, Konstanze took out a heavy iron key and went up the two stone steps to the pale blue front door, pausing to touch the driftwood of the porch. She remembered studying it as a little girl. She had no other real memories of the house, and only brief flashes of her great-uncle that could have been as much imagined as recalled.

The key worked easily in the lock, and the door swung open on the sitting room with its whitewashed walls and wooden floors. The dark, warped beams of the low ceiling came to within a few inches of the top of her head in places, making her glad that she was not a tall woman. A massive stone hearth dominated the end wall, and beside it a tiny staircase led to the upper floor.

Bright Cornish sunlight shone in as well as it could from the small, deep-set windows. The furniture, such as there was, was covered in dust sheets. At the far end of the wall on her right a doorway opened into the kitchen. It was a mirror image of the sitting room, including staircase, only in here the covered shapes suggested cupboards, a worktable, and the tools of cooking. There was also a door, leading out back to a yard and outbuildings.

She caught the musty smell of mice, and spiders had made free use of beams and corners, but other than that the cottage looked to be in good condition, with no water stains upon the walls or around the windows. Someone had taken care to shut up the house after her great-uncle had died, and she supposed she had the executor, Thomas Trewella, to thank for that. She would have to speak with him soon, for he and his solicitor and hired agent were the only links between Cornwall, herself, and Bugg, and given her own evidence of his diligence in his duties as executor, she assumed he would soon be asking questions about the new tenant at the cottage. She didn't want him sending those questions to Kent, to Bugg.

She climbed the narrow, creaky kitchen stairs to the room above, with its pitched ceilings painted white and its small bed. There was a faint scent of decay, and she found the dried remains of a small bird beneath one of the windows. Likely it had flown down a chimney and been unable to find its way out. A narrow doorway, devoid of door, led into the other bedroom. As below, there were no signs of water damage, which put to rest any concern about leaky roofs. The wood floor was dark with age and severely warped—a ball would have rolled a strange, irregular path across its surface—but it felt solid beneath her feet, its planks still tight together for all that each footstep drew forth a different note from the squeaking timber.

She went to one of the casement windows and swung out the sash, fastening the metal latch upon the peg that would hold it open against the wind. She rested her forearms on the deep sill and leaned outside. Hilde was below, issuing gruff orders to the wagoner,

Mr. Mogridge, as he dragged their trunks inside. He appeared to be ignoring Hilde, though Konstanze caught one fiery glare of annoyance he shot at the maid.

Konstanze turned her face into the breeze, catching its damp saltiness tinged with the scent of green growing things. She knew that the coastline was only a few minutes' walk away, just around the shelter of the hill, and yet she could not hear the surf. She closed her eyes, the sunlight red through her lids, goose pimples from the breeze on her arms even as the sun warmed her skin.

She had been forced to stay with Bugg for only three more days after his experiment with the riding crop. The moment he left town to attend to business, she and Hilde had set to work packing, both her own belongings and any portable wealth upon which she could lay her hands. There was precious little.

In a perfect world she could have left Bugg with only her own meager possessions from before her engagement, counting on pride and a noble heart to carry her through. Her lack of funds coupled with memories of her final, increasingly hungry years with Mama, however, argued for taking the silverware, the coffee service, a hideous ormolu clock, and every scrap of jewelry in the house. She had pawned the lot in London, feeling like a thief as she did so. She was the lady of the house, and pawning the silver should have been her option, but however much she rationalized her actions she still felt guilty shame for taking the items. She knew, though, that Bugg's anger when he discovered the missing things would be only a dribble in comparison to the deluge of fury that would come when he discovered her absence.

She was glad she would not be there to see it. He had always been jealous of her company, keeping her all but caged up at home, needing to know where she was at every moment, making her swear to stay in when business called him away. Like a sheep she had agreed, counting her obedience as the cost of security.

The placid sheep, pushed too far, had finally bolted. It would do what it must to avoid both the wolves and recapture. She smiled at the image of a sly sheep, creeping along ditches and peering over hedges for signs of danger, its eyes narrowed in cunning wariness.

She opened her eyes and looked out upon the beautiful, bare Cornish landscape, not a Bugg in sight.

For two years her heart had been bound tight and buried under a rock, and the moment she had decided to leave Bugg she had begun to lift that rock away. For the first time in almost two years she felt the urge to sing stir within her. She heard in her head the three opening chords to one of her favorite pieces by Mozart, the fortepiano notes sounding as clear to her as if the instrument were in the room behind her. She opened her mouth and her throat to song.

*"Ridente la calma*
*Nell' alma si desti,*
*Nell' alma si desti,*
*Ne resti un segno*
*Di sdegno e timor."*

Smiling peace
Awake in my soul

Let no trace remain
Of anger or fear.

The song felt as if it came from the depths of her
heart, both a prayer and a thanksgiving. The high, pure
tones vibrated the bones of her face, the highest notes
seeming almost to come from somewhere above and
behind her, issuing forth into the bright, clear air. She
repeated the gentle, simple verse again and again, the
music filling her soul and her senses, leaving no room
for Bugg or misery or regret.

When at last she sang the final note, and heard in
her head the fortepiano's finish, she looked down and
saw that Mr. Mogridge was staring up at her with his
mouth agape. She felt a flush of mixed pride and embarrassment. Hilde was standing beside him, her lips
pressed tight together, her eyes blinking rapidly. "It
has been long since you have sung," the maid said
gruffly in German.

"Too long," Konstanze said.

"*Ja.*"

"They'll like you at Talland Church, Miss Penrose,"
Mr. Mogridge said. He had told them he worked a
farm a few miles outside of Penperro. "They're proud
of their singing in Penperro, like any good Cornish
folk, but they don't a one of them lay a finger on what
you can do."

"Thank you," Konstanze said, enjoying the compliment, but then she remembered that she should not be
drawing undue attention to herself, and felt a twinge
of unease. She and Hilde had changed transportation
three times since Exeter, in hopes of further confusing

any trail she might have left for Bugg to follow. She had taken her great-uncle's name, Penrose, and referred to herself as Constance rather than the more exotic Konstanze.

There seemed no way in which Bugg could follow them here, and while news of new residents might excite local curiosity and gossip, there should be no reason for tales of Constance Penrose and her foreign maid to find their way to Bugg. Still, that did not mean she ought to be making a spectacle of herself. It seemed wise to maintain some element of reserve.

*Penperro Harbor*

"The man is becoming a pest," Tom Trewella complained to his good friend Matthew Jobson, the vicar of Talland Church. They were standing on the low bridge over the stream that flowed into the small, narrow harbor, watching Robert Foweather as he directed his fellow Preventive officers in maintenance work on their boat.

"He hasn't the wit to track a cow through the mud. He's easily enough evaded," Matt countered. He was in his early forties, but looked much older due to his wild head of pure-white hair. They watched as Foweather laid his hand down upon freshly varnished wood. He pulled his palm quickly off and wiped it on his blue jacket, permanently marring the wool.

"He may have the brain of a jellyfish, but he's tenacious," Tom said. "He's going to find all our caves sooner or later." Just last week the man had stumbled upon a favorite hiding place of the local smugglers. The caves were used for quickly storing smuggled goods unloaded off fishing boats or privateers in the dark of night. The goods would wait there until they could be safely hauled inland, to barns or cellars, and thence sold to private citizens or to those who would haul the goods even farther inland to be sold.

Foweather and his seven-man crew had arrived two months ago. They were members of the newly formed Preventive Water Guard Service, and had been permanently stationed to Penperro. According to Foweather, king and country had had enough of Cornish smuggling, by God, and he was here to see that the Crown got its rightful due. They were at war with France! The king needed his taxes!

The folk of Penperro had not been sympathetic to this patriotic cry, although they had been a bit more amenable to one of the Preventive Service's other purposes, which was to help preserve life in the event of shipwreck. It was perhaps only that fact that kept the crew from encountering real trouble.

"Hallo there, Mr. Trewella!" Foweather called from the boat, spotting them and waving happily. He was a tall man with fine bones padded with a layer of fat that made him look clumsy and childish. His dishwater blond hair was white at the ends from sun and salt, his nose and plump cheeks were permanently red, and he had the deep creases around his eyes of a man who spent much of his time squinting against the glare of sun off the water. He trotted across the gangplank to the pier, daintily picked his way through the fish piled in front of the packing house, then came up to join them on the bridge.

"I'm almost getting used to the smell of fish!" he

declared. "I never thought I'd say that." Foweather had erroneously fastened onto the notion that Tom was his friend, and a man he could trust in his efforts to rid the Cornish coast of the scourge of smuggling, by God!

"Still no luck with finding lodging in town?" Tom asked. The entire Preventive crew had been forced to live on a confiscated, derelict smuggling sloop hauled in from Fowey, as no one in Penperro would rent them rooms. He felt a curious mix of pity, fondness, and annoyance for Foweather. By profession the man was his enemy, and yet he was too simple and innocent a being for Tom to hate him, or to even wish him harm. He was a pest and a problem, but like a shoe-chewing puppy, one could not in good conscience do him a serious injury.

"There is the most damnable shortage of housing in this town that I have ever come across. We did get an offer to use a storage room in the Old Pallace," he said, nodding over his shoulder at the packing house, "but it smells worse in there than out here. If I didn't know better, I'd almost think no one wanted to rent to us."

"Surely that cannot be the case," Tom said, trying to look astonished. He would not endanger Foweather, but that sure as hell didn't mean he couldn't take out his frustrations in other ways, like a bit of too-subtle ribbing. "I know that the folk of Penperro care deeply about the welfare of the men sent to us on the king's business."

"There are prayers in your name said nightly," Matt

concurred. Tom knew the prayers might not be favorable, but they were prayers nonetheless.

"Truly?" Foweather asked, his face brightening. "I had started to worry that they might be more against us than for us. Some of my men say that you Cornish don't consider yourself part of England, and see us English as invaders, set on squeezing you dry of every last penny."

"Nonsense!" Tom declared. "Why, my great-grandmother was English. That makes us nearly brothers."

"Quite right! Quite right!" Foweather said, cheerily clapping Tom on the back. "Brothers with one goal in common: ridding the Cornish shores of the scourge of smuggling, by God!"

"By God!" Tom and Matt both agreed.

Foweather's chest puffed up, and he gazed with pride for some moments at his boat. Then, abruptly, he turned to Tom and Jobson. "I say, do you know where my men and I can get a decent meal? Mrs. Popple at the Fishing Moon has served us rancid meat nigh on a dozen times now."

"Shameful," Matt said, shaking his white head and staring at the ground, lips pursed in disapproval.

" 'Tis a miracle she and her husband stay in business at all, serving food like that," Foweather said.

"Wiggett does decent pasties," Tom said, referring to the baker whose shop was up the narrow lane behind them. "Other than that, though, I'm afraid there are not many options."

"Wiggett's pasties it is, then. My thanks to you."

"Anything you need, just let me know."

33

"Right! Best I get back to the boat, else my crew will shirk their duties." He seemed reluctant to go, but when neither Tom nor Matt said anything more he uttered another "Right!" and trotted back to his boat.

Tom and Matt watched him reboard. "How did he manage to live into adulthood?" Tom wondered aloud.

"God protects fools and children," Matt answered. "Do you need any further proof of His existence?"

After a few more words they parted ways themselves. Tom stepped off the bridge and turned right, up the lane on the west side of the stream. The stream itself was blocked from view by the houses and shops that pressed up against it, their foundations making up the banks of the narrow waterway. Penperro was situated in the bottom of a rocky cleft, and those houses and shops not at the bottom or surrounding the harbor were forced to cling to the steep slopes above. Narrow stone stairways had been hewn out of the rock, winding between and behind the houses.

Tom's house was one of those clinging to the steep side, some ways up the stream from the harbor. Its stone walls were covered in gray slate shingles as protection against the sea air, the window sashes painted a vivid ultramarine. His housekeeper had insisted on having flower boxes on the low wall in front of the house, which now spilled a profusion of orange and yellow nasturtiums. The public stairs passed below this floral bounty and then continued behind his neighbor's house, and thence to the path that led to the rough shoreline. The flagstoned yard before his front door was only two feet wide, and used only by visitors.

Tom went in through the kitchen door in back, sniffing appreciatively at the odors of cooking that met his nose. He went to the hearth and found the Dutch oven, its open face turned to the flames, a chicken roasting within. Further investigation revealed a bubbling pot of mushy peas—his favorite—as well as boiled potatoes and a sweet pudding with dried apples and nuts.

Mrs. Toley, his housekeeper, appeared suddenly from the pantry with a chunk of cheese in her hand, making him start. She was a painfully thin, intense woman in her late forties, widowed eight years ago when her husband, a fisherman, was lost at sea. She had never had children. "Dinner will be ready shortly. Can I get you something to hold you over? I could heat the fish stew from yesterday. There's a beef pie and biscuits, as well."

"No, thank you, I'll wait," he said, moving away from the open range, feeling the dread of a child caught in a misdeed, and the same desperate need to escape. He knew what was coming.

"Cheese? You could have cheese, and I bought some Spanish oranges today—"

"No, Mrs. Toley, please, I'll save my appetite for dinner—"

"The peas are ready; you could have those now—"

"I'll eat in half an hour," Tom said, panicky, holding up his hands palms out as if he could hold her back as she approached, her face blank while she pursued inner visions of culinary possibility, no doubt picturing him seated at a table mounded with food, eating for hours on end. He began backing out of the kitchen, pushing against the door with his shoulder blades.

"Or there's a nice bread pudding with currants I was saving for your supper tonight, although you'd have to do without the custard sauce, but cream would do nicely—"

He escaped into the hallway and dashed into his office at the front of the house, slamming the door behind him and barely stopping himself from wedging a chair under its handle as final protection. Mrs. Toley would stuff him from daybreak to midnight if he let her. At the end of her first month in his employ he'd had only one pair of old breeches that still fit, and he'd had to restrict his food severely for several months afterward to return to his regular size. There was something unbalanced in her obsession with feeding him, as if somehow the other losses in her life could be made up for by pouring gravies down his throat.

He slid into his heavy oak desk chair and tried to calm his beating heart, the oversize mass of the desk sitting before him with all its pigeonholes, drawers, slots, and trays, its papers and account books and correspondence. He always did his best thinking here, where the organization of his desk provided a model of mental order to the hundreds of thoughts and concerns flashing through his mind.

His eye lit on the Failes family ledger. Jeremy Failes was a minor baronet, and the owner of a vast estate. Tom had been put in charge of that family's accounts, and he had, he hoped, saved it from bankruptcy. In the next week he should pay the children's boarding school fees.

His eyes flitted to the ten-pound note sitting atop a stack of papers, a note that he had issued himself against his own bank. Within the month he would have to have more of them printed. His private bank was doing well, the farmers and fisherfolk of Penperro taking his advice to save what money they could in hopes of buying the land beneath their rented homes if the opportunity arose.

On a shelf near his desk were the ledger books where he kept track of his seagoing barges, which sailed from Plymouth. He dealt in coal, linen, seed, corn, pilchards, and timber, his barges traveling to the coasts of Ireland and, when breaks in the war with France allowed, Italy. There had been no such breaks for a year now, and the fishermen of Penperro suffered for the lack of the Italian market.

And then as well there were the books for the smugglers.

He himself did not sail a smuggler's craft, although he invested in several, and in their trade. His true role in the smuggling was that of manager and, to some extent, caretaker. When a local smuggler landed in jail, Tom hired a lawyer and sent money. When a Guernsey trader doubted a smuggler's trustworthiness, Tom vouched for him. When smuggled goods were sold, Tom forwarded the money to those awaiting their share. He hired horses and workers to come down to the beach caves and haul goods inland in the dead of night. He arranged for safe hiding places in the town and countryside. He found buyers for the goods.

Many of the smuggling details remained in his head alone, never set to paper. He enjoyed organizing and planning, and balancing hundreds of pieces of information at once. The risks and challenges of his work made him feel alive, and knowing that others benefited from his efforts gave his work a sense of meaning.

Apparently he had been a little too good at his work with the smugglers, though, if it had brought the Preventive Water Guard to their harbor. There had been revenue men in Penperro since the beginning of the fifteenth century, but they had always been men like the present agent, Edward Stephens, who was happy to take the king's taxes from the goods brought through town in daylight, and leave the nighttime goods to the locals. In this way Stephens secured for himself both a cellar filled with brandy and the high regard of his neighbors.

It was a great pity that Foweather could not be so easily persuaded. Attempts at bribery had been made, subtly at first, then with increasing boldness as it became apparent then he was oblivious to innuendo. Matt had even made the man a blunt offer, although it was unclear if Foweather realized the vicar was not speaking hypothetically. In any case, Foweather had made it plain that he did not simply earn a living as an officer in the Preventive Water Guard Service: he *was* the Guard, a living embodiment of all for which it stood.

The man had all the wit of a dead pilchard, but that very dullness allowed him to pursue his ends with a methodicalness that would drive a more intelligent person insane. One of his superiors had apparently told him to search out the caves the smugglers used. When they were not out in their sloop patrolling the waters, that was what he and his men did. Inch by inch of coastline, they searched and scrambled and pried. When they had covered every rock and shadowed indentation and wave-echoing crevice within their range, they started over.

Fortunately for the people of Penperro, Foweather's men grew more easily bored than he, and had begun to show a greater interest in local women and drink than in seaweed-slimed caves. He could almost feel sorry for the men, as Penperro's young women met their advances with stony glares and curled lips. No girl would dare bring a Preventive man home to her family. The rebellion of youth was one thing, but the girls relied on the smuggling trade for many of their own creature comforts.

Even if Foweather did manage to find all the caves and the half-hidden coves where the smugglers landed, he could not patrol them at all hours, and he would run himself ragged if he tried to search them every day. The thought was a small consolation. All the smugglers really needed to keep themselves out of jail was a way in which to predict or control Foweather's presence, both on land and at sea. The obvious solution of spreading false rumors of where and when boats were to come ashore had backfired the one time they had tried it, as Foweather had called for reinforcements from Fowey, and the entire coast for two miles on either side of the harbor had been crawling with revenue officers and militia.

Tom nibbled on a hangnail, and his mind clicked through the possible remedies for the Foweather situation.

# Chapter Three

"Enough. You are sweating like a goat," Hilde said in German, taking the stiff-bristled brush away from Konstanze. "Go rest. Get some fresh air."

"I should do more," she protested, gesturing around her at the kitchen, where there were several tasks yet to be completed. The stone sink in front of her still held several pots that had to be scrubbed clean before either she or Hilde would be willing to cook from them. There were linens to be washed, trunks to be unpacked, furniture to be polished, windows to be cleaned.

"Let me work in peace! Go!" Hilde commanded, shooing her out the door to the back garden.

Konstanze gave up and let herself be shooed, pausing only to unpin her apron from her dress, which was a white cotton sprigged with tiny green clusters of lily of the valley. She admitted privately that she was glad

41

enough to be done with chores for the day. She had grown soft living her stationary life on the sofas of Bugg House, and had forgotten the stamina required to care for a home. Her muscles ached, and the skin of her fingers felt raw from soap and cold water, her knuckles stiff.

She glanced back through the open door to the kitchen, and saw that Hilde was inspecting Konstanze's pots and shaking her sandy blond head in dissatisfaction. Hilde was a firm believer in the adage that if you wanted a job done well, you did it yourself. While the maid never disobeyed a direct order, she nevertheless mothered Konstanze and did not hesitate to tell her young mistress, in her abrupt Austrian manner, what she thought was best.

The day was sunny and warm, and whenever the gusting breeze stopped fresh perspiration broke out over her skin, only to be cooled by the next brush of air. Konstanze felt as though she had been outdoors more in the past two days than she had in the entire two years of living with Bugg.

Between the privy, the unoccupied chicken house, the well house, and the overgrown patch where vegetables had once grown, the back garden was far from lovely to look upon. It was not too late to grow some of their own vegetables, although Konstanze did not relish the thought of putting hand to spade and overturning that tangled growth of weeds. There was also a decrepit barn that she had yet to investigate. Her great-uncle had been a farmer, one of the few fortunate enough to own the land he worked. Konstanze spared a passing thought of wonder that he could make a living from this small acreage.

She set her feet in the direction of the headlands and began to warm her voice with a series of scales, then arpeggios, feeling cheerful and carefree. She slipped from chest voice to head voice, and on the passage after that her voice went even higher and purer, taking on the character of a flute. Her mother had found work mainly as a lyric soprano, singing the sweet melodies of the innocent heroine, her head and chest voices often mixed. Konstanze herself was more fitted for the coloratura soprano roles, her voice at its best when at the highest reaches of human sound, bouncing or sliding agilely between notes.

The ocean came in sight over the next rise, its waters close to shore an intense turquoise green, speaking of currents warmer than those to be found anywhere else in England. The waves sloshed lethargically up against the dark gray rocks of the shore, the waters today calm. She picked her way carefully down the sloping green to the drop-off where the rocks began, looking down at the short cove some twenty feet below.

She had found the cove yesterday, its beige sands stretching only thirty feet or so between rocky arms. It took a bit of care to descend to it without harm, and she did so now after taking a brief glance around the deserted countryside behind her. As yesterday, there was not another soul to be seen. She and Hilde had not, in fact, laid eyes upon another human being since Mr. Mogridge had delivered them to the cottage.

"Ev'ry sight these eyes behold does a different charm unfold," she began to sing.

It was the aria sung by the Queen of Sheba upon arriving in Solomon's court, in Handel's *Solomon*. It was not a coloratura piece, but had enough drama to satisfy her, and the words suited her mood. To her eyes, the lovely cove was as wonderful as any palace shining with gems.

She slipped her shoes and stockings off when she reached the sand, tucking them neatly into a cleft of rock near where she had climbed down. She could tell by the narrow strip of wet upon the sand that the tide was coming in, and did not want to risk her shoes floating away while she dawdled amongst the rocks.

"Does a different charm unfold; flashing gems and sculptured gold," she sang.

The water was frigid upon her toes at first touch, but a few seconds later the coolness was pleasant, not half so startling. She lifted her hem and waded to the west end of the cove, the water splashing up her legs with each step, the energy she had thought drained by chores coming back full-force now that there was play at hand.

She cast a glance over her shoulder, up to the top of the rocks. There was no one there, and likely there would not be anyone there all of today, and tomorrow too. Though she knew there were footpaths across the green downs, she had seen none anywhere between her great-uncle's cottage and this cove. No one had reason to come this way, and even if someone should cross the land above, they would have to come to the very edge of the low cliff to see her here down below.

The weather was sunny and warm.

The water was pleasant.

She was in need of a bath.

She was as alone as she could ever hope to be.

It was a perfect chance for a swim. She felt an anxious, excited rush at the thought. Did she dare?

Her grandfather had taught her to swim when she was a small child, telling her that it was a foolish thing for anyone who lived near the water to be unable to save himself should he have the misfortune to fall in, and that went for little girls, too.

Grandmother had protested, fretting at the shoreline as Grandfather led her into the water, her chemise billowing around her thighs as the water deepened. She had been frightened at first, scared to put her face into the water, but Grandfather had gruffly told her to do it, to quit her fretting, and done it she had.

By the end of that first lesson she had learned how to float on her back, arms spread like a starfish, her potbelly a small island in the waves. With the knowledge that all she ever had to do was flip onto her back to be safe, the water had quickly lost its terrors.

Poor Grandfather. She had caused him endless grief from Grandmother, for as a young girl she had not completely understood the dangers of currents, undertows, jagged rocks, or the cold that robbed the body of its heat and life. She had been, however, an obedient child, and had kept her swimming to coves that her grandparents deemed safe.

All that had been close to twenty years past, and when her mother had directed her to be sent to boarding school in Switzerland at the age of ten, her swimming days had ended.

Konstanze waded out of the water and put her hands to the buttons at the front of her high-waisted gown, hesitating as she looked up again at the unvisited ledges above her. Logic argued that no one would see her, but still she was nervous about disrobing outdoors. There were but a few minutes in the day when she was not covered shoulder to ankle by clothing, and those minutes were within the privacy of home.

She remembered again her grandfather ordering her to put her face in the water, never mind her fear. He had known there was no danger, just as her logic told her there was none now. She teetered a moment longer on a point of indecision, just long enough to grow tired of her own waffling and to toss her worries to the wind.

She slipped the buttons through their holes and unfastened the inner, built-in panels of the gown that supported her breasts. Up, over the head and off, and after a moment of contemplation her chemise went, too. She rolled them into a neat little log and put them on top of her shoes in the crevice, safe from wind and tide. She pulled the pins from her hair and tucked those up there, too, as her heavy mahogany hair fell from its coiffure to hang around her body in thick, snakelike locks.

She was Medusa! She was Judith! She was Circe! She ran down the sand and splashed into the water, the chill against her skin only half as shocking as the feel of her bare skin in the open air, her breasts bouncing as she ran. She was Aphrodite, born in the waves, and wondering where her clothes were. But no, above all she was Konstanze Crécy, the Bugg-free woman of Cornwall!

She dove into the low waves, the water a cool massaging caress down her body, her hair dragging as she glided underwater. She kicked and pulled, going farther and farther until her breath gave out, and then she came to the surface with a gasp. She stood on the sandy bottom, the undulations of the water's surface rising and falling over her breasts, which had gone tight with the cold. Her hair floated and swayed around her like fronds of seaweed, its touch against her bare sides both tentative and intimate.

She swam out into slightly deeper water and lolled on her back. She dove and surfaced and dove again, and when she tired she swam over to the end of one of the outthrusts of rock that surrounded her cove. The weight of her body was heavy on her arms as she pulled herself up out of the salt water. She sat on a low rock, her legs still half submerged, and looked out at the sea.

She dug her fingers into her hair, making them a crude comb as she worked at the worst of the snarls. Bugg would have a fit if he could see her now, preening nude on a rock. The thought brought her a wicked delight. The emotion begged for expression, something vengeful and impassioned.

In her head she heard the violent, crashing introduction as an orchestra hurled itself into the opening bars of a furious Mozart aria. She flung out her hands and raised her head in an arrogant, queenly gesture as she gathered a deep breath.

*"Der Hölle Rache Kocht in meinem Herzen,"* she belted out, startling a small flock of seagulls into flight. *"Tod und Verzweiflung flammet um mich her!"*

She threw all her soul into the song, feeling it in a way she never had before. She was singing the part of the Queen of the Night from *The Magic Flute*. The queen was singing, "Hellish revenge boils in my heart/ Death and desperation are flaming around me!" as she tried to persuade her daughter to murder her father, Sarastro.

The aria was a favorite of Konstanze's, its passages some of the most difficult in the repertoire. The highest notes of the piece were produced by air moving across motionless vocal cords, much as a flute was played, and the result was eerily inhuman.

*"A a a a a aaaaaaaaaaa,"* she sang nearly three octaves above middle C, the notes rising, falling, and rising again in steps to ethereal levels and then finally doing a frantic dance of ascension to the high F.

She was at the end of the second major run of such notes when she heard a shout behind her. She jerked her head over her shoulder, and to her horror saw a man in a blue coat and white trousers gaping at her from back on the grassy shore. In panic she flung herself into the water.

She heard him shout again as she came back to the surface. She had to hide, and quickly! Horror upon horrors, to be caught like this.

There was nowhere on the rock outcropping to secrete herself. She swam around the rock arm, beyond sight of the cove, thankful that the waves were calm enough that she would not risk being battered against the rocks. The land rose higher in this direction, the shoreline irregular. The man was out of sight for the moment, so if she could just find a place to hide before he appeared again . . .

*There!* A dark, upright shadow in the next headland bespoke a cave, the opening all but hidden by a tall rock before it. She swam desperately for the opening, and with the help of an incoming wave slid easily inside. She clung to the slick rocks of the wall as the wave retreated, leaving her waist-deep in the water, in a passage no more than three feet across.

When she perched the rocks beneath her feet were jagged, so she lowered herself back into the water to take her weight off them. With the next wave she allowed herself to be carried farther inside, seeking a more comfortable resting place. The water sloshed and echoed weirdly in the confines of the crevice, the sound almost metallic.

She clung to the rocks again as the wave retreated and water drained out of the cave, leaving her this time in only a foot of water, lying atop slightly smoother stones. Looking back over her shoulder showed that she was ten feet or so from the opening, probably deep enough in the darkness that she could not be seen from outside.

Ahead the passage continued, darkening as it went. The next wave carried her just a few inches farther, but when it receded she froze in place. In the center of the darkness before her there had appeared a narrow sliver of light.

In the blackness ahead without landmarks she had no way to tell how far off the light was, or how large.

She pulled herself slowly forward, floating just above the rocks, pushing with her knees and forearms, and as she progressed the sliver grew wider as the passage turned to the right, and she realized that what she was seeing was the opening at the other end. This was not just a cave; it was a natural tunnel through the headland. The light from behind her was cut off as she rounded the corner, but the opening at the far end kept her from being frightened, even though it was too distant to throw any light into the tunnel itself.

Although her clothes were well behind her, the knowledge that there was another escape from the cave was a relief. She would not have liked to have risked being trapped inside by the incoming tide, or forced to exit while the blue-coated man still searched for her.

The water progressed only a few feet more, ending at sand. She crawled up onto this unexpected beach within a headland, her eyes still blind from the brightness outside. She felt her way forward, patting the sand with her hands, and then her touch landed upon something warm and alive.

She yelped and jerked back at the same time a male voice cried out. The man's cry startled her anew and she screamed, scrambling backward toward the water, splashing into it with all the grace of a turtle returning to the sea, shrieking all the while.

Hands fumbled at her, then plucked her from the water and dragged her back to the sand. She struggled, and one of the strong hands slid over her breast and her cold, stiff nipple. "Good Christ!" the voice exclaimed, and dropped her abruptly.

She landed on her rump, and after a moment's surprise scrambled again in the direction she hoped the water lay—she was turned around now, her only landmark the far oval of light—but then her ankle was suddenly clasped and pinned to the sand by the man's strong hand. Konstanze tugged against it like a fox in a trap but could get no leverage, and she started to shriek again.

"Shh! For God's sake, be quiet!" her captor said, just barely audible over her screeching. "I won't hurt you."

"Let me go!"

"Don't scream, please! I implore you. You'll draw him right down on us."

She was drawing in a breath to scream again, knowing that if she tried she could produce a sound that would echo through the passage and out into the open air. It was that thought coupled with his last words that gave her pause. She held the breath. Fear was making it difficult to think of anything but escape, but it occured to her that a man in the dark who was pleading with her was perhaps better than one in the daylight who could see her.

"Please," he said again.

Although his grip on her ankle was firm, he made no other move to touch her. She realized that he didn't want to be found by the blue-coated man any more than she did, and molesting her appeared to be the last thing on his mind. "Get back and I won't," she said, the words an experiment, a test of his intentions.

He let go of her ankle. She quickly turned around and inched backward toward the water, keeping her eyes open wide to catch any hint of movement, the urge to put distance between herself and the man irresistible. Her eyes were becoming adjusted to the dark, and she could faintly make out her companion's outline as he sat on his knees and watched her. She felt vulnerable without her clothes, despite the blackness of the cave, and fear continued to flush through her veins and muscles.

"Did you come in here to hide?" the dark shape asked. "Did he see you swimming?"

She didn't answer, her feet finding the edge of the water. It felt warm in comparison to the chill of the cave and the cold, damp sand.

"He may be out there for a good time yet," the man said. "You'll be chilled to the bone if you try to wait him out in the water."

As if in answer to his words she felt a hard shiver shake her body. "I cannot remain in here with you," she found voice to answer, through teeth that had suddenly begun to chatter. She was surprised the words came out sounding as calm as they did, given the way her heart was thundering in her chest.

"Of course you can." He started doing something with his arms. She found herself opening her eyes even wider, trying to catch his movements in the dark. A shadow suddenly flew at her and she crouched down, covering her head with her hands.

Something heavy and warm landed on her head. His coat.

She pulled it off her head and immediately slipped it on, too glad for clothing to question his generosity. The silk lining was still warm from his body. Unlike the stylish short-fronted coats that men in London wore, this one was long in front and back. She was grateful its owner was either unaware of the current fashion or chose the country style intentionally. Judging by the fine feel of the materials, she was guessing he chose it.

She ran her hand under her hair along the back of her neck and tugged her wet locks out from under the coat, letting them drop onto her back. Her eyes carefully on the shadow that was the man, she walked on her knees to a dry patch of sand a safe distance from him, the coat wrapped tightly around her, then sat, tucking her feet up beneath herself. "Thank you," she said.

"My pleasure." He made himself more comfortable. "It is not every day that I have the chance to offer my coat to a lady in such needy circumstances."

She could hear the amusement in his educated, yet still faintly Cornish-accented voice. "I imagine not," she replied, having no witty repartee with which to deflect him. Cautious fear and an embarrassed horror at her situation were taking all her brain power. She huddled down into his coat, catching the faint scent of lavender from the collar. Her shivering was no longer constant, but coming now in short, bone-jarring bursts.

As the minutes passed and it became apparent he was not going to try to approach her, her fear faded and she wondered what he was doing in the cave himself, and who the man in the blue coat was from whom they both were hiding. The situation, however, did not seem appropriate for asking questions. As long as he stayed away from her, he could keep his business to himself.

"Are you quite all right there?" he asked into their mutual silence. "Are you warm enough?"

"Yes, thank you. Your coat is more than adequate."

"I didn't hurt you, did I?"

"No. I am uninjured."

More silence; then she heard him shifting again. She could see him just well enough to know that he was facing her now, one arm resting on an upraised knee. "I have never in all my days seen a woman intentionally take a swim in the sea. I don't suppose you were in a boat that capsized, were you? But no, you would not have been able to strip off your clothes if that were so. So swimming it must have been."

Why was he talking to her? Why couldn't he just be quiet and let this horrible situation play itself out in silence, so she could pretend it wasn't happening? "Excuse me, but I really don't think we should be speaking," she said. "Our voices may carry outside the cave."

"I doubt that, as long as we keep them low," he said, and blithely continued on. "You gave me quite a start when you came crawling out of the water."

"*I* gave *you* a start?" she asked incredulously, startled out of her embarrassed reticence. *"I?"*

"Yes, you. Visions of all manner of terrible creatures entered my mind when I heard you splashing about in the shallows."

Terrible creature? She? "Do you think I expected to find *you,* lurking in the shadows like . . . like some type of bat?" Woefully inadequate, "bat." She could do better than that!

"Oh, I am nothing like a bat, I assure you. They hang from their feet, you know," he said.

"That is not the point."

"It's not? I was sitting here quite calmly, keeping to my own affairs, waiting for Foweather and his men to go away, and then you turn up like some sort of confused sea lion, flopping itself onto the sand and scaring me half to death."

She made a little grunt of offense. She did not flop! And she was nothing like a sea lion. "What are you doing hiding in here, anyway?"

"Oh, that," he said, and she saw him wave his hand airily. "It's not important."

*Fine.* Let him keep his secrets, and she could keep hers. Silent moments passed, and she began to relax, thinking he had finally caught that she was not in the mood for social chatter.

"Do I have the honor of addressing Mrs. Konstanze Crécy Bugg?" he suddenly asked.

"Ug—" she gurgled. *"O Gott!"*

"I suspected as much. Allow me to introduce myself. I'm Tom Trewella, the executor of your late uncle's estate."

"How . . ." she tried, but could not finish the question, horrors of embarrassment cascading through her.

"How did I know it was you?"

"Mr. Mogridge," she said, answering her own question.

"Yes, I happened to see him and he said how he had delivered you and your maid to the cottage."

Konstanze saw in a flash how this one man with all
the pieces could figure out her identity so easily. Her
accent had marked her as an outsider, and then between that, Mogridge, and the proximity of the cottage
it had been a simple puzzle for him to piece together.

"Mr. Mogridge did say, though, that you gave your
name as Miss Penrose," he continued.

She stared at him in the dark, the statement hanging
between them. "Yes," she said, and closed her lips.

"But you *are* Konstanze Bugg."

*Unfortunately.* "Yes."

He wanted, but she waited longer. She was good at
silence.

"I wouldn't have had any questions about a Miss
Penrose," he finally said, "except that I knew that Konstanze Bugg was the only living relation of Mr. Penrose." He sounded as at ease as if he were at the tavern
sharing a beer with his friends, whereas she was growing more alarmed with each word he spoke. "I had
actually been intending to pay a call on you later this
afternoon, to be certain that this Miss Penrose was
someone with a right to be in the cottage, and was not
just a clever squatter."

"You are a conscientious executor, Mr. Trewella,"
she said through a tight throat. "I had intended to call
upon you myself tomorrow." She paused, debating the
wisdom of the question she wished to ask. "Tell me,
do others in Penperro know to whom the cottage was
left?"

"I have not discussed your affairs, nor those of your
uncle," he said with the first trace of sharpness she
had heard in his voice, as if he were offended at the

mere suggestion that he would share private information. "Mr. Penrose himself let it be known that a niece would be his heir, although he did not know it would be you, and not your mother, who inherited."

"Ah." She chewed her bottom lip, considering. With the exception of the fact that he was presently hiding in a cave, by all other evidence Mr. Trewella seemed an honorable enough man, and perhaps worthy of some small degree of trust. He had, after all, taken the care to track her down and ensure that she was made aware of her inheritance. "Would it trouble you greatly if I were to request that you keep my true name in confidence, and refer to me only as Constance Penrose should the need arise?"

"You want me to lie for you?"

"Well, not lie, exactly," she said, "just stretch things a bit. My mother's maiden name was Penrose, and Constance is simply Konstanze in English. It will be much easier for me to fit in here if my name is Cornish, don't you think? And I did spend my childhood in Mousehole, so it is not as if I have not in some degree earned the name."

"Mmm. Where is your husband, Mrs. Bugg?"

"Husband? Mr. Bugg is at home," she said lightly, but did not like where this was heading.

"Please pardon my impertinence in asking, but did he not protest your traveling, with just a maid as escort, all the way to Cornwall to take up residence on a remote farm? Your home is in Kent, I believe. Mr. Rumbelow wrote to me that your husband is a man of business there, and of no small fortune. I am surprised that he would be content to let you live in such conditions as are to be found in your great-uncle's cottage."

"Not that it is any of your affair, Mr. Trewella," Konstanze said, her voice rising in pitch with her nervousness, "but the truth of the matter is that my husband and I have separated." She nodded her head. That *was* true. "I am trying to start a new life, one where I am not burdened by the mistakes of my past. Surely it is of no consequence if the people of Penperro know me only as Miss Penrose. It will do them no harm, whilst saving me a multitude of embarrassments."

"Is your husband going to divorce you?"

"It is my sincere hope that he does so, only I doubt he wishes to spend the vast sums of money such an action demands. He is an old man, Mr. Trewella, and has no reason to marry again. A separation is financially more prudent." *There.* True statements all, albeit lending a false impression. "So will you keep my secret?"

He was silent, and she waited tensely. "If you wish to be Miss Penrose," he said at last, "then I shall not call you otherwise. My only request is that if there comes to be any trouble that follows you here from this past you are so set on escaping, that you come to me at once and tell me. As the executor of Mr. Penrose's estate, and as a former friend of the man, I feel a certain responsibility for your well-being."

"I doubt that any trouble will follow me. I am certain I will fare perfectly well."

"All the same—"

"Yes, I will tell you if there is trouble," she said, feeling a wild relief that she had weathered the worst of his questions, and he had responded so well. Perhaps he would accept the entire truth as easily? He could perhaps be of some assistance to her in hiding from Bugg. She felt the urge to tell him everything building in her chest, the possibility making her heart pound, but then it occurred to her that he would want to know exactly why she had left a comfortable home with a wealthy husband. She could not tell him what Bugg had done to her with the bindings and the riding crop—she could not imagine telling anyone, not even Hilde. It would be too humiliating.

Tom stood up and started toward the far cave opening, where the light was visible.

"Where are you going?" she asked, unaccountably wishing not to be left alone in the cave. Their conversation had made her forget the awkward inappropriateness of the situation.

"To check if Foweather is gone. He's had enough time. If he hasn't found the cave by now, he likely won't this time around."

She got to her own feet, the muscles around her knees stiff and making her stagger a few steps until they loosened. "Who is this Foweather?" she asked, brushing the sand off the back of the coat.

"He's with the Preventive Water Guard Service. Not a bad fellow, actually, but he has a tendency to put his nose where it does not belong."

Her lips parted in a silent *O* of understanding. She had not spent her childhood on these coasts without learning a thing or two about that most Cornish of occupations: smuggling. She could remember occasions when her own grandparents had hidden contraband in their cellar. She had been too young at the time to think anything other than that it was normal, and it had been beyond comprehension that her grandparents would engage in activities that others might find immoral.

She followed Mr. Trewella toward the entrance, the sand cool under her feet and studded with the occasional half-buried rock. As they approached the opening he gestured behind him for her to stop, and she obeyed, standing in place as he stepped into the light and peered out.

It was her first real chance to see him, and her eyebrows went up, her chin tucking into her neck in surprise. Somehow in her mind she had formed an image of Tom Trewella as short and a trifle thick through the chest, like most Cornishmen, and of middle age because he had been her great-uncle's executor. The easy confidence of his voice had spoken of a more mature male as well, for while self-assured it had lacked the abrasive cockiness she had long noted in young men. And once he had finished with his sea lion comments, his conversation had been reassuringly civil.

She had been decidedly misguided in her notions. Tom Trewella was as fine-looking a man as she had seen in a very long time. He was perhaps five-foot-ten and slender with hard, narrow hips, but with wide shoulders and an easy grace to his movements that spoke of physical agility and strength. His hair was black—that at least she had imagined correctly—and cut short, ruffled and disordered by the wind. He wore a tight waistcoat that showed off his form to great advantage, and the white sleeves of his shirt billowed and then flattened against his arms as the sea breeze caught him outside the cave entrance. His trousers were close-fitting buckskin, disappearing below the knee into his tall black boots.

When he turned his head she caught a glimpse of his profile, and she saw he could not have been over thirty years in age. He had a hawkish, high-bridged nose, a clean jawline, and wore an expression animated with intelligence and energy.

He moved out of her sight, and she waited where she was, hidden in the shadows in case anyone other than Mr. Trewella should enter the cave. Several minutes later he returned.

"All clear," he said. "Tell me where you left your clothes and I'll fetch them for you."

"Do you know the small cove just to the east of here?" When he said he did, she explained the location of the crevice. He left again, and, knowing she would have several minutes to wait, she went back to where they had been sitting, intent on seeing what she could see.

Her eyes were fairly well adjusted to the dark now, and as she moved up the sandy beach she found the pile of contraband goods that Mr. Trewella must have come to check. She could make out a few dozen small casks, and investigation into other boxes and packages turned up tea, tobacco, and a carefully sealed package that, when put to her nose, declared itself to be scented soap. Altogether, a store of goods that would well line the pockets of the smugglers involved, provided they could be safely sold.

The tide was still incoming, each gentle swell bringing the water closer to the stored goods. She thought the entrance through which she had swum was likely tall enough that even at high tide she would have been able to swim out, but she was happy to have Mr. Trewella retrieve her clothes for her. Never again would she swim nude, ever! She had learned that lesson well enough, thank you.

"Are you still here?" she heard him ask, and turned to see him approaching, a silhouette against the light.

"Yes, over here," she said.

"I'm half blind from the sunlight," he said, but seemed to find her easily enough despite that. He held up one of her green slippers. "You have tiny feet."

"Not particularly so," she said, uncomfortable to have him handling her clothing with such interest, but also a little flattered by the comment. It made her feel dainty, rather than like the great flopping sea lion he had mentioned earlier.

He handed her her things. "Perhaps it's been too long since I've taken notice of women's feet. I forget they are not the same size as my own."

She gave a small laugh. "They would not look too attractive, sticking out beneath the hems of our gowns." She imagined a roomful of such young misses, their long feet slapping the ground with each flat-footed step. The curled edges of carpets would be a constant trial. She laughed again.

"I suppose not," he agreed, and he sounded almost as if he wanted to join in whatever thoughts were amusing her so. She did not explain, and after a moment he said, "Well, then, I'll leave you to dress. Your hairpins are in one of the slippers. I'll be just outside to help you up the rocks."

She dressed quickly, her clothes feeling warm and soft and infinitely welcoming on her skin. There was little she could do with her hair, so she just twisted it into a coil and pinned it to her head. At least that would keep it from dripping on her back and soaking through the shoulders of her dress.

As she stepped out of the cave she saw that the entrance would be impossible to see from land, as there was a wall of natural rock blocking the view. One would have to be at sea, and at just the right angle, to catch a glimpse of the dark crevice. Mr. Trewella was sitting on a rock, face turned up to the sun as she emerged.

The inside of Mr. Trewella's coat was damp from where it had soaked up the salt water from her body. "I'll replace the lining in your coat for you, if the salt water stained it," she said, handing him the garment.

He opened his eyes and looked up at her, and she saw that he was even more striking than she had thought. His eyes were an unusual amber, rimmed in dark brown, their shape somewhat narrow and slanting slightly upward at the outer corners, like on a fox. He was not beautiful in the pretty way of a painting of a man, all pastels and round blue eyes, but had instead something raw and alive about him. Even while reclining, apparently at his ease, there was nothing lazy or lethargic in his attitude.

"I shouldn't stay up nights worrying about it if I were you," he said as he took the coat, and then his eyes ran quickly over her face and dress and he grinned, his teeth straight and white. "I almost feel as if we should introduce ourselves all over again, Miss Penrose. You are quite transformed."

"And in this form I intend to remain until the end of our acquaintance, Mr. Trewella."

"Ah, well, sad news for fishermen sailing by and the Preventive crew alike."

He stood and drew on his coat despite its dampness. "Follow me up the rocks. I'll help you where you need it, but otherwise you'll keep your balance better if I leave you on your own."

She nodded in agreement, and holding up her skirts in one hand she followed him up the steep face of the headland.

# Chapter Four

*Kent*

John Bugg gave his hat, greatcoat, and walking stick to Deekes, the butler, and tramped up the stairs to his wife's sitting room. "Konstanze, darling, come give me a kiss," he said, opening the door. "Konstanze?"

She wasn't there, and there was no fire in the grate. Frowning, he went through to their bedroom. "Konstanze?"

Something seemed a little off about the room, but he did not know what, other than that his wife was not in it. He stomped out to the gallery that looked down on the main hall. "Deekes!" he called down. "Deekes!"

"Sir?" Deekes asked, emerging from a doorway.

"Where's Mrs. Bugg?"

"You did not receive her message?"

"What message, damn you?"

"Your pardon, sir. She told me she had dispatched a message to you to inform you that her aunt in Scotland was ill and she must depart immediately to go to her."

"Scotland! Aunt? She has no aunt, in Scotland or elsewhere."

"Sir?"

"Damn her! When did she leave? Who drove her?"

"She's been gone a week. Mr. Hanley drove her to the Shepherd, a coaching inn on the mail route to Edinburgh," Deekes said. "Sir, was she not to have gone?"

"Of course she was not to have gone, you fool!"

"Dear me. That does raise a few questions."

Bugg did not like the sound of that. "What? What questions?"

"She took the silver coffee service, sir. And the flatware. And the ormolu clock that belonged to your late wife."

"What!"

"She said she was going to replace them with something she liked better. I thought it odd, but it was not my place to question her."

*"Arg arg arg,"* Bugg barked, incoherent. *The bitch, the lying French trollop!* Quarles was right about her: she was the daughter of a whore and no better than the polluted loins from which she'd sprung. But she was his trollop, *his*, and she would not run away from him, or steal his silver either!

He would punish her when he caught her—oh, how he would punish her! She had cringed at the riding

66

crop, but that was nothing to what he'd do to her when he caught her. The stupid, cold-blooded tart. She couldn't please him in bed, and didn't even have the sense to know what a failure she was. He'd chain her to the bedposts, he'd smack her with his own hand, he'd have her begging him for mercy.

There was a stirring in his trousers. He reached down and felt himself. By God, it was the best erection he'd had in five years, and it was going to go to waste all because of her!

The injustice of it infuriated him further, and he felt the blood pounding in his head, his face going hot. He could almost feel his eyes bulging from the pressure, vessels on the verge of bursting.

Pain clamped his chest, and he could hardly breathe. The world started going dark.

"Konstanze!" he cried on a wisp of air, and then he collapsed on the floor, unconscious.


John Bugg II sat on the hard wooden chair beside his father's bed. Why couldn't the old man hurry up and die?

His father took a rasping breath, exhaled, and then there was no sound or movement of his chest. Bugg II straightened and stretched his neck forward, examining his sire for signs of life. Was he finally gone? He lifted the candle and held it up to where it would shed better light on the pale figure, unconscious now for two days.

There was a hitching sound, then slowly his father sucked in another weak breath.

Bugg II slapped the candlestick back onto the bedstand and leaned back, his arms crossed petulantly over his chest. It was just like the old man to take his time about it. Bugg II's eyes went to the pillows on the bed. It would take only a moment to snuff out the miserable little flame of life still in the codger. No more than a minute, surely.

That would be when Deekes would walk in, or the doctor, just when he had his hands pressing the pillow over his father's face. He'd be hauled off to prison and then either hanged or, if he was lucky, transported to Botany Bay. No, he'd have to be patient and let the old fool kick the bucket in his own sweet time.

And then . . .

He's send a private thank-you to his lovely young stepmother, Konstanze. Not only had her departure brought about this present happy state of affairs, but as she in all likelihood had no intention of coming back, he needn't worry about actually paying her whatever widow's portion his father had set aside for her in his will.

Konstanze. He would have liked to have taken her to his own bed, but the haughty bitch had the insulting habit of looking right through him, as if she couldn't even bother to take notice of his existence.

He touched his protruding front teeth in a self-conscious gesture. He did not have much luck with the ladies. When he was only fourteen a young girl he had admired had told him quite bluntly that his face looked like someone very strong had squeezed his head from the sides when he was a baby. He rubbed his large nose, and blinked his deep-set eyes against the memory.

All women really cared about was money. He'd have that soon, and then he could have his pick of the lot of them.

# Chapter Five

*Penperro*

"Tell us again about the mermaid," Mrs. Popple said, pulling another beer for Foweather. She was behind the bar at the Fishing Moon, and the tavern was full of locals and Preventive crew alike. Tom and Matt Jobson sat at a table against the wall, their chairs tilted back on two legs, Tom with one foot braced against the edge of the table as he observed the scene.

"My men and I were searching the coastline just east of here for caves," Foweather said eagerly, taking a sip of his fresh beer. He was happily oblivious to the glint of derisive amusement in the eyes of the locals, who were enjoying themselves thoroughly at his expense. He had told the mermaid story over half the town already, but no story was truly told until it was told in the Fishing Moon. His men, sitting in a sad

70

huddle at the long table in the center of the tavern, had begun to sulk at the jolly reception their commander was getting. They seemed to sense that it was not as sincere as it appeared.

"We had spread out, and I came down to a small cove, thinking perhaps there might be signs of smuggling near such a smooth landing place," Foweather explained, gesturing with his free hand. "And then I heard the most magical song—like something from another world! I cannot explain it, except to say that it was in a voice such as the angels might have, pure and light and thoroughly unlike any you will ever hear coming from a human throat. She sang in some strange mermaid tongue, unknown to me and unknown, likely, to any living man." Foweather's gesturing hand froze in a raised position, and tears glistened in his eyes as he silently relived the unearthly music.

"And then I saw her sitting on the rocks below, her tail dangling in the water. She had long brown hair, still wet from the sea, and when in my startlement I called out, she turned and saw me. Such a face! Plump and youthful as a girl's, her skin pale but tinged with pink, and her breasts were high and full." He set down his beer and cupped his hands in the air.

"That's the part we want to hear!" someone in the room shouted.

"No, you do not gawk at something so beautiful, so precious!" Foweather scolded, dropping his hands. "She saw me, and, frightened, she slid into the sea and swam away. I understood then, though, why it is said that such sirens can lure men to their watery graves, for I would gladly have leaped into the sea to pursue her."

"It's not a likely story," a local scoffed. "Mermaids!"

"I saw her; I would swear it on the Bible! I saw her and heard her sing!"

A bit more scoffing, and then Foweather was persuaded to recite the tale yet again. Tom lowered his chair to all four legs and narrowed his eyes, the idea that had been forming in his brain suddenly coming into clear and perfect focus. "Matt," he said to the vicar, "I have a most devious plan."

Matt's chair came down to the floor as well, and he leaned across the small sticky table. "By the look on your face it's more amusing than devious."

"You'll like this, I promise you." He outlined his thoughts to his friend, and before he was halfway done Matt was choking with laughter. "Do you think it will work?" Tom asked when he finally got the vicar to listen to the rest.

"It won't hurt anyone to try," Matt said.

Tom tilted his chair back again as Matt got up to fetch a fresh beer. He watched his friend wend his way through the locals, pausing here and there to whisper a few words into likely ears.

He knew of course that it was Konstanze that Foweather had seen sitting on the rocks. The only part he hadn't known was that she was singing at the time, and apparently with some skill. Mogridge had waxed on about her voice, but Tom had put the comments down to the man's fondness for telling a story. Perhaps he had been mistaken to do so. Since Foweather had begun his talk of a mermaid with an angel's unearthly voice, he had recalled that Konstanze's mother—the original heir named in the will—was an opera singer. He doubted anyone else knew that. Robert Penrose had not been particularly proud to claim such a relation, and had only told Tom because such information would be necessary in finding her in the event of his demise.

How much talent for performance had mother passed on to daughter? Tom wondered. He hoped a great deal, for what he had in mind. Certainly the young woman had the other requisites for his plan: she could swim; she apparently lacked some degree of modesty; and she had a sense of adventure, if coming alone to Cornwall and hiding in caves were any indication. She had shown remarkable self-possession for being naked with a stranger.

She had also scared the wits out of him, creeping out of the water in the dark as she had. His mind had gone blank when he first heard those distinctive splashing noises of something large coming out of the water, breathing heavily in the confines of the cave. Her cold wet hand had then come down over his own, and thoughts of drowned sailors coming back to pull the living into the depths of the sea had overwhelmed his imagination.

Then she had yelped, and he'd thought it was a boy who had swum in to hide from Foweather, for whatever reason. He'd gotten his second shock when he pulled her from the water and felt his hand slide over a firm, full breast and the hard pebble of a nipple.

When he'd seen her in the daylight, he'd had a moment's wish that he hadn't been so quick to drop her. Her Cornish heritage showed in her short stature and the dark of her hair, but there her resemblance to local women ended. She had the pale, smooth skin of a woman who spent her life indoors, and she dressed in the current high-waisted mode whereas local girls were mostly still in stays. Her face was softly square with full cheeks, and she had enormous gray eyes from which it was difficult to look away. In her movements, in the modulation of her voice, and in her words themselves it was apparent that for all that she may have been a child of Cornwall, she was a creature educated in farther places and used to finer things.

And she was also, obviously, running away from her husband. He would have liked to have known the full story, but could hardly blame her for wishing to keep such information to herself. Perhaps he could pry it out of her at a later time. As it was, he thought it likely that a woman in her situation might be short of funds, a condition that would give him just the leverage he needed to persuade her to what he had in mind.

The thought passed through his mind that there might be other things he would like to persuade her to, as well. He had a brief image of her naked, on her hands and knees in the sand, water glistening on her skin, her gray eyes peering back over her shoulder at him with unspoken invitation as he approached her from behind. She'd cry out when he entered her, then push back, wanting more....

Tom shook the thought from his mind and watched as Matt, fresh beer in hand, sat down at the end of the table where the Preventive crew were sitting. Matt gazed seriously into his tankard, waiting for the right moment, the exact lull in the conversation that would serve his purpose. Tom felt, as he always did, a deep admiration for his friend's sense of timing and ability to capture an audience. With such talent, it was little wonder that the majority of Matt's parishioners actually remained awake during his Sunday sermons.

A small pocket of quiet spread around Matt, as others noticed his grave absorption in thought. Matt enjoyed bawdy humor as well as—or better than—the next man, but his position as vicar and the fact that he seemed to have a true calling for God's work tended to make others watch their behavior near him. If he seemed to disapprove of something, then it wasn't quite so easy to enjoy it while he was around. Matt's sense of right and wrong, however, were not always what one might expect.

"A mermaid," Matt said into a momentary hush. Those who still talked were hushed by neighbors. Everyone turned to look at the vicar, the man of God with his wild white hair and smile-creased eyes. "A mermaid is an intriguing puzzle. The Church has long had an interest in mermaids. You know yourselves of the ancient oaken chair in Talland Church, with the mermaid carved upon its side." There were nods and murmurs.

"Why was she carved there? Some say that a mermaid is a symbol of vanity and lust, sins of which man must ever be wary. Others, pointing to her human flesh paired with that of a fish—a symbol of Christ—say that she represents the union of God and man. And

75

still others would say that she is no symbol at all, but a living creature like ourselves, only lacking in a soul."

"The Mermaid of Penperro," a local said with feigned awe into the following silence. He was one of the men into whose ear Matt had whispered. "She was supposed to be a fairy story, nothing more," he said. Tom winced at the stilted delivery of the line, but no one else seemed to notice.

"The Mermaid of Penperro?" Foweather asked, taking the bait. "What's this?"

"It's a story that parents tell their children, that once upon a time there was a mermaid who came to services in Talland Church, dressed in the finery of a noblewoman, her gait halting and awkward under her skirts, her feet newly formed for walking upon land. They say she came in hopes of earning for herself a soul. Instead she fell in love with a young man in the choir, and he with her. He followed her into the sea, and there they were said to live out their lives. She was seen only once more, when a fisherman had anchored near a headland. He says a beautiful woman appeared in the water, and asked him to please move his boat, as the anchor chain was blocking the entrance to her cave, and she could not return to her husband and child."

Another local spoke up in forced tones of wonder. "Do you think she has returned?"

And then Matt cast the hook that Tom hoped would snare Foweather fast and hard. "Perhaps it is her child who has returned these many years later, to find herself a husband as did her mother."

"By God!" Foweather said. "By God!"

"Eh, now wouldn't that be the life?" Dick Popple, the tavernkeeper, said, and gave Foweather's arm a nudge. "Married to a mermaid! I'd give my right arm to be that lucky. Hell! I'd give both legs, if she wanted me to turn fish for her, as long as I got to keep what was between!"

"As if she'd want the likes of you!" his wife said, and snorted. "She wouldn't want a dirty old dog; she'd want a fine young fellow, someone handsome and strong."

"You'd better watch out, Mr. Foweather," Wiggett the baker said. "Looks like she may have set her eye on you."

"You'll be making your home in a sea cave before long!" someone threw in.

"You said yourself you almost went into the water after her," Wiggett reminded him.

The bantering was taking a turn that Tom hadn't expected. He had wanted to feed Foweather's burgeoning obsession with the lovely mermaid, not scare him away from her. Matt, realizing the same problem, stepped back in. "I'm not saying the stories are true, and I'm not saying Mr. Foweather saw what he thought he saw. It could have been a seal down on those rocks, barking, and the sun on the water tricked his vision into thinking he saw a woman."

"No, it was her!" Foweather insisted. "It was the Mermaid of Penperro—or her daughter. I would swear my life on it!"

"What are you going to do?" Mrs. Popple asked, seeming to catch on that there was more at play here than the simple joy of harassing Foweather. "There could be danger for you near the water, if you're not wanting to bed down with the mermaid. You'd better beware."

*Clever Mrs. Popple.* If the mermaid was not a lure or distraction, then she could be used to frighten Foweather from his course. As long as he was stunned by his sighting, as long as they could keep him fascinated by the possibility that a mermaid lurked offshore, they might be able to either push or pull him where they pleased.

"I cannot forget my duty, mermaid or no," Foweather said, and raised his tankard with a shaking hand. In his voice there was an uncertainty that Tom had not heard before.

The stage was all but set. All he needed now was the heroine.

# Chapter Six

"You are ripping out your hair," Hilde scolded. "Give me the comb."

Konstanze obeyed, and sat up straighter on the low stool before the coal fire in the sitting room. With Hilde's help she had heated bathwater in the kitchen, and had sat in the shallow round tub that was shaped like an oversize saucer, washing the salt from her skin and hair. She wore her nightgown and wrapper now, and was soothed by the feel of Hilde's hands at work on her hair. The only light came from the fire and from the candle that burned on a small table.

She rocked gently against the pull of the comb through her damp hair, Hilde's touch far lighter than what she had used on herself. It was a moment of such peace and comfort that she could almost forget the rest of the day.

Almost.

Hilde had been appalled to hear that she had swum in the ocean, and had spent a good half hour enumerating for her the dangers of such an activity, ranging from man-eating sharks to drowning to contracting a fever of the lungs. Any mention of the possible therapeutic effects of immersion in salt water were brushed away, for surely immersion and active swimming were two entirely different things.

Konstanze did not dare tell her the rest of it, except to say that, thoroughly clothed, she had briefly spoken with Mr. Trewella while walking upon the headland, and received his assurances that her true name would be kept secret. When Hilde had asked her to describe Mr. Trewella, Konstanze had said only "dark" and "not old," and then tried to change the subject. A mistake, to be sure, for Hilde's hazel eyes had narrowed with suspicion, although she had said no more.

Of course, Mr. Trewella had been filling her thoughts since the moment she had laid her hand on him in the dark. She felt a desperate urge to speak with him again, to try to amend the faulty impression of her that he could not help but have formed, but reason told her it would be no use. One could not amend having met a man while outdoors and naked. Not that indoors and naked would have been much better, but at least some excuse was conceivable.

And what would be the use of amending the impression, anyway? Her sense of him was that he was gentleman enough to tell no one of their encounter, which meant there was no public reputation to be saved, so the only opinion she could wish to change was his. The reason for *that* was as clear to her as the amber of his uptilted eyes.

Folly. It was pure folly and foolishness to give even a moment's notice to a handsome man. It did not matter what he thought of her, because there was no possibility of anything respectable growing between them. Even building a friendship would be a pretense on her part, done only to gain more chances to drink in the contours of his face. After spending all those months with Bugg, fantasizing about handsome young men coming to rescue her, she could hardly trust herself when she encountered one in the wild.

Men were not as women, her mother had repeatedly explained to her. They took a smile as an invitation to a kiss, and a kiss as an invitation to your bed, so it was best to keep one's eyes averted and one's smiles hidden lest intentions be misconstrued.

Konstanze had no wish to take a man to her bed, even one as attractive as Mr. Trewella. She already knew what that was all about, and thought she could live out her life quite happily without it, thank you very much. It was the romance of simply being near and gazing upon such a specimen that was the temptation, and then down the slippery slope she would go, casting him smiles and getting herself into trouble. She was a woman separated from her husband, who swam naked and asked a smuggler to lie about her name. Mr. Trewella must think her terribly fast already, without her gazing calf-eyed at him as if in invitation.

Someone knocked at the door. Konstanze jumped. Hilde's hands froze on her hair.

"Who's that?" Hilde asked her.

"I don't know."

Hilde stood and gave her a patting shove on the back. "Go upstairs. You should not be seen so."

Konstanze stood, pulling the wrapper closed over her breasts, which were faintly visible through her sleeping chemise. "I'll go in the kitchen."

Hilde nodded, waiting until she was out of sight before taking the candle and going to the door. "*Ja? Who ist dere?*" she asked through the door in her stilted English.

"Tom Trewella, miss."

"Ah." Hilde opened the door, holding up the candle and squinting. "*Was für ein fescher Bursche!*" she said in surprise, and Konstanze cringed just around the corner in the kitchen, praying that the educated Mr. Trewella did not speak German, and so did not know that Hilde had just declared him a decidedly fine-looking piece of manhood.

"Excuse me?"

"Vhat do you vant?"

"Er, is Miss Penrose home?" he asked.

"Just a moment, Mr. Trewella," Konstanze called from the kitchen. "Hilde, let him in," she directed in German.

She heard the maid grunt; then the door swung wide with a creak. Konstanze grabbed a large, fine wool shawl hanging from the peg near the back door and draped it over her wrapper in a way that covered her to a satisfactorily modest degree. She went back into the other room.

Hilde and Mr. Trewella were both standing just inside the door, Mr. Trewella with his hat in his hand, ducking to avoid the low beams. Hilde frowned at her state of dishabille, but Konstanze warned her to be quiet with a slight emphatic widening of the eyes and jerked her head toward the long, high-backed oak settle.

"Sit," Hilde said to their guest, and gestured toward the settle. "You vant tea, eh?"

"Thank you, that would be most welcome," he said, taking a seat and laying his hat on the bench beside him.

"Be nice," Konstanze whispered to Hilde as the maid stomped by on her way to the kitchen, handing her the candle as she went. Konstanze put on a smile for Mr. Trewella, and after setting the candle on the mantel went to sit in the shepherd's chair opposite from him.

"I seem to have disturbed you on your way to bed," he said. "I do apologize." He wrinkled his brow and sent a worried glance toward the kitchen, where the overloud and unnecessary clanging of pots could be heard. "I do not think your maid approves of my late visit."

"She is protective," Konstanze said, enjoying the firelight playing on the edge of his features. She probably should have heeded Hilde's direction to go—and stay—upstairs. She should at least have gotten dressed and put her hair in a cap, or she should have asked him to come back tomorrow, but at the sound of his voice all she'd been able to think was that she didn't want him to leave before she could talk with him. She was at least more thoroughly covered in layers of cloth now than she would have been in one of her day dresses.

"Then I am certain she will not like the reason I have come here."

Konstanze's lips parted, her eyes widening. Was he going to make advances? Offer her a dishonorable arrangement? Her heartbeat quickened. She hadn't expected him to want her that way, or at least not so quickly. She didn't think she'd smiled so obviously at him, once they'd left the cave. She was surprised that Cornish men were so very forthright. Bugg had taken months to court her.

"I have a proposition for you that I think in your present circumstances you might find beneficial."

Good gracious, here it was! She felt a flutter in her stomach, her breath coming more rapidly. She was being offered a place as his mistress, a kept woman. How did one respond? Should she be offended and slap him? Be polite and thank him, but decline? Of course she would decline, and explain how mistaken was his impression of her.

In the space between one moment and the next she imagined him kneeling before her, one hand going beneath her shawl to lie against the side of her rib cage, just beneath her breast, the other reaching behind her neck, pulling her face down to his, his head tilting, amber eyes half closing, his lips—

"It occurs to me that your husband, Mr. Bugg, may not have . . . ah . . . provided you with sufficient funds with which to take care of your needs during your separation."

Should she stop him now? But it would be presumptuous to decline before hearing him out. He might say she had misconstrued his offer, and then she would be the one looking the fool. She cocked her head, examining him. He did not look particularly overcome with desire for her. Perhaps, for all his forthrightness on the issue, he was better at hiding his animal desires than either Bugg or Bugg II.

"Yes?" she prompted.

"Is that the case?" he asked. "Do you have enough money?"

"I do not think that is any of your concern."

"I know I have no right to interfere in your life, but I truly do believe I can be of some assistance to you. My proposition, however, is somewhat shocking."

She was no longer certain she wanted to hear the actual words spoken. Whatever thrill or flattery she might get from hearing of his desire, it would likely be overwhelmed at the shame of his assumption that her favors were for sale. She did not want to hear him offer money for a place in her bed. It would be so embarrassing for them both.

"Mr. Trewella, I think you have said quite enough. You will kindly leave now," she said, and stood, her shawl grasped tightly in both hands. "Hilde! Show Mr. Trewella the door!"

He looked up at her with confused startlement, and then his face cleared and he jumped to his feet, narrowly missing a beam with his dark head. "Miss Penrose, you've misunderstood me. I wasn't trying to suggest that—"

Just as she'd thought! He was trying to deny it!

"Please, say nothing more. Go, and we won't speak of this again."

Hilde appeared from the kitchen, frowning fiercely. "*Ja,* you go now." She opened the door and stood beside it like a fierce medieval guard. "Go. *Schnell!*" When he made no move toward the door, Hilde began to march toward him.

He held up his hands, palms out, in a gesture saying he meant no harm. Hilde kept advancing. Trewella gave Konstanze a desperate look, saying quickly, "I want to hire you to be a mermaid!"

It took a moment for the word to make sense, but even then she couldn't believe she had heard him right. "A mermaid?" she asked, confused.

Hilde got a grip on his arm and began to haul him toward the door, his feet fumbling as he tried to find purchase against her impressive strength. "Foweather thinks he saw a mermaid today," he said, desperation in his voice. "You."

"Hilde, stop," Konstanze ordered.

"I throw him out," the maid said, still pulling.

"No, wait."

Hilde reluctantly released Tom. He closed the door and gave a slight bow of the head to Hilde, then returned to the settle, sitting down once Konstanze had resumed her own seat.

"Start from the beginning," Konstanze said. She wanted to hear what this nonsense about being a mermaid was. He wanted her to play a part? Her? Inside she was cringing at the assumption she had made about being his mistress, but greater even than that embarrassment was curiosity about what he had to say.

"Foweather returned to town telling everyone that he had seen a mermaid singing on the rocks. We have him all but convinced that this mermaid has come to shore in search of a husband. He's fascinated by the idea, half afraid that she has set her sights on his own handsome self and intends to drag him off to her home beneath the waves. This is the first time I've seen him distracted from catching smugglers. If we had you to sing the role of mermaid at specific times, we could ensure that no one got caught and sent to jail."

"You could ensure that just as well by not smuggling," she said.

"You grew up here. You know that it is part of the way of life."

"If smugglers wish to avoid getting caught, perhaps they should rethink their way of life," she said primly, in no mood to be sympathetic.

"And do what instead?" he asked simply and without rancor. "What few pilchards have come this year cannot be sold to Italy, due to the war with France that has blocked off all trade through the Mediterranean. There's a tax on salt that makes it nearly impossible for women to preserve enough of the pilchards to feed their own families. The farming has never been profitable, and few own their own land. What's left but the mines, none of which are owned by the villages any longer and which do not offer wages to support a family? All a man has to look forward to there is an early death. The king may lose a bit of revenue to Cornish smuggling, but there are many here who would starve without it."

"I had no idea things were so bad," Konstanze said

softly, embarrassed by her own holier-than-thou statements. She looked around herself at the cottage. "My great-uncle, was that how he managed to survive?"

"That cove where you swam is a good landing place. Goods would be hauled from there up to the barn."

Konstanze grimaced, visions filling her mind of revenue men searching the barn, finding a dozen casks of French brandy, and then hauling her off to jail. "Is that still going on?"

"Not without your agreement, no."

"I could never give it," she said quickly, the image of herself locked up in a damp, dark cell making her feel slightly ill. "I don't want to end up in prison any more than you do."

"You wouldn't be risking that as a mermaid. All you'd be doing is singing, and when was that ever considered breaking the law?"

"I would be an accessory. I would be aiding smugglers."

"What judge would even listen to a case of a woman impersonating a mermaid? And who could ever prove it? Foweather would embarrass both himself and the Preventive Service if he ever made a statement against you for such a thing."

"But the entire idea is ludicrous," she said. "Get a local girl to do it, if you must have someone."

"One who can sing like you can? Not likely. Mogridge said you sang like an angel. I thought he exaggerated until I heard the tales that Foweather was telling."

She tried not to show it, but the compliments heard

secondhand made her preen a bit. "I was trained at my boarding school in Switzerland, and then when I joined my mother she taught me. She made me promise never to go on the stage, though. She wanted me to lead a respectable life." She looked at her guest, wondering exactly how far from respectable he considered her.

"It's not as if you would be standing on a stage, hundreds of pairs of eyes on you. You'll be visible for only a few moments, and all the job will require is a bit of singing, and perhaps a bit of swimming here and there."

"You want me to *swim*, too?" No, no, not in a hundred years, not after today. "And I suppose I'd have to be naked except for a big fake tail and some pearls wound in my hair," she said.

"I hadn't thought about the pearls. That would be a nice touch," he said, and smiled charmingly.

Did the man not even see how insulting he was? It was beyond humiliating that he thought he could pay her to bob around bare-breasted for the sake of misleading the sitter of the Preventive boat. That he thought of her that way—that she wasn't just imagining it in another of her diverting daydreams—made her feel cold and sick. She wrapped her arms around her waist, wishing she had taken the time to dress. "I think you should leave now," she said.

"I warned you it was a shocking proposition. If you'd give yourself a minute to think on it—"

"Leave, Mr. Trewella. I do not want you in my home."

He stared at her, his expression losing its cheery

easiness. A nature far more determined and calculating showed itself now. "Let us be frank, *Miss Penrose*. We both know that you ran away from your husband, and that likely he is looking for you even as we speak."

She sucked in a breath and then forgot to exhale, cold flushes of fear washing over her body. Little pinpricks of light danced in her vision. "You'd tell him where I was?" she asked, her voice barely audible.

Hilde came in just then with the tray of crockery tea things, setting it with a clatter on the small table. "Do you want me to get rid of him?" she asked in German.

Konstanze shook her head and gestured for the maid to return to the kitchen.

All Mr. Trewella had to do was send a note to Bugg, and her freedom would be at an end. She'd go back to Bugg House, back to endless days trapped indoors, and back to nights where he tied her to the bedposts and beat her for his enjoyment. She was caught between two despicable choices.

"What type of man do you take me for?" Tom protested, visibly angered by her accusation. "I should hope I had not sunk so low as to blackmail a woman," he said.

She did not trust his words. Her impression of him as an honorable man had been wrong, and formed too quickly. "Then what is your meaning? Why should you mention my husband to me in such a way?"

"What I meant to say—and would have had you not been so quick to jump to conclusions—was that I thought it likely you would be in need of cash. Your husband obviously will not have provided you an allowance, and whatever money you have with you will not last forever."

"Neither would whatever you offered to pay me for this disgraceful stunt."

"Play the mermaid, and I will give you two percent of the profits from each cargo you help to preserve. You could take home anywhere between one and ten pounds for a few hours' work. At the end of the summer I will give you any aid you wish to ensure that you have escaped your husband forever. I'll see what can be done about an annulment of the marriage, or a divorce. Or I'll help you sell the cottage and take ship to America, or Europe if you wish it. Whatever you want."

"And if what I want is to stay here and live in peace?"

"Winter is the height of the smuggling season. Open your barn to us, and you can live on those fees as your great-uncle did. Even I wouldn't ask you to swim in the winter seas, and I doubt Foweather's interest would hold for that long anyway."

Her head ached, and she pressed her fingertips against her temples and closed her eyes. There was too much here, too many possibilities both good and bad. She could not think. For all her repulsion at the idea of playing a bare-breasted mermaid, even worse was the idea of going back to Bugg. She would be a fool to trust that Trewella would keep her secret if she refused to do as he bade. "Must I decide tonight?" she asked, opening her eyes and letting her hands drop down to her lap.

"Not tonight, but soon. All I ask is that while you deliberate, you avoid the town. Let your maid go if you need to buy things, but keep your own self hidden. It will all be spoiled if Foweather sees and recognizes you, or if there is too much talk of a new, pretty young woman in the area."

She nodded, the notion forming that she could escape this neat little trap by "accidentally" letting herself be seen and recognized by Foweather. A glance at Mr. Trewella's face, however, warned her that he would see through such a feeble plot.

He stood and picked up his hat. "I won't trouble you further tonight. I'll return tomorrow evening for your answer."

"Tomorrow evening," she echoed, her impossible situation overwhelming her mind.

He gave a short bow and showed himself out. She watched him go without paying attention to what she was seeing, and it was several moments after the door had shut behind him before she returned to her senses.

Hilde came back from the kitchen. "What happened today that you did not tell me?"

"I wish that nothing had, Hilde. You do not know how much I wish that."

"Tell me."

# *Chapter Seven*

Konstanze sat at the kitchen table, poring over sheets of paper covered with her own fine script. A small pile of banknotes and coins sat in the middle of the table. The afternoon was growing late and the headache left over from last night more painful. She refilled her cup with tea and defiantly dropped in three lumps of sugar, the irregular white cubes splashing drops of tea onto the table and the edge of one of the papers, blurring the figures written there.

She sat back and sipped the too-sweet drink, hoping it would somehow help the headache as well as her worries to go away. She had thirty-four pounds, eight shillings, and sixpence to her name. It was enough to see both her and Hilde through a year of frugal living, but there would be no wages for Hilde out of that. The maid had received a paltry sixteen pounds a year from Bugg, and at times in Europe had received nothing when Konstanze's mother had trouble finding work. Konstanze knew that Hilde would stay with her even without wages, but she hated having to ask that of her. It had been Konstanze's decision to leave Bugg, and Hilde should not have to pay for it.

She had a year's leeway until the money ran out, and had thought that in that time she would think of what to do next. Now, unexpectedly, Mr. Trewella was offering her a job. A job! Not a respectable job, but a job nonetheless. She'd never had one. With the money from it she could pay Hilde and save enough to stay on at the cottage for another year, perhaps even two. She wouldn't have to sell it. Money was security, and money was freedom.

Ten pounds for a few hours' work—it was more than Bugg's scullery maids earned in a year.

She did not like the idea of floating around naked, though. She'd be too embarrassed to utter so much as a squeak of song. Really, it was quite unthinkable.

She sipped tea, and thought about it anyway. She and Hilde could design a costume, something silky and green that clung to her from the hips down but left her feet free underneath, so she could swim. Maybe some sort of shell bodice could be constructed to cover her chest. And pearls in her hair, that would be nice; she could wind them in amongst braids and dangling locks as she had seen in portraits from the Renaissance.

She saw herself sitting on a rock as the sun lowered to the west, casting the water and sky in an orange and pink glow, the light soft on her skin. She'd sing something of Purcell's, perhaps. She liked Purcell. Mr. Trewella would be waiting in a cave nearby, but as she sang he'd be drawn out, lured by her voice. When he saw her he would forget that she had a husband; he'd forget everything except how beautiful she looked, his eyes roving over the curve of her hip, the dip of her waist, the slight, gentle swell of her belly that was not covered by the shell bodice. He'd come toward her and—

And what? Probably tell her to sing a little louder, as he wasn't certain the Preventive sitter could hear her.

She clunked her cup onto the table and gave a sigh of frustration directed solely at herself. Mr. Trewella was no one about whom she should be spinning fantasies. He was not to be trusted, and she only wished she had known that sooner. Surely the only reason she was even allowing herself to think of accepting his "offer" was the fear that if she didn't, he would tell Bugg where she was. It did not matter that he had claimed he would not. That determined look in his eye told her he got what he wanted. She'd rather not find out how far he would go to ensure it.

It was a rotten world where escaping one man landed her firmly in the clutches of another.


Hilde could smell the town before she could see it. She was used to cities that held the stench of human habitation and streets filled with horses and livestock, but this was completely different. This stench was like a belch of warm air from the belly of a whale.

Fish. Rotten fish. There was no other smell like it.

She crested the hill and looked down on the town, which was wedged into the bottom of a crack in the land where a creek flowed down to the sea. The harbor was nothing more than the widening of the creek's mouth, protected from the force of the sea by three stone piers staggered on either side. The buildings inside the protection of the harbor came right down to the edge of the water—or of the mud, as the case was at the moment. The tide was out, and several fishing boats sat balanced on their keels in the mud.

The path zigzagged down the steep rocky slope, turning to stairs and then back again to an uneven slope of stone, winding between houses as she approached the bottom. She had come to buy food, that which they had brought with them having been finished off this morning.

Hilde trod steadily through the town, heading for the center. Town, village, or city, the food was always to be found at the center. She had moved through half of Europe with Marguerite, Konstanze's mother, and foreign towns and people held no fears for her. She rather enjoyed being the outsider in a new place. Although she often found the mannerisms of the local people annoying, she liked the challenge of getting what she needed in a new environment.

She explored the town, which consisted of a street on either side of the shallow creek, buildings on both sides of each street. There was a bridge crossing the creek at the landward end of the harbor, right next to a tavern that backed onto the creek, the Fishing Moon. The smell down here was worse than elsewhere. Any thoughts of buying fish for dinner fled her mind.

She made her way back to the one small butcher shop, its goods hanging from hooks in the low ceiling. A middle-aged man was grinding meat at the counter against the back wall.

"Sausages," Hilde said loudly in English. "Four pounds of sausages."

"Eh?" the man said, and turned around. "Pardon me, what was that?"

Hilde looked the man over. He had good muscles in his biceps, and a belly that was large enough to make you feel like you had a man in your arms, but not so big that it sagged. As he came closer she saw that he had bad skin, though. His nose was marred by large black pores, especially profuse on the sides, in that crevice around the nostrils. She gave a little "umph" of disappointment.

"What was that you wanted?" he asked again.

His teeth were about average, a couple missing, one or two gone a spotty gray. It was too bad about the skin. She liked good skin on a man. "Sausages. Four pounds. Please."

"Eh?"

"Sausages!" she said more loudly.

" 'Zah-zahg?' "

"Yes, beef. Four pounds."

"Where are you from? Are you Scottish or something?"

Hilde rolled her eyes. She could understand English much better than she could speak it. She knew what he was asking, but she wasn't about to go into an explanation of who she was. She would be here all day with this simpleton. "Sausages! Four pounds!"

He scratched at his hairline, right above the temple, looking confused and a bit embarrassed. "I'm sorry, could you say it one more time?"

"Saaa-saaa-je."

He screwed up his face and hunched his shoulders a bit. "Once more?" he asked in a small voice.

She sighed and looked around the shop, spotting a looped collection of what she wanted. She went over and tapped them.

"Ohhh, sausages!" he exclaimed, relief all through his voice and body. "Why didn't you say so?" he scolded, taking down the links.

*O Gott.* This was going to be a long day.

The sausages purchased, she moved on. Cheese was next on her list. She would try to find one of the soft French cheeses that Konstanze liked so well, but she knew it was a fairly hopeless endeavor in a place such as this.

*Poor Konstanze.* Like her mother, she was a lamb at the mercy of wolves, and in need of a shepherdess such as Hilde for protection. The child had no sense of how to protect herself, her head always in the clouds, her thoughts far from the mundanity of life. Konstanze would be unable to get along without her Hilde, that was for certain. She was quieter than her mother, more subdued, but Hilde knew she was just as helpless and in need of her care. The poor thing likely hadn't even given thought to how long her money would last.

A large chunk of white cheddar was purchased after much ado and a few barked orders on Hilde's part. The woman she bought it from did a bit of her own barking in return, which Hilde appreciated. The woman was red-faced and had her arms crossed over her chest, her jaw set as she watched Hilde put the cheese in her basket. Hilde gave the woman a curt nod before she left, feeling that she might have made a friend there.

She finished her purchases and was walking back

up one of the twin streets when she caught sight of a lush, beautiful head of white hair. She stopped, standing still, her basket hanging heavily in her hand and tilting her off balance.

The man was conversing animatedly with another man through a cellar doorway. She paid no attention to the words—they were too quick and too heavily accented to understand anyway—and just stared. Now *there* was a man to crawl into bed with on a cold winter's night. He looked to be about her height and had that stocky, barrel-shaped chest that she could not resist. There was something so very primitive about it, something strong and solid that made her think of godlike men with war hammmers, or great bulls stomping through the fields.

The man finished his conversation and turned toward her. Bliss upon bliss, he had a clear complexion, pinkened by sun and wind, deep lines spreading out from the corners of his eyes and down from the corners of his nose. He saw her staring and frowned.

Hilde hiked the basket back up her arm and resumed walking toward him, her gaze intently on him. With her free hand she ran her fingers lightly over her hair, tucking a stray strand of graying blond behind her ear. She moistened her lips and straightened her back, pushing forward her breasts as well as she could.

Her chin raised, she walked up to him and paused, meeting his eyes with a gaze of arrogant approval. She saw his blue eyes widen, and she grinned, her eyes roving over his body, and then in German told him, "I could eat you in one night."

"I beg your pardon?" he said, confusion in his eyes.

She nodded once, a promise in the gesture, and then

left him. It wouldn't do to come on too strong. She knew he watched after her as she mounted the steps between houses that led up to the path: She could feel his eyes on her back. She swung her hips for his enjoyment, then bent down as if to adjust her shoe, giving him a good view of her backside.

Perhaps Cornwall was not such a bad place, after all.

"Come on, move it, you mangy donkey," Tom said, yanking on the halter of the beast in question. The donkey flattened its ears and made a move to sit down. "Oh, no, you don't, not again." Tom reached into his pocket for his last remaining carrot, and used it to coax the creature forward, the small cart with its cages of squawking chickens and bags of feed trundling behind.

The donkey had been cheap even by donkey-purchasing standards, costing him a mere five shillings. He could understand why, now that he had shared the creature's company for two miles in the near dark. He had bought it and the chickens and cart from one of the farmers from whom he often hired horses to haul smuggled goods.

The livestock was for Konstanze, more a move of practicality on his part than of generosity. All of Penperro was talking of Hilde's visit to town, of her brusque ways and her incomprehensible speech. Tom had found Matt tossing back whiskeys, the light of a hunted creature in his eyes. "That woman's going to track me down and haul me off to the forest to have her way with me," he'd said. "And she looks strong enough to do it."

"She probably is. She left a bruise on my arm from where she grabbed it last night."

"Oh, God."

Tom had laughed, but when one of the Preventive crew overheard speculation about Hilde, it became necessary to concoct an explanation for her foreign presence on the off chance that questions might lead anyone to the Penrose cottage.

Keeping as close to the truth as possible, Tom had the information spread that Hilde was maid to the lady who had inherited the Penrose cottage. The lady was, unfortunately, an invalid, and had come to the cottage for the sea air and for the utter quiet and privacy in which she hoped to regain some of her former health. He would have to ask Mogridge not to talk to any more about the young singer he had brought to the cottage, and warn others to watch their words near the Preventive crew.

He had little doubt that Konstanze would agree to his plan eventually. She would not have listened to him half as long as she had last night if she were not in need of money, and he had seen proof enough in his time of what a person would do to ensure a full larder. She already swam around naked and sang sitting on the rocks, so allowing a man to glimpse her from afar while she did so should be but a slight change for her, and worth the profit. If he were in her place he'd do it, no question.

The cottage came in sight, and after a little more argument with the donkey he persuaded the creature to go around to the back. Tom unloaded the chickens into the chicken house and stored their feed by the last light of day, then unharnessed the donkey and put it and the cart in the barn.

"Who is dere?" Hilde demanded from the back

101

doorway, as he emerged from the barn. She had a fire poker in her hand, both she and the weapon silhouetted against the warm light from the kitchen.

"Tom Trewella. Good evening, Hilde. I hear you went shopping today."

Distressingly, she appeared to be getting a firmer grip upon the poker. Its angle rose, as if she was contemplating the best position from which to take a whack at his head. "Vhat do you vant?"

"To speak with Miss Penrose."

"Hilde, put that down," he heard Konstanze say from within the kitchen. Hilde turned her attention to her mistress, and a short argument ensued in German. Hilde reluctantly moved out of the way, and Konstanze stepped out onto the stone step.

"Mr. Trewella. Is there a reason you are skulking about in the yard instead of knocking upon the door?"

"I've brought you chickens and a donkey and cart."

The message was greeted with long moments of silence. "Have you?" she finally asked. "And why, pray tell, did you do that?"

"May I come in? We can talk about it inside," he said, coming up the steps and forcing her to move back. She pressed herself against the edge of the door frame, staring wide-eyed as he turned sideways to fit past her, their bodies just inches apart. When he met her gaze she quickly looked down and turned her head slightly away.

Now that he was close enough to see her well in the kitchen light he had to admit she dried off very nicely. Her brown hair showed hints of red now that it was dry, and was pulled sleekly back into a bun surrounded by a braid. A few short ringlets framed her face on either side. Her dress was white with yellow stripes, the yellow sprinkled with tiny red flowers. The neckline showed the curves of her breasts, pushed up high by whatever underpinnings this new style required. He had not thought to investigate the issue when he had fetched her clothes from the rock crevice.

He moved past her, and she slowly followed, pushing shut the door. She said something in German to Hilde, then preceded him into the sitting room, where they resumed their seats from last night. He wasn't certain if he was relieved or disappointed that she was not fresh from the tub, as she had been last night, the damp soapy scent of recent bathing still in the air. He'd had to fight to keep his eyes off her body, hidden so well under the shawl, wrapper, and nightgown, and yet seeming so very accessible simply because she was in her nightclothes. His hand had tingled with the desire to touch her, to lay his hand upon her breast and feel how soft and warm it was, in contrast to what he had felt when she'd been chilled and fresh from the sea.

After he'd left her last night his mind had followed its own happy male course, imagining the two of them on the floor before the fire, his hands digging into her wet hair as he buried himself within her. It had been longer than he cared to think since he'd been with a woman. His idle fantasies during the past months had made casual use of whatever attractive female he came across, but they had all been interchangeable in his mind, mere mannequins without faces or personality. No one had caught his attention in quite the way Konstanze had. He doubted she'd be flattered.

Tonight she was all formality: during their brief acquaintance, she had gotten progressively more securely dressed. He would be well advised to keep his eyes on the curves of her cheek and chin, and allow his gaze to go no farther down. He didn't need this type of distraction in his life, and she was married besides. A personal involvement with her was far more trouble than he needed, and doomed to a bad end.

"Now, Mr. Trewella, do you care to explain about the animals?"

"It occurred to me that you would be buying them yourself sooner or later, so I've saved you the trouble."

"I'm quite capable of purchasing my own chickens."

"So you are, but your maid has a hard enough time with sausages and bread. You would be the one buying chickens, and I want you to stay out of sight. Hilde can use the donkey for carrying purchases from town."

"You assumed that I would accept your offer."

"I assumed you would have the intelligence to see that it was to your benefit to do so, yes." Her lips tightened with, he assumed, some degree of annoyance at his comment. He supposed it did sound a bit presumptuous, but what the hell. This was business. There was no time for playing dainty. "And have you decided to agree?"

Hilde came in and all but dropped the tea tray onto the small table. She gave a sniff, then stomped back to the kitchen.

"Sugar?" Konstanze asked, and began to pour the tea.

"No, thank you."

She handed him his cup, poured one for herself and dropped in three lumps, then sat back with her cup and saucer balanced easily in her hand, looking for all the world as if she were the one in charge of this conversation, and not he. "I will agree to play the part of mermaid upon certain conditions," she said. She took a sip of tea, then set the cup and saucer down on the small table at her side with a lethargic grace that implied she had hours to spare.

"One," she said, counting it on her pinkie, "I will design my own costume. Two: the locals will not be permitted to gawk at me—no one will see me except for the Preventive sitter, Mr. Foweather, and his crew, and they only from a distance. Three: if I am ever charged with wrongdoing, you will pay for all legal representation necessary to prove my innocence."

She paused to stare at him with raised brows, apparently gauging his response so far. "Four: even should a cargo be lost, I will be paid one pound for my efforts. Five: I will be the one to determine if the water is too dangerous for swimming at any given time, and I will choose which songs to sing. And six: you will never, under any circumstances, inform my husband of my whereabouts or make any attempt to contact him. Do *you* agree to *my* terms, Mr. Trewella?"

He blinked at her. For such a frivolous-seeming young woman, she certainly had a practical head on her shoulders, not to mention a way of getting to the bare bones of what she wanted. He had been expecting at least half an hour of sham protestations of modesty and offended sensibilities, and then a willing acceptance of his proposal along with a demand for a higher percentage of the profits. He felt a bit of cheer at her demands. Now *this* was a woman with whom he could do business. "I want approval of the costume design."

"I really think that Hilde and I will be able to devise something appropriate on our own. Hilde has spent two decades in the world of the stage."

"And I have a much better sense of what a man would

105

expect of a mermaid than either you or she would, with all due respect to Hilde's talents. I am asking only that the costume meets with both of our approvals."

"Very well," she said grudgingly. "You agree to the rest?"

"All except that no one see you. You must realize that someone will have to take you to the proper locations, and help you escape should the need arise."

"I will not be paraded about like a maritime Lady Godiva."

"I wasn't suggesting that you should be. I'll take you."

"*You'll* take me?"

Why did she have to say it as if it were an insult? He'd already shown her in the cave that he could keep his hands to himself. "Was there someone else you'd prefer?"

"Are there no women who know the caves and landing places who could do it?"

Damn, he hadn't thought of that. There *were* women who helped with the unloading and transfer of goods. He'd been looking forward to watching Konstanze's mermaid performance, though, and wasn't about to let go of the prospect. "It's best that you have someone strong with you, in case of danger. I know how to swim, too, and I don't know of any women who could claim that."

She didn't look pleased, but did seem to accept his excuses. "Then I suppose I will just have to trust you, Mr. Trewella, to behave as a man of honor."

"I always endeavor to do so."

She raised an eyebrow in what he could only describe as skepticism. "Then I suppose we have an agreement."

# Chapter Eight

*Kent*

"Son . . ." Bugg wheezed.

Bugg II jumped up from his chair and leaned over his father, turning his head so his ear was near the old man's mouth. Was there a hidden safe in the house, or a lockbox full of jewels and gold? Were there properties held in another name, of which Bugg II must be told before it was too late? "Yes, Father?"

"Find her. Bring her back to me," Bugg said.

"Find who?" Bugg II asked, just to be difficult, feeling thoroughly annoyed. He knew damn well whom the old man sought.

"Konstanze! Find my darling. Bring her back."

"No one knows where she has gone. It would be impossible to trace her. She's probably gone off with a young lover." It wasn't a great pleasure, provoking a critically ill man like this, but it relieved some of his spleen that his fool father hadn't died as the doctor said he would. *Prepare yourself for the worst, but pray for the best,* the idiot had said.

"Find her!" Bugg demanded, a bit of color coming into his cadaverous face. "If you want anything more than ten pounds for your inheritance, you will find her and bring her back to me."

Bugg II's eyes widened in horror. A ten-pound inheritance? "What do you mean?" he demanded, tempted to choke the life out of the withered old snake with his bare hands.

"Ask Quarles," his father said, and gave a gurgling chuckle that sounded like rocks boiling in a pan of gravy.

He would, damn it. He left his father and went in search of the solicitor, finding him drinking by the fire of the drawing room. "What's this my father says about my inheritance?" Bugg II demanded without preamble. "I'm to have everything except the widow's portion, am I not?"

Quarles looked up from his drink, his eyes narrowing in malicious delight. "Are you? Your father is leaving everything but ten pounds a year to his wife."

"He can't do that!"

"He most assuredly can."

"But why?" Bugg II cried. As if he didn't know. But he had never figured that his father would be so stupid and self-absorbed as to leave all the money to his wife. What a spell she must have woven over him in the bedroom! A son had no way in which to com-

pete with the obsession of an old man with a young
woman.

"It has lately become his opinion that the anticipation of inherited wealth has robbed you of your native
ambition, and he believes it is ultimately in your best
interest to be forced to find your own way in the
world. Konstanze, on the other hand, he believes in
need of the protection of a comfortable income. Her
wealth will be held in trust for her, so that no unscru-
pulous young man can either kiss or kick it out of her."

"He only lately came to this conclusion?" Bugg II
asked, his suspicions rising.

"Your father does take my opinion quite seriously."

"You foul, dung-eating dog! What business is it of
yours to whom—" Bugg II stopped himself, a thought
hitting him. "And who will administer this trust for
Konstanze?"

Mr. Quarles smiled.

"Greedy, prick-licking pig—"

"There, there, Mr. Bugg. Such language!" Mr.
Quarles said with a smirk.

Bugg II stomped and swore for a few more minutes,
then settled down enough to start thinking again.
There had to be a way out of this. There just had to.
It was too much of a nightmare to be true. "But Konstanze has run off. What will happen to the money if
she never comes back?"

"It will remain in trust."

"Indefinitely?"

"Until proof of her demise can be given."

*Demise.* He liked the sound of that. "What happens
in the event of her death?"

Mr. Quarles shifted in his seat, and took a swallow of his drink. He didn't look quite so happy anymore. "In the event of Mrs. Bugg's death, the estate reverts back to you."

"Ohhh . . . does it, then?" Bugg II said. "And you wouldn't have a trust to administer, if that happened." To administer, and from which to skim a comfortable living for himself.

"As your stepmother is young and healthy, I don't think I'd rely on her death if I were you. It would speak ill of you even to contemplate the prospect."

"Heavens, no," Bugg II said mockingly. "I surely would never wish for the least bit of harm to come to dear Konstanze's pretty head. Why, just now my father begged me to go in search of her and return her to him. Out of filial devotion, I will have to obey. Why, who knows what may have befallen the poor creature, out all alone in the world? I would hate to think that some dread accident had occured, of which we were unaware, and that she was lying ill or injured somewhere, on the very brink of death."

Mr. Quarles snorted. "You don't have the spine to even try it."

Bugg II tried to look smug. "Don't I?"

Did he? He didn't know. He'd have to find Konstanze, though, before he had a chance to find out. The threat of ten meager pounds a year might be enough to push him to extraordinary deeds.

Father and Quarles were right about that, at least. Lack of funds did wonders for one's sense of enterprise.

# *Chapter Nine*

*Cornwall*

"What's that you're drawing?" Konstanze asked, curious.

"Fins for your feet," Hilde replied, hunched over a piece of paper that was covered with a multitude of small drawings.

"I thought we'd decided it would be too difficult to swim with legs in a tail." They had spent the entire day at the kitchen table, discussing costuming ideas. Konstanze was having more fun than she had for a very long time. Living with Bugg had encouraged her to fantasize, but she'd never done anything about those phantasms of the imagination. She rather liked the idea of bringing something created in her mind to life. So to speak.

"I did not say it was a tail. I said it was fins for

your feet. If someone does see you and you must swim, it would not do to have your human feet splashing about."

"True enough, but Mr. Trewella said I shouldn't be seen, except from a distance."

Hilde snorted.

"No, I don't trust him either," Konstanze said. Hilde had been very much against Mr. Trewella's preposterous plan, and they had argued about it well into the night after Mr. Trewella left. Hilde still refused to give her approval to it, but when Konstanze started making her own designs for a mermaid costume, the maid had been unable to resist taking charge. If it was going to be done, Konstanze knew, Hilde would want it done right. Hilde wouldn't want her charge appearing in less than the perfect habiliment.

She set down her own pen and massaged her cramped fingers. She had splotches of black ink on them, and there was a dent pressed into her reddened writer's callus. "I don't think Mr. Trewella is going to like our ideas," she said, cocking her head and looking critically at the small sketches that she had circled as her preferred options. There was not a bare bosom to be seen, each and every mermaid modestly covered. Trewella's comment about what men expect in a mermaid had given her plenty of warning about what he himself would want to see.

"Then he can find someone else," Hilde said. "Your mother is rolling in her grave already, without you showing your breasts to men."

Konstanze felt a twinge, wondering if her mother could indeed see her from the afterlife. No, she would not be happy about this, not at all. She would have rather Konstanze sold the cottage, or let the smugglers use her barn if she needed money. She felt another little twinge, and shifted on the hard seat of the chair as she recognized that she was enjoying the drama of the situation.

No, that could not be right. She was the lady her mother had sent her to boarding school to become. She was a good girl, one who desired stability and peace and respectability. Singing to an audience of herself and Hilde should be excitement enough for her.

She slid off the chair and went to the window, looking out through the rippled green glass at the hills. It had drizzled all morning, the air damp and cold and pushed along by a gusting wind off the ocean, but the late-afternoon sun was showing itself now, and the winds had died down.

"I think I'll go for a walk, Hilde," Konstanze said, turning away from the window. She was suddenly impatient with the confines of the indoors. "My legs ache from sitting in that chair all day." They ached with the desire to move, in a way that she remembered from Bugg House, where there was noplace to go.

"Mr. Trewella won't like that."

"Mr. Trewella will simply have to recognize that he cannot keep me in a cage." No more cages for her, not ever. "There is no reason I should not take a walk, as long as I avoid the shore and the town. I shall simply be a woman out and about, unworthy of anyone's notice."

Hilde shrugged. "As you wish. I would be happy to have his plans foiled."

"They won't be. I'll wear a veil on the off chance that I do come across someone. If I've learned one lesson, it's that there are people where you least expect them," she said wryly.

A few minutes later and she was on her way, wearing a dark green dress and a black velvet spencer, the short jacket coming to just beneath her breasts. She wore a smart black hat with an overabundance of veiling, the long tails of the netting lifting and flapping in the slightest breeze. She felt independent and strong, striding off across the countryside.

She found a narrow path and headed westward, in the direction of Penperro. She would be good as her word and avoid the village itself, but that was no reason not to explore the space in between. She hummed under her breath, tempted to sing a lively song or two as she marched along—perhaps something Scottish, to fit the patches of heath—but then thought better of it. It was a disappointment, but it wouldn't do for anyone to hear her singing.

After a good two miles or so she came over a low hill and looked down upon a long valley covered in bracken fern. Gray stones poked out of the greenery here and there, speaking of the rocky soil beneath. The bracken was all but useless, inedible to most livestock and prone to invading otherwise grazeable land. Her grandmother had said all it was good for was stuffing mattresses, and Konstanze had spent years sleeping upon the rustling, crunching dried fronds.

The path, narrow and covered in small loose stones, continued down the hillside and then along the valley floor, leading to somewhere out of sight behind the curve at the end. She decided she would go that far, just far enough to see what was at the end of the valley, and then turn back.

Still humming contentedly, she let her palms brush along the tops of the ferns as she walked, setting the plants swaying. Many of them reached to chest height. Nuisance though the bracken might be to farmers, she thought there was something rather magical about the way it coated every inch of ground, the green walls of the valley rising up on either side of her. She would have had great fun playing here as a little girl.

She came around the curve at the end of the valley and saw what had been concealed from her sight. The land dropped off to the ocean except for one headland, upon which sat a stone church, its square tower short and squat, as if built to withstand the buffeting of the coastal winds. The late-afternoon sun, cutting through breaks in the clouds, touched the small leaded windows with reflections of gold. This must be Talland Church, which Mr. Mogridge had mentioned.

Konstanze stopped where she was, knowing that to indulge her curiosity and enter the church would be foolish. As she stood taking in the scene, a chorus of male voices started up, the notes of their song reaching her faintly from the church. She was surprised to recognize it as a sea chantey that her grandfather had sometimes sung. The choir was more skilled that she would have expected, and she smiled behind her veil and found a rock upon which to sit and listen.

Time passed quickly as she listened to the choir practice and watched the sunset begin to color the sky in yellows and oranges. She was feeling relaxed and peaceful when, several songs later, two figures emerged from the church. One wore a blue coat and white trousers, which meant it was likely Foweather, and the other's black hair and frock coat told her he was none other than Mr. Trewella.

*Damn.* She had the worst luck when it came to those two. Peace and contentment fled, replaced by heart-thumping anxiety.

She started to rise, then decided against it, afraid the motion would draw attention. Perhaps if she sat very still they would not look in her direction. Her green dress was very nearly the color of the bracken that rose up nearly to her shoulders as she sat on the stone, and perhaps the black hat and veil would appear as a shadow only. Maybe Mr. Foweather had poor eyesight—he had after all thought she was a mermaid.

One could hope.

"It's astounding, perfectly astounding!" Foweather declared as they emerged from the church. They had been inspecting the famed "mermaid bench."

"I had always thought it a legend, myself," Tom said, "built up around a curious piece of furniture with an inexplicable carving. I had never believed the tale to be based on fact. I'm still not certain I do." He gave himself a mental kick. He was not supposed to be the voice of reason; he was supposed to be deceiving. Somehow, though, it wasn't much fun when the target was as credulous as Foweather.

"But it is, Mr. Trewella. I saw her with my own eyes, and heard her with these very ears. I cannot blame you for not believing, based upon the words of another. I never did, either," Foweather said, and gave Tom a consoling pat on the back. "When I read in the *Sherbourne Mercury* about those fishermen up in Scotland, why, I didn't believe what was there in print."

"What happened with the Scottish fishermen?" Tom asked, although he already knew. The *Sherbourne Mercury* was the only news sheet to regularly make an appearance in Penperro, and its articles were read by—or read to—every living soul. People still talked about articles they'd read five years ago.

"They caught a mermaid in their nets, and hauled her right up onto the decks. She was obviously from a different class than mine, though. They say she was a small thing, and bald, with spines that ran in a row down the back of her head. She hissed and made the spines stand up whenever anyone came close. Mostly, though, she cried, and so piteously that the fishermen threw her back into the sea. It's bad luck to kill a mermaid, you know."

"So I'd heard. And bad luck to see one. Or good, depending on to whom you speak."

"Which do you think it is for me, Mr. Trewella?" Foweather asked, in the voice of a little boy in search of reassurance.

"I think it's—" He cut himself off, suddenly noticing the motionless figure sitting upon the rock amidst the bracken. She was unnervingly still, facing in their direction with a gaze hidden by black veiling, as mysterious and eerie as some dark figure from the depths of Cornwall's past.

Konstanze, of course.

He had to hand it to her: the girl had an instinct for

117

being at the worst—or best, depending upon your view of it—place at the worst time.

A moment later Foweather saw her, too. "I say, who's that?" he asked. "Doesn't look like a local girl, does she? Unless it's one of the Failes women." Even Foweather could recognize such a distinctly different style of dress from that to be found in the village.

"No, she's not a Failes," Tom said, angry to see her there. There was no time to indulge the feeling, though. He thought quickly, trying to find a way to turn the situation to his advantage. "I can only guess at who she might be," he said, trying to inject a bit of dire warning into his voice.

"Hmm, yes?"

"Mr. Foweather, I think it would be best if you went back into the church. You'll be safe there," Tom said urgently.

"Safe from what?"

Tom jerked his head in the direction of the motionless figure, as if afraid she would know he spoke about her. "From her. She's been drawn here by the singing."

Foweather blinked at the motionless figure, then blinked at Tom as the gears of his brain got into motion. "By God!" he exclaimed, and stepped backward and then forward again, then turned to Tom, clamping his hand down on his shoulder. "We should warn the others. She might be after any one of them, with the way they sing."

"It's you I am concerned about," Tom said with as much seriousness as he could muster. "It's you she is watching even as we speak."

Foweather's eyes widened, and he cast a frantic look back at the figure. Konstanze stood up and took a step, and that was all Foweather needed. He dashed back into the church and sent up a cry that stopped the choir midnote. "The mermaid, she's out there!" Tom heard through the door before it swung shut under its own weight.

He gave Konstanze a furious look and made an exaggerated "shoo" gesture with both his hands. She apparently needed no second reminder and, picking up her skirts, ran the few steps through the bracken to the path and quickly disappeared behind the curve of the hill. She was just out of sight when the entire choir poured out the door behind him.

"Where is she?" Clemmens demanded. He was a fisherman, with a boat often turned to other catches than pilchards.

"Did you see her?" Wiggett the baker demanded.

There were fifteen men in the choir, and all were scattering about the churchyard, seeking some sign of the mermaid. Tom and Matt had told them all it was a trick, yet at this moment they seemed to have forgotten that fact, their faces as eager as Foweather's was scared. The Preventive sitter was peering out from behind the protection of the heavy door.

"She went down the rocks, there," Tom said, pointing to the rocky drop-off to the water. Surely they didn't all believe she was real?

Half the choir dashed over to see. "I don't see her!" someone called back. "There's no sign of her at all. Are you sure this is the way she went?"

119

"She moved so quickly," Tom said helplessly, taken aback by their sincerity.

"She must have made it to the water," Foweather said, inching his way out of the safety of the church. "We won't catch up to her now."

"I thought that would have been the last thing you'd have wanted," Tom said, turning to him.

"I'd be safe in this crowd."

"Would you? Ulysses' men had to tie him to the mast of his ship and stop their own ears with wax to make it past the sirens." He said it without conviction, but Foweather was beyond needing help to believe.

"I'm not saying I'd face her alone! By God, I'll not be spending my life in a mermaid's cave if I can help it. You've got to help me, Mr. Trewella. There must be some way to divert her interest."

"I don't know the ways of mermaids. I don't know how to help you."

"Think on it, man! I should not like to see what would happen if I came upon her while at sea! She might bring the entire crew down to the depths with her."

Tom shook his head sadly, trying to maintain his role. "They are dangerous creatures, it's true. I'll see if there's anything I can learn that might help you. In the meantime, I think you would be wise to stay clear of the water. If you can see the water, then likely she can see you."

Foweather's lips pursed and released like those of a fish, his eyes blue and bulbous. "But my work. The smuggling must be stopped. I cannot remain inland."

*The Mermaid of Penperro*

"Then take care, sir, and beware the song of the mermaid luring you to your doom."

Foweather pulled out a kerchief and patted his perspiring forehead. "Good advice. I shall heed it well."

"Good man," Tom said, and slapped him on the back. "Go to the Fishing Moon and get yourself a drink. You need to settle your nerves." He wanted Foweather out of his sight so he could stop feeling guilty for duping him.

Foweather nodded, and with a last wary look toward the cliff scampered off toward town.

When he had gone Matt was the first of the group to ask, "What was that all about?"

Tom put his palm to his forehead and ran his hand back through his hair, releasing a sigh. "Our mermaid was apparently drawn by the singing of the choir. She was out here listening when Foweather and I came out, sitting on that rock," he said, pointing for everyone's benefit. "She just sat and stared, and Foweather took fright."

"With a little prompting, I'm sure," Matt said.

"She was really here?" Clemmens asked.

"She's not a true mermaid, you dolt," Dick Popple said.

"I know," Clemmens said. "But I haven't seen her with my own two eyes, and neither have you."

"She sounds a beauty, from Foweather's account," Wiggett put in. "I'd like to see her myself, especially if she's got titties like he said." He held his hands in front of his puffed-out chest in the form of two breasts, and sashayed in front of the others.

"Stop it!" Tom ordered, incensed. "You are none of

you to speak of Miss Penrose in such a manner, nor am I to hear that any of you have gone snooping 'round the cottage. Miss Penrose is a lady prepared to render us a great service, and you will treat her with all due respect."

"Didn't mean to tread on your toes there," Popple said. "We didn't know as it was like that between you."

The choir let out a collective "ooh," and more than one elbow was nudged into a side.

"It is not 'like that' between us," Tom said sourly. "This plan hangs by a thread as it is. If any of you accidentally let on that the mermaid is anything but real, it is liable to fall apart."

"Are you certain she *isn't* real?" Clemmens asked.

Tom kept himself from rolling his eyes, if just barely. The sarcasm, however, he could not keep out of his voice. "Why, you're right. She may be off eating seaweed somewhere at this very moment. How could I be so foolish?"

"There's no call to be getting snippy," Clemmens said. "I was just asking."

"Bernice's sister's husband's cousin saw a mermaid once," Popple put in. "I hear she had a sort of grayish tail, spotted like a mackerel. She cut a hole in his nets and let the fish out."

"I wonder how mermaids have sex?" Wiggett asked of no one in particular. "Like dolphins? Come to think of it, I don't know how dolphins do it, either."

"Do dolphins have dicks?" Clemmens asked.

"Does Foweather have one?" Popple asked. "That's the true mystery."

"And if he came upon an unsuspecting dolphin, would he try to use it?" Matt asked, to a great outburst of laughter. Long minutes of ribald speculation and descriptions of Foweather, dolphins, and mermaids in outrageous combinations closely followed. Tom pulled a grinning Matt aside.

"I'll leave them to you. I'm going to go have a talk with our maiden of the sea."

"Beware the German dragon. I'd ask to meet the girl myself, except it would mean facing *her*."

"Maybe Hilde's what you've been looking for all these years, and you just didn't know it."

"God save me."

Matt herded the group back inside the church, and Tom set off in the direction Konstanze had taken. He was unsurprised to find the bracken valley deserted in the fading light—if she had kept up her pace, Konstanze should be halfway home by now. And she *should* run, if she knew what was best for her. Although the incident had worked out to his advantage, he was decidedly displeased that she had ventured so far from her cottage.

He kicked a stone as he went down the path through the quiet valley, diverting himself from his annoyance with the idle pastime of a boy.

A movement from the corner of his eye slowed his step, and the stone rolled to a stop. Fronds of bracken were swaying as if disturbed by some creature beneath their cover, and the disturbance was coming toward him. He stepped back, alarm tingling all over his body, his mind running through a quick list of possible creatures in the bracken, none of them fitting this low, rapid motion.

A goat burst out of the ferns, bleated at him, then turned and trotted away down the path. He let out a breath and dropped his shoulders at his own foolishness. He was as bad as the choir, believing in monsters when he should know better.

"Mr. Trewella!" a voice whispered.

He jerked around, eyes wide.

"Is it safe to come out?"

*Oh, Lord. Konstanze.* "What are you still doing here?" he whispered toward her voice. "And where the hell are you?"

There was another rustling of ferns and then her veiled head appeared above the green. "I was afraid someone might try to follow me, so I hid."

"It wouldn't have been an issue if you'd stayed at home," he said, then realized it was pointless to keep whispering, and raised his voice to its normal volume. "Come out of there, will you?"

She waded her way to him through the ferns. "I heard all the shouting. What happened?"

He explained the scene to her briefly, leaving out all reference to mermaid breasts and dolphin sexual apparatus. "You could easily have ruined everything."

She looked down, her face invisible beneath hat brim and veil. "I suppose you want me to apologize."

"Don't you think it appropriate?" he asked, incredulous.

"I should think that my hiding in ferns with a bunch of goats would be an obvious enough acceptance on my part of my error. I see no reason to belabor the issue," she said, raising her head. He could just make out the shadows where her eyes were, and sensed that they were glaring at him with defiance.

"I would still like to hear you say you were wrong," he said. Really, the woman was unbelievable.

"That is one of the greatest pleasures known to man, it is true, to hear another admit their error. I must, however, be getting home. Hilde will be worried."

He felt his eyebrows rise up his forehead. She wasn't going to apologize? She wasn't going to beg his forgiveness? His lips parted in amazement as she started walking away from him, her short legs moving with surprising speed. "I hadn't figured you for such a proud, stubborn little thing," he said, catching up to her and finding himself caught between amusement and annoyance at her behavior.

"Mr. Trewella, I feel I have shown a distressing lack of either pride or backbone during our acquaintance. I am certain you must have formed a most inaccurate picture of my character."

"How so?" he asked, surprised. He was quite certain his picture was accurate in the extreme.

She waved one hand lightly through the air. "Despite appearances to the contrary, I like to think of myself as a reserved and cautious person, and one who prefers calm to drama. And I have, until recently, been quite circumspect in my behavior. The present situation is highly unusual, and I do not like to think that your opinion of me is based upon it."

He tried to take her seriously, but it was hard. "I have always been of the opinion that one's true character is most likely to emerge when one encounters unexpected circumstances."

"I am *not* the type of woman who roams about unclothed and takes part in illegal plots."

"Apparently you are." He tried not to laugh.

She clenched her fists, shaking them at her sides and giving a little grunt of frustration. "If you had seen me a month ago you would never have said so."

He shrugged. "Perhaps not. Does it matter?"

She was silent for several steps, then: "No. I don't suppose it does."

"I much prefer your present self to whatever silent creature you may have been before."

"You do?" she asked, looking up at him.

"You wouldn't have been much use to me the other way, now, would you?" he said, deliberately misunderstanding her desire for flattery. It wouldn't do for her to know that he was beginning to enjoy her company very much indeed. "Foweather would still be combing the coastline looking for contraband, instead of studying mermaid benches and worrying about whether he'll be safe from you when he goes to sleep on his boat tonight."

"I see."

"Mrs. Bugg—"

"Please don't call me that," she interrupted, her voice going cold. "Call me Miss Penrose, or if that seems too false for you, then even Konstanze is better."

"Konstanze." He tried it out on his tongue, giving the name three syllables as she did, the accent on the

126

second. "How did a woman with Cornish roots end up with such a name?"

A tilt of hat and veil betrayed her glance at him. "Do you truly wish to know?"

He shrugged. The name didn't matter to him, but he was curious as to what she would tell him. Konstanze might be many things, but so far she had never been boring.

"My mother was singing the role of Konstanze, in Wolfgang Mozart's *Die Entfuhrung aus dem Serail*—that's *The Abduction from the Seraglio* in English—when I was conceived. It was her first major role, and being cast as Konstanze was doubly exciting, as she was the first Englishwoman anyone had ever known to sing at the Kärntnertortheater in Vienna."

"What is a seraglio?" He almost didn't ask, embarrassed to display his ignorance.

"A harem," she said, and he thought he heard a smile in her voice. "It's quite the risqué opera. Konstanze is captured by a pasha who desires her, but she yearns for her lover. The lover plots to rescue her, but they are caught in their escape attempt by the pasha, who is understandably upset and orders the lover put to death."

"Does this have a happy ending?"

"Naturally. The pasha has a sudden change of heart and releases them both so they can go off together and live happily ever after. Much joyous singing ensues."

"That's rather farfetched, don't you think?"

"I do not believe that plotting was the point of the thing."

He gave a grunt of assent. That was clear enough.

"And what of your father?" he asked. It was a delicate question to ask of anyone whose mother had been on the stage. She might not even know who he was. As long as she was in the mood to talk, though, he was happy to take advantage of it to learn what he could of her.

"His name was René Crécy. He and my mother had been married for less than a year when I was conceived. He was an actor, and worked as a stagehand when he was not in a role. Mama said he could have been great, if he hadn't had such a fondness for drink. He died in a brawl three months after I was born, so of course I don't remember him. Mama came home to Mousehole, and left me in the care of my grandparents until she had enough money to send me to boarding school in Switzerland. From then on I spent my holidays with her."

"That must have been quite a change from the boarding school." He surprised himself by feeling a bit of envy for her colorful past. What must it have been like to be raised in Europe, traveling with a group of opera singers during one's holidays, moving from country to country?

"It wasn't like you think," Konstanze said. "Everyone assumes that opera singers are women of questionable morals, and that the stage is peopled with wicked, hedonistic types who are unworthy of respect. It's not true. There are some like that, but there are some like that everywhere. My mother, for all her liveliness, was never loose or casual in her behavior. Evenings in our apartments were far more sedate and ordinary than I think you would imagine."

"I really hadn't thought about it," he said, in a slight bending of the truth.

They walked a few minutes in silence; then she said, "I didn't mean to bore you with all that."

"On the contrary. You've led a fascinating life. Most of the people in Penperro have never been farther from home than Liskeard, if they've made it even that far."

"Are you a native of Penperro, yourself?"

"No, Marazion," he said shortly. The town was half-way between Penperro and Land's End, and held a wealth of unhappy memories.

"Why did you leave?"

"I was looking for new opportunities," he said. There was no need to say any more than that. She doubtless thought him scoundrel enough without hearing his dismal history. "I should think it perfectly safe to remove your veil if you wish. I don't know how you see the path in front of you with all that netting."

" 'Twasn't a problem, but it is getting dark now," she said, unwrapping the veil and then giving a sigh. "This is much better, although the veiling does help keep one's face warm. What type of opportunities were you seeking?"

That was a safer topic than his past in Marazion. "I thought to start a small school, but the venture failed. People did start coming to me to draft letters or help manage their affairs, however, as they apparently thought that anyone educated enough to teach must know more about the world in general than they themselves."

"And was that the case?"

"I kept them fooled long enough for me to make up the difference. Desperation makes for a quick-witted student. The business with the smuggling grew out of that, but I assure you the bulk of my work is perfectly legal. Especially now with the war."

"How do you mean? I thought the war was pushing you further into smuggling."

"It's not the only way to turn a profit upon the seas. Piracy becomes privateering once you lay hands to a letter of marque."

She looked at him aghast, her rosy lips parted.

He laughed. "I'm not a pirate. I have invested in a few sloops that have taken French prizes, though." He regretted the words as soon as he spoke them. Why had he told her that? He realized that he was bragging, trying to impress her—though it was stupid to think she'd be impressed by legalized piracy—and immediately sought a change in subject. "Have you had time to work on the costume?" he asked. They were drawing near to the cottage.

"Hilde and I have sketches awaiting your approval. Do you wish to see them, Mr. Trewella?"

His little comment about the privateering seemed to have brought back her formality. "If you are to be Konstanze to me, please call me Tom, as my friends do."

The look she gave him held no softening, and she did not reply.

"Yes, I'll see the sketches. I can get you whatever materials you need to construct the costume, the sooner the better."

She nodded, and he followed her through the back

door into the cottage. Hilde the harpy was there, and the two women exchanged a brief, heated conversation in incomprehensible German as Konstanze removed her hat and spencer. Hilde set her jaw and gave him a dirty look, then went to the pile of papers at the end of the table and pointed something out to Konstanze, apparently explaining. She then scooped up the entire pile, thrust it into Konstanze's arms, and returned to tending her cooking.

They went into the sitting room, and he took his usual place on the settle. To his unspoken delight she sat down next to him, the papers in her lap. Her lips were pursed in displeasure.

"What was that all about?" he hazarded to ask.

"It's just Hilde being Hilde."

That actually explained things quite well. He wondered how Konstanze stood living with the woman. He'd take his food-obsessed housekeeper Mrs. Toley over Hilde any day. "Let's see what you have," he said, and reached for the sketches.

She pulled them away from his outstretched hand, and thumbed through them herself, choosing and pulling out a sheet that she handed to him. "There, this is my first choice," she said, pointing to the circled drawing in the corner of a sheet covered front and back with sketches.

"What's this on her chest?"

"A shell bodice."

"Mermaids don't wear bodices, shell or otherwise," he said with exaggerated patience. He'd suspected she would try to pull something like this.

131

"How would you know? No one knows what mermaids wear."

"You don't see carvings or drawings of them with shells on their chest," he pointed out. "Mermaid figureheads on ships are bare. The carving on the church bench is bare."

"That doesn't mean that this mermaid can't wear shells. Figureheads are nothing to go by. They're carved for a bunch of sailors stuck out at sea with no women."

"But mermaids don't wear clothes," he insisted. It was such an obvious point, he could hardly believe they had to discuss it. "We have to stay with what is known."

"I think you're confusing fact and fantasy. Mermaids aren't real. They can be however we want them to be."

"Foweather saw a mermaid without shells or anything else covering her chest."

"He didn't see a real mermaid."

"You know what I mean. That's what we all expect," he said, and couldn't help looking at her breasts, high and full beneath her gown. "I want you barebreasted." He paused. That hadn't come out sounding quite like he meant it. He glanced at her face and saw that she had narrowed her eyes at him, her lips pressed tightly together.

"You've made your point," she said, "and quite clearly."

"I didn't mean it like that," he said. "I'm talking from a man's perspective, from what a man wants to see." Oh, God, he was digging himself in even deeper.

"I can't expect you to like it, but I can expect you to try to understand it."

"Oh, I understand well enough." She riffled through the papers, then pulled out another sheet and thrust it at him. "This, then. At least it's not a bodice."

The drawing showed a mermaid wearing such a profusion of necklaces that her breasts were completely buried. "Konstanze. You know this won't do."

"She's naked. Mermaids are known to like jewelry, and perhaps she plundered the necklaces from a sunken treasure ship."

"You are forcing me to be blunt. Have you ever once seen a depiction of a mermaid where you did not see both her nipples?"

She stared at him, cold and silent.

He shifted, uncomfortable under her gaze. She looked as stern as Hilde. "Have you?" he asked again. He was beginning to feel like a boy caught thinking about sex while in church.

"I can see we're not going to agree on this today. Shall we move on to the tail? What do you think of this tail?" she asked, holding out a piece of paper.

She was doing it again! She was changing the topic as she had when he had wanted her to apologize in the fern valley. He gritted his teeth, irritation crawling up his skin. Couldn't she just admit she was wrong? "I'm the one who will be paying your wages. I think my opinion is paramount in this."

"And I am the only mermaid on offer. Hilde designed some interesting fins for my feet. What do you think?" she asked, thrusting a new sheet of drawings beneath his nose.

133

"Breasts. Two bare breasts," he said, and slapped the sheet down.

"We'll not discuss it now," she said, and her jawline firmed. "I think a gray-green material would suit best for the tail—"

"You can't just discard our discussion because it's not going the way you like!"

"This drawing right here I think shows best what I—"

"Konstanze!" he shouted, trying to break through her intentional disregard. He leaped to his feet, knocking his head on a low beam. "Ow! Dammit!" he cried, raising his arm to feel for the sore spot.

Her eyes suddenly went wide and she cringed away from him, her forearms raised protectively over her face, the sheets of paper spilling from her lap onto the floor.

"Konstanze?" He stared at her in surprise. She looked as if she thought he was going to hit her. He slowly lowered his arm, despite the urge to rub at the tender spot on his head.

Is that what her husband had done when upset? Hit her? It was hard to imagine anyone striking that big-eyed face, but it would certainly explain her eagerness to escape the man.

She must realize he was nothing like that. Or did she? She knew him as a smuggler, a liar to the law, and now as one who profited from privateering, as well. He did not think there had been anything amiss in his treatment of her, but he had to admit that she had perhaps not seen the best side of him.

"Konstanze?" he asked softly. "Are you all right?"

She straightened, a flush coming to her face. "I am not accustomed to being yelled at."

"Did your husband beat you?" he asked. The question was intrusive in the extreme, but he had to know.

Her eyes widened. It looked like a confirmation. He felt a slow burn of rage start in his chest that anyone could have treated her so. "Did he strike you when he was angry? Is that why you cringed, because you thought I'd do the same?"

"He never struck me in anger," she said.

"But he hit you," he said, a little less certainly. The man had plainly done something to her to make her shy away from an upraised arm.

"I really can't see that there is any reason for us to discuss it further. It has no bearing whatsoever on our arrangement."

"I would never harm you," he said. Whatever had gone on with her husband, he could not bear the thought that she might fear him because of it. "Surely you know that. I have never done anything to make you think I would physically hurt you."

"What worth does that have?" she asked, the bitterness in her voice taking him by surprise. "I haven't known you long. You haven't had much opportunity." He started to protest, but she held up her hand, stopping him. "Let me continue," she said, the bitterness replaced now by exacting precision, each syllable careful and emotionless. "I was startled by your shout and your leaping up, that's all. It won't happen again. My reaction was nothing to do with you, and I am quite recovered."

He was tempted to believe her, as she looked entirely in control of herself, as if that moment of cringing fright had never occured. Still, he wanted her to have no doubt about her safety in his company. He reached out and lifted her chin with the tips of his fingers, looking steadily into her eyes, trying to communicate the sincerity of what he was about to say. "I swear to you I will never harm you. Not under any circumstances. You have my word."

As he watched, a fine sheen of tears coated her eyes, making them glisten in the candlelight. She had not been as self-possessed as she had appeared, and the realization gave his heart a gentle wrenching. "I believe you," she said.

He gave a firm nod and dropped his hand, affecting a tone as businesslike as hers had briefly been. "All right then. The tail. Is it a single or a double tail you have in mind?"

She gave him a weak smile, and with a faint unease he recognized that that small curve of the lips, so shakily given, was worth more to him than winning any number of arguments on breasts and nipples.

# *Chapter Ten*

Konstanze was deep asleep, nestled warmly under her covers, when a pounding at the door woke her. It took her several seconds to make sense of the sound and to separate it from her dreams. She threw back the covers and ran barefoot over the warped floorboards to the window that looked out over the front of the house. A grumbling Hilde joined her as she unlatched the window and pushed it open into a night blanketed heavily by fog.

"Who's there?" she asked, although there was only one person it was likely to be.

"It is I, Tom! Konstanze, we need your help. Get dressed and come down at once."

"The costume isn't finished!"

"You won't need it tonight. Be quick!"

"But what will you have me do?"

"I'll explain on the way. There's no time now. Will you come?"

"I'll be but a minute," she said, and pulled the window shut. She stood there dumbly for several seconds, heart pounding, not believing it had already started.

"What does he want, pulling you out of bed at this hour?" Hilde asked.

"I'm not certain, but I think the smugglers are having trouble."

"Then you should stay here. There's no reason to put yourself at risk for them. Let the thieves do as they will, and hang as they will."

Konstanze brushed the comments aside. Her own grandparents had on occasion been such "thieves." Tom's explanation of the plight of the people of Cornwall had touched her sympathies.

The chill of the night was already setting her skin to goose pimples, and she felt a deep longing to return to her comfortable bed. But no, she had agreed to do a job, and this was her first chance to prove herself.

"Light a candle and help me dress," she ordered.

By the time she was dressed and opening the front door she felt as if she'd been running in a footrace, her heart was beating so rapidly. It was a wild mixture of fear and excitement she felt, the one emotion urging her to stay safely at home and out of trouble, the other entrancing her with the adventure ahead.

"I'm counting on you to keep me safe," she warned Tom as she stepped out of the cottage. "Whatever it is that's going on, don't make me regret doing this for you."

"There are no guarantees," he said, and before she

could protest he took her hand and pulled her after him into the dark and the fog.

*"Sei vorsichtig!"* Hilde called after her. Konstanze turned and could see only the faint yellow light of the candle Hilde held, its illumination diffused through the fog.

"What did she say?" Tom asked.

"She says to be careful," Konstanze said, jogging after him, her hand still held firmly in his strong grip. She held up her skirts with her other hand, her braid flopping on her back. The fog was a cool mist against her face. "Where are we going?"

"To the cove. Sounds carry well in the fog—you'll have to keep your voice down once we come 'round the hill."

She didn't know how she'd be able to tell when that was. She could see next to nothing, and was surprised she hadn't already tripped and fallen. Tom, however, seemed to have no trouble finding his way.

She was panting by the time they reached the cove, too anxious to catch her breath to try to talk. Tom helped guide her down the rocks, reaching up to grip her around the ribs and half lift her down. She clung to his coat and his shoulders, more concerned with slipping and breaking an ankle than with propriety or even her unwilling attraction to him. There was no time for either, and in a few moments they were down on the narrow rim of sand.

"Into the boat," Tom whispered, leading her to the gunwale of a small wooden rowboat that was pulled up on shore.

She wanted to question him—surely it was not wise

Lisa Cach

to go paddling about in such lightless conditions?—
but thought better of it. It was pointless to quibble
when she knew she would agree to get in anyway.

As soon as she was seated he hunched low and put
his strength behind sliding the boat into the water, and
she felt a small jolt of nostalgia as the water took the
boat's weight and it began to float, gliding easily over
the surface. Tom jumped in a moment later, the boat
rocking as it always had when her grandfather took
her out. She knew she was smiling in the dark, thrilled
despite her better sense. If she were the proper girl she
was supposed to be, she wouldn't be itching to take
the oars into her own hands or eager to head bow-first
into a good, splashing wave.

Tom unshipped the oars and with a few expert
moves had them turned around and heading out of the
cove, the paddles making only the faintest of noises
as they slid in and out of the water, a few drops hitting
Konstanze where she sat in the stern. She guessed he
had wrapped cloths around the oarlocks to keep them
so quiet. The sea was calm in the still fog, with no
waves to impede their progress.

"Can you tell me now what's going on?" she whispered, her voice barely audible even to her own ears.

"A lugger loaded with goods from Guernsey is offshore, but it can hardly move in these windless conditions. Its men are pulling as well as they can on the
long oars, but the going is slow. Foweather and his
crew are out in their cutter, in similarly becalmed conditions, only he has put his crew in a small-oared boat
and has them towing the armed cutter. It makes for a

slow chase, but if Foweather stumbles across the lugger, they'll be caught."

"How did Foweather know they were there?"

"With no moon and plenty of fog, tonight's a perfect night for smuggling. Even one as dim-witted as he can see that . . . or one of his men pointed it out to him. It was by pure chance that he caught a glimpse of the lugger, before the fog hid it again. One of the lugger's men swam to shore to give the alert."

"But why is Foweather towing the cutter? Surely it would be faster to row something small like a pinnace."

"A pinnace wouldn't have the guns of the cutter."

"Oh." She'd conveniently forgotten about the guns, and didn't much like the idea of one of those cannons being fired at her. "Are you certain that my singing will frighten him away?"

"It will either frighten or draw him; I'm not sure which at this point."

"That's not terribly reassuring."

"Either way, he'll be distracted and the boat will have a chance to come to shore—perhaps even to sneak back to the harbor, if Foweather is sufficiently bemused. Do you know what you'll sing? Something lovesick would do. It needn't be in English."

"I'll be ready," she said, and then they both lapsed into silence, the only sounds the muffled oars and the soft sounds of water moved by Tom's rowing. Her excitement was waning as they moved forward, the reality of the situation coming home to her. Those men on the Preventive cutter would be very angry indeed were they to discover the trick that was about to be played on them.

And then as well there was the less deadly but equally troubling anxiety of giving a public performance, something that was fairly new to her. Recitals in front of her boarding school chums and for Bugg's friends were not in quite the same league as duping the king's men. Her eyes went to Tom, a shadowy form bent to the oars. She wanted to impress him with her voice, never mind saving the smugglers. She wanted him to have a reason to look at her with admiration.

She was still a bit ashamed over the way she had reacted the other night when they had argued over the costume and she had shielded herself, acting as if he were going to hit her. She had sworn to herself that she would never again cringe away from another's anger, or shut her mouth because of it. No more cages!

"We should speak as little as possible. When I tap your foot with mine, sing," he whispered. "When I tap it again, stop."

"All right."

He let the boat drift a short distance, and she knew he was listening for sounds of the cutter. He dipped the oars back in the water and changed their course. She thought he must be one of those men who seemed to carry a compass around in their heads, always knowing which way was north and exactly where they were.

She imagined him as the captain of a ship, maybe in Elizabethan times, as a contemporary of Sir Walter Raleigh. She could see him standing on the high poop deck at the stern, his hand raised to shield his eyes as he gazed into the distance, nothing but ocean waves as far as the eye could see. He'd be wearing black hose, formfitting, and those funny, short, blousy breeches with an embroidered codpiece. He'd have a pointed black beard, and a single pearl-drop earring. She liked the image very much, especially the part about the tight-fitting hose.

She felt a tap upon her foot, the signal startling her out of her reverie.

Unprepared, she opened her mouth and out came a crackling, rough note. She shuddered at the sound and tried again, and within a few notes was in her usual form, singing Purcell's "If Love's a Sweet Passion."

She was only a few bars into the piece when the sound of startled male voices came to them over the water. The voices suddenly stopped as if shushed, and then a few notes of singing later Tom tapped her foot.

She shut her mouth abruptly, and Tom gave the water a loud slap with his oar. A shout rose up from the unseen men. Tom bent to the oars, rowing hard and silently. Konstanze could hear the voices on the other boat, becoming louder as the Preventive men drew closer, then going silent as they listened.

Tom maneuvered the rowboat around so that they were on the opposite side of the cutter from where they had begun, judging by the murmur of voices that carried through the fog. The Preventive boat was now between them and the shore.

The tap came again.

She picked up where she had left off, projecting

toward where she now knew the cutter and the small boat hauling it to be.

Again a cry went up, and this time an argument ensued, angered male voices coming through the fog. She kept singing, reaching the end of the song and starting over, aware all the while of Tom sitting tense before her, the oars held poised and ready above the water.

As the arguing died down Tom put his back to the oars yet again, almost silently moving them out to sea. She guessed that any sound of the oars that did carry to the cutter would be misinterpreted as her swimming. He tapped her foot with his, and she stopped, hearing as he must have the sounds of the Preventive men laying into their oars, coming toward them.

They settled into a game of cat and mouse with the Preventive boat, starting and stopping, singing and silence, listening and rowing. Foweather and his crew chased after them, never getting too near—although whether that was due to caution on their part or to Tom's careful positioning of their rowboat, she was not sure. At one point they dipped close to shore, passing close by an outcropping of rocks, the type that would have been deadly in foul weather. The crew cursed and Foweather gave frantic orders when they came suddenly upon the rocks in the fog.

The game went on for well over an hour. Konstanze fell prey to the thrill of it, wanting to laugh aloud each time Tom had her stop and she heard the Preventive crew's frustration, and their heated arguments. "Where'd she go?" "I think I heard something over there." "Quiet, I can't hear!" When Tom rowed she

144

found herself gripping her thighs, as if doing so might make their little boat go faster.

She had no idea where they must be in relation to the shore, or how far down the coast they might have traveled. Tom cued her to stop singing and then gave another of those splashes of the oar against the water, as if the mermaid were diving. He rowed on for a short way and then they sat in silence, listening.

The Preventive boat drew closer, the voices of the men hushed, growing more uncertain as the minutes ticked by with no mermaid song. She heard them ship their oars, sitting silent as she and Tom did, waiting. They could not have been more than fifty feet off. She glanced at Tom, trying to catch some expression of his in the dark, but he made no move, sitting as still as stone.

Konstanze shivered, her clothes damp from fog and the accumulated drips off the oars. As the minutes crept by she came to understand without Tom's having to tell her that they were through with their game for the night, and it was a matter now of waiting until Foweather gave up and went back to shore.

With each silent minute Konstanze grew more tense, and the muscles around her ears pulled tight as she strained for any sound from the Preventive boat. Her buttocks were sore from sitting for so long on the wooden seat, but she dared not so much as shift her weight. Her imagination began to work on her, convincing her that Foweather was drifting closer and closer as they sat there, easy targets in their tiny boat.

"Give it up, men," a voice that must be Foweather's said, coming from what might have been no more than

145

twenty feet through the fog. "She's gone."

There were murmurs of assent, and the sound of oars being unshipped. Konstanze spent an anxious few moments trying to guess if she and Tom were on the landward or seaward side of the cutter and if the crew would row right into them, but as the men rowed the splashing of the oars grew quieter, the boats moving off without coming any nearer.

She held her silence, knowing how easily sound carried over calm water, but the tension drained from her muscles and she allowed herself to rearrange her position. They were all but safe now, the worst of the danger past. She trusted that Tom could get her back to shore without stumbling into the path of the cutter.

"Well done, Konstanze," Tom whispered at last, and began to row them back to shore.

"Thank you," she said, pleased with herself and with his appreciation. "Was my singing what you had hoped?" she asked, unable to resist digging for a few more compliments.

"It was adequate."

"It was more than that!" she whispered fiercely.

"If you already know it, then you don't need me to tell you so."

She wrinkled her nose, glad he could not see her face. How was she supposed to argue with that? *Stupid man.* He made her sound vain, when all she wanted was a few minutes' worth of adulation.

"When do I get paid?" she asked. If she couldn't have fawning praise, she'd settle for cash in hand.

He laughed softly. "After the goods are sold. It should be a week or so."

"How much are they worth?"

"Figuring your percentage, are you? You can expect to get about three pounds."

She made a little noise of assent. That was certainly decent pay for the night. In her heart of hearts, she knew that she would almost have done this for free, for the sheer thrill of it. Now that it was all but over, her moments of fear were easily discounted, relished instead as part of the fun. She felt energized and alive, and began to fidget.

"It's exciting to face danger and escape, isn't it?" Tom said.

"It's better never to be in danger in the first place," she said, but did not mean it.

He laughed again, still keeping his voice low. "There are some who find they can't live without that excitement, once they taste it."

"That is not I."

"Then why are you bouncing your knees like that? I think you've enjoyed yourself. You would be collapsed in the bottom of the boat if this had been as much of a strain on you as you like to pretend."

"It's nervous energy, that's all," she said, bringing her bouncing legs to an abrupt halt.

"Oh, I see."

He rowed in silence for some minutes, then asked, "In what language was that song that you sang?"

She gave a grunt of offense. "English!"

"Was it? I thought I could make out a word or two, but thought that might have been my imagination."

"I'll have you know that my articulation is excellent."

"I'm not complaining. I'd rather have Foweather think you were using some foreign deep-sea tongue, anyway."

"I would like to hear the singer who could have done it better!" The man obviously had a tin ear when it came to music.

He laughed, long and low, and managed to gasp out between breaths, "Konstanze, you are a treat. You have a beautiful voice, and if I had been in Foweather's shoes I'd have thought you a mermaid myself."

The compliment smoothed her ruffled feathers. She was not accustomed to being teased, and once her irritation began to settle she felt a curious warmth toward him for having teased her so, his compliment feeling the more sincere for having come out in such a way. His teasing bespoke a playful friendliness that she had not encountered in her few dealings with men. She liked it.

She searched her mind for something clever to say, something about which she could tease him in return, but with examination every thought turned childish or awkward, and she feared her words would fall flat. She held her tongue and instead repeated in her mind his praise of her singing.

The fog was beginning to thin out a bit, the difference visible to her as a few stars appeared faintly above. She wondered how far off dawn was, and with her waning excitement began to think longingly of her bed and dry clothes. Going home would mean that Tom would part company with her as well, though, and she was not certain that the warmth of a cup of tea and a fire in the grate were an adequate exchange.

She gave herself a silent scolding for thinking that way. She really had to keep a firmer hold on her romantic tendencies. There were a dozen and a half reasons that she should not allow herself to become attached to the man in any way. As she had told herself before, nothing honorable could come from any attraction she felt. She was a married woman, and therefore even if he ever wanted to, Tom would not be able to offer her anything other than a shameful affair. As Mama had warned, such entanglements had landed many a good girl pregnant and in the poorhouse.

And besides, Tom seemed to think of her as little more than a tool—a talented tool—for his schemes. The man did not seem to spare a thought for women other than to analyze the degree to which their breasts were visible.

She was busy working herself into a froth of indignation against him when she noticed Tom had stopped rowing, the oars poised inches above the water. Tension had come back into his silhouette.

"What is it?" she whispered.

"Shhh!"

She shut her lips, straining along with him to listen into the darkness. She picked up the soft slosh of the calm sea against the rocks, then heard what had set him on the alert: subdued voices and faint splashings.

She caught only a few words as they drifted across the short distance between their rowboat and the craft near shore. *East, harbor*, and *patrol* were a few of them, and they told her that it was the Preventive boat to which they had caught up. The fog thinned for a moment, and Konstanze felt her eyes widen in horror as the shadowy shape of the cutter became visible against a short stretch of pale sand.

Tom dipped the oars back in and changed their course. Konstanze needed no warning to remain silent. The thought that all those men need do was take a careful look seaward and they might see the rowboat made her sit stiff with fear, as if she were a rabbit who thought that she might pass unnoticed if she did not move. She was intensely grateful for the layers of fog that built between them and the shore as they moved away.

"That's deuced inconvenient," Tom said when they were well beyond earshot.

"Was that my cove they were in?"

"Apparently Foweather thought it a good idea to go back to where he'd first seen you."

"Are they going to stay there all night?" She realized that she really had been looking forward to returning to the warmth of home.

"From the sounds of it, Foweather is letting off a few men to patrol the coast on foot, likely to look for where the lugger lands. He and the rest will remain with the cutter: now that there's some sign the breeze may pick up, they have a hope of traveling under sail. I suspect they'll be at it until dawn."

"So what does that mean for us?"

"It means, my dear Konstanze, that we get to spend a bit more time in our lovely little boat."

"How much more time?"

"Until Foweather and his friends are gone."

"But you said that wouldn't be until dawn," she protested, the warmth of the grate getting farther and farther away.

"Yes."

That wasn't what she wanted to hear. "Aren't there places we can land other than my cove?"

"There are, but I don't particularly wish to risk it with the men patrolling on shore. If they should spot us, we would raise considerable suspicion."

"We are doing nothing illegal."

"No, but there is no reasonable explanation for our presence out here in the middle of the night."

She understood that, but still didn't like the thought of drifting around out here for several more hours. Her buttocks were beyond sore, and her feet were wet from the inch of water in the bottom of the boat. Why was it that boats always had water in their bottoms? "We can't be out here at dawn," she pointed out. "Can't we row farther down the coast, beyond the patrol?"

"You can, perhaps, but I think it's a bit beyond my power at the moment."

"You're tired?" she asked, somewhat incredulously. For some reason it had not occurred to her that he, a man, could be worn out by rowing.

"I know you thought I was a man of great physical prowess, a veritable Samson and Hercules rolled into one, but I do have my limitations."

She gave a little snort. "Hardly Hercules. If you'll trade me seats, I'll row for a while."

"I am not yet that enfeebled."

"Don't pretend to be chivalrous. I've rowed a boat before, and won't faint from the effort."

151

"I wouldn't feel right about it."

"Don't be stupid. What else can we do? We can't be drifting around out here when dawn comes."

"There's a cave down the coast a short ways. We'll tie up inside and wait."

She supposed that was a reasonable enough idea. "Will you let me row to the cave, then? It's not just to save you the effort," she admitted. "I've been wanting to take a hand at it since we got in the boat. I remember enjoying it as a child."

He paused in his rowing. "You think this is fun?"

"I used to. Please, will you let me?"

He hesitated. "You're not doing this just because you feel sorry for me?"

"Feel sorry for Samson? Never! No, I only offered before because I want to row. I don't care a farthing for the state of your shoulders and arms."

"Nor my back?"

"I would gladly feed your whole body to the sharks for the chance to put hand to those oars," she said, happy that she seemed to be getting the hang of this teasing business.

He shipped the oars. "Then to save myself from the fishes I suppose I could let you give it a try. Tell me as soon as you feel the strain, though. A few minutes' rest should have me ready to go."

*Wunderbar!* She slid to the side while he stood and, moving low, sat down beside her as she rose, moving with equal care to the center seat, her hands on the gunwales. The transfer accomplished, she rearranged her skirts and the hem of her pelisse, making sure she wasn't sitting on them in such a way that the movement of her arms would be hampered. She found the smooth wooden handles, still warm from his touch, and maneuvered the oars into the water. The oars were heavier than she expected, and she remembered rather belatedly that when she was a child her grandfather had taken one oar, and she the other.

But she'd been only a child then, and was a woman full-grown now. She would do fine handling both.

"Keep me on course," she directed Tom, and dug in.

Her muscles strained, pulling against the oars, and she braced her feet for leverage. The left oar moved unevenly, that arm weaker, but she corrected it, endeavoring to keep the force even on each side. She completed the stroke and lifted the oars out of the water, and was rewarded with a little noise of surprise from Tom.

"Sorry," she said. She must have splattered him with water.

She dug in again. It wasn't so bad. It wasn't as hard as she'd feared, either. A few more strokes and she thought she had the hang of it.

"A bit to port," Tom directed.

She corrected course, silently proud that she had not had to ask which way was port. She was no landlubber, not she!

Five minutes later she was wondering if she had perhaps been a bit precipitous in claiming she could row them to wherever they were going. She was sweating, the chill from earlier long forgotten, and her entire upper body was beginning to feel heavy and drained of strength. Her strokes became progressively shorter and slower, the oars dipping less deeply each time.

"A little to starboard," Tom said.

She took a breath and bent back to the task. She wasn't so proud that she wouldn't give the oars back to him, but she'd be damned if she'd do so after five minutes, especially after arguing to get them.

She rowed on despite the growing pain in her muscles, pausing briefly between each stroke and settling into a rhythm. In her mind the tiny rowboat became a Mediterranean galley and herself but one of many workers upon the oars. She closed her eyes and imagined the burning sun overhead, beating down on her bare shoulders as she rowed, rowed, rowed. Tom became a foreign prince, reclining on a pile of pillows as she and the others slaved away.

*The girl in the third row back,* she imagined him saying to one of his officers. *Where did she come from? I have never seen a female so fair, and yet with such strength in her arms.*

*We bought her in Algiers,* the officer said. *Does she interest you?*

*Bring her here! I would see her up close.*

The officer approached her in her fantasy, and she looked up, taking a hand from her oar long enough to wipe the sweat from her brow.

The real Tom spoke then. "Easy, Konstanze. We should be hitting the rocks at any moment."

She opened her eyes for real and saw that much of the fog had dissipated. The coastline was dimly visible, the black bulk of the nearest headland blocking out the stars.

"Trade places with me," Tom directed.

She obeyed, knowing he could much more easily guide them to the hiding place than she could. She didn't know if she had ever been so happy to be back in the stern as she was at that moment, arms hanging limply.

The boat bumped against rocks, Tom pushing them off with a well-directed oar. They inched along the side of the headland for several more minutes; then all at once they were at the opening and Tom moved the boat inside to the utter blackness. The small sounds of water against the boat and the rocks were magnified in the cave, reverberating strangely. She felt Tom moving around, the boat rocking.

"There," he said, settling down. "Now we sit and wait."

"In the boat?"

He laughed. "Would you prefer in the water?"

"I thought there'd be a beach in here, like in the other cave."

"No such luck. I've tied us off as well as I could to a rock."

"Oh. How long until dawn, and the Preventive crew goes home?"

"I should imagine another three hours or so. I know it's longer than you had counted on, but I'm afraid there's no avoiding it."

"At least I will feel that I've earned my three pounds," she said, and wrapped her arms over her chest. The heat of exertion was already passing, and now she had weariness to add to the discomfort of the cold. She was glad she'd had the foresight to use the chamber pot before going out.

"What happened with the goods in that cave where I found you?" she asked, hoping to distract herself from her discomfort.

"They were hauled out and sold. It's not a good hiding place, though. Too difficult to bring things in and take them out, and in very high tides there's a danger of it all floating away."

"Ah." They both fell silent, and she searched her mind for something else to say. "That choir at Talland Church. They're very good. Have they been singing long?"

"They would be flattered to hear a mermaid praise them. They haven't been singing so long with regular practice—only a year or so. It was a good way to bring a wide group of men together without arousing suspicion."

"You mean—"

"Bloodthirsty, thieving smugglers, all," he said cheerfully.

"But they sing so well!"

"I don't know that the two are mutually exclusive. They sing at festivals in town, and at the church on Sundays. We even sent them over to Fowey once, to show those rusty-throated fakers what real singing sounds like."

"Does the vicar of the church know they are smugglers?"

"Matt? I should say so."

"Good gracious." If even the vicar was in on it, then who wasn't? Just Foweather and his crew, apparently.

Knowing Tom, he'd probably manage to turn even the crew to his purpose, given half a chance.

"Your Hilde seems to have taken an interest in the vicar, Matt Jobson. Is she looking for a husband?"

"Hilde? Not that I know of. What do you mean she's 'taken an interest' in him?"

"She gave him the eye."

"What eye?"

"You know, the one you women give a man when you're interested."

"I assure you, I have no idea of what you're speaking. Giving 'the eye,' indeed."

"Oh, come now, Konstanze," he chided. "Even convent-bred virgins are not that innocent."

"I may know of what you speak," she admitted grudgingly, "but my mother warned me about that sort of thing, and she said that men mistake even a casual meeting of the eyes as an invitation. I'm certain that is all that has happened between Hilde and your Mr. Jobson. For all that she thought you yourself were a fine specimen, Hilde does not flirt."

"She said I was a fine specimen, did she?"

"Not in those exact words," Konstanze said, grimacing. She had not meant to let that slip out.

"The woman has admirable taste."

Konstanze rolled her eyes in the dark. "I suppose that now you'll be adding Adonis to the list of legendary men you resemble."

"You said it, not I."

She could not help it; she laughed.

"Now you're offending me," he said. "I think it fits quite well."

"So, Adonis, if you're so wonderful, why is it that you have not married?" she asked.

"How do you know I don't have a wife waiting for me at home at this very moment, fretting over my absence?"

She shrugged, the gesture invisible in the dark. "It's just a sense I get," she said. "Something about you says you are a bachelor still." As she said it, she wondered how she did know. Perhaps it was his subtle flirtation that made her think that way, but she would be a fool to count on that alone to guide her. As Mama had said, marriage bonds tied the wife more firmly than ever they tied the husband.

"No woman who can sense that can be innocent of using 'the eye.' "

She decided to let that pass. She admitted she was perhaps not so pure of thought as she would like to pretend. "I can still disbelieve that Hilde used it on the vicar. But you are changing the subject. Why is it, O Great One, that you have never married?" She was grateful for the dark that hid her face from him, for she was certain she was casting a bit of "the eye" in his direction at that very moment. She only hoped he had no sense of how very interested she was in the answer to her question.

"I thought to, once," he said, "but it ended badly."

"That is not much of a story."

"I never claimed it was worthy of an opera."

"Tell me anyway," she said, "if you're willing. I don't want to pry." That was a lie, but he didn't need to know it. Besides, hearing about his past romances would help keep her mind off her wet feet and damp clothes. Surely he owed her that?

He sighed. "I don't suppose it makes much difference if you do know," he said, making her wonder exactly at his meaning. Had he worried over the impression he made on her? "I was a young idiot, head over heels in love with a girl who had no particular interest in me. I pined for her. I wrote atrocious poetry. I planned out my day to increase the chances of meeting her 'accidentally.' I even ingratiated myself to her parents.

"I had had an education, and with a former school chum was trying to start a school in Marazion. It was going well until I fell in love with Eustice, at which point I became so obsessed that I let my duties fall by the wayside."

Eustice? He'd been madly in love with a woman named Eustice? It sounded so . . . unromantic. How did one write poetry to a Eustice? It didn't rhyme with anything romantic. Eustice, avarice, artifice, prejudice . . . Clearly not a romantic name.

"Then Eustice fell in love with my old school chum, and he with her. I didn't handle it well, I'm afraid. The school was already folding due to my neglect, and then when Herbert told me that he and Eustice were to wed, I lost what little sense I had left. I got drunk, there was an awful fight, and in the end poor Herbert had a broken arm and I had worn out my welcome in Marazion. I left and came here."

"Gracious, I don't know why you don't think that has the makings for an opera. Jealousy, passion, violence, disgrace—you have everything."

"But I'd be the villain. It's a role I've since sought to avoid."

"And very commendable of you, Adonis, although it does seem you have your own ideas of what constitutes villainy. Breaking the law apparently does not qualify."

"That is getting to be a tired refrain."

That stung a bit. She didn't like to think she was sounding like an annoying old prig, and a hypocritical prig at that, considering that she had put herself in league with the smugglers for the promise of three pounds. "Surely all that drama must have happened some time ago. Why have you not married since?"

"No time, I suppose. I have too much to do to waste my time on such things."

"But don't you hope to have children of your own someday?"

"Perhaps. I am in no hurry. It has been my observation that such a relaxed attitude is largely incomprehensible to women, however, and so I'll beg you now not to continue digging for an explanation."

"Are you still pining for Eustice?"

He barked out what might be called a laugh. "Enough, Konstanze. Eustice is part of the past. I can't even recall what it felt like to be in love with her. I look back on that time and can hardly believe that I was the person who did and felt those things."

She liked the idea that he had forgotten all his feelings for the unknown Eustice. The little green demon of jealousy that had been stirring in her chest settled back down, reassured.

"If you feel so free to pry into my personal life,"

he said, "perhaps it is only fair that you tell me something more of yours. Why exactly did you leave your husband? Was it that he beat you?"

"I—" she started, and then stopped, trying to find words to explain without having to explain absolutely everything. She wanted him to know she had had just cause to run away, and that she had not taken her decision lightly. "I did not like the way he treated me," she said, and felt how inadequate that was. "He allowed me no freedom. I spent all my time cooped up indoors alone, with no chance to make friends of my own. We never went out, and only rarely had guests, and when we did they were his friends, and all his own age. I felt like my life was draining away while I sat by and watched it go."

"You were bored?" he asked, his incredulity apparent even in the dark.

"It was more than that. He frightened me," she explained. "On occasion he would drink, and when both angry and drunk he threatened me. I thought he might do me harm."

"Might? You mean he didn't?"

"He never broke my arm," she said.

He was silent for long enough that she wondered if she had gone too far, referring to his past like that. "Fair enough," he said at last.

"I know when I describe my life with Bugg, it doesn't sound so terrible. I had clothes and food and a big house, and servants to wait upon me. I know there are many women who would have happily traded their lives for mine, but I couldn't stay. I simply could not. I might as well have been dead, for all the living I was doing in that marriage."

"Why did you wed him in the first place? No one forced you into it, did they?"

She heard the hint of accusation in his tone, and imagined that as a man he was sympathizing with Bugg. "My mother had asked me to, on her deathbed. For all that he has forty-five years on me, Bugg seemed to her—and to me at the time—a good enough match. He had been kind to us, and paid our rent those last two months. I thought he would treat me well. Whatever doubts I had I forgot about when Mama died. I didn't want to have to think about anything, or worry about taking care of myself." She shrugged, remembering the alternating grief and numbness of that time. "Bugg was there to take care of me, and I let him. I suppose I should feel grateful to him for that."

"He took advantage of your vulnerability to get what he wanted, and I don't know that that particularly deserves gratitude. On the other hand, you got what you wanted as well. It sounds like you both bought yourselves a boatload of misery, if you don't mind my saying so."

"Why should I mind?" she said faintly. Instead of painting herself in a sympathetic light, she'd apparently managed to come across as self-serving.

"Marriages of convenience seem invariably to turn out inconvenient," he said.

"I shouldn't have thought there would be so many in Penperro to observe," she said, glad to turn the conversation to a more general discussion.

"The lives of the few big landowners are forever a

topic of gossip, but marriages of convenience occur regularly enough on a small scale. The girl who gets pregnant, the boy who seeks a bride with a dowry, the fathers who want to combine their businesses, small though they are—there are a dozen reasons it happens even in poor Penperro."

"So you think that couples should marry only for love?"

"I have yet to meet the man who could think straight while in love. They're damn fools, and I can tell you that from personal experience. They make terrible choices."

"Then who should get married? Who's left?" she asked, genuinely curious as to his answer.

"I suppose it could be decided by committee."

She made a disgusted noise. "I cannot see agreeing to wed someone a committee had chosen for me. The very idea is repellent."

"I doubt you would have ended up any worse than where you are now."

"At least it was my mistake to make, and I won't be making another like it. Would you marry someone chosen for you by others?"

"I might do so if Matt was the one who did the choosing. I don't think I'd trust anyone else to do it."

"I don't think I'd trust Hilde. She'd pair me with Napoleon if she could. She likes commanding types."

"I'll have to tell Matt that," he said, and the boat rocked as he moved around. "It's getting light. The Preventive men will have returned to the harbor by now."

She turned and looked out the cave entrance, and

indeed the blackness had lightened to a dark grayish blue. She was surprised that they had been talking for so long. "Does no one smuggle during the day?" she asked.

"Of course not," he said, in a voice that said she should know better.

"I wasn't trying to sound stupid," she said, resenting the tone of his answer. She realized she was getting tired, and bad-tempered as well. "It just occurred to me that if no one expects smuggling during the day, it might make it possible to do so once or twice without getting caught."

"How?"

"I don't know," she said, irritated that she had said anything at all. It did sound stupid, now that she thought about it. "You're the master smuggler. You figure it out."

"I thought I was Adonis and Hercules," he said, using an oar to push off the walls and send them drifting toward the entrance.

She rolled her eyes. "Just take me home."

They were both quiet as Tom rowed them back to her little cove. The dawn air was no warmer than the night's had been, and was made chill by a freshening wind that kicked up small waves. Konstanze huddled on her seat in the stern, shivering and thinking of warm fires and hot cups of tea. She was surprised when the rowboat finally nudged up against the sandy shore; her attention had been so securely focused inward on her discomfort.

Tom leaped out and pulled the boat farther up the beach. She stood and, stiff and hunched over, stepped through the bilgewater up to the bow of the boat, her balance uncertain. Tom was waiting to take her hand as she climbed over the gunwale.

"Good Lord!" he exclaimed as she put her hand in his. "Your hand is like ice. Is your blood even moving?"

As soon as she was standing on solid ground he took both her hands and held them between his own, pressing the warmth of his palms against her fingers. "I've never known anyone whose hands get as cold as yours."

"Thank you," she muttered sourly. "That makes me feel so much better." She refrained from mentioning the equally frozen state of her buttocks. She couldn't even feel them, they were so cold. A long, shuddering shiver racked her body, and her teeth began to chatter audibly. His hands felt hot against her skin, the simple pleasure of a bit of warmth outweighing any more licentious thrill she might have gotten from his touch. She'd welcome those hot hands on her chilled buttocks for the same reason, except he'd likely be repulsed by the feel of them. They probably felt like two dead fish.

He removed one of his hands from hers and touched her cheek with the backs of his fingers. "You're frozen half through. We've got to get you home."

She let her teeth chatter noisily at him in response, enjoying his concern and hoping he felt a little guilty for keeping her out all night.

Her fingers were so stiff she could barely grip her skirts to raise them for the climb up the rocks. Tom put his arm around her waist, cursing softly at the dampness of her pelisse. He felt warm and strong beside her, and she let him help her up the rocks. Once at the top he scooped her up into his arms.

She could have walked, but she was tired and Tom was warm. Despite the long night he was still somehow full of energy, carrying her in a smooth lope back toward the cottage. She shut her eyes and wrapped her arms around his neck, nestling her face against the wool of his coat. No one had carried her since she was a child, and she planned to savor the experience. She wasn't making eyes at him, so surely it was an innocent enough indulgence.

Her mind was already in that bleary state halfway to sleep when they reached her cottage. She knew she should have him put her down before Hilde saw them and made a fuss, but it was so very nice being carried she did not say a word. Tom managed to open the door with her in his arms, and carried her into the warm kitchen. She was vaguely aware of Hilde jumping up from her chair near the fire.

Tom set her down in the vacated seat, and she looked up into his eyes while his face was still near hers. For a criminal, he was awfully attractive. She reluctantly took her arms from around his neck, and thought she might have felt the slightest hint of reluctance in him as well, before he withdrew his arms from beneath her knees and behind her back.

"Thank you," she said.

He gave her a wry smile. "My pleasure."

"Where have you been? Why did he carry you? Are you hurt?" Hilde was barking in German.

"I'm fine, just cold and tired," Konstanze answered in the same language.

"She needs to get out of those wet clothes," Tom said to Hilde. "She should soak her feet in warm water, too."

"You don't need to tell me what to do," Hilde said in her own tongue. "As if I don't know how to take care of her! You were the one who got her in this state, you with your plots and schemes—"

"Hilde, enough," Konstanze said, glad Tom couldn't understand the maid's words. By the angry set of his jaw it was apparent he understood Hilde's tone well enough, though.

"I'll be going, then," Tom said. "I see you're in capable hands."

"Stay and warm yourself. Have a cup of tea, at least," she said, laying her hand against his sleeve.

He looked down at her hand, then at her, and as she let her hand drop he stepped away. "No, you need to get into dry clothes and be put to bed. I'll not hold you up."

She stood as he moved toward the door. "The costume should be done by tomorrow evening. Will you want to see it?"

He gave her a short nod. "I'll come by after dark."

"Tomorrow evening, then."

"Tomorrow," he said, and then he was gone.

Konstanze sat back down, her clothes suddenly feeling more damp, her limbs wearier than when he had been in the room.

"He is trouble, that man," Hilde said. "You should not be making eyes at him."

"I wasn't."

167

Hilde snorted, and poured hot water into a basin.

"I know enough to stay out of trouble," Konstanze said. She knew enough, and she hoped she would heed her own good sense.

# Chapter Eleven

*London*

Bugg II woke with a smile on his face. He rolled onto his back and stretched, then turned his nose to his armpit and sniffed, enjoying his own scent. He smelled like a man who had performed admirably in bed.

The prostitute he had hired the night before was long gone, departing while he slept, sated from his exertions. He yawned, then grimaced at the sticky, cheesy taste of his mouth, and rubbed his tongue over his front teeth. He sat up, swinging his legs over the side of the lumpy bed in his rented room and reaching under it for the chamber pot. He sighed as the pressure on his bladder was released, and winced as the hot acid fumes of his urine met his nose.

Yesterday had been a day of victory, and his hiring of the prostitute his celebration. After two weeks in

London he had finally found the pawnshop where Konstanze had sold the family silver, jewelry, and the ormolu clock that his mother had left to him. Although he had been unable—and unwilling—to buy the items back with his cash on hand, he had bribed the pawn-broker to write out a letter confirming Konstanze's actions, and to give him copies of the pawn tickets.

Not only had finding the pawnshop put him on Konstanze's trail, but it had given him the means to see her hanged for theft. Although it was debatable whether the silver and jewelry were hers to do with as she wished, it was beyond question that the clock had been his. There were those who got transported to Australia for as little as stealing a few linen handkerchiefs, and a theft of more than two pounds from a house was a hanging offense. Why do the dirty work of killing her himself, if the Crown would do it for him? And transportation to Australia was as good as a death sentence. She'd never survive.

He nodded to himself. It was a brilliant plan. He had the upper hand now, and he'd use it, once he found her. The pawnbroker had given him the name of the inn that Konstanze had given as her address. It was only a matter of time now.

He set down the chamber pot and stood, stretching again, then looked around for his clothes. Where had they gone? He'd been drunk as well as horny as a bull last night, and dimly remembered dropping them to the floor as the prostitute helped him strip.

There were no clothes on the floor. A short search of the small room revealed that his bag was present, but empty except for one ratty old handkerchief, a pair of stockings with holes, and the pawnbroker's letter and tickets. He dropped to his knees, searching for the shoes he knew he'd left under the bed.

Gone. And in the toe of one of them had been stashed all his money.

He stood and gave a mighty roar of anger, and yanked all the covers from the bed, throwing them on the floor in a fit of pique. His foot caught the edge of the chamber pot, spilling its contents. He kicked the offending pot away, then threw himself upon the stained mattress and wept, his bare, hairy butt exposed to the chilly air.

# Chapter Twelve

*Penperro*

"It was like she was taunting me," Foweather said, and took a sip of his tea. He was sitting on a settee across from Tom, in Tom's parlor. "We'd hear her on one side; then there'd be a splash and a silence, and then we'd hear her from a different direction. She must have swum under the boat a half dozen times!"

Tom nodded sympathetically. Foweather looked pale and weary, purple shadows under his eyes. "And this went on all night?"

"Nearly. She tried to lure us onto the rocks, even. If it had been rougher weather we might have perished!"

Tom shook his head and made *tsk*ing sounds. "I fear you may be right, and it is you she has set her cold, fishy heart upon."

172

Mrs. Toley came in with a fresh pot of tea and a plate of cakes and biscuits. She set them down near Tom. Foweather's head lifted at sight of the goodies, his eyes roving avidly over the assortment. With the edge of her hand Mrs. Toley pushed the plate closer to Tom. She gave Foweather a narrow-eyed glare and went back to her kitchen.

"May I?" Foweather asked.

"Please," Tom said, and handed him the plate.

Foweather sat back with the plate on his lap, his tired features showing the first hints of life. "You don't know how long it's been since I've had a decent meal," he said. "My clothes are hanging on me." He selected a small cake and devoured it.

"You don't look like you've been sleeping well."

"I can only nap when the tide's out. It's the only time I'm certain she will not be swimming up to the boat."

"But surely you are safe with all your men around you?"

"I remember what you said about Ulysses. She may tempt them as much as me. They were the ones who persuaded me to chase after her last night. They wanted to catch sight of her."

"If she's as lovely as you say, and her voice so sweet, perhaps becoming her husband would not be such a bad thing," Tom suggested.

Foweather stopped chewing a mouthful of tart, and spoke with crumbs falling from his lips. "Become her husband! I could not! I don't want to spend my days under the cold waters. It is every mariner's nightmare." He shuddered. "Her husband. Indeed!"

173

"Isn't there some small part of you that is tempted?"

" 'Twould be an unholy match."

Tom just looked at him, waiting.

Foweather's cheeks began to pinken, and he dropped his eyes to the half-empty plate, selecting another cake. " 'Twould be a sin against God to mate with such a creature," he mumbled, and popped the cake into his mouth. He glanced up under his brows as if checking for Tom's approval of the statement.

Tom shrugged. "Her mother went to church. Perhaps she would become Christian to secure your heart."

Foweather dropped his eyes and selected another biscuit, chewing vigorously on the cake in his mouth.

"Come now," Tom coaxed. "Can you honestly say you are not the least bit tempted?"

"But it's wrong!" Foweather suddenly declared, throwing wide his hands and knocking over his cup of tea. "Damn me!" he exclaimed, and jumped up. The plate of goodies fell to the floor and he took a step toward the mess of tea, stepping on a tart and squishing its contents into the carpet.

"Don't fret yourself!" Tom said, and gave Mrs. Toley a shout. "Mrs. Toley will take care of it. Please, Robert, sit down."

"A damned mess, I've made a damned mess," Foweather said, sopping up the spilled tea with his handkerchief.

"Sit, Robert."

"And the cakes!" he said, lifting a foot and spying the mess attached to his sole.

"There are more. Sit, please."

"My apologies. Look at your carpet—"

"Forget the damn carpet, Robert. Sit down!" Tom ordered.

Foweather gaped at him, blue eyes bugging, then obediently moved to the end of the settee and sat.

Mrs. Toley came in, saw the mess, and gave a great sigh. As she was going out to get cleaning supplies Tom asked her to bring more cakes. She was back in a minute, and Tom gave the fresh goodies to Foweather, who sat with a sad and guilty expression. He let the plate sit on his lap untouched while Mrs. Toley made a show of cleaning up the mess.

"My apologies," Foweather offered again in a small voice.

"There are more important things at stake here than cakes on the carpet," Tom said. "It sounds as if part of you is secretly attracted to the mermaid. We must discuss this. These are dangerous waters, Robert. Dangerous!"

"I know," Foweather said mournfully, and turned his attention to the plate and reluctantly selected a biscuit. "Nothing like this has ever happened to me before." He stuffed the biscuit into his mouth sadly and chewed unhappily.

Tom almost felt sorry for him.

Tom saw Foweather off through the front door, the Preventive man trudging wearily away as if he were a Greek hero burdened with the weight of a tragic, inevitable fate. Tom had him half convinced that his encounters with the mermaid would someday become the stuff of legend. Foweather seemed equal parts hor-

Lisa Cach

rified and fascinated by the notion of such fame.

Tom retreated to his office before Mrs. Toley could catch him and try to press some fried eggs or fish on him, or perhaps some of the leftover trifle from last night. He slipped into his chair and propped the soles of his boots up on the edge of the desk, leaning back on two legs of the chair and staring out the window to his right, ignoring the piles of papers on his desk.

He was troubled by the interview with Foweather. His own blatant lies to the man ate at him a bit, but not too much. The smuggling would happen with or without his mermaid plan, but at least with the deception there was less chance of anyone getting hurt. Smugglers caught red-handed were liable to panic and fire off a shot or two, thus putting themselves at risk for getting shot in return or hanged for firing on a revenue officer. The mermaid plan protected the Preventive men as well—it kept them out of dangerous situations.

No, it was something else that was gnawing at him, something that left him feeling unsettled. There was something about the way he had badgered Foweather into admitting an attraction to his mermaid—Konstanze—that had him feeling squirmy in his own skin. He had been unable to stop himself from harping on the topic, when that hadn't been his plan at all. He had thought to take a more passive role today, and let Foweather spill all his thoughts without much prompting. He had thought to take on the role of benevolent listener and wise older brother.

He had not thought to nag the man into admitting he harbored secret lusts for the mermaid.

176

# GET YOUR 2 FREE BOOKS
# NOW—AN $11.48 VALUE!

*Mail the Free Book
Certificate Today!*

## TWO FREE BOOKS

# *Free Books Certificate*

**YES!** I want to subscribe to the Love Spell Romance Book Club. Please send me my 2 FREE BOOKS. Then every other month I'll receive the four newest Love Spell selections to Preview FREE for 10 days. If I decide to keep them, I will pay the Special Member's Only discounted price of just $4.49 each, a total of $17.96. This is a SAVINGS of at least $5.00 off the bookstore price. There are no shipping, handling, or other charges. There is no minimum number of books I must buy and I may cancel the program at any time. In any case, the 2 FREE BOOKS are mine to keep—A BIG $11.48 Value!

Offer valid only in the U.S.A.

Name _____

Address _____

City _____

State _____ Zip _____

Telephone _____

Signature _____

If under 18, Parent or Guardian must sign. Terms, prices and conditions subject to change. Subscription subject to acceptance. Leisure Books reserves the right to reject any order or cancel any subscription.

A $11.48 VALUE

# Get Two Books Totally
# FREE —
# An $11.48 Value!

▼ Tear Here and Mail Your FREE Book Card Today! ▼

PLEASE RUSH
MY TWO FREE
BOOKS TO ME
RIGHT AWAY!

**Love Spell Romance Book Club**
P.O. Box 6613
Edison, NJ 08818-6613

AFFIX
STAMP
HERE

So why had he done it? And why had he felt a spark of angry jealousy when Foweather admitted his stirrings of passion?

He chewed a hangnail, frowning out the window at the bright nasturtiums, and did not like the conclusion to which he came: not only did he feel a normal animal attraction for Konstanze, but he was beginning to feel possessive of her as well. That was not a good sign, not a good sign at all.

It was that long talk in the cave that had done it, most likely. Or maybe it had been the way her eyes filled with tears when he'd sworn he would never harm her. Or maybe it was walking home with her from the church, hearing her talk about her life.

Hell, he didn't know. Somewhere along the line she had stopped being some rich man's runaway wife and had started being an interesting woman, and God knew how long it had been since he'd had a real conversation with a woman he found interesting.

Come to think of it, had he ever talked with a woman for as long as he had talked with Konstanze last night? The strange intimacy of the situation—working together, waiting in the dark—and her apparent friendly interest in him had prompted him to pour out information he had thought to keep bottled tight inside. Why, for God's sake, had he told her that pathetic tale about Eustice and the failed school? He cringed to think of it.

He didn't need this. He would have to keep an eye on himself to ensure that he didn't become the same obsessed fool he had become over Eustice. Being in love had been a painful, terrible experience during which logic had gleefully abandoned him, and if he valued the life he had built for himself here in Penperro he would do well to avoid repeating past errors.

Besides, Konstanze was married, and, even if she somehow had it annulled or obtained a divorce, she had already shown herself to be decidedly lacking in loyalty to her spouse. She was trouble, and any interest he had in her would best be limited to their business dealings and the conscientious concern he felt for her as the great-niece of Robert Penrose, a former client and friend.

He remembered carrying her back to the cottage, her arms around his neck, her body soft and curvaceous against his chest. She had seemed deliciously vulnerable and trusting, her face close enough that if he had but bent his head he could have taken her lips with his own. He had thought his concern was that she not fall ill from being so thoroughly chilled, but his body had paid detailed attention to the feel of her. Once back at the cottage he had scampered out of her kitchen like a frightened rat, unwilling to stay and sip hot tea while she went upstairs and stripped off her wet clothes. The very idea of her undressing had given him a glorious, brief image of her naked on her bed, her legs parted, an inviting smile on her lips.

This would have to stop. No more imagining having sex with Konstanze. He was enjoying it far too much. He had found over the years that thinking of doing something made one much more likely to attempt it. He didn't want to find himself actually making a pass at her at some opportune moment.

No, he would just have to remind himself as often

as necessary that she was married. Her husband sounded like he was a real monkey's butt and undeserving of her, but married she still was. As far as he was concerned, such women were forever forbidden fruit.

Now if only he could convince himself that he wasn't looking forward to seeing her this evening.

Konstanze took the pins from her hair and unwound the coils she had just finished arranging. She tugged the string of fake pearls free of the twisted tresses, a few strands of hair getting caught around the string. She picked at the hairs with fingers made shaky by too many cups of tea.

"Let me," Hilde said, and came over to where she was sitting on the floor of the kitchen, in front of a mirror propped against the stones of the hearth. Hilde deftly untangled the hair and dropped the pearls into Konstanze's lap.

"Thank you."

"You are going to too much fuss," Hilde said. "Why are you trying to impress him?"

"I'm not," Konstanze lied, and picked up the curling iron, quickly touching its surface to test the temperature. She wound one of the short tresses near her face around the iron rod, trying to repair the damage done to the ringlet by her last attempt at a hairstyle.

"Mermaids don't have curling irons," Hilde grumbled.

"But they might have natural curls in their hair. I'm enjoying the chance to be in costume is all, Hilde. This has nothing to do with Mr. Trewella. Didn't Mama

179

take forever to prepare for a performance?"

Hilde gave a mutter that Konstanze took for reluctant assent. The maid went back to putting the final stitches in the costume they had both been working on for several days.

Konstanze released the ringlet from the iron and sat staring at her reflection, feeling the flutterings of a sort of stage fright in her chest. She did not know what Tom was going to say about what she had come up with to solve the issue of the bare breasts. She did not know quite what she thought of it herself. She looked over her shoulder at the bodice that lay over the back of a chair, and felt a nervous giggle bubble up her throat.

Hilde heard her and looked up, and saw where she was looking. "It's disgraceful," she said, nodding toward the bodice.

"It's properly concealing," Konstanze said. But yes, it was disgraceful, too. She giggled again, nervousness and too much tea making her feel almost sick, her emotions overbright, her underarms damp with perspiration.

She took a small hank of hair from each side of her face, twisted them separately, then brought them together at the back of her head, winding them into a small coil and pinning it in place. She wound the pearls around the twisted tresses and through the coil. She cocked her head and examined the results, then turned around and with a small handheld mirror examined the arrangement from the back.

It would have to do. It was at least the eighth style she had tried, and her arms were getting tired.

The privy was calling, and she got up off the floor, her knees and hips creaking and stiff, and went out the door to the back. She had just returned to the kitchen when the expected knock came at the front door. She gestured for Hilde to remain seated and went to go answer it herself, her heart thudding in her chest. She wiped her damp palms on her skirts and opened the door.

"Tom," she said. He was a dark shadow in the driftwood-sided porch, just enough candlelight coming from the sitting room to softly paint the planes of his face and illuminate his white shirt. Her heart thumped painfully.

"Konstanze, good evening," he said, and nodded, his dark-rimmed amber eyes meeting hers. She felt a tremor of excitement run through her.

She stepped back to allow him to enter. He doffed his hat as he stepped into the cottage, the scent of fresh sea air coming with him, his head bent down to avoid the beams of the low ceiling. She felt the absurd urge to step close to him and soak up his presence with every pore of her skin.

Instead she stepped back and avoided his gaze, not wanting him to guess what wild fancies were dancing through her head. She tried to remind herself that he was a criminal mastermind with warped morals, but the thought only set her blood to racing all the faster.

She really shouldn't drink so much tea.

"Tea?" she offered Tom, and gestured him toward his usual seat.

He hesitated, then nodded. "Thank you. Are you feeling quite well? You seem a bit flushed."

181

"I've recovered completely from the chill of last night. I've been sitting too near the fire, is all."

"Good. I shouldn't like to think I'd caused you to fall ill. I wouldn't be able to sleep with such a heavy guilt on my conscience." He gave her an amused look from the corner of his eye.

"It would be the least of your sins," she said, knowing him well enough now to know that he was teasing her. "I'm surprised you can catch even a wink of slumber, with the life you lead. The angels must be wailing 'round your bed all the night, imploring you to reform."

"I usually hear them down in my cellar, breaking into the French brandy."

She laughed. "You are a wicked man, and will surely come to a bad end."

"I have a feeling you'll be leading the way."

"Now what is that supposed to mean?"

"Nothing at all," he said, and turned away, going to the hearth and warming his hands over the fire.

She frowned at him, not certain of what he'd meant by his teasing comment. Did he mean she'd be leading him to hell? It wasn't a flattering notion. Or was it? She gave a little shrug and went to fetch the tea things. He'd been joking, and there was no sense in putting significance where none was meant to be.

Hilde gave her a knowing look while she was putting together the tray. "You giggle like a foolish girl," the maid said.

"I do no such thing."

"You think he won't take advantage of you if you let him, just like Bugg? Eh?"

182

"I doubt he'd want to, and I wouldn't let him if he did."

Hilde gave a mimicking giggle and tossed her head.

"Stop it!" Konstanze ordered. "Do not mock me."

"It's for your own good," Hilde grumbled, her tone resentful and contrite both.

"It is unkind."

Hilde gave a guilty shrug and focused her attention on tying off a thread. "I've finished the last alteration." Konstanze took the comment and the shrug as Hilde's form of, if not an apology, at least of an acceptance that she had been in the wrong.

"Thank you. I'll be back to put it on in a few minutes. Will you help me with that?"

*"Ja, freilich,"* she said. *Yes, of course.*

Konstanze returned to the sitting room with the tea tray and sat down, Tom waiting until she had done so before he also took a seat. It was becoming a familiar scene, having him sitting across from her while she poured tea. She would not have believed it if someone had told her a month ago that this was how she would spend half her evenings.

"What did I do to anger Hilde this time?" Tom asked.

Konstanze glanced at him as she handed him his cup, then turned her attention back to serving herself. "Nothing."

"So she's always that way?"

"What way?"

"Angry."

"Her bark is worse than her bite. German is not a

language that sounds particularly soothing even when used in gentleness."

"Teach me to say something."

"You want to learn German?"

"Just a word or phrase. Teach me one."

"All right then. *Bitte*."

"Bih-tuh?" he repeated.

"Yes. *Bitte*. It's very useful. It means 'please,' and *bitte schoen* can mean 'you're welcome' or 'here you go.'" She gestured to a plate with biscuits. "Would you like some?"

"*Bitte*," he said, smiling.

She held out the plate, offering them. "*Bitte schoen*."

"And 'thank you'? How do I say that?"

"*Danke*.'"

He nodded. "*Danke*."

"*Bitte schoen*," she replied.

"Wait a minute. Are you offering again? Which *bitte* was that?"

"'You're welcome.'"

"I am?" He smiled, letting her know he was joking. "*Danke* Konstanze. *Danke* for teaching me *bitte*."

"*Bitte schoen*."

He laughed. "I've gone 'round the circle again, and don't know where I am. Is all of German so confusing? I thought if I could use a little of it on Hilde she'd soften toward me."

"I doubt it."

They sipped tea for a minute; then he gestured toward the pearls in her hair. "Are you performing a dress rehearsal?"

She tossed her head, her hand going up to touch and smooth her hair, the gesture embarrassingly involuntary and reminding her of Hilde's mockery. She dropped her hand, hoping her flirtatious gesture hadn't been as obvious as it felt. "Do you think it suits?"

"Turn around."

She shifted in her seat, twisting to show him the back, wondering despite herself if he liked her hair, pearls or no. Did he find her attractive? Or was she just an average woman to him, with an average face and figure, and worthy of no special notice?

"It's quite nice," he said. "Wear it that way if you wish. I like it all down, myself."

She turned back to face him. Her gaze went to his straight, long fingers, and she imagined the feel of them touching lightly at her temple, then carefully working both pins and pearls free. He would comb out the twisted locks with his fingers, the tips trailing gently across her scalp, then down to the back of her neck.

"I'll wear it down," she said. She looked at his hair, ruffled by the wind. She'd like to run her own fingers through it. Her eyes met his, and she found that he was watching her with a strange intensity. She held his gaze, her lips parting and her breath coming heavily, and felt a contraction at the very base of her loins. The surprise of that sensation made her break the stare, her cheeks heating to think he'd been looking at her when such a thing had occurred.

"Good," he said at last, and they both remained silent for several seconds. Then all at once they both spoke.

"Can I—" he said.

"How did—" she began.

"I'm sorry," they said in unison. Konstanze ducked her head, smiling, and he chuckled, the tension broken.

"Please. What were you going to say?" he asked.

"I wanted to know how our performance went over. Did you hear anything?"

"It turned out even better than I could have hoped. Not only is Foweather beginning to consider the advantages of life as a merman, but his crew is now convinced that you—by which of course I mean the mermaid—exist. They had been more suspicious than Foweather, not having seen you themselves, but now they are as eager as he to recount to anyone who will listen the night spent chasing you through the fog. They are spending inordinate amounts of time at the Fishing Moon, accepting free beers in exchange for repeating the tale once again. I think it's the most fun they've had since they arrived here."

"I almost feel sorry for them, being played for such fools by the entire town."

Tom shrugged. "One might say the townsfolk are the bigger fools. They are beginning to believe the stories themselves."

"But don't they know—"

"Yes."

"But—"

"Don't try to puzzle it out. For a few moments in the fog even I almost thought you would leap overboard and swim away."

"I suppose I can try to take that as a compliment," she said.

"At least you don't smell like a fish, for all that you sing like one."

"You're making it difficult to feel flattered."

He wiggled his eyebrows at her, his mouth crooking in a wicked grin, and she found herself smiling along with him. She felt like a cat at the cream, hungrily lapping up his teasing, and she wished she could stop. It was so new to her experience, though, and so pleasing that she knew she would encourage it beyond the limits of decorum. Her fanciful imaginings of handsome strangers had never had this element of playfulness to them, for she hadn't known it could exist between a man and a woman.

"Is the costume finished?" he asked.

She stood, with a quick gesture telling him to remain seated. "I'll go put it on."

"You don't need to do that. Just bring it out here."

"No . . . I really think you need to see it on me, for the full effect."

"I don't want to embarrass you," he said, sitting forward as if prepared to stand and stop her, his expression concerned.

She wondered what he was expecting her to be wearing. Necklaces or shells, as she had shown him in the drawings, her breasts loose beneath? "Trust me. You won't embarrass me. *Bitte* have a biscuit while you wait," she said, and with a barely contained smile left the room.

Tom sat and stared at Konstanze's empty chair, his hands flat on top of his thighs. They had never come to a spoken agreement about what the costume would be. She wasn't going to come out wearing nothing but a tail and her hair, was she? He both prayed and dreaded that it would be so. He didn't want to have the image of pink nipples showing through that glossy dark hair haunting his nights, and yet what a vision it would be to behold!

*No, no, no.* He had vowed not three hours ago to stop this nonsense of thinking of Konstanze as other than a business partner and an inherited responsibility. He was apparently greatly lacking in willpower. He hadn't been inside her cottage for more than two minutes before he had started making suggestive comments to her about being led down the path to damnation.

He was even, Lord help him, beginning to convince himself that she looked at him with some of the same desire that he felt for her. It was ridiculous, of course. She thought him a scoundrel, a "master smuggler," and endured his company only because she had to.

But for a moment there, he could have sworn . . .

Why was he even thinking about it? She was married. She could come out of that kitchen wearing nothing but a pair of gartered stockings and a smile, and he would do nothing to act on the invitation. He had standards, by God.

Now he was sounding like Foweather. It was a bad sign, a very, very bad sign. The idiocy of romantic obsession was digging its claws into him.

He grabbed a biscuit off the plate on the tray and chewed furiously, trying to think of other things than Konstanze in white stockings with red garters. Konstanze with her hair loose around bare shoulders. Konstanze, naked, coming to sit on his lap and wrap her arms around his neck, whispering "I'm yours" into his ear.

He plucked at his buckskins, trying to find some give in them for the part of him that had swelled against the confines of the narrow trousers. If he didn't get control of himself he'd have to sit with his hat in his lap. He crossed his legs.

This would all be so much easier if he didn't enjoy her company, as well as find her so damned attractive. Her being shrewish or dim-witted would have been such a help. Hell, it would even have helped if she didn't speak with that educated accent that proclaimed her special simply by the way she said the word *tea*.

After the Eustice debacle he had thought—rather vaguely, it was true—that he would someday find a farmer's daughter and settle down to raise a family. He had put his dawdling on the issue down to being too busy with business affairs to bother with courting a woman.

His reaction to Konstanze, however, was making him think that it had been something else at work. Without even knowing it, all this time he had been waiting to meet someone extraordinary, someone who had more to her background than eighteen years of tending sheep and salting pilchards. He'd been waiting to find someone who might have read some of the same books that he had, and who had seen a world beyond the shores of Cornwall. Even Eustice could not claim that.

Fate, being of a contrary nature, had chosen to put before him a woman he could not have. If he were wise he would learn from the situation, and move on. But when had he ever been wise when it came to women?

"Are you ready?" Konstanze asked.

Startled from his thoughts he turned to her voice, and then felt his jaw gape wide, his entire body going stiff in surprise. She was standing there in a silvery green narrow skirt, its waistline low across her hips. Tresses of hair fell forward over her chest, partially obscuring the hands she held over her bare breasts.

"Good lord!" he said. "Konstanze, you don't need to do this!"

"Oh, but I do!"

And with that she flung her hands wide, baring her chest to his eyes. He twitched and blinked and tried to look away, but his eyes were pulled back and he was powerless to stop himself from staring at the two large nipples so proudly on display. They were larger and darker than he had imagined, unsettlingly so.

Konstanze lifted her chin, one hand defiantly, proudly on her hip. "Do you like them?"

He gurgled. "Cover yourself! Good God, Konstanze, have you no shame?"

"I thought this was what you wanted. 'Show me breasts, I want to see your breasts,' you told me. 'Bare breasts, mermaids have bare breasts with nipples showing.' "

"I never meant you to parade them before me." He couldn't stop staring at them. He managed to glance up at her face for an instant, but with an eerie power those nipples drew his attention back downward. "Please cover yourself," he begged. "Please."

"Don't you want to get a closer look?" she asked, and started to come toward him.

He tore his gaze away and stared determinedly at the fire. "No. I've seen enough." He could see her, dimly, from the corner of his eye, standing close.

"The light is much better over here. Come, you want to get a good look. You might not have another chance."

"No."

"Don't be shy," she coaxed, and he heard laughter in her voice. It was that hint that she thought she had somehow played him for a fool that got him to turn his head a mere inch, just enough to see a blurred vision of nipples from the corner of his eye.

They really were unnaturally large and dark. He turned his head a little farther. There was something wrong about the color and shape of her breasts, as well. He turned enough to get a full view, and his eyes widened.

"They aren't real," he said in utter amazement.

She laughed, a vaguely hysterical sound, and put her hands back up over the false breasts. "It almost feels like they are, especially with someone gaping at them the way you are."

"In the poor light, I couldn't tell," he said, still not quite believing he had been so thoroughly taken in.

"That's the very idea. From a distance or in dim light, no one would be able to tell they were not real."

He could see now that what she wore was a tight-fitting sheath of material dyed a fleshy tone, then carefully darted, padded, embroidered, and appliquéd to resemble a bare female torso, complete with navel.

191

Except that she wore no sleeves, she was as covered as she would be in a dress. The effect, however, was anything but modest.

"It's indecent," he said.

"It's far more decent than what you had in mind!"

He knew his feelings were illogical, but he couldn't help it. Those nipples were like beacons, and he hated the idea of someone seeing them and thinking they belonged to her. He hated the idea of Foweather leering at her torso, thinking he was catching an eyeful. "You can't go out like that."

"I can and I will. Hilde and I worked hard on this. It is the perfect solution."

"Konstanze, you don't know how you look. There . . . there is no subtlety to this," he said clumsily, gesturing awkwardly toward her outfit. His eyes kept going back to the bits of dark nipple showing through her fingers.

"I didn't think you wanted subtle. What good is subtle in a mermaid, if you want her to be a distraction? Really, Tom, I don't understand you," she complained.

"Are you getting angry with me now?" he asked incredulously.

"I think I am. It took me a long time to come up with this idea, and I think it deserves a little more consideration than you're giving it."

"What about the shell bodice? Did you make one of those, too?"

"Shells! Pah! You said yourself this is what men expect." She dropped her hands from her fake breasts.

He winced and turned his face away, taking unwilling glances at her from the corner of his eye.

"I want to wear this. It does everything you said you wanted. You have no idea how much time Hilde and I put into this, and I won't have our efforts wasted. It's a brilliant costume, and I'm going to wear it." She crossed her arms under her breasts, the nipples peering over her forearms like the eyes of a lurking beast.

Tom hunched down in his coat, feeling queerly defeated and wondering just how he had gotten himself into this situation. "Anyone who sees you will assume they're seeing you naked," he tried once more. "They won't think it's a costume they're looking at. I don't see how that is any better than being naked to begin with."

"*I* know it's just a costume. And you know."

Yes, he knew, but somehow he hadn't considered the reality of his plan when he had proposed it to Konstanze. At the time had thought there was nothing wrong with having her splash about half-naked for another's eyes, but now some part of him was saying there was something very wrong with it indeed.

He frowned. Was he jealous of what Foweather thought he would be seeing? It couldn't be that—or at least, it shouldn't be. Konstanze was not for him, and he had no right to be possessive of her . . . attributes.

He straightened up, determined to set aside his qualms. "Have it your way," he said primly, then gestured toward the green-gray skirt that narrowed toward her ankles. "That's your tail?"

Konstanze unfolded her arms and pulled aside the

long, V-shaped front flap of the skirt, revealing slender green-gray trousers covering her legs.

Tom blinked, again seeing much more than he expected. The trousers fit closely to her legs, revealing hints of their gentle curves and drawing his eye inevitably upward toward her groin, which the front flap of skirt barely covered as she brought a leg forward to show off her handiwork.

He swallowed. "It doesn't look much like a tail," he said.

"Yes, it does. You have to imagine me sitting on a rock, wet from swimming. The fabric will cling to my legs, and from a distance it will look like I have a tail. With the skirt slit like this I'll have no trouble swimming. I can easily spread my legs," she said, demonstrating.

Oh, good Lord, why did she have to do that? Now he had that to imagine, her spreading legs encased in wet, clinging fabric. "What about your feet?" he asked, silently imploring her to close those plump little thighs.

"Hilde is making fish fins for them," she said, standing straight and dropping the skirt flap back into place. "They aren't finished yet." She rested her hands on her hips, arms akimbo. "Well? What do you think?"

"I think you've taken to being a mermaid like a fish takes to water," he said glumly.

She went to her chair and sat down, her hands resting neat as you please in her lap, her legs and ankles properly together. She seemed to have momentarily forgotten what her chest looked like.

"I think there's more of my parents to me than I

thought," she said. "I hadn't realized that dressing up could be so much fun. I love it!" she suddenly shouted, and flung her arms wide.

He put his hands over his face, his fingers pressing in on his eye sockets. What had he done to her? What manner of creature had he prodded her to become? He peered through his fingers at her. Her eyes were sparkling, and she seemed to be silently laughing at his distress.

"What of the promise you made your mother never to go on the stage?" he asked, dropping his hands.

Her smile faded. "This isn't exactly the stage."

"But it goes against the spirit of what she wanted for you."

She frowned at him, resentment in the set of her features. "I don't know why you of all people bring that up."

"Despite what you may believe of me, I do have your best interests at heart," he said. "Your great uncle would not have wanted me to open the gates to your own perdition."

"I hardly think I'm on the road to ruin because I donned a costume and liked it."

"I think you like it a little too much."

"Why are you never happy?" she accused. "I'm doing what you asked. Why can't you say, 'Thank you, Konstanze, that's a brilliant costume. I appreciate all the hard work you put into it'? Why instead do you have to try to find a way to take the fun out of it? I should think you'd be relieved I had so enthusiastically joined in your plan."

"I don't want to think that after you leave Penperro

you'll end up on a stage somewhere, and that it will be all my fault."

"You take too much credit for your own influence. And who's to say that I'm going to leave Penperro at all? Or are you hoping that I'll leave, after you've gotten all your use out of me?"

"I didn't mean that at all. And I'm not saying I have so much influence on you. You're obviously quite capable of finding your own way to ruin, if recent history tells me anything."

"What is that supposed to mean?"

"I think you know."

"Are you referring to my leaving my husband?"

He shrugged a shoulder, realizing he had said something he did not entirely mean. He had forgotten for a moment that the man might have beaten her, but he was in no mood to admit his error. This entire encounter with Konstanze had put him into an irascible humor. His insides felt like the coals of a fire, vigorously stirred by a poker, and there was nowhere for the flames to go.

"Get out," Konstanze said, standing up and pointing toward the door.

He looked up at her in surprise.

"Get out, I said." She was trembling.

He stood. "Konstanze—"

"Go!"

He saw tears filling her eyes, and felt like a complete heel. "I shouldn't have said that," he admitted.

"No, you shouldn't have. You have no right to judge me. Now get out."

"I didn't mean it," he said.

"You of all people," she said. "You asked me to take part in your foolish plan, and then you berate me for doing so, implying that I have no honor, no self-respect. I thought you were a better man than that."

Her words struck a telling blow. Since coming to Penperro he had made it his purpose to live a life that followed his own internal code of decency. "I'm sorry, Konstanze," he said, reaching out to grasp her by the shoulders. "I don't know why I said that. I didn't mean it."

"You did mean it."

"I'm an idiot. Please forgive me," he said, leaning closer. With his fingers he touched her cheek, and she looked up at him, her gray eyes swimming with unshed tears. "You have every right to be angry with me. You've taken me by surprise, is all, and I haven't reacted well."

"Then you don't truly think I'm a wanton?"

"Only the very best kind," he said softly. Against all his better intentions he lowered his head toward her, his mouth nearing her lips, so full and pink and slightly parted.

He could feel her breath, coming fast now, and felt as well his own heartbeat in his chest. He slid his hand into her hair, feeling the silky locks between his fingers, the warm curve of her skull fitting neatly into his palm. Her head tilted back, her lips and throat vulnerable and bare.

At the last moment a faint prickling of sense and conscience intruded. To kiss her now, to treat her as a woman who could be taken, would be to negate the very apology he had just given. However wanton her behavior might seem from the outside, he knew in his heart that there was an innocence to it. For all that she was married and had lived on the fringes of the stage, there was something about her that said the world had not quite touched her, as if she had somehow escaped its laying its dirty finger on her soul.

She was soft and close, and he wanted to let his other hand move down her back to cup her buttocks. He wanted to pull her against the arousal that still strained his breeches, wanted to bridge that last short space and claim her mouth, to delve his tongue inside that warm wetness, but he would be discarding honor if he did.

He shifted his mouth over an inch, and laid a gentle kiss upon her cheek, letting his lips rest against her smooth skin. He closed his eyes for a brief moment and inhaled the scent of her, then drew back.

One tear had spilled over onto her cheek, and with his thumb he brushed it away. "Do you forgive me?" he asked.

She gave a halfhearted shrug, then nodded.

He gave her a quick smile and released her, stepping away. He took his hat from the settle and held it in his hands. She had not moved, and an awkward silence lay between them.

"I'll go now," he said. "I'll let you know when we need you."

She nodded and looked away. He felt as if he had bungled whatever beginnings of a friendship they might have had. His jumbled emotions would not settle. It seemed as if every time he was with her he somehow managed to put his foot wrong.

"If you need anything, have Hilde bring a note to me, or to the vicar."

"Thank you," she said, sparing him only a glance.

"I'll go, then," he said again.

She led him to the door and opened it, and he paused on the step outside, turning back to her.

"It's a wonderful costume, Konstanze. It truly is. It took a clever mind to think of it."

She smiled at that, a small expression but he hoped a sincere one. "Thank you."

He nodded, realized he was lingering like a fool, and stepped out into the dark.

# Chapter Thirteen

Hilde kept her eyes out for Matt Jobson as she strode into Penperro. Konstanze had told her the man's name and occupation, and the information had served only to further her interest in him. Not only was he a sturdy piece of male flesh with a fine head of hair, but he was a man of God, too.

Hilde wasn't sure what it was about priests and ministers, but she invariably found them immensely attractive. Maybe it was the challenge of seducing a man of such pure thoughts, or perhaps she liked the implied power of his position. He did, after all, work directly for God.

Whatever the reason, Matt Jobson was firmly in her thoughts. She imagined he was likely the type of man to make a lot of noise in bed—or at least, she hoped so. Maybe he was one of those who used dirty words in the heat of the act. She gave a little shiver.

Unfortunately, she had seen neither pink hide nor white hair of the vicar by the time she reached Tom Trewella's house. She was here at the invitation of his housekeeper, Mrs. Toley, whom she had met several days ago in a shop. They had fought over a wheel of soft French cheese, and when Hilde had heard for whom the woman worked, she had forced her friendship on the woman. She had even offered to split the cheese wheel.

The result was an invitation for tea. At least, Hilde thought she'd been invited to tea and a chat. She couldn't be sure. The woman's accent made it difficult to understand much of what she said.

Mrs. Toley had pointed out the house to her, and it was easy to recognize with the abundance of orange and yellow nasturtiums overflowing their planters atop the surrounding wall. Hilde gave a grunt of approval as she looked up at the house. It was in fine repair, and the smell of fish was less prevalent here. It spoke well for Tom Trewella.

Hilde had every intention of seeing every inch of the house. If her Konstanze was going to be so involved with this man, Hilde thought it best if she discovered as much about him as she could. There was no better way than a good, old-fashioned snoop in someone's private quarters.

She went around to the kitchen door in back, aware that neither she nor Mrs. Toley warranted using the front door. It had never particularly bothered Hilde, being considered a servant. In her heart of hearts she believed that servants were all that kept their "betters" in their superior place. Masters and mistresses were like exotic animals who did not realize they were in cages, being fed and brushed and cleaned and kept from harm. They didn't know how much they depended upon their keepers.

She knocked on the door and waited, listening to the approaching sound of footsteps on a flagstoned floor. Mrs. Toley opened the door a moment later, her eyes going wide in surprise.

"Good day," Hilde said firmly and clearly.

"Oh, good day, Mrs. Hoffman," Mrs. Toley said, still looking at her with that surprised expression.

*"Ja,"* Hilde said, and waited. Was the woman going to ask her in? She tried to get a glimpse of the kitchen over her shoulder.

"Er, was there something I could do for you?"

"Tea, *ja?"* Hilde asked. Had the woman forgotten? "Tea?"

"Tea. Talk. *Ja?"*

"Oh. Oh, of course," Mrs. Toley said, and stepped back from the doorway. "Do come in. It's not often that I get visitors. You'll have to forgive the mess."

Hilde came in, her eyes scanning the kitchen. Everything was in order, and there was an assortment of brightly polished pots, pans, and cooking paraphernalia. Trewella kept a good kitchen, and Hilde gave a nod of approval.

Mrs. Toley continued to blather on about something, but too quickly for Hilde to understand. She ignored her and did a little more in-depth investigation of the kitchen. Mrs. Toley fussed, talking rapidly about whatever Hilde looked at. Hilde opened the door to the hallway.

"See house?" she asked.

"Oh. Oh, I don't know if Mr. Trewella would like that. He's a very private man. You can see the sitting room, though."

Hilde marched through, and with Mrs. Toley making bleating protestations behind her she made a complete circuit of the house. Trewella's bedroom upstairs was unremarkable except for the piles of books on his bedstand and stacked on the floor. Hilde grunted at that. Konstanze was the same way, reading into the small hours of the night when she should be sleeping.

When she and Konstanze had fled Bugg House there had been space for only a few of Konstanze's favorite books. Hilde looked at the rich piles of reading material on Trewella's bedstand and floor. Surely he would not mind lending a few to Konstanze?

Hilde squatted down and selected four or five, guessing as well as she could by the English titles which were fiction. Mrs. Toley began spluttering behind her.

"I say, Mrs. Hoffman, what are you doing? You put those books down! Those are Mr. Trewella's!"

"You say, 'Hilde took.' "

Mrs. Toley blocked the bedroom doorway. "I cannot let you take those."

Hilde stood and stared at her, the books tucked under her arm. "You say, 'Hilde took.' "

"I will do no such thing, as you are not taking those books out of this room." The woman was quivering with anger and, Hilde judged, a bit of nervous fear.

"Mr. Trewella say, 'Hilde, you take the books.' "

Mrs. Toley frowned at her. "Do you mean Mr. Trewella told you to take the books?"

Hilde was quite aware that that was not exactly what she had said. She stared at Mrs. Toley.

"Oh, well, in that case," Mrs. Toley said doubtfully. "If he said you could borrow them, then I suppose it's all right." She stepped aside, and Hilde continued her snooping through the rest of the house.

All in all, there was nothing in the dwelling to cause alarm or suspicion. For all that he was a nefarious mastermind smuggler who had drawn her Konstanze into his crimes, the man kept an orderly, innocuous house. He must not be all bad. Perhaps she could release a bit of her worry.

Back down in the kitchen she sat at the table while Mrs. Toley went to work preparing the tea and setting out things to eat. The woman plainly hadn't been expecting her, and Hilde admitted that it was just possible she had misunderstood whatever it was Mrs. Toley had said to her in the shop and while walking up the lane.

Not that it mattered. Mrs. Toley looked like she could do with a bit of company. The woman was all nerves. She obviously needed a man on whom she could expend all her energy at night.

As if in answer to the thought there came a knock on the kitchen door, and then Matt Jobson poked his head in before Mrs. Toley could answer.

"Good afternoon," he said. "How are you doing today, Mrs. Toley? Baking up any special treats?"

Mrs. Toley giggled, and Hilde's eyes narrowed. These two seemed awfully friendly.

Matt stepped into the room before he saw her. When he did, his expression was even more surprised than Mrs. Toley's had been, and he seemed to lose the power of speech.

"Mr. Jobson, this is Mrs. Hoffman," Mrs. Toley explained. "She's come to have tea with me."

"Mrs. Hoffman. It's a pleasure to meet you," he said clearly and slowly. Apparently he knew enough about her to know her troubles with English. Maybe he had been asking about her. She liked that thought. "I believe I've seen you in town a couple times these last few weeks."

"*Ja, freilich.* I remember. Call me Hilde," she said, making what was for her a long English speech.

"Hilde." He swallowed. "Perhaps I'll see you in my church some Sunday. Or are you Catholic?"

"Not Catholic," she said. Neither was she Anglican, but God would not mind in which house she chose to worship, should she attend one of Matt's services.

He smiled and nodded, then turned to Mrs. Toley. "Is Mr. Trewella home?"

"He's gone over to the Faileses'. I don't know when he'll be back."

"Let him know I came by, will you? Well, then," he said, nodding to them both, "I'd best be off. Mrs. Hoffman, it was a pleasure to meet you."

"Would you like to stay and have tea with us?" Mrs. Toley asked. Hilde didn't like the eagerness in her voice. Was she after the vicar, too?

"Er, there are some things I need to put in order at the church. I really can't stay."

205

Hilde stood, gathering up her books. "I walk with you."

"What? Oh, it's out of your way, surely."

"I walk with you."

"You'll miss your tea. You wouldn't want to miss Mrs. Toley's biscuits and tarts."

"That's quite all right," Mrs. Toley said. "They'll keep for another day. You go ahead and walk with Mr. Jobson, Mrs. Hoffman, if that is what you want to do."

"We walk," Hilde said. He was plainly a bit of a shy one, and it would take some coaxing to draw out the animal she sensed beneath. This could be even more fun than she'd thought.

Matt swallowed and gave a weak smile. "We walk."

Konstanze jammed the point of the shovel into the ground, wedged it in further with her foot, then when it had sunk a few inches climbed on with both feet and bounced up and down on the top edge of the blade, trying to force it farther in. It sank another two inches.

"Stupid, stubborn piece of dirt," she muttered, hopping off and using her full weight on the shovel to lever out the clump of dirt and grasses. Her back protested as she lifted the shovelful of dirt and flung it to the side. It landed on top of the small pile of such clumps she had made, then rolled down the front and back into her tiny garden patch.

She sighed and reached down, tossing it back onto the pile with her bare hand. What did a little more dirt on her matter?

Lacking either books or company, and unable to go wandering about the countryside, Konstanze found that boredom and restlessness had gotten the better of her and she'd decided to do something about the fallow patch of ground behind the cottage that had once been a garden. Hilde was off in town visiting some woman she had met while shopping, and Konstanze hoped to have a respectable showing of turned earth by the time she returned.

She drove the shovel in again, the blade scraping on a buried rock. The only thing about this confinement to the farm that made it bearable was that she had chosen it herself, as part of her "job" as the mermaid.

It had been a week since Tom's visit. Usually she could fill such time—and more—with her own private musings and stories. She could spin away months in daydreams, even without the help of books. Since Tom's visit, though, every daydream centered on him.

They were pleasant daydreams, there was no arguing that. However they might start out, they always ended with touching, or kissing, or undressing and letting him explore her body with his hands. It was quite shocking, really, what went on in her head. Thank God no one could see into it.

It was in part the very fact that she enjoyed those illicit daydreams so much that made her anxious to escape them. She had never thought that she was the type of woman who lusted after men or invited dishonorable attentions. It was the romance of love that had always appealed to her, never the physical aspect.

Her experiences in the marriage bed with Bugg had confirmed that.

She had been brought up to be modest and to take care with her honor. The required behavior had come easily to her, and she had never, not once, had cause to consider that she was the type of woman who might one day become an adulteress. A mistress. A wanton on the road to ruin.

She saw herself living in a small, overdecorated apartment, pillows strewn everywhere. She would spend her days lounging on her bed, half-dressed, waiting for her lover to come use her body. He'd give her gifts of jewelry, over which she'd coo and sigh, and then she'd stash them away against the day he abandoned her, and she found herself alone on the streets with a baby held to her breast. She'd read a novel like that, once, and Mama had warned against such a life, pointing out the singers and actresses who fell into such traps.

Konstanze shuddered at the thought that she could become one of those women, but that was what her fantasies about Tom were telling her: disgrace was but a few tempting touches away.

She heaved a shovelful of dirt, sweat trickling down the sides of her face. She was wearing her oldest dress, a faded dark red one that now had holes cut out of the hem from where she and Hilde had taken the material for the nipples. Her skirt and chemise were tied up to the side, her feet bare inside a pair of old leather shoes. Dirt had trickled down inside the shoes, gritty and uncomfortable. It had turned to mud down where her toes were sweating.

She stood back to survey her work. Pitiful. After what felt to be half a day's work she'd cleared a space no more than six feet long and three feet wide. It looked more like the beginnings of a grave than a garden. She supposed she'd have to retrieve as much dirt as she could from the clumps she'd removed. Who knew that gardening was so much work?

Too tired to continue for the moment, she stabbed the shovel upright into the ground and stepped around her pit to the lush grasses growing on the bottom slopes of the hill that came down to the edge of the yard. She collapsed there, kicking off her shoes and lying back, staring up at the puffy white clouds in the blue sky.

As she had done a hundred times already, she replayed in her mind those long moments when Tom had stood up next to her, his hand cupping her head, his mouth so close she could almost feel his lips on hers. She'd been angry and hurt at the implications of what he'd said, but those emotions had transformed themselves quickly into a longing for his kiss, her desire to kick him turning to one to hold him.

She was a stupid, lustful girl. All she'd been able to think as he had lowered his head was *yes, yes, yes.* How easily pacified she was! He had insulted her, and she'd forgiven him the moment he put his hand on her and said he was sorry.

She was the one who should be sorry. She should be apologizing to dear dead Mama right now for letting her teachings fall so easily by the wayside.

She closed her eyes and felt again his hands in her hair, his mouth coming down to kiss her cheek, her own lips pressing against skin made rough by shaven whiskers. A liquid rush of desire ran through her, pleasantly thrilling, but not as strong as it had been the first few days. She'd conjured the image too often, and was wearing it out.

At her boarding school the teachers had once given a vague, embarrassed lecture about the evils of self-pollution. She had not understood it, and it was only a few years later when the girl in the bed next to hers started making strange movements under her covers that she had gotten an inkling of what their teachers had been speaking about. The next time she had bathed she had taken more time and care when she washed, paying attention to what she felt as her soap-slick hands slid over herself. Her body's response to her own touch had startled her, and she'd quickly moved on to scrubbing legs and arms. During the nights she'd been tempted to try what her classmate had, but the thought of anyone catching her at it had been enough to stop her.

Now Konstanze wondered if her recollections of Tom's kiss hadn't become her own touchless form of self-pollution. She was a wicked girl.

And wicked as she was, she could not help but wonder what it would be like to share a bed with Tom. Would it feel as terrible as it did with Bugg, or would it be more like those times she let her hands linger while washing?

She threw her arm up over her closed eyes, embarrassed even to be thinking about it. *Wicked, wicked, wicked.*

"Digging your own grave?" a familiar voice asked.

*O Gott.* Her heart gave a painful thump, and she pressed her arm a little more tightly over her eyes. Would the man never leave her in peace? If Tom wasn't in her mind, he was in her presence. She didn't want to look at him, didn't want to talk to him when her mind had so recently been on such intimate imaginings, and yet she could not deny that she was glad he was here.

But how was one supposed to behave with a man who had held one's head and gently kissed one's cheek the last time one had seen him?

Perhaps if she just kept her arms over her eyes he would go away, and she wouldn't have to worry about it. Maybe he'd think she was sleeping.

"You look ready to be rolled into that hole over there. Want me to give you a shove?"

The mood between them was to be one of teasing, was it? Perhaps she could face that.

She brought her arm down and squinted up at him where he stood above her. After having her eyes closed, she noticed that he and everything else in the bright sunlight looked queerly washed out. "It's to be a garden."

"A very small sort of garden, to be sure."

"I've spent all morning turning that soil, and I'll not have you casting aspersions upon it. It's a beautiful garden, and will give me all the cabbages, carrots, and peas that my heart could desire. And flowers, too. There will be a lovely knot garden over by the chicken coop when I'm finished," she said, waving vaguely in that direction.

"It's a long hole in the ground. You'll be lucky to get so much as a turnip from it."

Konstanze pushed herself into a sitting position, saw her knotted skirts, and quickly undid them, covering her bare feet and calves. "As if I should take your word on gardens. I doubt you've ever done so much as pull a weed. What are you doing here, anyway? Is there a boat coming in?"

"No, I was just in the neighborhood and thought I'd see how you were doing."

She gave him a doubtful look.

"How are you doing?" he asked, sitting down beside her and resting his arms across the tops of his knees.

"Fine, thank you," she said, wary of his close presence and her own reaction to it.

He gestured to her trench. "Are you truly trying to dig a garden?"

"I don't have much else on which to spend my time."

"I should think you would enjoy being a lady of leisure, lolling about with nothing to do all day."

"Leisure, I've found, is best enjoyed when there is work elsewhere in one's day. I shouldn't imagine that you yourself would do well confined to a cottage without visitors for weeks on end."

"I might surprise you there," he said. "I sometimes think I would enjoy such a retreat very much indeed."

"Nonsense. You'd be so desperate for lives in which to meddle that you'd resort to messing up your own affairs just to break the tedium."

"I am not a meddler."

"Of course you are, and the worst kind, too," she

said. "You convince yourself you are doing it for the good of others."

"I should like to think my efforts help people."

"You've proven my point."

"That does not prove I'm a meddler. You make me sound like an interfering old woman."

She smiled. "I like that image."

He looked at her. "You're in a strange mood, Konstanze."

"Am I?"

"Most strange, indeed. Are you feeling quite well? Headache? Stomach troubles? Bad dreams?" He reached over and pressed his hand to her forehead. "Fever?"

Her breath caught at his touch. She knew he was still teasing her, but some intuitive sense suspected that he was using his words as an excuse to touch her. The skin all over her body came alive, tingling with awareness and expectation.

"No, no fever," he said, "although you are a bit warm." His hand moved down to briefly touch her cheek, then withdrew.

She had to stop herself from leaning after that departing hand. She didn't say anything, her meager ability to be witty vanishing with the desire his touch had roused. It was hard to be clever when all she could think was that she could not let him know how very much she wanted to touch him right now. She was, she realized, on the dangerous verge of making eyes at him.

The slippery slope was beckoning, and oh, how very enticing it was.

She tried to remind herself of his true nature: he was a smuggler, a liar, a criminal mastermind. He hired women to swim half-naked. He partook in the profits of privateering. And he was, she hoped, dishonorable enough to make advances toward a married woman.

*No, no, no!* She must stop thinking that way!

"I should get back to work," she said, standing up and stepping into her shoes, the leather heels crumpling as she tried to wiggle her sockless feet back in. She bent down to slip a finger behind her heels, easing them on. "I tell you, I have a whole new respect for farmers," she said into her skirts.

"I don't know any farmers who till soil with a shovel. Isn't there a plow in the barn? I thought your uncle had one," he said, standing as well.

Konstanze straightened. "I saw one when I went to find the shovel, but I haven't the first idea how to use it."

"How big a garden were you planning?" he asked. "Truly. No more talk of yew mazes or reflecting pools."

"It was a knot garden," she said. "I was originally thinking to dig something about five feet by fifteen."

"It will take you until winter to get that done, at your present rate."

"I'm quite aware I was overly ambitious in my thinking, thank you. I'd be happy with something half that size." She frowned at the shovel standing upright in the dirt. "Or a quarter."

"I doubt you'll be able to manage even that."

"Thank you very much for your input," she said

214

crisply. "If you're not going to be either helpful or encouraging, then why don't you run along and go play in your caves?" She made shooing motions. "Go on, run along."

"But my dear, I do intend to be helpful," he said, and began taking off his coat.

"You're going to dig?"

"Of course not. Do I look like a fool?"

She narrowed her eyes at the implied insult. "Then what, dear sir, do you propose to do?"

"You have a donkey and a plow. I see no reason not to put them to work." He began marching off toward the barn.

She trailed after him. "You know how to use a plow?"

"No," he replied over his shoulder. "But how hard can it be? I should think I have sufficient intelligence to figure it out."

"I didn't ask for your help."

"Certainly you did," he said, entering the stone barn, then stopping for a moment to gaze around the dim, dusty place. The plow was in a corner with other forgotten equipment and junk, covered in cobwebs and a fine layer of dirt. "How could a gentleman see a lady prostrate from exhaustion and not offer to be of assistance? I seem forever to be coming to your aid," he said, smiling beatifically.

She rolled her eyes. "You have more to do with creating my difficulties than with solving them."

"Nonsense. I consider myself your benefactor, as well as your employer." He grabbed hold of the plow handles and began to pull. When the plow didn't

215

budge he braced his feet against the ground and hauled with all his weight, a long groan of exertion coming from between his clenched teeth.

"My Samson! My Hercules!" Konstanze said, and clasped her hands together between her breasts. "My heart is all aflutter."

He gave her a dirty look, and stopped straining. He stepped around the long handles and peered at the pile of junk.

"It's probably caught up on something," Konstanze said, coming closer.

"Thank you for that astute observation."

"Getting testy already, are you?" Konstanze said. "I shouldn't like to see you in half an hour's time."

He shook his head at her. "You are in the damnedest mood today."

"You've informed me of that once already."

"And apparently there is no explanation forthcoming." He began moving tools and farming implements away from the plow.

She wasn't about to tell him that she was expecting her monthly any day now. It wasn't that she was put into a foul temper by it, but whatever emotions she did feel seemed to be amplified at this time, and her tolerance for irritations was minimal. She didn't know why precisely she was being so unpleasant to him, unless it was to drive him away so she wouldn't have to feel this annoying attraction to him. She didn't want to be lusting after a man, or finding it queerly touching that he was trying to help her with her garden.

And maybe as well she was being unpleasant to see how he dealt with it, to see if he would put up with her at her worst. She pursed her lips, not liking that thought.

Or maybe she was being unpleasant because if she seemed to reject him first, she would save herself the humiliation of being rejected herself, later. She liked that thought even less. What if she had misread his gestures, and he had no interest in her at all? What if she made eyes, and embarrassed him by it? He had not wished to stay for tea after their night in the rowboat, after all. He had seemed positively eager to get away.

*Damn it, stuff it, bugger it all*, she cursed in her mind, using privately the words she would never be caught uttering aloud. Her mind was all a muddle where Tom Trewella was concerned.

He lifted away an empty crate, in the process knocking loose a heavy old ax head. The blunted corner fell directly atop the toes of one foot. "Good Christ!" he cried, hopping about with the injured foot raised off the ground. "Frig—" he started to say. "Blood—" he tried, then bit down on the words, and furious, half mumbled, unintelligible curses caught behind his teeth as he hopped madly around the barn, one hand holding on to his foot.

"Are you all right?" Konstanze asked worriedly, her irritation with both herself and Tom immediately forgotten.

"Frig—"

"Put your hand on my shoulder and come out into the light," she urged, anxious that he might have done himself a serious injury. Had he managed to lop off a toe?

"It's nothing," he gritted out.

"Don't be stupid. Let me take a look."

He put his hand on her shoulder and hopped alongside her out into the yard, then dropped down to the ground and pulled his shoe and stocking off. Konstanze knelt down and took his foot into her lap, gingerly inspecting the reddened toes. The nail bed of his big toe was turning a dark, ugly red. She gently wiggled each toe in turn.

"Ow," he complained.

"Can you move them?" she asked.

"I don't want to. They hurt."

"I'm trying to see if any are broken. Be a hero and wiggle them for me."

He curled his toes under, the digits barely moving.

"Is that all you can do?"

"I'm not a monkey."

She gave him a look from under her brows. Mama had always maintained that men were babies when it came to pain, and turned petulant at the least little ache. "I don't think you broke any, but you're bleeding under the nail of your big toe."

He scowled over his knee at the digit in question, then looked away.

She gave the bare skin on top of his foot a quick, encouraging rub, taking surreptitious enjoyment from the feel of his skin under her palm, the sparse, crisp black hair near his ankle brushing the edge of her hand. She could feel the structure of his foot, the tendons and bones larger and nearer the surface than on her own feet. His feet were remarkably well cared for, nothing like the yellow, horn-clawed things on Bugg that had gouged her calves in the night. "Come into the cottage. I know how to treat this."

"I'm fine," he said, giving his toes another brief, unhappy look. "You really don't think I broke any?"

"No, but this bleeding should be taken care of. It's the pressure of it under the nail that's making it hurt so badly. Hilde showed me how to relieve it."

He narrowed his eyes at her. "I don't like the sound of that. I think I'd be better off leaving it alone."

She lightly tapped his toenail, and he flinched. "It's only going to hurt more if you leave it. It'll turn black and fall off."

He retracted his foot and took a quick look at the splotch of darkness under his toenail, wincing at the sight of it. He started to pull his stocking back on. "I've seen others with black nails. It will go away eventually."

Konstanze gave a noisy sigh. "You're suffering needlessly."

"I like it that way."

She rolled her eyes. He sounded like a stubborn five-year-old, and she had half a mind to tell him so. She watched him carefully pulling up his stocking, then loosening his shoe and trying to put it on over the swelling toes, his face going through all manner of contortions and grimaces. "You think I'll make it worse, don't you?" she asked.

"It's not that."

"You don't trust me to know what I'm doing. You think I couldn't possibly know how to help you."

"It's not that," he repeated, getting testy.

"Then what is it?" she asked, her own ire rising. *Try*

*to do something nice for the man and look what you get: distrust and rejection.*

"It'll be fine. Just forget about it."

She shifted on her heels, her jaw tightening. She glared at him.

He glared back.

"Fine," she said, and stood up. "Suffer all you want." She turned and marched back toward the cottage.

"Where are you going?" he asked.

"To make myself a pot of tea," she said without turning. She needed it to soothe the frustration of dealing with him. "You may do as you like." He could leave if he liked; that would suit her just fine. He could limp away, weeping over the pain in his toe, and she would laugh. Yes, laugh!

When she got to the stairs she stopped and turned. "Just you think about this, Tom Trewella. People don't like to be helped without the opportunity to return the favor. If you can't let someone do something nice for you, they're left feeling very low indeed." And with that she tramped up the stone stairs and into the kitchen, slamming the door behind her.

Tom's toe pulsed with agony. Damn it all, he should have stayed clear away from the Penrose farm. The farm had not been on his way back to Penperro from the Failes estate, not by a mile, but his feet had pointed him in this direction as surely as the needle of a compass pointed north.

He'd succeeded for all of five days at staying away from Konstanze, a feat he had thought admirable and to their mutual benefit. His last visit had proved that he could not be trusted with her and that whatever his noble intentions, his body had a way of circumventing them. As did his mouth. He had no trouble maintaining diplomatic relations with even the most pugnacious of Penperro inhabitants, yet with Konstanze he found himself constantly treading off the safe path and into the mire.

There was something about her that damaged his ability to think. She gave off an energy akin to the charge in the air before a storm, capable of winding him tight and sluicing anxiety through his veins. It wasn't much like the warm, intoxicated bliss he had felt in the presence of the half-forgotten Eustice. With Eustice he had been full of the impetuosity of youth, placing no floodgates on his passion. There had been no reason to, as there had been no obvious barriers to their future together.

No barrier, except that she didn't care a rotten fish head for him.

He knew the situation was different with Konstanze. He knew all the reasons he should curb his desires, all the reasons he should not let his interest in her grow, but it was as if his passions had a will of their own, and they waged a bloody, ruthless war against his common sense. No, this was not warm, intoxicated bliss he was feeling. It was more akin to a bout of cholera.

He tried to shove his foot farther into his shoe and yelped. He let loose a string of curses under his breath, easing his foot back out.

He didn't want to like her as much as he did. He

didn't want to wish to be inside her mind, to see what thoughts so often gave her that look of secret amusement, as if she lived half in another world to which he was not privy.

He climbed unsteadily to his feet, his injured foot barely touching the ground, and picked up his shoe. He started the long hobble toward the cottage.

She was wrong in thinking he did not trust her to care for his toe. She had perhaps hit upon a hidden truth when she said he did not like to accept help from others. He had at least enough self-awareness that he could admit that he liked to be the one others came to for assistance, rather than vice versa. That wasn't the reason he had refused her offer, though.

The truth was much less complicated, and far more humiliating.

He was afraid of the sight of blood.

One of his earliest memories was of being a small child and falling, skinning his knees rather badly. He couldn't remember the pain, only the hysterical fit he had thrown at sight of his bloody knees, and his mother's frantic attempts to calm him. His reaction to the sight of blood—especially his own—had grown quieter with age, but no less severe. There was no rhyme or reason to it: he knew perfectly well that a bit of leaking blood was no danger, and had grown up seeing animals slaughtered, noses bloodied, and fingers cut.

He liked to think that he could brave a hundred dangers, take a thousand necessary risks without flinching, but cruel fate had given him this inexplicable weakness over which he had no control. How could anyone have expected him to admit that to Konstanze, after already making a fool of himself trying to move the plow?

He'd always been better at laboring with his mind than with his body, and it was nothing of which to be ashamed. Even a hen-brained half-wit could see that the better life in smuggling and privateering was on land, organizing, rather than out on the ocean, making oneself a target for a bullet or vulnerable to one of the miscellaneous, dreadful sailing injuries that took fingers and limbs from the unlucky.

He reached the steps and braced his hand on the cottage wall for support as he climbed them.

Konstanze knew none of that. She was probably sipping her tea right now, thinking he was an uncoordinated pansy who was too stupidly proud to let another ease his suffering. If he let her help him, at least the impression of unmerited pride might be erased. If he did not disgrace himself utterly while she tended him, even the pansy part might be somewhat amended.

There were a few ways he could think of to show her he could use his body with adequate coordination, as well, but those methods would tear down the last tattered hangings of nobility he was trying to keep upon the walls of his soul. It was better not to dwell on those thoughts, however pleasantly distracting from one's throbbing toe.

He gave the door a rap, and a moment later Konstanze opened it, her expression one of blank surprise.

"If the offer still stands, I would appreciate your help," he said.

He watched her expression transform to one of

knowing, secret delight. He felt a moment's trepidation at that evil glee, wondering just what exactly it was that she had in store for him. On the other hand, at least she was smiling. If he could make her happy by sacrificing his toe to her ministrations, so be it.

"Come sit by the fire," she said, and came around beside him, her side pressed up to his, her arm around his waist. He laid his own arm over her shoulders, tilting his head down to brush his nose and lips against the top of her head as she tried to help him over to the chair. He all but forgot about his toe, his senses distracted from pain by the feel and scent of her. He could hobble all the way to China if she were helping him like this.

She turned her face up to his when they reached the chair, their cheeks nearly brushing. Her gray eyes were wide, the cheery energy there for a moment softening to something else, her pupils large and black. Whatever pull he felt toward her, he understood in that momentary gaze that she felt at least some of the same in return. Whether she knew it or not, she was making eyes at him. He wanted very much to take her up on the offer.

He should have limped home.

It took a determined effort to pull away from her, his body and hers separating with the slow tearing of a plum in two. He forced himself to sit down, breaking their contact, her arm sliding free of his waist as she bent to ease him down. He caught a faint scent of her body, warm and musky, coming from the neckline of her gown. He closed his eyes against the primitive reaction that rushed through him, images of lowering

her to the floor and making love to her cascading un-
bidden through his mind.

"What is it you're going to do?" he asked.

"I have to relieve the pressure of the blood under
the nail. I'll heat an embroidery needle in the fire
and—"

"Don't tell me," he said, grimacing. *Oh, God.*
Blood, a red-hot needle, and his toenail. He closed his
eyes and took a deep breath, trying intentionally now
to think of Konstanze naked, Konstanze with her legs
spread wide, Konstanze with her skirts pushed up as
he lay between her thighs—anything to get Konstanze
with a red-hot needle out of his mind.

"Are you sure—"

He opened his eyes. "Please do it, but don't nar-
rate."

She gave him a curious look, then shrugged. "All
right. I'll go get the nee—" She caught herself. "I'll
get what I need." She gave him another look, then
disappeared into the sitting room.

Tom slouched in the chair and pressed his hand over
his brows. There was a fine film of sweat there, and
he was feeling queasy. It was too late to back out now,
though. She was as pleased as if he had given her a
gift, happy to be able to "help." He spread his fingers
and peered through them at the back door. He could
make a run for it.

Footsteps heralded Konstanze's return and the end
of his opportunity to flee.

He wouldn't watch. If he kept his eyes averted,
everything would be fine. He wouldn't think about it;
he wouldn't pay any attention at all to what she was

doing. He turned his face from her and stared at the bare wall across the room.

She moved around, arranging he knew not what, her dark red dress moving in and out of his peripheral vision. Each second of anticipation felt a dozen times as long, her preparations both endless and too brief.

At last he felt her fingers upon his stocking, pulling it carefully down his calf and off over his foot. Her touch was gentle, almost tentative. An unsettling suspicion popped into his tense mind.

"You've done this before, haven't you?" he asked, risking a glance at her where she knelt by his bare foot. He avoided looking at his injured toe.

"I've seen it done a few times. Stagehands used to get their fingers smashed with fair regularity."

That was not the answer he had wanted to hear. "But you know what you're doing."

"Oh, yes. I'm all but certain of what to do."

"Splendid," he muttered. He shouldn't have asked.

"Are you ready, then?"

He waved his hand for her to proceed, then brought it up to tent it loosely over his eyes, needing the extra protection against the gruesome urge to watch. He felt her lift his foot onto her lap, onto what felt to be a rough towel spread over her skirts. She shifted, and between his splayed fingers he saw her lean toward the fire, removing one of several needles that had been heating there. She held it in a scrap of cloth to protect her fingers, and with her other hand he felt her get a firm grip upon his foot, down near the toes.

He shut his eyes, fingers pressed tightly over the lids. He felt a slight increase in pressure directly on top of the throbbing nail, instead of at the end of the toe as he'd expected. He kept waiting for the burning feel of the needle. And waiting. He could feel slight movements of her body through his foot. She was doing something, but what?

She shifted, the pressure easing for a moment; then it started up again. Curiosity got the better of him, and he lowered his hand down his nose enough that he could peer over and see her.

Her dark head was bent to her task, her concentration absolute. He flicked his eyes downward, and at that precise moment the needle she held finished boring its way through the center of his nail, releasing a tiny spurt of blood like a miniature red fountain.

"There!" she cried in triumph.

He barely heard her, stars appearing in his blackening vision. He felt the strength drain out of his limbs, and his body swayed to the side as he began to tumble from his chair.

He slowly came to his senses as Konstanze patted him lightly on the cheek. He was flat on his back, on the floor. "Tom, Tom, can you hear me? Tom, wake up!" she was saying. He opened bleary eyes to see her unfocused face above him.

He lifted his heavy arms and enfolded her within them, pulling her down so that she rested against his chest. She was stiff against him, her forearms caught between them, her backside in the air.

"What are you doing?" she asked, her voice squeaky.

"Shhh. Lie still."

"You fainted," she said, tilting her head and speaking to his chin. "Did I hurt you so badly?"

He spared an ounce of internal attention for his toe. "No. Actually, it feels much better," he said, surprised. There was still a dull throb, but nothing like what it had been.

"Then what happened?"

He didn't want to tell the truth; he didn't want to say anything at all. Maybe she would believe it if he claimed he'd been ill and hadn't eaten for three days? But no, he couldn't lie to her. He sighed. "I watched."

She was silent for a moment; then he felt her begin to quiver against him. She tucked her face down into her hands, shaking atop his chest.

"Are you laughing at me?" he asked.

She gasped for air. "No, no, of course not."

"You are." The humiliation of it was too much to even try to escape. He lay supine, letting her laugh on top of him.

She raised up, and he let her. She held his face between her hands and looked down into his eyes, her own teary with laughter. "Oh, Tom," she said, and then she kissed him.

It was a kiss masquerading as friendly affection, but in the soft touch of lips that lingered a moment longer than necessary he sensed the desire beneath. He moved his lips briefly against hers, just enough to let her know that he responded.

She pulled back, laughing again, as if to preserve the shield of humor that made her action acceptable.

He smiled and let her go, the previous humiliation a worthy price to pay.

# Chapter Fourteen

*Penperro*

"If you start to get tired, I want you out of the water," Tom said urgently.

Konstanze nodded, her own nerves making her limbs quiver. She was shivering, although she was not cold. The day was overcast, but temperate.

"It should be no more than an hour—but remember, your safety comes first."

"I know," she said, appreciating his concern but getting frustrated now with its repetition. She didn't want to dawdle any longer. It was time to set aside the stage fright and begin.

Tom had surprised her at the cottage thirty minutes ago, riding bareback on a borrowed draft horse. Someone in his network had sent word that Foweather and some of his crew were searching caves that they had searched two days earlier: caves that had been empty that first time, but one of which was now full of smuggled goods worth nearly seven hundred pounds.

Tom explained that it had seemed a safe bet to use a cave that had been so recently checked, as it was unlikely to be searched again so soon. Alas, Foweather had either managed to think of that as well, or simply did not mind the repetition of tasks, as a dog did not mind the repetition of fetching a stick again and again and again.

He had given her only a moment to grab her costume; then with Hilde hurling German insults at his head he had dragged her out of the cottage. They'd pushed the heavy horse to a faster pace than it was used to, skirting Penperro and tearing down the coast on the southwestern side of the village, stopping about a mile before where Foweather was searching.

With a stone fence and the horse making up the meager walls of a makeshift dressing room, Konstanze had changed into the mermaid outfit, letting her hair fall free. There had been no time for any preparation but the most basic, which was something of a disappointment after the hours she had spent dressing herself so precisely in her mind.

Tom gripped her shoulders, looking her in the face for long moments as if there were things he wanted to say. At the end he just gave her shoulders a squeeze and nodded. "Good luck," he said.

She tried to look confident and smiled, and then he was leaving, mounting the tired horse and heading down the coast to Foweather. He would tell the Preventive man that he had heard that the mermaid had been sighted, and bring Foweather and his crew to this part of the coast to hunker down and watch her antics. It was late enough in the day that if she could keep the Preventive men distracted for an hour, likely they would head back to Penperro at the end of her performance rather than continue their search of the caves. Tonight Tom's network of inland workers would remove the goods, and a couple weeks from now she would be fourteen pounds richer.

It wasn't the fourteen pounds she was thinking of, though, as she climbed down the rocky slope to the shore; it was Tom. She didn't want to disappoint him. Preposterous a scheme as this was, and for as questionably moral a purpose, he was counting on her to play her part, and she would not let him down.

Never mind that the water looked cold and choppy, or that she was having her period. She had heard that sharks could scent blood in the water, and she had a dark fear that one would come after her and take a bite out of her leg. Her grandfather had perhaps shared one too many sea stories of that kind with her, of castaway men being consumed one by one as they drifted in the currents.

*Stop it*, she told herself. She mustn't let her imagination run away with her, especially not now. For all she knew, sharks could smell fear as well as blood, and she'd have a whole swarm of them after her.

She sat at the edge of the water and laced onto her feet the fish fins that Hilde had finally completed. They were light tan, made of oilskin ribbed with boning taken from an old pair of stays. They did look like the fins of a fish, extending nearly a foot beyond her toes.

231

If fish could swim with such things, she supposed that she could as well.

Of course, no one who had ever put on a pair of wings had been able to fly, but she'd be better off not thinking of that, either. She didn't need to add a fear of drowning to her thoughts of blood-scenting sharks.

She stood up and took a high step with the fins on her feet, nearly falling in the process. Instinct prompted her to turn around and walk backward, which was a little easier, but the uneven sand and stones under her feet made it a difficult endeavor. When she was ten inches deep in the chilly water she took a deep breath and plopped down.

She bit back a shriek at the cold. She supposed it was no colder than that first day she had taken a swim, but attitude seemed to play an important role. She had actively wished to swim on that day.

She tilted her head back, wetting all her hair, then turned onto her stomach, using only her arms to swim against the chop, not wanting to risk banging her knees on the rocky bottom. She felt the water seep through her costume, turning it heavy and rough against her skin, and making it cling uncomfortably. She thought she might almost rather swim naked. At least her own skin did not drag against the water like the wet fabric and padded breasts did.

A hundred and fifty yards out from the low-tide line there was an outcropping of rock, a small island inaccessible by land. Tom had suggested she swim out to it and wait there for him to return with Foweather. The seaward side would also provide a hiding place for her when the show was over, and if worse came to worst and she could not swim to shore due to Fow-eather's lingering presence, she could wait there until dark, and one of Tom's allies would pick her up in a boat.

Safely beyond the knee-banging shallows now, she gave an experimental kick with her finned feet. To her utter surprise she shot forward, getting a mouthful of salt water as she plowed into a wave.

She coughed and spat, legs kicking as she treaded water and tried to regain her breath. With her move-ments her body rose several inches above the waves, as if she were a sea otter rising up to survey the ocean surface.

She sank back down, feet slowing, mouth opening with amazement. She rolled onto her side and kicked, plowing smoothly through the water at incredible speed, the waves breaking around her head as if it were the prow of a ship. A wake formed from her passage. The fins were propelling her in a way her own bare feet never could.

This time she did not try to contain the shout that rose in her throat, a shout of pure joy that resounded across the water. She laughed and whooped. She let herself sink underwater, then kicked fast and furious toward the surface, rising up out of the waves to waist height before falling back into the water. She arched her back and turned a backward somersault, then came up and swam on her stomach, letting her arms trail at her sides as she used the fins to propel her, her hair streaming behind.

A wild, exuberant glee filled her. She hardly felt like a mortal human in the sea: she was a true sea siren, a mermaid, a creature born and bred in the briny deep.

She was at the rock outcropping within a minute, and pulled herself up onto a low seat. She reached up behind her, found the buttons hidden in their placket, and undid her bodice, peeling off the garment and stuffing it in a crevice above the tide line. *Modesty be damned.* No one from shore could tell the difference anyway, just as she'd told Tom. She wanted to swim as fast as her fins would let her, and the bodice and fake breasts only slowed her down. She was a mermaid!

"Where is she? Where?" Foweather asked, his breath hot on Tom's ear as they rode double back to where he had left Konstanze.

The man was as awkward on a horse as he was on the ground, and several times Tom had been certain Foweather would pull him off the draft horse's broad back as they bounced along. Foweather had clung tightly to Tom's waist the entire ride.

"Shush," Tom scolded, Foweather's clumsiness and incessant questions only adding to his darkening mood. If the man would have stayed on his Preventive boat where he belonged, none of this would have been necessary, and Konstanze would be safely on shore. He drew the horse to a halt. "Dismount," he ordered.

"Is this where she is?" Foweather asked, sliding off behind him.

"Almost," Tom said, and dismounted himself, then tied the horse to a bush. The other members of the crew were following on foot. It had gone without question that Foweather should of course see the mermaid as quickly as possible, the belief having spread amongst the Preventive crew that their leader had a special bond with the creature. Which was not to say that the crew themselves were not more than eager to abandon their tiresome search of the caves in favor of spotting a frolicking half-naked mermaid. Their curiosity had been well fired by the night spent chasing Konstanze's voice in the fog.

" 'Twould be best not to ride where she could see us, don't you think?" Tom asked.

"Oh, aye," Foweather agreed. "I don't want to frighten her away."

"You're not worried that she will come for you?" Tom asked, cocking an eyebrow.

"Not with you here," Foweather said. "And I can count on you not to let me go to her. You will restrain me, won't you?"

"Most assuredly, to the best of my ability," Tom said in his best imitation of the Noble Friend. "You're a strong man, though. It could be that I will be unable to hold you back. Remember, Ulysses had to be tied to the mast."

"I haven't any rope," Foweather said with some concern.

"Nor a mast. I suppose I could crack you on the head with a rock, if the need arose," Tom offered, cheering a bit at the prospect. "But let's hope it doesn't come to that." He led Foweather along the path, privately worrying about Konstanze and how she was faring in the cold water. The water was a little rough today—she'd be careful of the rocks, wouldn't she?

She seemed confident of her swimming abilities, but there was so much that could go wrong, alone in the water.

Within a few minutes he and Foweather were in sight of the curve of coastline with the rock outcropping, and Tom pulled Foweather down onto his knees. "We'll crawl from here up to the edge."

"Right."

Like two dogs they hunched down and crept toward the edge, dropping down to their elbows as the water came in sight. An exuberant, warbling cry drifted up to them from the water, and they both dropped flat.

"Good God," Foweather said on a released breath.

Tom could only second the sentiment, his own jaw dropping at the spectacle that met their eyes. Down below and a hundred yards away from shore, Konstanze was splashing about and frolicking like a demented dolphin. There was something weirdly unnatural about the speed with which she moved and the height she obtained when she propelled herself out of the water, splashing back down like a breaching whale.

"Good God" was right. No one human could move like that. What a fool he had been to worry about her in the water! And he had to admit, she had been right about her bodice, as well. From this distance, her breasts looked perfectly natural. If he hadn't known better, he himself would think she was a mermaid.

"She is even more spectacular than the first time I saw her," Foweather whispered. "I cannot believe I am witness to this."

"Nor can I," Tom said, watching entranced as Kon-

stanze turned a backward somersault, her fake breasts
kissing the open air as she arched her back. Her torso
went underwater and her fins came out, waving gaily
in the air for a moment before disappearing after her.
She came up again thirty feet away.

He heard thudding footsteps behind him, and looked
over his shoulder just as the rest of the Preventive
crew came into sight. He gestured them down, and the
men crawled up to join Tom and Foweather at the
edge. The lot of them were sweaty and breathing hard,
and Tom knew they'd run the entire mile to join them.

Hushed exclamations flew with whispered vehe-
mence as they sighted Konstanze cutting through the
water. Disbelief and awe mingled, and Tom could feel
their excitement vibrating in the air. The force of their
emotion sent a ripple of discomfort through his own
awe of Konstanze's swimming, knowing as he did that
at least half their wonder was due to a hoax. He hoped
the men would never discover that they had been
played for fools.

Still, better this fraud than an armed encounter. The
hidden cargo was worth enough that if not for this
plan, a number of those involved in the smuggling—
from fishermen to farmers to shopkeepers—would
have been willing to use force to retrieve their goods
from the Preventive men.

Konstanze rolled onto her back and with seemingly
no effort began gliding nearer the shoreline, then in a
path parallel to the coast. Her finned feet appeared
hardly to move, only the smallest splashes of water
occasionally appearing. She came within twenty yards
of where they lay hidden in the grasses and pink flow-

ering thrift, no more than the tops of their heads visible should she choose to look up. They were, he thought, like a pack of wolves greedily observing their prey.

As she swam by below, his eyes were drawn as always to her breasts, and he knew the others were looking there as well. He was unaccountably glad to know that those were false breasts Foweather and the others were seeing, and that Konstanze had not given in to his wrongheaded idea that—

*Wait a minute.* That *was* the costume bodice he was looking at, wasn't it? He narrowed his eyes, squinting at the light brownish pink nipples as Konstanze swam idly by. Brownish pink, not dark red. And they were a normal size.

A flush of shock washed through him. Those were her own breasts!

"Have you ever seen such a fine pair of bubbies?" one of the men asked on a sigh.

"I'd give her my soul if she'd let me touch 'em," another replied.

Tom felt his blood heat, his face burning as jealous fury built within him. These men should not be gazing upon Konstanze's unclothed body, should not be privy to such secrets of her flesh. They had no right to see her. She was not for the likes of them, she—

She what? He pressed his forehead down onto his fisted hands on the ground, his nose pressing into the grass as he tried to gain control of himself. She was doing exactly what he had first asked of her.

His muscles trembled with the need to act, to drag the men away from the cliff edge, to pluck out their staring eyes with his own fingers.

He could do none of that. He had neatly made this bed with his own hands, and he shuddered as he forced himself to lie still in it. If he could do nothing else, at least he could keep his own eyes from spying upon her, stealing glimpses of what she must not know she so clearly revealed.

He remained with his face averted until he heard her voice floating to him across the water, singing pure notes in an unknown tongue. He raised his head and found her perched out on the rock island, her wet hair trailing down her chest, concealing her lovely breasts.

He didn't recognize the song she sang and could not understand the words, but that did not matter either to him or, apparently, the other men. The melody was lyrical, lilting, and went straight to the soul. No one made a sound as they all strained to catch each and every note as they floated across the water. Tom wished there were some way to hush the sounds of waves and wind that stole tones from her voice.

"I must go to her," Foweather said, his voice raw.

"What?" Tom said, the words breaking him out of Konstanze's spell. He turned to the man, the others echoing his sentiment of surprise. Foweather was gazing intently out at Konstanze, tears seeping from his eyes.

"I must go to her," he repeated.

"You cannot!"

"I cannot bear it any longer," Foweather said. "Do you hear how she sings to me, how she calls me to her?"

"Get a hold of yourself, man!" Had the fool lost his mind? "You don't want to live with a mermaid!"

"How can I deny her?" Foweather asked, and made a move to get up as sounds of alarm came from his men.

Tom grabbed his arm. "Stay down, for God's sake. You cannot go to her. She was not meant for you— nor for any mortal man!" Had he really just said that? Perhaps Konstanze was not the only one who was meant to be on the stage.

"She is my destiny!" Foweather cried, and, throwing off Tom's hand, he struggled to his feet. Tom and the others rose as Foweather yelled out across the water, "I'm coming, my darling! Your bridegroom is coming!"

The singing abruptly stopped, even as Tom and two of the others lay hold of Foweather, restraining him as he pulled against them. The man struggled madly, trying to shake them off. "Let me go!"

"I swore I would not," Tom said through gritted teeth. "I cannot let you do this."

"She is my destiny!" Foweather cried, trying to throw himself from their grip.

"She would be your death!" Tom said, feeling a melodramatic fool for saying it. He suspected that Foweather would not have been half so eager to throw himself into the water if there had been no one present to restrain him.

Out on the rock island, Konstanze slipped into the water. She bobbed for a moment, watching their struggles, then dove under, her fins flashing in the air. Foweather saw her go as well, and stopped his struggles, his attention all on the surface of the water. They all waited for her to reappear, holding their breath against

240

her absence, their grips on Foweather loosening.

A minute went by, and then two. She was not coming back.

"She's gone," Tom said.

"No!" Foweather cried, and lunged for the cliff's edge.

The move caught Tom and the others loosely holding him by surprise, and he threw himself after the man and barely snagged him by the back of his coat. They both crashed to the ground, mere inches from the edge and a very long and bumpy fall down to the rocks.

"Let me go! Let me go! She needs me!" Foweather wept, tossing his head back and forth as the rest of his men piled on top of him, pinning arms and legs.

"No, listen to me, Robert," Tom said, grasping the man's face between his hands, wondering if he had misinterpreted the depth of Foweather's obsession. "You were under her spell. She's gone now. You must regain your senses. You do not want to go to her. Can you even swim?"

Foweather's pale blue eyes met Tom's. "Swim?"

"Yes. Can you?"

"No."

"Do you understand, then? If we had let you go, you would have drowned before you ever reached her."

"She would have come for me. She would have saved me. She loves me."

"How can she love? Can a turtle love, or a fish? It takes a human soul to love, Robert, a human soul. She does not have that."

241

Foweather tried to shake his head against the hands that held him. "She is my destiny. I feel it. It is the reason I came to Penperro."

"You came here because the coast around Penperro is rife with smuggling, with men who would cheat the king of his revenues," Tom said, not believing he was reminding Foweather of that particular fact. He should be encouraging Foweather's mania, not trying to bring him back to reason. "That is your purpose, to protect the coast against the pernicious influence of smugglers. You are a member of the Preventive Water Guard Service, by God!"

"Hear, hear!" the men cheered.

"But why me?" Foweather asked, plaintive. "Why did she choose me?"

"I do not know," Tom said, releasing him and gesturing to the others to do the same. "You will have to consider it your greatest challenge—to resist her unholy allure." He helped the man get to his feet.

"Her mother went to church," Foweather said. "Her mother must have had a soul, else surely God would have struck her dead for crossing the threshold of his holy house."

"Without such evidence of your own, you had best beware. We none of us want to find you washing ashore with the seaweed. You're too good a man for such a fate, Foweather," Tom said, slapping him on the back and finding to his surprise that he actually meant it.

Foweather turned and cast a longing look back out over the water.

"She's gone," Tom said. "Go back to town; get

some rest." He sent a meaningful look to the men, one that said they should keep a close eye on their leader. They all of them looked little better off than Foweather himself, their expressions bewildered and uncertain, frightened, Tom was sure, of the momentary insanity that had come over their leader.

"Will you come, too?"

"I have to return the horse. I'm sorry now that I came to tell you of the mermaid being sighted. I can see it has done nothing but bring you grief."

"You mustn't think that!" Foweather said. "Please. This has been the most wondrous day of my life. How many men ever see such marvels as we have today?"

No men ever did, by Tom's reckoning. He slapped Foweather's shoulder again in an effort at manly camaraderie and understanding. "You get some rest—and don't go alone to the shore."

"We won't let him," a crew member said, the sentiment seconded by others.

Tom watched as the group headed back down the path toward Penperro, then went to fetch the horse. By the time he got back the group was out of sight, but he waited a good ten minutes more to be certain they were gone before he raised his arms above him, signaling to Konstanze that all was clear. Her head and a waving arm appeared at the side of the rock island, a few feet above the waterline.

He went to where her clothes and a towel were hidden, gathering up the bundle and tucking it inside his coat. He found the same safe route to the bottom that he had directed Konstanze to use and climbed down, reaching the shore just as Konstanze herself swam up and pulled herself to a sitting position at the waterline. She looked every inch the mermaid. The fake red nipples were glaring at him from beneath her heavy wet hair.

"How did I do?" she asked gaily. "I was wonderful, wasn't I?"

"What—" he began, then had to take a breath and try again, his temper tied down tight. "What do you think you were doing?" he asked with feigned calm.

Her brows drew together, her smile fading. "Didn't I do as I was supposed to?"

He looked pointedly at her chest. "And what of those?"

She looked down at her chest, then back up at him, her eyes going wary. "What about them?"

"Where were they?"

She pursed her lips as if whistling and looked away, then lifted one of her finned feet out of the water, droplets spraying. "Did you see how fast I swam?"

"Konstanze!"

"What?" she snapped back, dropping the finned foot into the water. "What, Tom? Are you going to try to tell me you're upset because I did exactly what you wanted me to do?"

"You said you would wear the bodice. You insisted upon it."

"It looked unnatural."

"But we agreed—"

"I changed my mind. I decided you were right at the very beginning about how a mermaid should look. I should think that would make you happy," she said and, turning away, started yanking at the laces on her fins.

"Don't you try to ignore me," he said. "Konstanze!"

She dropped her hands and turned to look at him from under her brows. "What?" she asked again with exaggerated patience.

"Do you even realize that we could see you, all of us? We were right up there," he said, pointing to their hiding place. "You swam not twenty yards away, your bosom in plain view."

"Did you enjoy the show?"

"No, I did not! I turned away. I could not watch you shame yourself so." He felt the anger draining away, revealing something deeper and more painful. "Konstanze, where has your modesty gone?"

She shrugged. "What use was it? They would have thought they were seeing my real chest whether I wore the bodice or not."

"But I knew."

She ducked her head, resuming work on the laces. "You didn't look."

"You couldn't have known that I wouldn't." He knelt down beside her, out of reach of the lapping water, a new suspicion forming. "Or did you mean for me to see?"

"For God's sake, Tom, you think awfully highly of yourself! I thought I was too far away to be seen; that's all there is to it. The bodice drags against the water," she said, plucking at the wet material. "I wanted to see how fast I could go with the fins. It had nothing to do with you!" Her words were fierce, but her throat and cheeks were red with embarrassment.

245

"You swam along this entire section of coast on your back," he said. "Wherever we were, you must have known I would see you and know you weren't wearing the bodice."

She met his eyes, glaring. "I wasn't thinking of that. I was enjoying myself, that's all."

"That's not all," he said softly, some instinct telling him that she was bending the truth, that she *had* been aware he would see her and know the difference. "If you want my attention, you don't have to put yourself on display to get it."

"You're insufferable!"

"And you're a bad liar," he said, touching her cheek with his fingertips. She held still as he trailed his fingertips down to her lips, lightly brushing over their full curves. They parted and then her wide eyes met his, uncertainty and hunger in their depths. He felt the gentle warmth of her breath on his skin, and she leaned toward him.

She was irresistible. He pulled her gently into his arms and used his lips this time to caress hers, sliding softly across them, kneading tenderly. Her hands were caught flat against his chest; then as he continued to kiss her they slid up behind his neck, digging into his hair and pulling him closer.

He knew he shouldn't be doing this; it went against every promise he had made to himself. He knew it could lead to nowhere but trouble, but he wanted her, every inch of her flesh, every thought in her head, every beat of her heart. He wanted to devour her, heart, body, and soul, and when he had done so he would do it all again and again, until there was nothing left of either of them but exhausted satisfaction.

He traced his tongue along the line where her lips met and they obediently parted, allowing him the freedom to explore as he pleased. He tasted her own timid tongue, stroking it with his as his hand behind her back searched for and found the buttons to her wet bodice. Only one was fastened, and as he continued kissing her he undid it and slid his hand inside to lay it against her chilled skin. At his touch she arched toward him, a muffled sound coming from her throat. Her fingers tightened in the hair at the nape of his neck.

With his tongue he touched the roof of her mouth, distracting her, her hands loosening in his hair as he continued to play inside her mouth. He slowly pulled the back of the bodice open and then shifted her so that she lay across his thighs. His hand moved around to the front of her waist, massaging her flesh in gentle circles.

She was every bit as soft and shapely as he had imagined. He trailed kisses down to her neck, sucking on her earlobe, pausing to trace the whorls of her outer ear with his tongue and then touch lightly upon the center of it, setting her squirming in his arms. He moved his lips down the side of her neck, stroking her salty skin with his tongue, his hands moving to draw down the wet bodice, the fabric coming over her shoulders. She did not protest, her head arching back to allow him greater access to her neck and the vulnerable, sensitive point where it met her shoulders.

He bent his head, nibbling at that tender bend, his hands pulling the bodice all the way off her and flinging it away. She shivered, and he laid his hand against her bare belly, his palm and fingers spanning the width of it. He returned to her mouth, kissing her deeply as he moved his hand up to cup her breast, playing with the erect nipple between his fingers.

He ducked his head, taking the hard nub within his mouth, suckling at it as his hand went around her buttocks. She held him tight against her breast, deep sounds of pleasure forming in her throat. Far from reluctant, she showed every sign of wanting to continue this course to its natural end.

He slipped his hand inside the back waistband of her costume. "How do we get this off you?" he asked, raising his head and looking at her.

There was a dreamy, faraway look in her eyes. He slid his hand down to the top of her buttocks, bare under the wet material, and she blinked at him, her thoughts refocusing as he watched. Her eyes widened, and she suddenly pushed away from him, sitting up, her hands going over her breasts. *"O Gott,"* she said softly.

"Konstanze," he said, reaching for her.

She leaned away. "Tom, no. We can't do this. It's not right.•

His body disagreed with its every fiber, with every sinew and nerve, but against his wishes part of his mind awoke to echo her thoughts. Rationally he knew that this wasn't right, but the logic seemed no more than empty words to his heated senses. It was only his own trust in his mind to make better decisions than his body that had him reluctantly setting her off his lap.

He released a long, shuddering breath. He felt her bundle of clothes still in his coat and pulled it out, placing it on the ground between them. "I had no right to take such liberties. My apologies." He was not sorry, and knew she had been as eager as he, but the brain knew what was best and he obeyed its orders.

She snatched up her clothes, unfolding them with her bare back to him, pulling them on over her head. "I am as much to blame," she said over her shoulder, and then he heard another muffled, *"O Gott!"* and realized that her distress was very real, and of a different order than his frustrated desire. She sounded like a woman ashamed of her own behavior, and her shame made him feel sick inside.

"It's not your fault," he said.

"It is. I knew better than to behave as I did." She looked over her shoulder at him. "Turn away."

He obeyed, sitting with his forehead in his hands as he listened to her trying to dress, her breathing audible, catching on what sounded like sobs. What had he done? He had known that to touch her would be to dishonor her, and to dishonor himself as well. She was married, for all that she had left her husband. All that had kept her from becoming an adulteress was a thin layer of wet green material.

Her sobs were growing louder. "Konstanze?" he asked.

"I cannot untie them," she said.

He turned around again and saw that she struggled with the fish fins, their laces swollen with salt water. She was wearing her dress, but the mermaid costume was bunched down around her ankles, trapped on her by the fins.

He knelt at her feet and gently pushed her cold hands aside. "It will be all right. Don't fret, Konstanze. It will be all right."

*It will be all right*, he'd said. Konstanze pulled the covers up over her nose, her body curled into a fetal position in her bed. She was washed clean of salt, and of the traces of Tom's mouth upon her body. Still, she knew it would not be all right.

Something had been happening to her since she'd come to Penperro. She didn't know who she was anymore. She had always been a good girl, obedient and moral. Modest. Her reputation was above reproach, her honor unsullied.

What was happening to her? It was as if the secret fantasy life she had once lived was slipping free of the confines of her mind, intent on taking over her real life. The naughty Konstanze, the Konstanze she had always kept safely bottled deep inside like a dangerous genie, was showing every sign of having pushed out the cork and escaped.

Why had she taken the bodice off, and why had she swum where she knew Tom would see her? She pulled her knees up closer to her chest, remembering that exhilarating sensation of being bare to the world and not caring. She had looked down at her own body and thought it beautiful, and had wanted to show it off to any who would look. She had made excuses in her mind, but that was what the truth had been. She had had no shame. None at all. She had stuffed the bodice in a crevice and reveled in her nakedness.

And she had wanted Tom to look at her and to want her.

When he had touched her she had wanted more. It was only when he made to remove her costume that she had come to her senses, and only then because she had recalled her monthly flow, and had not wanted him to see evidence of that. Otherwise she would have let him take her there on the rocks and sand, not a thought in her head except the glorious feel of his hands and mouth on her body.

*O Gott.* She was not going to be all right.

# Chapter Fifteen

*Exeter*

"You should be using condoms if you're bedding down with whores," Dr. Cox chided.

Bugg II pursed his lips over his protruding teeth, watching with impatient ill humor as the physician took a sample sheep-gut sheath out of his bag, its red drawstring dangling. They were in a tiny room in yet another seedy inn, this one in Exeter. He had traced Konstanze this far by finding the coaching service that had taken her and Hilde as passengers from London, and felt in his bones that he was getting close. He was running her to ground like a terrier after a rabbit.

So intent had he been on pursuing her, he had been unwilling to stop and take the time to seek out a doctor. As a result his condition had worsened, his penis dripping a nasty yellow-green substance, the opening at the end an angry, inflamed red. It hurt every time he took a piss—which he found he needed to do with annoying frequency.

"See, it covers the penis entirely," the good doctor patiently explained. "You pull the drawstring tight, and tie it around the scrotum to keep it in place. If you use these, you'll have less need of the services of those in my profession. Even better, though, I'd advise you to find a wife and take your pleasures in one place."

"I am aware of my mistake," Bugg II gritted out as politely as he could manage. The doctor had yet to treat him, and it would be no good to antagonize the man before he inflicted whatever medical punishment was in store.

He'd spent many hours fantasizing about finding the thieving whore who'd both stolen his money and passed on her dose of the clap as a parting token of her appreciation. He'd kill her. First he'd make her and Konstanze pleasure each other while he watched; then he'd kill her. And kill Konstanze. He'd kill Dr. Cox if he could get away with it. He'd kill every damned inhabitant of Exeter.

"The treatment is threefold. First, you must rest, dining only on gruel and water until the symptoms have all passed. Do not touch alcohol. Second, hot baths for up to two hours, three times a day."

"And third?"

"Mercury," Dr. Cox said, "taken by mouth, but also as a solution applied inside the affected member."

"Inside?" Bugg II asked, worried. "How do you get it inside?"

# Lisa Cach

Dr. Cox reached into his bag and took out a large brass syringe an inch in diameter, with a thick, hollow needle six inches long. "With this," Dr. Cox said.

Bugg II gave a little cry.

"I'll slide it up the urethra as far as it will go," Dr. Cox cheerily explained, "then irrigate the passage and bladder. You will feel a certain amount of discomfort."

"Discomfort? How much discomfort?"

Dr. Cox handed him a wooden dowel, pocked with teethmarks. "Here, bite on this. It'll keep you from screaming."

# Chapter Sixteen

*Penperro*

"The woman is a menace," Matt Jobson said. "It's gotten so that I can't take a step in the open without fear that she will swoop down upon me. I've come across some bold women in my day, but Hilde—good God, even Admiral Nelson would turn his ship around and flee from the likes of her."

Tom played with his pint of cider, twisting the glass in its ring of moisture on the table. They were in the Fishing Moon, the room nearly empty, as it was midday. Mrs. Popple cleaned glasses behind the bar, and her husband could periodically be heard in back, doing the heavy work of moving kegs up from the cellar.

"I told you she 'borrowed' some of my books from my bedroom, right under Mrs. Toley's protesting nose, didn't I?" Tom said.

"I saw them myself, tucked under her arm. I think they were all that saved me. I don't like to think what would have happened if she'd had both hands free. It was bad enough as it was."

At that Tom looked up from the rings he was making on the table, distracted finally from his own troubling thoughts. "What did happen? You never said, specifically."

Matt downed half his pint of cider before speaking. "I feel like a teenage girl pursued by an older man. 'Oh, please, sir, I'm a good girl, please let me be,' " Matt cried in a falsetto. "And of course she has no idea how to stop the man, and may even succumb if he proves persistent enough."

Tom stared at his friend. "Do you mean you might?"

Matt looked into his nearly empty glass, swirled the contents around a few times, then drank the remainder down. "She backed me right up against the door of the church, chest to chest. She's a little taller than me, did you know that?"

"No. What did she do then?"

"She sniffed me."

"What?"

"Like an animal. She put her face right against my neck and sniffed me, and then she made this little growling sound deep in her throat."

"Good Lord."

"That's not the worst of it. The worst of it was that I almost enjoyed it."

Tom began to laugh. "You're joking."

"I started thinking of she-lions and bears and wild

pigs, and how they must go about their mating, all that squealing and biting and rolling around in the woods. They do what comes naturally, and to hell with the consequences."

"Wild pigs? You're aroused by the thought of wild pigs?"

"It's been a while since I've had a woman, Tom."

"Less than a month, by my reckoning."

Matt frowned at him. "As I said."

"But you would break your fast with Hilde?"

"Why do you think she makes me so nervous? It's not the giving in that is so troubling as what might happen afterward. I am somehow certain that should I give her what she wants, I shall never be free of her. I can see myself an old man, still being shaken awake in the middle of the night so that she might have her way with me. She is the type of creature whose hunger is never sated, who will drain a man dry till he is nothing but an empty shell, devoid of ambition or energy. She is an animal."

"You say that with a little too much enthusiasm."

Matt rubbed his forehead and sighed. "I know."

"I shouldn't worry too much about it. I cannot imagine her giving up her position with Konstanze, even for such a stallion as yourself."

"There is that," Matt said, brightening. "And how is our mermaid faring? I've grown quite curious about her. After her performance off the coast the other day, she's been the main topic of conversation around here. The stories keep getting better and better. If I didn't know better, I'd think the Preventive crew saw the real thing splashing around out there."

Lisa Cach

"You and half the town. I've given up reminding people that she's Robert Penrose's great-niece. It's as if, since they haven't met her, she doesn't exist except as the mermaid. I even heard one theory that although she's been living as a human woman for many years, she was actually a mermaid all along and has now come home, and since she is from these waters she has agreed to help the Cornish people against the foul English."

Matt shrugged. "You can hardly blame them. Times are hard, and there's something appealing in the idea of Penperro having a protective mermaid."

"I'm beginning to think that Konstanze herself would enjoy playing the role full-time."

"She's overcome her misgivings?"

"With a vengeance. It's as if all along she was a brilliant butterfly, trapped inside a smothering white cocoon. It's unnerving, watching her come out."

"Her mother was on the stage, and her father," Matt reminded him. "It shouldn't be such a surprise that she enjoys her part in your scheme."

"If you met her you'd understand my confusion. There is something confoundingly innocent about her, despite actions contrary to that notion."

Matt gave him a long look. "It sounds as if you have been spending a lot of time thinking about her."

"Too much time," he admitted, and rubbed his eyes with the heels of his hands. "I don't want to talk about it. I've got enough to worry about without throwing that into the mix." He was having a hard enough time accepting what he had done with Konstanze on the shore—he wasn't about to discuss it with Matt in the

258

Fishing Moon over pints of cider. The worst of it was, he didn't feel half as ashamed of himself as he knew he ought. His feelings for her were making it harder and harder to see the error in helping her to betray her cruel, elderly, and blessedly distant husband.

When he'd come to Penperro he'd promised himself never again to be the villain. It had been an easy enough promise to keep, until Konstanze came into his life. He'd also promised himself never again to let a woman so distract him that he let his friends, his family, and his business fall by the wayside. Yet at this moment he could barely manage to shove thoughts of Konstanze from his mind. Even while he devoted his attention to business, there was a part of his mind making love to her.

"You heard about the close call with the seaweed wagon, I presume?" Tom asked, trying to drag his mind onto another topic. In the back of his imagination Konstanze, naked, was lying in his lap, her arms wrapped around his neck.

"Clemmens and the others are lucky not to be in jail right now, and their wives, too," Matt said.

"It was sheer bad luck for Foweather to stumble across them like that." Clemmens and some farmers and their wives had been down on the shore, transferring goods to a wagon heaped with seaweed. When Foweather had come across their early morning activity and asked what they were up to, they had quite legitimately claimed that they were collecting the seaweed to fertilize their fields. Clemmens was a fisherman, however, and had been forced to claim he was there to help his friends. They were fortunate that the seaweed had been slimy enough that Foweather had not searched it.

"His movements seem more random than they were before the mermaid," Matt observed.

Tom sighed. "Yet another unanticipated consequence. I think he is becoming so obsessed that he cannot keep to his usual methodical methods. Wherever he is, he thinks the mermaid may be someplace else, and he has to go check."

"It would be more convenient if he'd stick to a regular schedule," Matt said dryly.

"It would be more convenient still if we could write the schedule for him. We could land boats in broad daylight if only we could be certain where he was going to be," he said, remembering Konstanze's ridiculous suggestion to smuggle in the middle of the day.

They were both silent, contemplating the problem.

"Even two or three hours would be sufficient," Tom said. "Especially if the boats knew several days in advance—especially if it were to be the same two or three hours each week, like, say, on a Sunday morning."

Matt seemed to understand the direction of his thoughts. "Foweather doesn't come to church, except sporadically. Do you have a way to insure his presence?"

"I'm thinking it's time our mermaid went in search of her soul."

"How's your toe?" Konstanze asked, unable to think of anything else to break the silence that weighed heavily between her and Tom. He was walking beside

her, taking her to Talland Church for a rehearsal of
her next appearance as the mermaid. Hilde walked a
few paces behind, urged to come along by them both,
as if neither trusted their actions if left alone together.

"It looks terrible but feels fine. I meant to thank you
for that."

"Don't mention it. I was happy to be able to help."
She couldn't contain the smile that pulled at her lips,
recalling his fainting spell.

"Don't laugh," he said, casting her a stern glance
from the corner of his eye.

"I would never." They continued on in silence, and
she wondered if that incident upon the shore preyed
upon his thoughts as strongly as it did upon hers. During the day she was apt to dwell on his amorous attentions with a fair trace of longing, but at night as
she lay in bed, unable to sleep, demons of thought
would come and plague her, scolding her for her sins
and laughing that she had already begun her short,
quick descent to hell.

As a runaway wife she supposed that some would
say she did not have much honor left to lose, yet it
did matter to her that she was not yet an adulteress.
In thought she was perhaps already guilty, but she
could still cling to the technical truth of being innocent
in deed.

She had once thought it would be no hardship to
live a continent life, abstaining from the intimate attentions of men. She had never guessed how wrong
she was. Was she now to live out her days plagued by
unfulfilled longings, or should she toss honor and caution to the winds and give in to her body's desires?

This would all be so much simpler if she were free to marry.

She cast Tom a sideways glance, wondering what manner of husband he would make. Hilde had said he kept a comfortable house and that he appeared to be well respected by the townsfolk. People liked him.

Which was not to say the man was above reproach. Beyond the obvious matter of the smuggling—about which she was no longer in a position to judge, taking part in and profiting from it as she did—was the matter of his choice in reading material. Of the four books Hilde had forcibly borrowed from his room, one was a treatise on mining, one a new book of poetry by Wordsworth, one an adventure novel, and the last was a scandalous bit of literature entitled *Memoirs of a Woman of Pleasure.*

She blushed even to think of the book. She had not read too far as yet, for the book embarrassed her even by being in her hand. Equally, she could not *not* read it. The heroine began the story an innocent, but a dozen pages into the novel was being initiated by prostitutes into the ways of the flesh. The author, John Cleland, had endeavored to explain each step in this initiation in titillating detail, and Konstanze was finding herself befuddled by several particulars. She read and reread the troubling passages, comparing them to her own meager experiences.

What, for example, was the stiff, erect machine that emerged from a man's breeches? She assumed it to be his penis, but Bugg's had been a soft, limp thing, more like a bit of wet sponge cake than a stiff, erect machine. Was Mr. Cleland simply using his poetic imagination?

And what of the milky effusion one character had left spilled over the heroine's thighs? What was that?

And the ecstatic fulfillment that the heroine had reached, touching her private parts while spying upon a man and woman engaged in sexual relations, what had that been? She had tasted bits of pleasure by her own touch, and now by Tom's, but she had not known there was a goal to be reached in such pleasures.

It was all quite confusing, but worse yet was that the book was Tom's. She wondered at what depravities filled his head that he would purchase such a book, but at least it was nowhere near as vile as that tome that Quarles had given her husband, where pleasure came only from a woman's pain. On the contrary, she had more than once felt a pulse of response as she read the *Memoirs*. But what was Tom doing with such licentious material? And more important, had he yet noticed that it was missing?

"Are you enjoying the books Hilde borrowed for you?" he asked.

*O Gott.* What to say? "I like the Wordsworth poems very much, and the adventure story is most entertaining."

He slanted her a knowing look. "And the other? I'm sure you've found it fascinating."

"I . . . I haven't quite made my way through it."

"I wouldn't have thought that was your usual choice of reading material."

"It's not! Of course it's not! I shall return it to you this evening, and shall be glad to be rid of it."

"You're certain you wouldn't like to keep it? I should think it made very good reading for when you go to bed at night. I keep it in arm's reach of my bed, myself."

Her jaw dropped. "You are being more frank with me than I perhaps could wish. I'll return the book to you tonight. I wouldn't want to deprive you of your entertainments. Now let us say no more about it."

"I don't know what is so frank about discussing reading habits."

Konstanze ducked her head and leaned toward him, whispering. "The book is scandalous. I have read only four chapters, and already I am quite horrified."

"That's why I don't take part in such things, myself. There are safer ways for a person to earn a living, ways that won't end in the worker's death from disease. You can't do much to change the situation if you don't understand it, though."

She blinked at him. He was a social reformer, and that was his purpose in reading the book? "I find much of the subject matter beyond my comprehension. All this mention of . . . of . . . fluids and such, and machines."

"I'm impressed that you're trying to learn about it. I find some of the mechanics quite confusing, myself."

She gave a little sigh of relief. "Truly? So it is not ignorance, or lack of intelligence on my own part that caused my puzzlement?"

"I've had to reread entire sections to get the gist of what was being said," Tom admitted.

"I, too! There was so little that related to my own experience."

"I shouldn't think there was. What chance would you ever have had to tunnel for copper?"

She frowned. Tunnel for copper? Was that a euphemism of some sort? "If you want to call it that, although I confess I have never heard the expression. Apparently there is much I do not know about the intimate relations between men and women."

"Intimate . . ." Tom stopped walking, forcing her to as well. "We are discussing Grant's *A Treatise on the Mining Techniques of Cornwall*, aren't we?"

It took her a moment to understand, to remember the barely glanced-at book to which he referred. Her mouth pulled down in a horrified grimace. "Oh, oh . . ." she said. She resumed walking, her pace quick and agitated. Tom quickly caught up.

"That was the other book Hilde took, wasn't it?"

Konstanze shook her head quickly from side to side, letting out little "ohs" under her breath.

"It puts me to sleep at night," Tom went on. "It's better than any number of sheep leaping fences. Was there another book she took?"

Konstanze moaned. She felt him looking at her, searching her face in the growing dusk for some hint of an answer. She spared him a quick glance, and saw his expression change.

"She didn't take . . . I didn't notice . . ." Tom stumbled. "It wasn't the *Memoirs* she took, was it?"

Konstanze cast him a helpless look. A chuckle started deep inside his chest, growing to outright laughter.

"It's a scandalous book!" Konstanze cried. "You should be ashamed to own it!"

"And you should be ashamed to admit you read and reread each scene!"

"I didn't reread each scene! And I told you, I've only made my way halfway through volume one, and that is quite far enough, thank you. You may take the vile thing home with you."

"And deprive you of your education? I wouldn't dream of it."

"There is nothing in that book about which I wish to be educated. I know quite enough already, thank you very much."

"Apparently not, if you found it as confusing as you say." He frowned down at her. "You did share a bed with your husband, didn't you?"

She made a noise of affront. "That is none of your affair. What an unspeakably rude question to ask!"

He grabbed her arm, forcing her to stop, his expression suddenly serious. "Konstanze, did you share his bed?"

"Well, of course I did."

"In, er . . . every sense of the word?"

"Yes!" Konstanze was aware of Hilde standing a few feet away, watching them closely but not, for once, interfering.

"I ask, because if the *Memoirs* is as confusing to you as you say, well, I just wonder—"

"Wonder what?" Konstanze asked, her own admitted confusion and ignorance on the topic of sex making her curious as to what he would say.

"I wonder if your marriage was ever properly consummated. If it wasn't, you have grounds for an annulment."

266

"Oh." She was silent for a moment. "I think it was consummated."

"You think? Or you're certain?"

"It hurt," she whispered. "It's supposed to hurt, isn't it?"

"The first time, yes," he said, just as quietly.

"Then it was consummated."

He placed her hand in the crook of his arm and they resumed walking. "The solicitor I hired, Mr. Rumbelow, said you didn't have any children."

"No. Perhaps there is something wrong with me." She was embarrassed to be talking about this with him, which seemed silly after she had so freely swum half-naked before him, and let him put his mouth to her breast. She felt sharply the difference between being free with her body and being free with her private thoughts. With Bugg she had had great practice in keeping herself locked away from whatever happened with her body. For all the fuss that society made about physical modesty, it felt like opening one's private, most intimate thoughts to another person—especially a man—was the far more revealing and dangerous act of the two.

"Do you want children?" he asked.

"Someday. Although I thought a child might make life with Bugg more bearable, I am glad now that we did not have any. I only hope I am not barren. He did, after all, have a son with his first wife."

"Bugg's an old man, past his prime. There's no reason to think you won't be able to have children someday."

She tilted her head toward Tom, a feeling of wick-

edness coming over her as she whispered conspirato-
rially, "After the first few months, he rarely paid me
any attention in bed," she confided. "I thought I had
done something wrong, but I'm beginning to suspect
that he was too old to fully play the husband."

"Serves him right, the old goat," Tom said. "So he
didn't have the energy to make proper use of the bride
he'd purchased, eh? Must have driven him half mad."

She couldn't fail to notice how very satisfied he
sounded with that piece of information. She knew it
was naughty to take pleasure in speaking with another
man of her husband's sexual deficiencies, but it was a
delicious little taste of revenge.

The first stars were showing in the deep blue sky
above them, and the last hints of the sunset were fading in pink and lavender to the west by the time they
reached Talland Church. A white-haired man was
waiting outside the front doors for them, a shielded
lantern dangling from his hand. Konstanze heard Hilde
give a little growl of what could only be described as
voracious pleasure. Tom's suggestions about her
maid's romantic interests were suddenly not half so
laughable.

Tom introduced her to his friend. Hilde and the
vicar obviously already knew one another.

"It's a pleasure to make your acquaintance at last,"
Matt said. "All of Penperro has been anxious to meet
you."

"I am equally eager to meet them," Konstanze said.
"Tom has been my only visitor since I arrived," she
said mournfully.

Matt laughed, holding her hand sandwiched between his own. "You poor child."

"Enough of that," Tom put in. "If you're going to speak ill of me, at least wait until I'm out of earshot."

"Now where is the fun in that?" Matt asked, and then to Konstanze, "You don't know how good it is to hear someone say she recognizes what a pest the man can be. Everyone else thinks he walks on water."

"In my experience he is far more likely to force a woman into the water than to risk getting his own feet wet."

Matt laughed again. "He doesn't much like to get his hands dirty, either."

"Did he tell you about his encounter with my plow?" Konstanze asked innocently.

"All right, enough!" Tom interrupted.

"What plow?" Matt asked.

"Never mind," Tom said. "Matt, show Konstanze the bench, will you?"

Matt exchanged glances with Konstanze, his look saying he fully expected to be told the plow story at the first opportunity. She smothered a smile. She was having entirely too much fun tattling on men this evening.

Matt led them into the church. There were a few candles lit, barely enough to illuminate the rough, whitewashed stone walls and arches. The floor was of dark yellow and black tiles, worn and dull. The ceiling was a barrel arch of wood, carved figures protruding from the ends of beams, but it was too dark to make out what they represented. On either side ran a row of pillars and rounded arches, parallel to the center aisle.

269

There was a choir at the far end and, off in the dim shadows to the left, an organ.

Matt led them through the arches on the center right to a small raised alcove where an old bench sat, the wood blackened with age. It was more of a chair, really, being only three feet wide with sides and a back. A white silk cushion was on the seat.

"This is the mermaid bench," Matt explained, and lowered the lantern to the side of the bench where a two-tailed mermaid was carved, a mirror in one hand and a comb in the other. She was remarkably buxom for a figure in a church, Konstanze thought. Hilde bent down with her, ostensibly to look, but more likely to be closer to Matt.

"Where did it come from?" Konstanze asked.

"No one knows for certain. All we do know is that it is very old."

"How old?"

"My guess is that it could be from as early as the thirteenth century, based on the style of the carving and the construction."

"Truly?"

Matt shrugged. "Then again, it could be no more than a hundred years old. Whatever the case, it's sat here in this alcove ever since I've been in Penperro, and for as long as anyone else can remember, as well."

"Does anyone ever sit in it?"

"There's never been any rule against a parishioner sitting here, but no one ever does. I think they feel there would be something vaguely sacrilegious in doing so, as if it were a holy relic passed down from another age."

They all straightened. "And now I'm going to sit here," Konstanze said. "Didn't anyone protest the notion?"

"They don't yet know you'll be here," Tom said. "But when they do, I imagine their response will be as it has been to anything else to do with the mermaid: they'll believe you're real. They'll want you to sit there, where you belong."

Where she belonged. It was hardly that, and yet she was feeling some of the same thrill of anticipation that came whenever Tom had a new suggestion for his ongoing mermaid scheme. Perhaps that bench was where she belonged more than she had thought, if it meant a chance to play another facet of the mermaid.

She was, she admitted, more the daughter of her dramatic parents than she had known. All those years of daydreams had been but her way of demurely living out the urges in her blood. Tom Trewella had no idea of the demon he had unleashed within her: at this rate, promise to dead mother or no, she would be seeking out a stage to earn her living.

At least it was better than earning money the way the heroine of the *Memoirs* did.

Too bad they were at war with France. That made working on the Continent a bit difficult. The Colonies were an option, though. Surely there couldn't be much competition for a talented singer in America—

"Konstanze?" Tom asked, in a tone that suggested it was not the first time he had called to her.

"Hmm? Yes?"

"Are you paying attention?"

She gave him a bright smile. "Of course."

He ran through again what she would do on Sunday, pointing out where everyone would likely be seated and explaining when she should both arrive and leave. Being a soulless mermaid, she wouldn't be expected to take communion. While he was talking Hilde grabbed Matt's arm and insisted he give her a tour of the church.

"Now let me show you where you'll hide before and after the service," Tom said, and taking the lantern he led her outside, then around to the back of the church where it faced the sea. The land sloped down, the back half of the church sitting high on stone foundations. There was a small wooden door, no more than three feet tall, set into the stones and mortar. Tom took out an iron key and unlocked it.

"I'm to wait in there?" Konstanze asked, appalled at the dark little entrance.

"It's dry and fairly clean," Tom said. "Come look." He held the lantern inside the opening.

Konstanze peered in, finding a space much larger than she would have expected. To one side, just within reach of the lantern light, was a stack of kegs. "Those aren't what I think they are, are they?" she asked.

Tom gave her an innocent expression. "Every church needs wine."

"And is that wine?"

He shrugged. "Some of it."

Konstanze just shook her head, deciding there was little that could surprise her any longer about the smuggling in Penperro. French spirits stored under the church—why not? Perhaps next she'd see the resident customs man helping to unload a boat. "It looks like there are spiders," she said, noting the cobwebs heavy between the stone groins of the low ceiling.

"They won't bother you. At least there aren't any snakes."

She flashed him a look. "Snakes?"

"There aren't any."

How would he know? Had he sat under here in the dark? "Rats?"

"Ah, well . . ."

"I don't mind mice, but I draw the line at rats," she said. "I won't be sitting in the dark listening to them scrabbling about."

"I'll take care of it."

They straightened up and Tom shut the small door. "There are a few small gaps in the flooring of the church, enough that you should be able to hear what goes on up there without any difficulty."

She nodded, thinking that it was too bad she couldn't hide in the bracken fern valley. The seaward side of the church had its advantages, though. If anyone did see her arriving, they would see her coming from this direction, and if anyone watched her go— and they were not chasing her too closely—they would think she disappeared into the sea. She would lock the little door from the inside, guaranteeing that no one found her under the church.

It was full dark now, and when she turned around she could see the crescent moon floating high above the horizon, the deep blue-black sky heavy with stars. A breeze off the ocean played at the curls about her face and the long fringe of her shawl, the air cool but not cold. "It's a beautiful night," she said.

273

"At times like this I forget what the rest of the year can be like," Tom said, standing close to her side. "In all your travels, did you ever see any place that was like Cornwall?"

She looked up at him, seeing only the faint glow of his skin and his white cravat. She recognized the pride of one who believed there was nowhere in the world that was quite like home.

"I saw parts of Cornwall abroad, in rocky shores or in blue water, or even in the color of the skies. Nowhere was quite the same, though. The hills would be the right shape, but the color of the rocks wrong, or the sky the same but the grasses and flowers different. There's something unique here," she said, looking out over the dark sea. Although they were only ten yards or so from the cliff edge, it was only a dull, faint thudding of the waves below that they could hear.

"What is it that's unique?"

She wondered at the need to ask, the same need that a person in any country or village seemed to have, as if they needed to be defined from outside by someone who had seen more and could tell them how they were different or special from anyone or anywhere else. "There's something barren here," she said. "Something hard-scrubbed, as if the wind has scraped away all that is soft."

"And the people?"

"Proud, of course. Hardworking. Pious. But also fond of fun, when they have a chance for it." She could almost feel him thinking, trying to decide if that description fit him as well. "Except for you," she amended. "A less pious man I have never met."

"Ah, but you wouldn't like me half so much if I were more so."

"Have you ever noticed that those with the greatest pride are often those with the least of which to be proud?"

He laughed and took her hand in his, bringing it up so he could kiss its back. "Ah, Konstanze, however did I amuse myself before you came here?"

"With naughty books," she grumbled, liking the feel of his lips on the back of her hand, and making no move to pull away. After all, Hilde the guard dog was right inside the church. They should be safe from each other.

She leaned in a little closer to him. He served as a shield against the sea breeze, creating a pocket of warmth. Surely it was innocent to enjoy that? "Do you ever think of leaving Penperro?" she asked, hoping that conversation would help hide the fact that she was drinking in the scent and nearness of him, her skin tingling with a yearning for closer contact.

"Sometimes." He still held her hand, and gently pulled her nearer, laying the back of her hand against his chest. "But there is no reason to leave. What is there out there that I do not have already? Nothing is so dire here that I would wish to escape it."

"You're more like me than I thought," she said softly.

"How do you mean?"

"That's how I was, with Bugg. It took a great deal of misery to spur me into leaving. Why is it we move on only to escape things? Why don't we move on to go toward something better, instead?"

"We both did."

"But if you had never fought with your friend, you would still be in that town."

"It's human nature, Konstanze. Change is hard. Starting over is hard. We don't give up what we have unless we're forced to."

"I don't want to be that way," Konstanze said. "I don't want to be trapped by security. I wish I had the courage to go off into the world without worrying about money or where I would sleep."

He laughed. "That's not courage. That's foolishness."

"For a woman, perhaps. Not for a man."

"You're not going to tell me you wish you were a man, are you?"

She looked up at him, her lips curling in a wicked smile. "If I were a man, I think you could get into trouble for holding my hand like this."

"There's a lot more than that for which I could get into trouble," he said, lowering his head.

His lips were soft against hers, playing gently at first. She closed her eyes, feeling the thrill of his kiss sinking through her veins. Half-formed thoughts fell apart in her mind, the pieces scattered by the wash of pleasure and a painful, aching desire.

He dropped the lantern, the metal casing clanking as it hit the ground. Tom released her hand against his chest and brought both his arms around her, pulling her hard against his body, her back arching against his supporting arms as he deepened his kiss. She felt something hard pressing against her belly, and had just enough sense to wonder if that was the "erect machine" of which the heroine in the *Memoirs* spoke.

If it was, she liked it. Her body recognized it even if she herself was not certain, and she found herself pressing harder against it. Tom slipped a leg between hers, the top of his thigh nudging thrillingly up against her. As his mouth moved down her neck, his hands roved lower on her back, going around her buttocks, cupping and massaging them, using them to pull her more firmly against his thigh.

Her hands went up around his neck, her body going weak as the ridge of his hidden manhood came so near to rubbing against her sex. She felt as if a thousand drops of pleasure were raining through her body, washing away her muscles and her ability to control them. Images from the book mixed with her own yearnings, and she knew that what she wanted was that "machine" deep inside her. She wanted to give herself over to whatever Tom desired, to offer up her body for his pleasure as well as her own.

"Konstanze," he murmured into her neck, and lowered her to the ground, her shawl forming a haphazard blanket beneath her. The shaded, tilted lantern was only a foot or two from her face, its muted glow reflecting in Tom's dark-ringed, amber eyes as he raised his head. His pupils were wide and black despite the light, and she saw in their depths the force of his desire. Knowing he wanted her as much as—perhaps even more than—she wanted him increased her arousal. Instead of being frightened as she thought she should be, she wanted to push him over the edge so that he would lose control and take her.

She slid her hands down from around his neck to

his chest, feeling the shape of him beneath his vest and shirt, then moved her hands around his waist to his back, reaching down to squeeze his buttocks as he had squeezed hers. She raised one knee to the side and pulled him against her, his hips settling between her thighs, that tantalizing ridge of flesh pressing exactly where she wanted it.

He shifted to the side, lying half over her and kissing her deeply, his tongue invading and exploring her mouth as his hand pulled at her thin skirt and chemise. Her knee lowered back to the ground as he found his way beneath her hem and smoothed his hand up her leg, fingertips curling around to brush the sensitive place behind her knee. His hand kept moving upward, the strong thumb pressing on the soft flesh on the inside of her thigh, lightening as it moved up, her skin anticipating each inch as she silently urged him forward.

She parted her thighs, allowing him room to touch her, but infuriatingly just as he was about to reach the very center of her—she could feel the side of his finger against the outer edge of her sex—he moved his hand up and over her pelvis, pressing small circles into the softness just above. The motion pulled at her sex, creating faint sensations that made her want to beg for more. She wanted to push his hand down there, but was torn between the wish for instant gratification and the seductive pleasure of leaving him in charge. There was a delectation all its own in being forced to wait for pleasure.

His mouth left hers, trailing kisses down her neck and then pausing in the hollow of her throat, his tongue darting out to swirl in the small pool. He traced a path down her breastbone, then ran his tongue along the scooped neckline of her gown, its tip dipping beneath to brush along the tops of her breasts. He bent lower still and let her feel the warmth of his breath through the thin cotton, then lowered his mouth over her breast, his mouth hot in contrast to the cool night, his teeth pinching gently at the sides of her nipple and causing an answering rush of wet heat in her loins.

He lowered his hand over her, she felt his fingers comb through her nether curls as he slid his hand downward, her folds parting and slipping into place around his long fingers. She moaned as his palm moved with gentle friction over the nub of her sensation, and when a fingertip ducked into her very center she arched her back, her knee coming up again as if on its own, her leg falling open to the side to give him all the access he could wish.

Slick with her moisture, his fingers came back up to her nub, stroking her with a silken touch. She wanted him to go faster, harder, and yet she could not bear him to stop this slow, gentle stroking, her hips straining to rise each time he touched her in just the right place.

She twisted her head to the side, closing her eyes against the lantern light, her fists clenched on the ground up beside her face. Tom slid his finger inside her, slowly, pressing deep until she could feel the knuckles of his other fingers nudging up against her. From somewhere within came a faint, nameless pleasure. She could feel the shifting of his hand outside her body, but did not know what he was doing deep within her that made the whole cradle of her sex tingle and shiver.

"Tom!" Matt called out. "Tom! Are you back there?"

Tom froze with his mouth above her breast, his hand stilling between her thighs.

"Tom!" The voice was coming closer.

Low curses flowed from Tom's mouth, curses she heartily seconded as he withdrew his hand and pulled down her skirts. He pulled her up off the ground, and she was still finding her balance when he flung her shawl around her shoulders. She felt the chill of the wet spot over her breast, and arranged the shawl to cover it, holding it tightly closed over her chest.

"We're right here," Tom called back, and a moment later Matt and Hilde appeared around the side of the church. "I've just finished showing Konstanze her hiding place. She's none too fond of it."

"Spiders," Konstanze said weakly, glad for the darkness that hid what she was certain was a flaming blush of guilt across her cheeks. Her sex felt swollen, throbbing with echoes of her heartbeats, and she could feel the trickling wetness of her arousal seeping onto her thighs. Was that the "milky effusion" of which the book spoke?

She hoped Tom forgot her offer to return the book tonight. There was so much more she needed to read.

*Hell, forget the reading.* There was so much more she needed to *do*.

# Chapter Seventeen

"Puss, puss," Konstanze whispered into the shadows. Where had the cat gone off to? "Puss, puss. Here, kitty."

There was a sudden crashing of wooden boxes behind her, then stillness. She huddled where she was, no longer so eager for the big tabby's company. Tom had promised to do something about whatever vermin might be lurking under the church, and the overgrown half-wild cat was his solution. Konstanze hoped it decided to eat whatever it had caught well out of her sight.

She'd been under the church for an hour now, staring at the boxes and kegs in the low light of a lantern. There had been footsteps overhead, but she guessed they were those of Matt and his deacon, putting all in order for the Sunday morning service. It was chilly under the church, and she wrapped her blanket more closely around her shoulders.

Since coming to Penperro, it seemed she had been spending an inordinate amount of time in dark, damp, rocky places, and almost always the reason she was there was Tom Trewella. Maybe hell itself was more like a damp cave than a fiery furnace. Her wicked thoughts and actions were linked to Tom, who was linked to dark rocky locales. Perhaps it was God's way of warning her.

Not that she was listening.

The entire way home the other night her swollen sex had been further aroused by her walking, her folds rubbing against themselves and the tops of her plump thighs with each step. Tom had walked beside her, but she could not bring herself to look at him for fear that he'd somehow see her state reflected in her eyes, and throw her into the ferns to resume where he'd left off.

And she probably would have let him, if Hilde hadn't been four paces behind.

She'd begun to worry that his fondling of her had led to a permanent change in her anatomy. The swelling had remained as she readied for bed, waiting impatiently for Hilde to settle in for the night. When she knew she had as much privacy as she could get, she'd reached for the *Memoirs*. Tom had apparently been too distracted by his own thoughts to ask for it back, for which she was grateful.

She'd read until her eyes stung, studying each passage where the heroine furthered her education, right up to the first time a man made his full penetration of her. Her ears straining to be certain Hilde still snored in the next room, Konstanze had let her own hand slip down beneath the covers, pressing against herself through her nightgown as she read and reread the critical passage.

Hilde had stirred and shifted then, and in fear of discovery Konstanze had shut the book and blown out her candle, sinking down under her covers with her mind full of wild and wicked imaginings.

She had eventually fallen asleep, her mind more on pleasure than on the rightness or wrongness of what she had let Tom do—and what further things she wished he might try. She had woken to a vanishing dream of being pierced by his manhood, pinned to the bed with the force of it, her body contracting in the mysterious release it had craved all the night. She was just conscious enough to realize that her body had reacted as if the dream were real, and she felt the final weak contraction of her sex around a member that was not there.

Now, sitting under a church with spiders and a rat-eating cat, she had plenty of time to sit and contemplate, and to repent. Or, if not to repent, at least to try to regain a grip on her common sense. She again ran through the reasons she should not be letting Tom within two feet of her person, but her heart and her body kept finding excuses that suited her desires.

She had already broken the spirit of her wedding vows; she'd broken them even as she made them, for she had made no attempt to love Bugg. What was one more sin stacked upon the rest? She was wicked, and she wasn't particularly sorry about it. She wasn't certain, though, that she could stand the names she would call herself if she did go to bed with Tom Trewella, for bed was certainly where things were headed. She had no illusions about that.

And what did she think of Tom, that he would engage in such a dalliance with a married woman?

She wanted to be able to say that he was dishonorable and that on those grounds alone she should restrain herself. She wanted to say that he was obviously a lust-crazed beast, with no care for anything but satisfying those animal drives of which Mama had warned her. She would be a hypocrite to say so, though; and besides, she did not believe it was half so true of him as it was of herself. At least to Tom her husband was nothing but a name, someone from her past and only tangentially a part of her future. She was the one who knew that an old man—however foul and bad-tempered—had given her a home for two years and had tried to be her husband.

She was going to have to decide which path to take: chaste married woman or wanton adulteress.

She listened to the sounds of footsteps overhead, and the murmur of voices. The noises settled down, and she assumed the morning prayer was about to begin.

" 'O send out thy light and thy truth, that they may lead me, and bring me unto thy holy hill, and to thy dwelling,' " the Reverend Mr. Jobson said, his voice loud and clear. It was, she thought, an appropriate choice of scripture for today. It almost sounded as if he were calling to the mermaid. She shrugged off her blanket and rose, walking with bent knees and hunched back to the small door. There was a bucket there full of seawater, and she paused to put the final touches to her appearance. She was wearing the same green dress, black spencer, and veiled hat that Foweather had seen her in before.

"The Lord be with you," the vicar said above. It was her cue to move. The Lord's Prayer would be coming next, and while everyone knelt in prayer, heads bowed, she would make her entrance.

She blew out the lantern and opened the door to the morning light. The tabby streaked past her, something dark and furry in its jaws.

Her attention was focusing on the part she was about to play, her heart beating rapidly in her breast. It was a touch of stage fright, but even as it made her stomach light with butterflies it also made her feel vibrantly alive.

She came out from under the church and made her way around to the front, one last thought surfacing on her choice of paths to the future: returning to Bugg was not one of them.

Head bowed, Tom opened his eyes and cast a surreptitious glance at Foweather kneeling beside him. The man had his eyes closed and was red-faced and sweating. His breath came raggedly, his body betraying the faintest of quivers. Nearly everyone in the church was in a similar state.

Matt had worked his usual storytelling wonder, bursting into the Fishing Moon yesterday with his tale of having met the mermaid on the beach, combing her hair and singing in as lovely a voice as any angel could have envied. And she had not swum away! He'd been stunned!

Matt had gone on to recount how he had entreated the mermaid to come to church and seek the grace of God. She had understood English, and after much persuasion on his part agreed to attend the Sunday service.

By now everyone but the Preventive crew knew in their minds that the mermaid was not real, but in their hearts they hoped she was. Even those who had clung more closely to reality were infected by their vicar's excitement, and plied him with ale as they had plied Foweather on many occasions, asking him to repeat the story.

When Foweather himself heard of the encounter he had nearly fainted. Tom hadn't been there to see it himself, but by all accounts the man had gone white as a fish's belly, and about as clammy.

There were so many men and women filling the church that it would be unlikely Foweather or his crew would notice that certain men were missing—men who were, at this very moment, waiting with wagons to receive the cargo of two boats that would be landing in Trennant Cove. It was the best landing place along the coast, second only to the harbor itself. If they were going to be brazen, Tom reckoned, they might as well be brazen as all hell. They would have gone for Penperro's harbor itself if the tides had been right.

Under the combined voices of the parishioners reciting the Lord's Prayer it was impossible to hear whether or not Konstanze had entered. He pricked his ears, straining to detect the sound of the door either opening or closing, but could tell nothing.

At the end of the prayer all stood, and as eyes came open an indrawn breath moved across the crowd in a wave, starting off to the right. One by one all heads turned to the alcove of the mermaid bench, and there stood Konstanze, veiled and motionless.

Whispers rustled through the congregation. "Her gown is damp. The hem, look at the hem!"

"There's a trail of water!"

"And seaweed by the door!"

"I swear I saw a fin where her foot should have been."

Foweather grabbed Tom's wrist, clenching it tight. "It is she. She has come!"

Matt loudly cleared his throat, continuing with the service. When it was time to sit Konstanze did so on the bench, to another collective breath of amazement. It was several minutes before even a few heads turned their attention from Konstanze back to the vicar.

"What should I do?" Foweather whispered frantically.

"Sit still. Don't look at her," Tom whispered back, speaking from the side of his mouth as he kept his face turned rigidly forward.

Foweather immediately turned to stare again at Konstanze, and Tom gripped the man's knee. "Control yourself! Do not let her know that you want her!"

"I cannot believe this," Foweather said under his breath.

Tom flicked him a wary glance, but Foweather's face was suffused with awe, not suspicion. Tom tried to pay some modicum of attention to the service, failing miserably. Although he did not look at her, all his senses felt focused upon Konstanze, and upon the reactions of those in the church. He and Foweather were seated in the center of a pew toward the front, the people on either side of them there to serve as obstacles should Foweather make a sudden dash for the "mermaid."

Matt began the administration of holy communion, and Tom allowed himself a silent groan. The high church mass always took so damn long. He could go through the required responses by rote, but with his attention elsewhere he found himself lagging behind the congregation by half a syllable.

And then it was time to sing the first hymn. Matt had chosen Psalm Twenty-nine, what should have been an evening prayer. He had apparently been unable to resist its mentions of the Lord ruling the sea, and the comparison in a later verse to young unicorns. Unicorns weren't mermaids, but fantastical creatures were the order of the day.

The organist gave the opening note, and the congregation and choir opened voice to sing. With the first sung notes, a purer, higher tone sang out from the mermaid's alcove. Konstanze was singing an octave above even the highest of females present. Voices faltered and died as the parishioners tried to hear the mermaid singing.

Tom saw Matt direct the choir to keep going, and with renewed energy they continued the hymn, the congregation halfheartedly following, no one wanting to risk drowning out the mermaid.

They needn't have worried. Not only could she sing

like a creature from another world—which was what she sounded like, her voice floating so strangely high above what the hymn called for—but she could project that voice with a strength that set his skull to vibrating. It was such a strikingly eerie and beautiful sound she made that it was two more verses before he realized that she was not singing the words of the psalm, but rather only the vowel sounds of those words.

She was clever; he had to give her that. His only instruction to her had been to try to imitate a mermaid on her first visit to church. She had found the perfect way to sound like a soulless creature, vainly pretending to be human. Although the mermaid could understand English, apparently she was not so skilled that she could read the words in the hymnal.

Matt launched into his sermon shortly afterward, and Tom and the others settled down to endure. Most knew that it would be a long sermon today: a very, very long sermon. The longer the better, as far as the smugglers in Trennant Cove were concerned.

Trapped in the church with nothing to do but sit and wait, with no distraction save Matt's sermon and Foweather's nervous shivering, Tom found his mind sneaking off to realms he had been trying to avoid: namely, the realms of Konstanze. Not Konstanze the mermaid sitting so prim and straight-backed in the alcove, but Konstanze on the ground behind the church, her thighs open to his searching hand, her breath catching with desire as he stroked her. *That* was the Konstanze he didn't want to think about.

It was as if she had become his own personal siren,

luring him to his doom. What had he been thinking, to go so far with her?

He hadn't been thinking. That was the problem. He had been left alone with her for five minutes, and all she had to do was lean close enough for him to catch her scent and he lost all control.

Had she known that would happen? Did she want him to ravish her? He couldn't be certain of anything with her anymore. He never would have guessed she would swim with her breasts uncovered, and never would have suspected that she so avidly read that licentious novel—even if she did claim to have difficulty understanding it.

Which brought him back to further puzzlement. She was married, and yet something about her was awkwardly innocent and naive. When he had slipped his finger inside her he had felt no evidence of a hymen, but then again he had never had personal contact with such a structure, and wouldn't know what it felt like to begin with. The entire situation with her would have been so much easier if she had never consummated her marriage.

What was he thinking? If she were still a virgin, and if her marriage were annulled, then she would be even more the forbidden fruit than she was now. If she were free and virgin, he could have her only if he married her. He would not want to do that, would he?

Would he?

His attraction to her was not purely physical. He liked talking with her, and despite the qualms it caused him he admired her adventurous spirit. She had a lively sense of humor, a practicality with which he could sympathize, and a quick, curious mind. She had courage and perseverance, too. He didn't know how well he himself would have done if asked to put on a performance like the one she was putting on at this very moment, in front of a crowd of strangers and an overexcited Preventive man.

All in all, she was everything he could have asked for. Her independence might give him worries that she would run off if she tired of him, but other than that he thought he could be very happy with her as a wife. He'd simply have to be certain to keep her happy, as well, so as not to lose her.

But what was the use of thinking of that? Konstanze had said that her first time with her husband had hurt, so surely she couldn't still be virgin, which meant that the entire train of thought was a pointless exercise in could-have-beens. However he felt about her, she could not become Mrs. Trewella.

He was beginning to build a respectable loathing for the unknown Bugg. He would, he thought sourly, be willing to lay money that Bugg was one of those men who had sex in the dark, all but fully clothed, giving no thought to the pleasure of the woman. Likely he had succeeded only in fulfilling his husbandly duties a handful of times with Konstanze, giving her no chance to learn anything of lovemaking.

He grimaced. He didn't like to think of some wrinkled, liver-spotted old goat having his hands on Konstanze, or her having to lie still and frightened while the old bag of bones shoved his way inside her. It made him want to soak her in a tub of soapy water, to wash away the contamination of her husband's touch.

And then . . . and then he would show her what it was supposed to be like between a man and a woman. He drifted off into an exceedingly pleasant daydream about exactly how he would do that. Matt's interminable sermon and Foweather's stink of nervous sweat faded considerably into the background.

Good Lord, would this service never end? Konstanze suppressed the urge to roll her shoulders and shake out the stiffness in her limbs. If it hadn't been for the standing and kneeling periodically required, not to mention the hymns, she likely would have fallen asleep in her alcove, ogling crowd of Penperro folk or no.

She was looking forward to this all being finished. Her skirt was still a little damp from the dousing she had given it, and her feet were cold. She was wearing an old pair of stockings to which Hilde had sewn a small set of fins, fanning out to the sides of her feet so as not to interfere overmuch with her walking. Her fins and stockings had been doused with seawater as well, making for that nice little trail she had left on the black-and-yellow tile floor.

*Hurry up, hurry up, hurry up,* she silently urged. She was about half-starved, on top of the rest. It was a pity she hadn't been able to accept communion. At least it might have taken the edge off her hunger.

*Wicked girl,* she chided herself. Oh, she was terrible. Cornwall was having the most deleterious effect upon her morals.

She tried to cheer herself with a thought of how much money she'd be making from this appearance. It should be enough to keep Hilde in sausages all through the winter. And money aside, she was glad that she had been able to attend the service. Although they stared at her, she liked to think that the folk of Penperro recognized her as a fellow conspirator, someone who was helping their cause. Although she could not talk to anyone, at least she had the pleasure of seeing new faces.

This was the first chance she'd had to get much of a look at Foweather, as well. It had been only glimpses from a distance she had had before. He wasn't a bad-looking man, but he lacked a sense of presence. In a crowd one's eyes would skim over him, drawn instead to someone like Tom, who fairly vibrated with energy and a working mind.

She squinted through her veil at him. She could see only a small portion of his face, but even from that wedge of expression he appeared to be about as numb as she was.

The vicar began reciting the *Gloria in excelsis*, the congregation all rising to their feet. *Thank God, the end is near! Hurrah!*

At the end of the *Gloria in excelsis* everyone knelt once again for the final blessing. It was her cue to leave.

Toes pointed outward because of her small fins, she held her skirt and stepped silently in her stockinged feet down the side aisle and headed toward the back.

"Do not leave!" came a shout from near the front of the church.

She turned her head and gaped at Foweather, standing up when he should have been kneeling along with the rest.

"My darling! Do not go!" he cried, and then he climbed up onto his pew and ran along the seat toward the center aisle, bypassing the other parishioners who were just now reacting to his outburst. She saw Tom lunge for Foweather and grab his coat, and then the cloth slipped through his fingers as Foweather leaped off the end of the pew.

Konstanze cursed in the frantic silence of her mind and ran for the door, her fins flopping on the tiles as she made her mad duck-waddle dash, in a race now with the demented Preventive sitter. Men and women murmured and shouted, rising, turning to watch, but no one thinking to try to stop Foweather.

She was almost there, the door was within reach—and then Foweather scooped her up into his arms.

"Marry me, my darling! Marry me! We'll call the banns this very morning," he said, and with clumsy jerks pulled the hat from her head, the hat pins yanking out her loose chignon. Her mahogany hair spilled down over his arm.

Over Foweather's shoulder she saw Tom stumbling free of his pew, then coming down the aisle toward them. Foweather pursed his lips and half closed his eyes, lowering his fleshy lips down toward her.

She did the only thing she could think of: she let out a shriek of a power and pitch to shatter crystal.

Foweather's eyes popped open, and Tom reached them, grabbing Foweather's shoulder. Foweather half turned, and stepped on the long frond of seaweed Konstanze had left by the door. She felt his foot slide as he lost his balance, and her shriek rose an octave as they went down together.

Foweather took the brunt of it, but still her head slammed against the floor. She was scrambling off the man and crawling for the door even before the pain had a chance to make it to her brain. A woman near the back, possessed of more sense than the others, rushed forward and opened the door for her, reaching down to give her a hand up. She gave the woman a nod of thanks as she found her feet and escaped.

Behind her, she heard Foweather shouting against the backdrop of Tom and others, pleading to be allowed to go to his bride. By the time she was halfway down the side of the church the roar of voices was spilling out the windows.

"She's escaping!" she heard shouted from a window. She ran around the far corner of the church and dived into her hiding place, slamming the little door shut behind her and turning the key in the lock.

She put her fingers up to the throbbing spot on the back of her head, feeling the stickiness of blood over the lump that was already beginning to rise. She took her fingers away, tested the tackiness between her fingers, then rinsed them in the bucket of seawater.

Outside, she could hear the shouts of men and women searching for her. Someone came and rattled the little door, making her catch her breath, but it was a halfhearted effort and abandoned when the door did not open.

She stripped off the finned stockings and put on her own shoes, and then found the blanket in the dark and, without even shaking it out to be rid of hiding vermin, wrapped it around her and curled into a ball against the wooden door, listening to the voices outside and trying not to think of the throbbing of her head.

Eventually the voices became fewer and fewer, and she waited with impatience for Tom to come tell her it was all clear.

And waited.

When the soft knocking finally came she jerked upright, having fallen into a doze. She could hardly believe that she had managed to overlook her discomfort enough to sleep. Her nest within her blanket was warm, the dark storage space feeling almost cozy.

"Konstanze?" a male voice said softly through the door. "Are you still in there?"

She frowned, realizing it was the vicar who spoke, not Tom. She turned the key, then squinted against the glaring square of daylight as the door came open. "Vicar? Where's Tom?"

"He went with Foweather. The man was overexcited, and didn't want Tom to leave him."

Konstanze felt her heart sink in disappointment.

"Tom had to ask one of the Preventive men to fetch the doctor," the vicar was saying. "I think they're going to have to give the man something to calm his nerves."

And what about her nerves, being swept into Foweather's arms and nearly kissed by him? Didn't Tom care about that? She didn't understand why he had chosen to go with Foweather instead of staying to be with her. After what they had done together behind the church, she had thought they had an unspoken understanding. She had thought he cared about her, at least a bit.

The vicar stretched out his hand and she took it, letting him help her out from under the church. "I hope Mr. Foweather will be all right," Konstanze said. "He may be a fool and a thorn in everyone's side, but I wouldn't like to see any harm come to him."

"That's generous of you," the vicar said, then started to chuckle.

"What's so funny?" Konstanze asked, standing up.

"I was imagining the look on his face when you let out that shriek."

"It was probably much the same as mine when I felt him slip," she said, hoping that at least the vicar would ask about her head.

Instead he laughed again, then led her back into the church. "I have the change of clothes for you," he said, bringing out a folded pile of clothing.

Konstanze shook out the skirt, of a dull gray-and-blue stripe. The bodice was of the same material, and there was a stained once-white apron to go with it, as well as a cotton cap and kerchief and an old pair of shoes. The plan was that she could wear this back to the cottage, so she could pass as a local girl should anyone see her. The green dress and black spencer were far too recognizable now as the clothing of the "mermaid."

"What happened to my hat?" Konstanze asked, remembering how it had been pulled from her head.

The vicar held up his finger, asking her to wait a moment, then went and rummaged behind the pulpit. "Here you are. Mrs. Popple—she's the woman who opened the door for you—saw it lying on the floor and thought it would be best if the 'mermaid' left no physical evidence of her presence. Other than seaweed, that is. And speaking of which, I suppose I'd better clean that up. You can change over behind the organ. I promise not to look," he said, and gave her a naughty grin.

Konstanze changed her clothes, realizing belatedly that she should have brought a pair of stays. She shrugged one shoulder and dressed anyway, trying to ignore the nagging little pain in her heart that complained of Tom's absence. What did it say to her that Foweather was more important to him than she was?

She was a tool for his schemes, and nothing more. She had mistaken physical affection for something more personal, and she was a fool to have done so after everything her mother had taught her. She hadn't even realized that along with her fantasies of Tom making love to her, she was fantasizing as well that he cared for her. It hurt to realize that his work—if she could call it that—ranked far higher in his mind than she herself.

Foweather was being coddled, attended by Tom and a doctor and a crew of men. She had blood matted in her hair and the company of a lecherous vicar engrossed in cleaning the floor.

Was she was reading too much meaning into Tom's absence? Perhaps. Her heart felt her perception to be true, though, no matter what cold rationality might say. It seemed she had been reading too much meaning into his actions all along.

She bit her lip and felt the sting of tears in her eyes.

It was all the worse to realize he might think nothing
of her just when she herself was realizing she thought
everything of him.

Fool that she was, she was falling in love with the
man.

She was upstairs when, through the open window, she
heard Tom's jaunty whistling as he approached the
cottage. It was past nine o'clock in the evening, and
she had given up all hope of his coming to see her.
Instead of being happy he had at last abandoned Foweather for her, with each note of his whistling she felt
as if a higher flame was heating the cauldron of resentment that was her heart. She'd like to slap that
cheerful tune right out of his head. He plainly hadn't
spared a moment's concern for her all day.

She let Hilde open the door, the petulant part of her
wanting to remain upstairs and send down word that
she was indisposed and did not wish to see him. Hilde
was scolding him in German for endangering her mistress, but he apparently was ignoring her. She traced
his progress across the sitting room, his steps loud in
the small house.

"Konstanze!" he called up her stairs. "I know you're
up there. Come down, will you? Or do you want me
to come up?"

She rolled her eyes and let out a pent-up breath. As
if she'd want him up here! Her general annoyance with
him was enough to override the petulance. She'd like
to be rude to him to his face. She tramped across the
warped floor and down the stairs, finding him waiting
with a silly grin on his face not a foot from the bottom

step, his head hunched to avoid the low ceiling.

"The boats made it safely to shore, and the cargoes were carted off without a hitch. The plan worked beautifully!"

She gave a closemouthed, sarcastic smile, but he didn't seem to notice her lack of enthusiasm.

"Foweather had to be given a dose of laudanum so he could rest. I almost felt sorry for the poor bugger. He should be all right, though—for all that he puts on a dramatic demonstration of his affections, I think he likes the fantasy of wedding a mermaid much more than the possible reality. He knew no one in that church would let him go off with you."

"*I* didn't know he might not make the effort," Konstanze said crisply, still standing on the bottom step.

Tom grinned. "He certainly took me by surprise, running over the back of the pew like he did. I suspect he was startled himself to have caught you."

"Not half so startled as I." Was he not going to notice that she was angry?

"You did a marvelous job, Konstanze. The strange singing, that fabulous screech you gave when he tried to kiss you—and the little fins on your feet! It was a brilliant touch." He stepped toward her and grasped her lightly by the upper arms. "If it weren't for you, this never would have worked. Even the idea of a daylight landing was yours."

She stared into his shining eyes, the praise she had once tried to pry out of him falling flat now, his appreciation meaningless because in his bright eyes she saw that he knew nothing of what was in her heart. It had not occured to him that she could be anything but as delighted as he.

"I don't want to be the mermaid any longer," she said, the words surprising her even as she said them.

He blinked. "What?"

She shook off his arms and stepped away from him, going to the small table and fiddling with the lid of the small sewing basket sitting there. She lifted her gaze back to him. "I don't want to be the mermaid."

"For God's sake, why not?"

Her thoughts were a muddle, her motivations unclear even to herself. All she knew was that she wanted to push him away. She wanted to reject him. To hurt him. To make him feel the same way she felt, and then perhaps he would see that he had hurt her. Then, perhaps, he would reach for her and seek to make amends. She knew all this only dimly, and there was too great a distance between her confused heart and her capability for verbal expression for her to be able to explain it. She could only act on it.

"I don't want that Foweather man coming after me again. I don't like being chased, or waiting in dark, cold places. I'm tired of living out here alone with Hilde, unable to go into town or talk to anyone but you. I might as well be back with Bugg, for all the freedom I have."

He looked stunned. "I thought you were enjoying the scheme."

She shrugged.

"When did you change your mind?"

"This afternoon. You know I hit my head when Foweather fell, don't you? My hair was full of blood."

The light could have been deceiving her, but she thought he paled at that piece of news. "No, I didn't know. Why didn't you say something? Why didn't you tell Matt? He would have fetched the doctor."

She hadn't wanted the vicar, or the doctor. She'd wanted Tom. "Hilde tended to it."

"How bad is it? Are you all right?" he asked, coming closer to her, his eyes roving over her hair, which was loosely arranged.

She softened a little at his obvious concern, and began to feel a bit childish for having hidden the injury and expecting him to guess at it. She lightly touched the back of her head. "It's here, under my hair. It's only a small split. I've got a lump the size of a duck egg, though."

"I should have kept a better eye on him. He was never meant to get so close to you. I won't let him harm you, Konstanze." Standing close, he lightly brushed her cheek with his fingertips.

There was caring in his amber eyes, and concern. Was it real? And was there anything there that went beyond the regard one would offer a friend? Perhaps he was giving her the attention he thought she required if she were going to be persuaded to continue her role as the mermaid.

She turned away, sighing internally and walking around the table to sit on the settle. She could not trust her perceptions where Tom was concerned. She wanted so badly to believe that he might care for her that she could read a thousand tendernesses into the most innocent of gestures. She did not want to encourage her hopes, yet neither could she douse them.

To do so would be even more painful than this torture of ambiguity.

"That is what this is about, isn't it?" he asked, coming around the settle and sitting next to her, a space of only a few inches separating them. "Foweather frightened you, and so you want to quit."

"It's more than that. It's as I said: I want to be with people. I'm tired of being alone."

"I can't say I'd want to spend a whole summer out here with Hilde, either."

She frowned at him.

"A poor joke," he admitted. "Could you not bear it until the end of the summer? It's not so very far away. Another six weeks, perhaps. Matt could come visit, so mine would not be the only face you saw. Come to think of it, there's really no reason why some of the women couldn't be encouraged to come calling."

"It's not the same as going into town." Now that she had started on this tack, she was finding that there was more truth to it than she had recognized. She was tired of being stuck out here. She did want to see new places and things, and not people who were sent to see her as if on a charity mission. "Even going to the market would be welcome."

"Foweather saw your face. If you came to town he might recognize you. Even one as lacking in wits as he might come to the conclusion that he had been duped when he saw the object of his obsession shopping for cabbages."

"It wouldn't be a concern if I was no longer the mermaid."

"No, it wouldn't. You did give your word, though.

You agreed to help us through the summer." He picked up her hand, holding it clasped between his as he gazed into her eyes. "I don't ask this just for myself. Your help has made a difference in the lives of dozens of people, many of whom were at Talland Church today."

She supposed that that should have meant more to her than it did. The folk of Penperro were largely faceless to her, an abstract concept in comparison to the man sitting beside her and holding her hand. If only he would say that he himself wanted her to do it, that it mattered to him—and not just because he cared about his income.

What she wanted him to say was that he wished her to continue because it gave him a reason to spend time with her.

He wasn't going to say that. She met his gaze and knew that he was unaware of the thoughts deep in her mind. The only way he would understand was if she told him she was falling in love with him, and there was no reason to do so, unless she were in the mood for humiliation. That left her with the choice of continuing as the mermaid to please him, or quitting to spite and wound the man—although he might never understand that that was her motive, which made the gesture meaningless.

Or she could please herself. She pulled her hand away from his, clasping it in her lap and looking down, considering. If she quit, she would see little of Tom thereafter. That wasn't what she wanted. Stupid as it had been to allow herself to fall for such a scoundrel with warped morals, she had done so. Stupid as it was to hope that he might grow to care for her, she did hope. She would rather suffer the pangs of unrequited love in his presence than in his absence.

But she still wanted to go to town.

She faced him again. "Couldn't I at least take a trip to a neighboring village?" she asked. "Foweather would not see me there. I could go on a market day, and wear those old clothes I wore back from the church today. No one would remark upon me."

"It's a long walk to the nearest town. You want to go so badly?"

She nodded.

Suddenly his expression brightened. "How about attending a fair instead?"

"Truly?"

He sat back, looking pleased with himself. "I don't know why it didn't occur to me sooner. Penperro's midsummer fair begins at the end of the week. People from half a dozen towns come for it—the streets are packed with people. I doubt that I myself would be able to pick you out in such a crowd. If you kept an eye out for Foweather I can't think that you'd have any trouble. Everyone will assume you are a visitor."

"I can do a wonderful Cornish accent," she said, speaking in one.

He blinked at her.

"I did spend my childhood here, after all," she said in the same accent. "The teachers at my boarding school trained me to speak otherwise, but I still remember. Will you be ashamed to be seen in the company of such an ignorant girl?" she asked playfully.

He was still looking at her strangely, but then his

eyebrows rose as he took in what she said. "Be seen with you? I can't be seen with you. You'll have to spend your time on your own, I'm afraid. Even Hilde's company would give you away as a local."

Her rising mood fell back to earth. "Oh. You're right, of course." She tried to smile.

"It's settled, then? You're happy? You'll continue playing the mermaid?"

What else could she say? "Yes, I'm happy."

# *Chapter Eighteen*

*Penperro*

Bugg II didn't know how much more of Cornwall he could take, which was a bit of a problem, as he had been in the blasted county for only two weeks. Two very long weeks. The place showed only the scarcest signs of civilization, and the people seemed as miserably hard and small as the stones that made up their fences.

He had been in constant fear for his life upon the roads, despite the pistol he carried. In the inns along his way the locals had sounded almost proud of their surfeit of highway robbers, bragging that one could not go a mile without being set upon. Bugg II counted himself lucky that so far he had gone unharmed, but he met every traveler with a wary eye, and fearing an ambush he galloped through any place in the road where the bushes came close or the trees were dense.

Why couldn't Konstanze have chosen Somerset or Dorset as her hiding place?

Hilde's overbearing German presence was what people recalled, and after a few exhausting and expensive days of questioning and bribing the landlords at inns in Exeter he had managed to find where Konstanze and Hilde had stayed. The landlord had helped the two to arrange for transportation through Devon and into Cornwall. Bugg II had worried that Konstanze might go south to Plymouth, and there take ship to some foreign land, but the landlord had assured him that she had been concerned only with finding her way into that most dismal and rough of counties, Cornwall.

Once in Cornwall the trail had seemed to go cold. Innkeepers along the one main highway were less than forthcoming with information, and for several days he could find no trace of Konstanze or Hilde. Then, finally, somewhere in the middle of Bodmin Moor he had found an innkeeper who recalled two women traveling together, and had said they were on their way to Penperro. The man had recalled nothing more about them, and considering the innkeeper's rude behavior toward him and the amount of money he had had to offer for that one tidbit, Bugg II had doubts that the man had been telling the truth. Still, he could not risk ignoring the information.

He left his horse at the small, overcrowded livery stables near a smithy and joined the flow of country folk down the lane and into the town proper. Apparently there was some manner of fair going on today.

How unspeakably amusing. He would get to see how the illiterate enjoyed themselves.

"Boo! Kill 'em! Boo!" Konstanze cried out along with the rest of the crowd, then took another bite of her jam pasty. She was sitting on a stone wall, thigh to thigh with women she did not know, watching a tragicomic play being performed on a raised wooden platform in the street, the painted cloth at the back the only set decoration. The players leaped and grimaced, fell, swooned, and sighed with enthusiastic melodrama.

She loved it. She was having a marvelous time. Despite her original disappointment at having to come to the fair alone, she was finding that it was exactly what she needed. She dallied where she wished, bought ribbons and cheap jewelry she did not need, ate sweets until she was sick, and eavesdropped on the conversations of women who lingered at the stalls or sat waiting for an entertainment to begin.

It was a day of greater freedom than she could ever remember. She was anonymous and yet part of the fair, fitting in as well as any of the other visitors. She had no chaperone and did not need one. There were plenty of men in the streets, but in such a crowd they were restrained from any improper advances toward women, and instead spent their energies in wrestling matches or rowing races down in the harbor, or drinking beer and engaging in garrulous conversations.

The play ended with the villain dead and the hero and heroine happily together, and Konstanze cheered with the rest of the audience, then hopped down off the wall and wandered down the street, pausing to consider the penny-peep show with its reenactment of grisly murders, then moving on.

The first thing she had done when she reached Penperro was to seek out Tom's house. Hilde had described it for her, and after a short search she had found the blue-trimmed house with the profusion of yellow and orange nasturtiums in the boxes out front. She had gone so far as to climb the stone steps to the slate-sided house, and had stood there staring, wanting to go up to the windows and peer in, hands around her face to break the glare. It had been hard to resist the temptation.

She thought of wandering back to the house now. Was he home? She guessed that he would likely be out here in the thick of things, having found some way to use even something as innocent as a fair to his advantage.

A young man with a lute was singing a ballad of lost love, to the dewy-eyed pleasure of several young women. Konstanze stopped to listen, but the boy's voice lacked range or expression, and she moved on. It was one of the drawbacks of being a singer herself that she was often too aware of the flaws in others' singing to enjoy it.

She wandered down toward the harbor, the smell of rotten fish growing stronger with each step, and the crowd denser. She made out the sign of the Fishing Moon, and saw that there were tables set out front, men gathered around them with their tankards of beer, ale, or cider. One man staggered off around the corner of the inn and relieved himself into the shallow river.

Unpleasant a sight as it was, she envied him the convenience. She had had to use one of the revolting temporary privies the town leaders had erected.

She wended her way through the people to the harbor's edge and looked down at the pile of wood and tar barrels that was being built upon the small beach. At dusk it would be lit for a blazing bonfire. Tom had suggested that she should leave at that time, as the night—and the accumulated effects of beer and cider—would bring out a wildness in the local men that it was best not to observe unescorted. She would take his advice, but wanted to stay at least to see the fire lit.

A roar of approval came from one of the tables of men, and she turned to look. They were drinking a toast of some sort, and as one of the men stepped to the side she saw that Foweather was in the center of the group. She quickly turned away, and with her heart thumping in her chest she eased through the crowd and back up the street, losing herself amidst a sea of white-capped women.

A big-bellied man stepped backward into Bugg II, jostling him and causing him to spill half his drink over his hand and his waistcoat. He cursed and moved the drink to his other hand, shaking off the wet one and glaring at the broad back of the offensive man. If the back had been less broad and the arms less brawny, he would have given the oaf the dressing-down he deserved.

As it was, he simply tried to preserve what remained of his pint as he squeezed through the men clogging up the Fishing Moon. The bright square of the open doorway looked liked heaven's gate, despite the stench of fish that awaited him outdoors. At least there was the hint of a breeze out there to carry away the smoke, body odor, and the sickening hints of rancid grease.

He was winding his way through the occupied tables when by a stroke of good fortune a man stood up and left his chair. Bugg II lunged and snagged the seat, beating out a nearer man by the slimmest of margins. The thwarted man gave him a glare, but Bugg II gripped his seat with his free hand, daring the local to try to dislodge him. The man made a rude gesture and spoke to his friends, the bunch of them giving Bugg II a stare and then laughing. Bugg II turned away and sipped at his drink, hoping his face did not look as red as it felt. They were ignorant yahoos, and it didn't matter what they thought of him.

Engrossed as he was in telling himself how much better he was than the uneducated peasants around him, it wasn't until he heard the phrase "she sings like an angel" that he looked up from his glass and started to pay attention to the conversation going on at the nearest table.

"She has glorious hair, dark brown touched with red, and gray eyes like the sea on a stormy day," a man was saying. "You've never seen a face so innocent or so pure."

Bugg II's eyes widened as he listened.

"And in place of her feet are the daintiest fins you ever could imagine. The poor thing, it must have pained her terribly to walk with them upon the dry land."

312

Bugg II's wide-eyed hope turned to consternation. *Fins?*

"She must have wanted to come to church very badly," another man said.

"She's besotted," a different one explained to the group, then nodded toward the first man. "With him. Can you believe it?" he asked good-naturedly.

"So what happened after the mermaid hobbled from the church?" someone asked.

*Mermaid?*

The first man answered. "We chased after her, but she was gone, back into the sea, leaving behind only a bit of weed and a puddle of salt water. She'll be back, though. I feel it here," he said, knocking his fisted hand against his chest. "She and I were meant to be together."

Bugg II was not certain whether or not mermaids existed, but he did know that mahogany-haired, gray-eyed singers were in short supply. Konstanze likely had nothing to do with this little fable—it was too preposterous—but there was enough here to pique his interest. It wouldn't hurt to learn a little more.

He pulled his chair closer and prepared to make a new friend.

The dusk was deepening the sky above to a rich blue-black as Konstanze found a place to stand along the harbor wall to watch the final preparations on the beach below. A row of young children sat in front of her, while older boys ran around the unlit bonfire, throwing mud at each other and shouting. More people came down to the waterfront, mostly men going down

# Lisa Cach

to the beach while the majority of women stayed up on the stones of the street and walls and bridge, safe from the impending merriment. Konstanze turned and looked at the houses and buildings lining the harbor, several windows crowded with faces.

She had caught sight of Tom several times during the afternoon, always surrounded by people, laughing and talking. As if pulled by some sixth sense, her eyes found him again now, amidst the men gathering around the tower of wood.

The vicar's white head appeared, and beside it Hilde's sandy blond one. Hilde moved to the side as the vicar spoke to a group of men, apparently ordering them into place. A moment later he raised his arms, and then brought them down, and the men began to sing.

The song started out low at first, then grew in volume and intensity. The noisy crowd, still growing, began to quiet as they listened to the sea chantey about a crew that by the grace of God returned to their port after a fierce storm. By the time the choir was into the fourth verse the crowd had begun to sing along, the song plainly a favorite. The voices echoed off the harbor walls and the stone buildings, the harbor making a natural amphitheater for the mass performance.

A roaring cheer went up as the song finished. The mayor, dressed in his chain of office, raised his hands for silence. Someone handed him a lit torch, which he held aloft, and the crowd waited with their breath caught in their throats. When the tension reached its height the mayor threw the torch into the pile of wood, and all eyes went to the flame to see if it would catch.

314

Moments passed, and then all of a sudden the fire caught hold of one of the tar-soaked barrels, flames shooting upward. The crowd shouted its approval.

The vicar raised his arms again, and the choir dove into another song. Boys linked hands around the bonfire, running in a mad circle around the growing flames, while brilliant orange sparks flew upward and across the narrow beach toward her. The children in front of her tilted their heads back, watching the dying sparks drift above.

Her eyes went again to Tom, standing back a ways from the growing fire, the orange light touching his features and the white of his shirt. He stood with arms crossed, talking to someone she did not know. It was strange to watch him with other people, and she saw that he was obviously a well-liked and popular man. He had an air of competence and easy confidence that drew people, even as her own eyes were drawn.

As if feeling her gaze he suddenly shifted his attention, looking in her direction. She doubted he could pick her out amidst the faces, with the glare of the fire so close to him, but in her mind she willed him to know she was there. He turned his attention back to his companion, then a moment later started to walk back up the slope of the beach toward the harbor wall.

Something shifted within her heart, a decision made without conscious thought. Konstanze edged her way to the back of the crowd, intent on making it around the harbor in time to catch him.

Sidestepping and weaving, she pressed her way through the people. For one heart-stopping moment she thought she saw Bugg II's face in the crowd, but then bodies shifted and she lost sight of the figure. It was too dark to have seen anyone clearly, and she shrugged off the possibility.

Standing on tiptoe she tried to see over the heads around her, but there were too many people between her and where Tom should have emerged. Instead of continuing, she backtracked and then went a short way up the street that led to his house, finding a quiet place to stand in the shadow of a shop porch. She took breaths free from the heaviest scents of fish and people, the fresh night air cool and welcome.

If he didn't come this way in the next few minutes, she might have to head home. Already she was sensing in the air the impending lawlessness of which Tom had spoken, and she admitted it must have infected her own blood, as otherwise she would not be waiting here for him.

Her day of freedom had been working a strange spell upon her. A lawlessness of her own had been seeping into her blood, silently chewing away the last binding shreds of propriety. Those bands had begun their first weakening many weeks ago, the night she had decided to leave Bugg, and had worn steadily weaker with each day in Cornwall. She was ready now to shed them entirely, releasing herself to follow her heart.

They said that blood would tell. She had never before agreed, as she seemed so different from her colorful parents. She had been well behaved at boarding school, she had been a dutiful daughter while traveling with her mother, and she had been a placid, obedient wife. Yet all the while, it seemed that there had been a different, wilder Konstanze underneath, surviving on the sustenance of music and daydreams.

It was that reckless Konstanze who had fallen in love with Tom Trewella, who had decided somewhere between the jam pasties and the bonfire that she did not want to live a celibate, reclusive life simply because a man she despised could legally call her wife. That Konstanze yearned for Tom, and the feeling she always had when in his company, showed that she was alive. Vibrantly, brilliantly alive. Even when she was upset with him a part of her enjoyed the emotional drama, as it was so much better than feeling nothing.

She knew Tom did not love her—although he lusted for her—and she could bear the knowledge. She would rather feel this passion than not, and would rather take what Tom could give than go entirely without. She knew it was not a wise choice, and she knew that she would have advised another against it, but the choice was her heart's and she would give it what it wished.

She waited, watching unfamiliar faces go by as some of the families with small children chose to leave.

And then he was there, speaking to a man, slapping his shoulder in farewell, and coming up the street alone, his eyes straight ahead. As he came abreast of her she stepped out of the shadow of the shop porch and fell into step beside him. It took him several steps to realize she was not just another farm girl headed home.

"Konstanze!" he said in surprise, glancing around in an apparent attempt to see if they were observed.

No one appeared to be paying attention to them. "What are you doing here? You should have been home by now."

"I wanted to see the bonfire. Then I saw you," she said.

"Do you want me to walk you home?"

"Will you take me to your house, instead?"

He frowned. "Whatever for?"

She shrugged as if she had no specific purpose. If it wasn't plain to him, she wasn't going to humiliate herself by spelling it out. "I saw it from outside. I should like to see where and how you live. You have certainly seen enough of where I spend my days."

"I don't think that satisfying your curiosity is worth the risk."

"What risk? Look around you. No one is paying us the least bit of mind. Even if they saw me go in with you, what would they think?"

"That I'd found myself a willing partner for the night. I don't particularly enjoy being the subject of gossip."

"It might be good for your reputation," she said, giving him a mischievous smile and trying not to feel embarrassed by how long the discussion was going on. You'd think he didn't want her sullying his sacred halls, the way he was hesitating.

"There's nothing of interest to see. You shall be quickly bored."

"If so then I'll leave. Won't you indulge me in this? It does not seem such a great thing to ask." Had any woman ever had such a hard time gaining admittance to a man's house? she wondered. A little more enthusiasm on his part would have been welcome. It didn't seem to have crossed his mind that her intention was to do anything other than snoop.

He sighed and ran his hand through his hair, looking over his shoulder to check again for observers. "All right, then. God only knows why it is that women are so consumed with going through others' houses."

"We're curious, nosy creatures, intent upon discovering secrets."

"How very reassuring."

It was only a few minutes more before he was letting her in the back door to his house. There was a lamp burning low in the center of a large worktable, several cloth-covered bowls and plates around it. Tom went to the table and lifted the edge of one cloth, then sighed.

"I told her not to bother leaving anything out for me," he said. "I gave her the day off, hoping she'd go out and enjoy herself at the fair."

"Your housekeeper?" Konstanze asked.

"Yes, Mrs. Toley."

"She lives here?"

"Actually, in a cottage a few houses away. She inherited it when her husband died. It had been in his family for generations."

"So she won't be back tonight?"

"I shouldn't think so."

*How terribly convenient.* "May I see the rest of the house?"

He lit a candle from the lamp and handed it to her, then held his open palm toward the door. "Be my guest. There's little to see."

That was a matter of opinion. She preceded him through the door and down the hall, then peered into the sitting room. Tom had brought the lamp with him, and he went in ahead of her to give her more light.

"Not very interesting, is it?"

She didn't say anything. The somewhat sparse furnishings were of middling quality, but not without a certain element of style. He might not put much effort into his decorating, but she guessed that was a matter of lack of time and interest rather than of lack of taste.

His office was more revealing, the massive desk, pigeonholes, shelves, and stacks of ledgers and papers speaking of how very involved his business interests were. Sailing ships were firing cannons at one another across a rough sea in a large painting above his desk.

"Do you dream of joining the navy?" she asked, nodding toward it. It looked like typical male art: they seemed to like paintings of battles, be they on land or sea.

He grimaced. "I should think not. I stay as far away from guns as I can manage, whether they be cannons or pistols. The painting was a gift."

"Would you have preferred one of a horse or cow?" Livestock was popular, too, among those of his sex.

"I should prefer something with people in it."

"I don't know why you insisted there was nothing of interest to see here. I am learning all manner of things about you."

He frowned at her.

"May I see upstairs?"

"I'm not certain—" he started to say, but she did not wait for his answer, heading up the stairs with her candle shaking in her hand. She tried not to think about what she was about to attempt. The only voices inside her that cautioned against her plans were those that belonged to other people: her mother, the teachers at the boarding school, Hilde, even Bugg. Her own heart was saying, *Yes, yes. This is what you want. Live your life; don't let it slip away.*

His room was as Hilde had described it, books piled on the floor. The bed itself had no hangings, just a simple tester of muslin atop the carved wooden posts. The coverlet was without wrinkle or flaw, and she suspected that Mrs. Toley had been at work. Tom did not seem the sort to make his own bed in the mornings, when it would only get rumpled again in the night. It was too inefficient a chore.

On the wall there was a painting, this time of a stern-looking man in the dress of a cleric. She looked from it to Tom, raising her eyebrows in question.

"My father. He died shortly after the Eustice debacle."

"I'm sorry."

Tom gave a quick shrug. "So am I. I would have liked him to know I did not remain the complete rotter he thought me at the time."

"Have you other family?"

"Not living, no. The Trewellas were never a particularly prolific line."

As interesting as this was, it wasn't the most conducive of topics to what she had in mind. Neither did she particularly relish the idea of making a seduction attempt while the disapproving Papa Trewella watched on. She set her candle down atop a short stack of books on the bedstand, pleased to see that the painting receded into the shadows.

"Are these all your own books?" she asked, squatting down and picking up a leather-bound volume.

He set his lamp on a dresser and came over to squat down beside her. "For the most part," he said, taking the tome from her hands and reading the spine. *"The India Sapphire.* It's an exciting story, if you want to borrow it," he said, handing the book back to her.

"Perhaps I will," she said, taking it and meeting his eyes. He broke the gaze and started going through the other books.

Konstanze frowned, chewing the inside of her lip. She had led him up here to seduce him—or at least to invite him to seduce her—and things were not going quite the way she had expected. Wasn't the mere sight of a woman in his bedroom supposed to inflame a man's passions? But Tom just searched through his books, as if she were a chum in need of reading material.

*"The Lost Land of Timbuktu.* It's about the legends surrounding the city, and the utter failure of any white man to reach it," Tom said, holding out the book. "Does that suit you?"

"Do you have anything like that other book?" she asked.

*"The India Sapphire?"*

"No, the . . . other book. The *Memoirs.*"

That caught his attention. "Are you serious?" he asked.

"Although it is only a novel, I am finding it quite informative. One always hears warnings against the way of life of the heroine, and yet no one ever offers to explain the details."

His eyebrows drew together, rising up over his nose. "And you want to read more of these . . . er . . . details?"

She shifted from her awkward squatting position onto the floor, her legs tucked up to one side. With one hand on the floor she leaned toward him. "I do."

He met her eyes, looking into them for a long moment, then abruptly stood, looking down at her with an almost angry expression. "What are you up to, Konstanze?"

She got to her own feet, her courage fading and embarrassment burning her cheeks. If he didn't know what she was up to, then it might be better not to continue. Despite what he had done with her in back of the church, and down on the shore, there was a part of her that was not confident of his desires. With an effort she tried to ignore that mewling voice of cowardice.

Instead of backing away, she stepped forward and laid her palm against his chest, and, leaning close, she looked up at him, her face mere inches from his own. She could feel the increase in his heart rate.

He took a hold of her hand as if to lower it, but held it where it was. "I should take you home."

"I don't want to go."

"Konstanze . . ."

"I want to stay here with you."

"You can't. We can't. There's no good to come of it."

"I think there is." She brought her other hand up,

323

# Lisa Cach

smoothing her palm over his waistcoat. She didn't know what manner of touch would please him, so she sought to please herself. She ran her hand under the open front of his coat, then up to his shoulder, his skin warm beneath the layer of fine cloth.

His grip on her other hand loosened, and she tugged it free, reaching up with both hands now to touch lightly over his face, exploring the contours and texture. He closed his eyes as her fingers drifted over his brow, down his nose, and across his lightly stubbled cheeks. She let a fingertip glide along his lips, then back again, fascinated by the smooth feel of them. She wanted to taste them for herself, and slid her hands into the hair behind his ears, holding his face and pulling him down to her.

She brushed her lips lightly over his, once, twice, enjoying the feel of them. She had not known there could be as much pleasure from touching as there was from being touched. Her worries about his reaction dissipated, her delighted senses blocking off all else but the man before her and her own body's reactions.

She kissed him then, gently, letting her lips speak silently of her love and desire. His arms came up around her, one in the small of her back and the other cupping her head. He deepened the kiss, taking her tenderness and turning it into something fiercer. He pulled the white cap from her head, his fingers digging into her bound hair and, unfortunately, her healing wound.

The pain made her jerk, and he loosened his hold on her, pulling his head back.

"Sorry," he whispered, his voice husky. His fingertips probed gently through her hair until they found the place of her injury, then retreated. The interruption seemed to bring a faint stirring of conscience back to him, and he loosened his hold further. "Why are you doing this?" he asked, looking as if he did not want to hear the answer.

"Why did you do the same to me?" she asked, playing with his earlobe, pressing her chest up against his. She wished she were wearing one of her own dresses rather than the stays that made a wall between them.

"I'm trying to remember that you're a married woman."

"On paper only. In my heart I am free. In my heart I know that this is what I want. You better than most should understand that what we know to be right is not always what we know to be lawful."

"I don't know if this is right," he said softly, and leaned his forehead down onto hers. "And I'm very near to not caring whether it is or not. I don't want to be the villain, but I want you, married or no. God help me, I do."

"There is no villainy in this." Konstanze tilted her face, breaking the contact with his forehead as she kissed him lightly, repeatedly, tempting him to take more. There could be nothing wicked here; she had been wrong before to chastise herself for her desires, and for giving way to his touch. She loved him, and that made everything permissible.

"I pray there is not," he said, whatever control he still retained breaking. He scooped her up in his arms and carried her toward the bed. "For if there is, you may count me damned." He set her on her feet beside

325

the bed and kissed her, this time taking charge and holding nothing back, hungrily exploring the side of her neck, the space behind her ear, the place where her neck met her shoulders in a gentle slope. He moved lower and traced his tongue over her collarbone, and then he was easing her bodice down her shoulders, his deft fingers having found the pins that held it closed over her stays.

She let him undress her, the experience widely different from the times that Hilde had performed the same task, her breath coming fast and strange currents of desire melting her muscles. Tom nibbled on her neck as he worked at the tapes fastening her skirt, and then when the material fell to the floor he knelt down, sliding his hands up her stockinged calves to the garters tied tightly below her knees. He pressed his face against the thin layer of linen chemise over her loins, and she swayed at the feel of his warm breath through the fabric.

She balanced with one hand on his shoulder as he made her lift first one foot and then the other and removed her stockings and shoes. His hands stayed under her chemise, rising up her legs as he again stood, his palms running over the backs of her thighs and then cupping her bare buttocks in their warm grip. He pulled her against him, kissing her deeply, his tongue exploring her mouth as his hands gently kneaded. Desire was a warm, wet rush in her loins.

He turned her around so he could unlace her stays, and when he had them loose enough he slid them over her hips, letting them fall to the floor. Her breasts felt heavy without the support, but then his hands came around and cupped them, lifting them against her chest, pulling her body back against his.

"You have no idea how much power you hold over me," he whispered near her ear, his thumbs stroking over the tops of her breasts.

"Nor you of the power you hold over me," she said, her eyes going half closed as he continued his caresses.

His hands moved down over her belly, one remaining there while the other covered her sex. Her legs parted. He lightly pressed his hand against the length of her, stroking up and down in short, gentle movements through the thin material, his middle finger a ridge against her own center of sensation, his fingertips touching against the entrance to her body at the end of each downward stroke. Her head arched back onto his shoulder.

He pulled up her chemise by the fistful, and she raised her arms to let him lift it off her. She turned in his arms, and felt the chemise fall in a gentle breeze behind her, onto the floor. With his arms around her she pressed close to him, enjoying the feel of his clothed body against her naked skin, feeling both vulnerable and liberated.

Her hair was next, his fingers moving with infinite care to find the pins and remove them, letting her hair fall in heavy locks about her. When the pins were all out he used his fingers as a comb, separating the strands and fanning them in a curtain over her shoulders and breasts, her hardened nipples showing through. He lowered his head and flicked his tongue against one, then the other, then took the tip gently between his teeth, his lips dampening her hair.

Just when she felt she was about to lose the strength in her knees, he went around her to pull the covers on the bed down, then swept her up in his arms again, depositing her on the mattress, kissing her until she was sunk deep into the pillows. He stood back then and stripped off his own clothes.

As his shirt came off she drew in a shuddering breath, her eyes taking in the planes of his chest and the movements of his muscles beneath the skin, illuminated by the yellow glow of the candlelight. He was nothing like Bugg, nothing at all. Her eyes were drawn to his nipples, small and flat compared to hers, and set upon broad, gently curved muscles. His chest tapered to a narrow waist and hips, and her eyes fastened to the bulge there as he undid the flaps of his breeches, dropping both them and the linen undergarment.

She felt her eyes go round. "Good Lord!" she cried. "What is *that?*"

He froze as he was bending over, the breeches still around the ankle of one foot. "Your pardon?"

Konstanze pointed to his crotch. "Is there something amiss with it?"

He stood straight, naked now, his penis protruding like the pole of a shop sign. He looked down at it, and it began to deflate, shrinking and sagging. "I don't think so."

"But . . ." she said, her eyes fixed upon it as if upon a snake, "it's so big."

"It is?" The member in question puffed up as if in pride, regaining its former stiff stature. "That's to make it the better to please you with, my dear," he said, and when she looked up at his face, he was grinning.

She pulled the sheet up, gripping it tightly. "It's not what I expected. It's like something out of that book, an 'enormous machine.'"

"Tell me more. You are delighting my vanity."

"I shouldn't see why," she said. "If Bugg's little thing caused me such discomfort, I cannot imagine what will happen with this." She was having second and third thoughts, her desire of moments ago fleeing under this mammoth threat to her person.

He came to the bed, and she moved over as he lifted the sheet and lay down beside her, propping himself up on an elbow, reaching out with his other hand to lightly stroke her cheek, his hand trailing down her neck, nudging aside her gripped hands and the sheet so that he could continue down her torso. "You'll be pleased with it in the end, I promise you. Would you like to touch it?"

She hesitated, but the truth was she would very much like to touch it and become acquainted. Perhaps it might not be so frightening if she did so. The thing might as well have been the appendage of a different animal entirely, compared to what had hung between Bugg's legs.

She pushed down the sheet and then, feeling like Sleeping Beauty reaching for the deadly spindle, touched the beast upon its head. It bobbed in response. Intrigued by the texture beneath her fingertips, she wrapped her hand around the shaft and slid her palm toward his body. He groaned, and she released him, jerking back. "What did I do?"

329

"Nothing wrong. I . . . liked it, was all."

"Did you?"

He gazed at her with desire, and she felt a little of her confidence return. It might not look as she had expected, but he seemed to think there was nothing amiss with his machine. She would trust that he was right. She scooted down in the bed, lying curled on her side facing it.

This time when she touched it she did not flinch at the sounds he made. She brushed the back of her hand along it, her own heartbeat picking up at the contact. She almost forgot that it was attached to Tom, she became so engrossed in exploring the contours and running her fingertips along ridges, and letting the dampened end nudge her palm like the nose of a friendly dog.

A wicked bit of curiosity got into her, and she bent her head down, flicking out her tongue to taste that salty, damp end. He grabbed her by the shoulders and pulled her back up even with him, rolling atop of her and kissing her deeply, his member hard against her sex.

She wrapped her arms around his neck, the size and feel of his rigid member against her welcome now that she had become acquainted with it. At the entrance to her body she felt a moistening—a desire rising within her to have Tom inside her, to have him filling a new and hungry emptiness the way the heroine in the *Memoirs* had been filled. The very interior of her felt as if it was alive with wanting, her flesh tingling with the need to be taken.

His hand stole down there, his fingers repeating the

same gentle game they had played upon her in back of the church. She parted her thighs, willing him to do as he wished. His mouth moved to the side of her neck, suckling above the point of her pulse.

His fingers moved smoothly upon her, dampened with her own desire; then he slid one of them within her, deep. She arched beneath him, the intrusion welcome but unsatisfying. She pushed her hips against his hand, trying to steal more sensation from that embedded finger.

A moment later it was gone, stroking once over her swollen folds before leaving her entirely. Tom came over her then, nudging open her thighs, the weight of his torso taken on his arm. She felt the back of his hand brush the inside of her thigh as he positioned his sex against hers, the head of it suddenly feeling three times as large as it had when it had been in her hand.

His elbows now braced to either side of her, his face was directly above hers, his amber-brown eyes looking down with an intensity that made her part her thighs a little further, her knees rising.

He pushed. She sucked in a breath at the surprise of it, the head feeling now like a veritable fist against her, it was so wide and her body so unwilling to receive it.

He drew back slightly and pushed again, gaining some small entrance. Again he pulled back, and again he thrust, and this time the stretching pressure was one of pain, and with her feet and palms she pushed herself up towards the headboard to escape it. "It hurts," she complained.

His own expression was one of concern, his voice

a whisper. "Does it hurt like the first time?"

"It's a little different. You're so big."

He kissed her cheek and brushed back the hair from her forehead. "I'm not too big. You're just not ready yet."

He moved down her body, her eyes growing wide as she saw where he was headed. He stopped with his face above that space between her thighs, and as she watched in horrified embarrassment he combed away her curls with his fingers and parted her nether lips. He glanced up at her, then with a wicked smile lowered his mouth.

She dropped back onto the pillows at the luscious contact, eyes closing and all thought melting away into a starry black galaxy of pleasure. His arms slid under her thighs, his palms holding her hips as he stroked and fondled her with lips and tongue. He went on and on, exploring and dwelling, caressing, suckling against her, drawing her into his mouth as his tongue flicked quickly against her. Anticipation built within her, her whole body tensing as if doing so could hurry her to the finish she knew must await. She didn't care now what Tom did, as long as he did not stop.

As she was approaching the very peak of her pleasure he took his mouth from her, coming back up her body and positioning himself as he had been before, only this time once he was seated at her entrance he kept his hand below, stroking her. He thrust, and this time gained greater ground. It hurt with a dull, burning pain, but mingled with it was the satisfaction of a stretching fullness, and the continuing touch of his hand.

He pushed again, and then once more, hard, seating himself fully within her as his fingers stroked, creating pleasure to counteract the pain. Tom moved within her, his hips thrusting against her in slow, hard thrusts, the strength of his motions taking the breath from her in small gasps, her breasts rocking on her chest. The combination of pleasure and fullness sent her over the edge, her body swept by pulsing contractions. Tom's pace quickened as if in response, then suddenly slowed. He grimaced and pulled out.

He came down on her, his member hard on her belly, and clasped her tight within his arms, his face buried in her hair. "Konstanze . . ." he groaned, and she felt his whole body go tense and hard. His manhood pulsed against her, and something warm and wet spread in spurts between their bodies.

She wrapped her own legs around the backs of his, her arms holding him gently as he shuddered against her. The tension drained from him, and he sank upon her. It was a welcome weight, secure and comforting, but he seemed to shortly sense that it robbed her of breath, and he rolled to the side.

"Stay here," he whispered, and got up from the bed, going to the dressing table where there was a pitcher, a bowl, and a towel.

She looked down at her belly, then sat halfway up in surprise, her fingers going to the substance spread there. "The 'milky effusion'! So this is what it is!" she exclaimed, touching it.

"Don't do that," Tom said, coming back to her quickly, a wet towel in his hand. "Here, lie back," he directed.

She rubbed some of the substance between her fingers, fascinated, then brought her fingertips up toward her face in the instinctual urge to catch the unfamiliar scent.

Tom stopped her, grasping her hand and cleaning off her fingers with the towel, then gently wiping clean her belly.

"I've never seen it before," Konstanze said. "Why haven't I?"

"Your husband had every reason to spend himself within you. I did not wish you to risk conceiving a child." He finished cleaning himself off, and threw the towel back to the dressing table. He got back into bed beside her, wrapping his arms around her and pulling her up close to him.

The feel of his skin next to hers, his smooth buttocks within easy reach of her questing hands, was almost enough to distract her, but the specifics of what had just transpired between them still intrigued her.

"It was never like this with my husband."

"It's selfish of me, but I'm glad to hear it," he said, kissing her cheek just below her eye, his hand playing in her hair.

She slid her thigh between his, and let her hand trail down to his member, much softer now and more malleable. She frowned, holding him in her hand. The sexual knowledge she had gleaned from the *Memoirs* merged now with her own experience, and she finally understood the basic workings of the male sex. "This is what Bugg felt like, those few times that we were together," she said. "Sometimes he seemed much smaller, even."

Tom's hand in her hair stilled, and he leaned his head back so he could see her better. "*Always*, he was like this?"

"Always."

"Konstanze . . . You said he hurt you the first time you were together. He had to have been erect to have hurt you, to have breached your maidenhead."

"I think—" she started, but could not quite believe what her thought meant, and sought to confirm it another way. "Are all men as large and hard as you when they are about to take a woman?"

"I'd like to say no," he said, grinning. "But more or less I believe that to be the case. We are none of us soft."

She took that in, turning it in her mind with her other knowledge, checking for flaws and finding none. "Tom, I think he never took me except with his fingers," she said, the words rushing out over a released breath. "That's what hurt, his fingers prodding at me. His penis was never hard."

Tom's face froze, and then he suddenly sat up, flinging the covers back.

"What? What is it?" she cried, pulling herself up.

"Blood. Do you see any?" he asked, getting out of the bed.

She moved aside, searching with him, then tentatively touched herself, seeking the telltale sign. "No, nothing," she said, feeling strangely frightened now by the abrupt change in her perception of her marriage and thus her world.

Tom shoved his hand through his hair, standing there for all the world as if he were unaware he was stark naked. "Perhaps his fumblings were enough to tear it."

"My maidenhead?"

He nodded; then his muscles went slack and he got back into bed with her, pulling the covers back up and bringing her close to his side. She rested her cheek atop his shoulder, her leg thrown over his.

"Do you know what this means?" he asked her.

"You were my first," she said.

"Yes. And it means you have grounds to annul your marriage."

Konstanze squeezed her eyes shut against the tears that suddenly formed there, but they slipped out regardless, trickling down her cheek and over her nose to drip upon him. She sniffed.

"Hey there, what's this?" Tom asked, and raised her chin up so she was looking at him. "Why tears?"

"I would never have known," she said. "If I hadn't followed my heart, I would never have known. I'm so happy." She gave him a watery smile. The shackles of her marriage could finally be broken. "I love you, Tom Trewella," she said.

His stared at her, his amber eyes like those of a fox at bay.

She gave a hiccuping little laugh and laid her fingertips over his lips. "You need say nothing. I understand." For this moment it did not matter if he could return her feelings. With her love for him had come the understanding, deep in her soul, that love asked nothing in return. She loved him, and she felt blessed that she could do so.

She laid her head back down on his shoulder, and

let herself weep with the relief of being released from her bonds, marital and emotional.

She was free.

Tom lay awake, Konstanze sleeping curled against his side, her hand on his chest as if to prevent him from slipping away from her. He was feeling little of that blissful relaxation that usually came with sexual release.

After Konstanze had dried her tears of happiness, she had in a broken voice described to him the night with her husband that had convinced her to run away. The thought of her tied up and beaten for an old man's lecherous amusement set his blood boiling. He was half tempted to hunt the villain down and deliver his own version of physical punishment—a punishment that would leave the man a bleeding pulp of broken flesh. Fear of blood be damned—this was one case where he would manage to stomach it.

The rage toward the faceless Bugg was only a distraction from deeper matters, though. It was easier to think about pounding a foul goat into the ground than about the delicate state of affairs between himself and Konstanze.

He had been her first. He had never been anyone's first before. It brought out feelings of possessive tenderness. That he had been the one to initiate her made him feel that she belonged to him. Not as a slave or as chattel, but more that she was joined to him now through experience, in bonds that time could never break.

He remembered his own first sexual encounter, with

an experienced woman several years his senior. When he had finished she had held him against her with all the tenderness of a mother holding a child. Were his feelings now like that woman's had been then? Their affair had been brief, but on the rare occasions that their paths had crossed afterward she had gazed upon him with gentle affection. For his own part he could remember his first time in awkward, embarrassing detail, but he had long forgotten whatever passions he had felt for his partner.

He tightened his hold on Konstanze. With an annulment she would be free to marry, and between her amiable—if slightly eccentric—nature and her pleasing appearance, he knew she would have no trouble finding suitors. He could be one of them himself, and he had an advantage, as she fancied herself in love with him.

He wasn't certain if he should believe her declaration, though, coming as it had on the heels of love-making and her realization that she would soon be free of Bugg. His impulse was to disbelieve her, and to think that she was confused by her turbulent emotions. He'd been stunned when she said it, incapable of responding.

He let himself consider that she might have known what she was saying, and meant it. What if her coming to him this evening had been because of love, and not merely desire?

The very idea made him tense, suggesting as it did that she might be aiming for marriage.

On the other hand, nothing was ever as one would expect with Konstanze. She might have every intention of sailing off to America, or of heading to London to go on the stage. She might decide she'd had enough of marriage altogether.

Marriage. He had thought the possibility to be comfortably far in his future. He was content with his life the way it was, with his tidy house and Mrs. Toley to tend to his creature comforts. He didn't know if he was ready to wed, if he was willing to disrupt his life to that degree.

He felt as if he were teetering on a precipice, his familiar, stable life underfoot and something new and frightening opening out in the vast and empty air before him. Were his feelings for Konstanze strong enough for him to leap and risk falling?

For all that Konstanze had been shaken by her discoveries of this night, he could not fail to notice that she was the one sleeping peacefully, content amidst the turbulence. She slept as one for whom the path into the future had suddenly become clear.

He wished he could be as certain of his own wishes.

# *Chapter Nineteen*

Bugg II stood hunched in the dark shadows of a shop, staring across the street and up the hill at the house into which Konstanze had disappeared with the black-haired man. The faint glow of candlelight lit one of the upstairs windows, and for several minutes there had been large shadows moving through it. As the minutes crept by he became more and more certain of what those shadows meant: Konstanze and the man were fornicating.

He'd expected it of her, of course, but to sit out here and see the reality was surprisingly distasteful. She was no better than a bitch in heat, and likely this was not the first man to make use of her person. She'd probably been supporting herself off the proceeds of such couplings.

He hoped she got a burning dose of the clap from it.

She would have to be gotten rid of. Although he had played with the idea of keeping her for himself once Father quit his dawdling and died, knowing she was up there sweating away with another man spoiled what little fun there was in the idea. No one wanted a whore for a wife. With his inheritance he would soon be able to afford much better.

A trio of rowdy drunks sang their way past, oblivious to his presence. He could still hear the faint sounds of carousing from down on the harbor, but this part of town was quieting for the night. Booths and stage platforms were clear of portable goods, but remained standing in preparation for tomorrow's continuation of the fair. No one was thinking of anything but having a good time.

The shadows stopped moving, and he tensed in anticipation. They might be coming back out soon. He felt for the pistol inside his coat, the weight of it heavy. It was big enough that if anyone had been looking, its presence would have been obvious, but no one did look. Even that fool of a Preventive man had not noticed.

Bugg II shifted, starting to perspire in anticipation of the confrontation with Konstanze and her lover. He didn't want to confront them alone. What if the man was dangerous? What if the man attacked him? And he still did not himself know exactly how he was going to deal with Konstanze. If he could to do so without risk of capture, he would just as soon shoot her. His hands would be kept cleaner and the risk of repercussions would be much less, however, if he could have her arrested for theft. Let the Crown hang her; it was skilled at execution.

Time moved slowly forward, and there was no change from the house. Perhaps they had fallen asleep. He pressed his knuckles against his lips and gnawed. Did he have time to fetch the Preventive man, Foweather? And would the man finally believe him well enough to help him?

The conversation in front of the Fishing Moon had been one of mixed satisfaction. The more Foweather spoke about the "mermaid," the more Bugg II had suspected that it was Konstanze of whom he spoke. The description of her visit to the church had all but confirmed it. Bugg II knew that one of her favorite outfits was an emerald green dress with a black velvet spencer. She had worn it often.

However, when he had suggested that the mermaid was actually his runaway stepmother—and a thief— and that an elaborate hoax had been played upon him, Foweather had not reacted well. He had flatly refused to believe such was possible, and had recited at length—for what must have been the hundredth time that day—every detail of his every encounter with the mermaid.

"I tell you, her mother was an opera singer," Bugg II had said. "She herself can sing in five different languages, and you'd think she wasn't human when you heard the notes she can reach." For a moment he thought he'd seen doubt in Foweather's eyes.

But then someone had chided the man not to listen to such nonsense, and to have another drink in honor of the mermaid.

He'd given up, and wandered through the crowd the rest of the afternoon, looking for some sign of Konstanze. It hadn't been until after the lighting of the bonfire that he'd succeeded in finding her; and he'd very nearly lost the advantage of surprise in the process. He'd been staring right at her, elated to have finally tracked her down, and then as if feeling his gaze she had turned toward him. He had looked away and hidden in the darkness and the shifting bodies of the crowd.

He'd followed her at a safe distance, and nearly missed it when she stepped into the shadows of a shop porch. He'd waited not thirty feet from her, watching, and then trying to eavesdrop when the man joined her. They'd been too far away for him to catch their words, and the man had looked uneasy. He hadn't dared follow any closer.

There was still no movement or change from the house. Perhaps it was worth the risk of losing Konstanze to go back and fetch Foweather. Even if Konstanze did leave while he was gone, he knew where the house was. The occupant could be questioned. Doubtless the sod didn't know what a gold-hungry little liar he had in his bed.

He gave the window one last look, then dashed down the street back toward the harbor.

Konstanze came awake to the slow stroking of Tom's fingers in her hair. For a moment she was disoriented; then memory returned and she smiled and nestled closer against his side.

"Are you awake?" he asked.

"Yes. How long have you been?"

"A while."

She let her hand drift down to his groin and found his member hard and full. She wrapped her hand around it and stroked down, loving the feel of it against her palm. He groaned, then took her hand in his own and brought it up to his mouth, kissing the back and palm.

"You're in no condition for a second time," he said, "although God knows I'd like to let you try."

She rolled on top of him, her breasts flattened against his chest, and wiggled her hips. "I didn't know that skin against skin could feel like this. I never want to get dressed again."

"Konstanze . . . You're making this hard."

"I can tell."

He rolled her over, coming to rest on top of her. "That's not what I meant."

"Let's do it again. I don't care if it hurts."

He made slow thrusts of his hips against hers, his manhood low enough to rub against her. She half closed her eyes and parted her thighs, throwing her arms above her head. "Please," she said.

He kissed her, deep and hard, then held her tight against him. She put her arms around his neck and held him close.

"Tomorrow," he said. "You may not care if it hurts you, but I do."

"I'd expected more rapacious behavior from you."

"Are you trying to taunt me into it?"

"Would I do that?"

He grunted, then rolled off her. "Hilde is going to

skin me alive for bringing you home so late."

"Probably. Unless she is not yet home herself. I saw her with the vicar in the crowd around the bonfire."

"That's right—I'd forgotten seeing them myself. I'll be looking forward to hearing all about it from Matt."

She gave him a look. "And will you be sharing any stories of your own?"

He picked up her chemise from the floor and tossed it to her. "Naturally. I shall share each and every detail with any who care to listen. I'm sure they'll enjoy the tale down at the Fishing Moon."

"Pig!" She threw a pillow at him.

He pounced on the bed and put his face to her bare belly, nuzzling and making snorting pig noises. She bent around his head, laughing. "Stop it! Stop!"

The rooting turned to kisses, and a moment later they were entwined in each other's arms, lips caressing and coaxing. Just when she was about to urge him to take her again he pulled away.

"I always said you would lead me down the road to hell."

"I would hardly call this hell," she said on a sigh.

He handed her the chemise, which had gotten pushed down to the bottom of the bed, then stood up and reached for his breeches. "I'll go see what Mrs. Toley left us to eat. Come down to the kitchen when you're dressed."

She smiled dreamily at him and stretched her arms above her head, arching her back so her breasts stood out, then collapsing in what she hoped was an invitingly relaxed pose.

"Stop looking at me like that," he ordered.

"I enjoy it."

He groaned and struggled into his shirt, then grabbed his stockings and shoes in one hand, the lamp in the other, and fled to the doorway. "What am I going to do with you?"

"I can hardly wait to find out."

He groaned again, then was gone.

"It's just up here," Bugg II said, hurrying his step, then turning to check that Foweather and his groggy men were following. He prayed the light was still there in the window.

"You're going to regret this if you're wrong, by God," Foweather said, without much heat. Like his men, he was still half-asleep.

The entire town was drunk or sleeping. By his pocket watch he knew it was near three o'clock, and except for a few bleary souls still nursing their cider or beer in front of the Fishing Moon, there was not an upright man to be seen. One of those bleary men had directed Bugg II to the old boat where the Preventive crew slept. He'd woken Foweather and told him what he'd seen, whereupon Foweather had told him to find the constable if it was an arrest for theft he was intent upon making.

The constable, unfortunately, was a loudly snoring man lying in the middle of the street who refused to awaken. With great annoyance Foweather had eventually given in to his pleas and proddings to come and at least see if the woman was the same as the mermaid, and had dragged half his men with him for good measure. Konstanze might convincingly plead innocence to the charges of theft—which had, after all, taken place far from here and were of no interest to the locals—but Bugg II was counting on Foweather being sufficiently incensed at being made a fool of by a fake mermaid that he would have her thrown in jail regardless of her tears and protestations.

"It's that house, right there," Bugg II pointed out, stopping. The upper window was dark, and he felt his heart plummet.

"That one? With the flowers out front?"

"Yes. That's where she went, with a dark-haired man."

"I ought to throw you in jail, that's what I ought to do!" Foweather erupted. "Telling lies about a man like Mr. Trewella! If he did bring a woman up there, I'm sure it's no business of yours."

"You know him?" Bugg II cried, flabbergasted by the violent response.

"Know him! I count him one of my closest friends. A better man you won't find anywhere in Cornwall."

"That's where she went, I swear it!"

"Perhaps she did, but the one thing I know is that whoever she is, she is not the mermaid." He turned back to his men, who had watched the interchange with some amusement. "My apologies! I did not know the man was insane," he said. They began to trudge back the way they had come, one of the men facing Bugg II long enough to make a rude gesture.

"But it's her! At least help me capture her for the theft! It was my mother's clock!"

Derisive snorts and insults were his only answer.

He stood in the street, furious and helpless. No one

would help him, and she had likely fled the house. *Damn her!* It bloody well wasn't fair!

He was still standing there fuming when a giggle floated to him on the night air. He looked up at the house and caught a faint light showing from behind it. He skulked into the shadows, heart racing.

Soft voices, one male and one female, grew louder as the couple came around the house and started down the stairs. He drew his pistol out of his coat and prepared to fire.

They stepped down from the bottom step to the street and turned to the left, away from the harbor. He let them go a few paces and then emerged from the shadows, pistol aimed at the harlot's back.

"Konstanze!" Bugg II said loudly.

She spun, the very act of turning proof in itself that it was her. He grinned, victory finally his. It took her a long moment to recognize him, and when she finally gave a gasp of horrified recognition, he fired.

Even as he pulled the trigger the man was shoving her aside, and as the pistol jerked in his hand, the report a thunderclap in the quiet street, the man stumbled, then fell to the ground like a sack of grain.

Konstanze screamed. "Tom! Tom!" she cried, then was on her knees beside him, hands fluttering over his body, searching for the wound.

Bugg II swore under his breath and fumbled in his coat pocket for the materials to reload. People would be emerging from their homes any minute.

The man on the ground, Tom, moved. His hand went to his side, touching upon the hole in his torso, the fingers coming away dark with blood.

"Help! Someone help us!" Konstanze cried into the night.

Bugg II fumbled and dropped his small horn of gunpowder. *Damn it all to hell!* He glared at Konstanze, who was still caterwauling. From behind him he heard shouts, running footsteps. He'd have to do this the hard way.

He jogged to the collapsed couple and, making a cudgel of the pistol, raised his arm high. He'd smash in her skull and be done with her.

Konstanze brought her forearm above her head as if it could protect her, and the pistol began its descent.

Something caught him at the knees, and he was falling, his own head smacking painfully on the ground. As the shouts drew closer Tom climbed atop him, the man's fist a cudgel of his own as he smashed Bugg II's nose, then his chin.

Then the man was being pulled off him, and they were surrounded by the men from the Preventive crew, and a growing group of locals, the air full of shouts and yells. Bugg II rolled onto his side, his hands going up to his face, feeling the damage. His entire head throbbed, his vision blurry with tears and pain.

"Grab her, too!" he heard Foweather say.

Bugg II managed to push himself up to a sitting position.

"He needs a doctor!" Konstanze cried as she was held between two men. "He's been shot."

"She's right, sir," one of the men said. Tom was hunched over in his grip, his hand to his side, not fighting the Preventive man's hold on him. The man lifted a lantern and looked at Tom's back. "Looks like

349

it might have gone through, but he's bleeding something awful."

"She's your mermaid, isn't she?" Bugg II asked Foweather, his voice sounding nasal even to his own ears. As he breathed, blood bubbled in his nose.

He watched as Foweather took a lantern from one of the men and raised it up near Konstanze's face. He pulled the white cap from her head, then yanked at her hair, pulling out her loose chignon. He reached out, hesitated, and then lifted her skirt high enough that he could see the normal leather shoes and white stockings. A look of utter bewilderment and hurt melted his features.

"Meet Konstanze Bugg, my stepmother," Bugg II said triumphantly, and climbed unsteadily to his feet. He took out a kerchief and tried to stanch the flow of blood from his nose. "Thief, adulteress, and liar."

It was Tom that Foweather turned to now. "Tom?" he asked, a plea in his voice.

"That man tried to kill her," Tom said weakly.

"She's not a mermaid," Foweather said, his voice quavering. "He was right; I've been played for a fool. It's all been an enormous joke. Why, Tom?"

"I did it myself," Konstanze said to Foweather, before Tom could speak. "I wanted to catch your attention. I thought I'd never do so unless I made myself into something magical. You were always so intent upon your job, you never even saw me when I was as I am now."

"She's lying!" Bugg II said. "And not doing a very

good job of it, either. Why would she be here with another man if she wanted you?"

"Please," Konstanze said, "let us talk about it later. Tom needs a doctor now."

Hearing his name, Tom raised his head, speaking to Foweather. "You were never meant to be hurt," he said, his speech slurring.

"Please!" Konstanze said.

A man from the crowd called out that someone named Wiggett had already gone to fetch the doctor. Foweather directed the men holding Tom to carry him back up to his house. Konstanze moved as if to go with them, but the men held her back.

"Whatever else she is, she's still a thief!" Bugg II said. "And I've got the proof of it. I have the pawn tickets for the things she stole from our house, with her name on them!"

"You're a murderer!" Konstanze shot back at him, then spoke to Foweather. "He tried to shoot me, and may very well have killed Tom. You have evidence enough of that!"

"I had my gun out to keep her from running," Bugg II said. "That man attacked me, and got shot by accident."

"Liar!" Konstanze shouted, but her gaze was on the figures disappearing with Tom.

Foweather looked at Konstanze, then at Tom being carried into the house. There was still hurt and confusion on his features, as if he could make no sense of anything that he saw or heard. He was silent for as much as half a minute, everyone quiet as they waited to see what he would say.

"Take her to the magistrate. I know she's a liar, for she's no mermaid. Let a magistrate decide if she should be tried as a thief, as well."

Bugg II met Konstanze's furious eyes and smiled.

# Chapter Twenty

*Launceston Jail*

The poet Richard Lovelace had written that stone walls did not a prison make, nor iron bars a cage, as long as he had freedom in his love and in his soul was free. It was a beautiful sentiment, Konstanze thought, but she was having difficulty accepting it as truth. The cold, seeping walls around her and the stinking, filth-slimed floors seemed to make for a very real confinement indeed.

She had been locked in the dank depths of Launceston Jail for a week now, and every moment, waking and sleeping, was spent in tortured worry about Tom. Her last sight of him haunted her thoughts: Tom on the edge of losing consciousness, eyes glazed, blood flowing from his body as the men carried him up to his house. Had he survived? She clung to the brief words of the Preventive man who said it looked like the bullet had gone clean through. Perhaps it had missed anything vital. Perhaps it had only grazed the flesh, and looked worse than it was.

Or perhaps however minor the wound, Tom had succumbed to fever and died, and even now lay in his grave while she rotted here in ignorance. She had received no word, no visits, had had no contact with anyone from Penperro since she had faced the magistrate, roused from his bed. Confronted with written evidence and an enraged Preventive officer, and with Tom unable to speak in her favor, the magistrate had concluded that there was sufficient evidence against her to warrant a trial for theft, and she had been hauled off to Launceston that very night.

She sat now in the decomposing straw with a dozen other women, thankful only that her nose had become somewhat accustomed to the stench. She was manacled around her waist and ankles, chains stretching between the bands of iron. Already the skin around her ankles was rubbed raw, and she had torn strips of cloth from her chemise and wrapped her inflamed flesh as best she could.

The door to the cell was suddenly opened. "Constance Bugg!" a guard shouted into the half-dark. "Which of you is Constance Bugg?"

"Here," Konstanze called, her heart leaping, a wild hope beating to life in her breast. She struggled quickly to her feet, swaying for a moment as her vision blackened, shimmering with stars around the edges. A moment later it cleared, and she stumbled forward even as the guard continued to speak.

"You have a visitor. Move lively now! I haven't got all day!"

*At last!* Could it be Tom? Launceston was over a day's journey from Penperro, and she doubted he could be well enough to make such a trip, but maybe it really had been just a flesh wound; maybe he was here. Or if not Tom, then Hilde. Or even the vicar. *Someone* had come for her, after a week spent alone with strangers, and they would have word of Tom.

The guard led her through the jail to a metal-banded door, then opened it to the bright sunlight and fresh air. Konstanze squinted, raising a hand against the glare, and stepped out into a small walled courtyard. She heard a cry, and then Hilde was enveloping her in her arms, weeping, pulling away to look at her and then holding her close again.

The joy of seeing a familiar and friendly face set Konstanze to weeping as well, and the two clung together for long minutes, until at last Konstanze pulled away, aware of time slipping by.

"What of Tom?" she asked in German.

Hilde sniffled once more, then contained herself. "It was bad the first two nights. He lost a lot of blood. The doctor said the bullet went through his liver, but that it missed any major vessels and he should make a full recovery. There was no infection."

Relief made Konstanze's knees go weak, and she staggered. With Hilde's help she sat on the cobbled ground, trembling. It was not entirely emotion that had her so weak, but lack of food. The prisoners were fed only once a day, and then only one pot of gruel to be parceled out between a dozen women. Launceston Jail had a reputation for being the worst of the worst, and Konstanze could well believe it after having spent a week inside its black-slimed walls.

"Thank God," Konstanze said.

"He cannot yet travel, and it is driving him half mad. He has barely the strength to hold a pen."

"Tell him from me not to risk the journey, please," Konstanze said. "I don't think I could bear it in here if I knew he were dead."

"He gave me this for you," Hilde said, holding out a letter.

Konstanze took it, her dirty fingers leaving smudges on the pristine paper as she broke the seal and unfolded the paper.

*My dearest Konstanze,*
*Do not fear. You shall be freed. I swear my life on it.*

*Your affectionate*
*Tom*

*Affectionate.* She gave a little gurgling laugh through her tears. *The poor fool.* He didn't want to commit his heart to her unless he knew he could follow through, even in such dire circumstances as these. He was willing to pledge his very life to freeing her, but was yet cautious of his heart.

She touched the black script with her fingertips, as if she could touch Tom himself through the curving letters. He might not be certain of his feelings for her, but she was. Despite his loathing for physical danger, he had used his own body to shield her from Bugg

II's fire, taking the bullet meant for her. Despite his debilitating terror of blood he had retained his senses long enough to knock Bugg II to the ground, saving her life a second time in the space of a minute.

He might argue he would have done the same for anyone, but the fact was that he had done it for her. He did love her, in some form, and between that knowledge and her own feelings for him she was satisfied. Whatever happened, as long as he lived, as long as she could love, she would not be conquered by her circumstances. Perhaps the poet had been right about that, after all.

The comfort of love had been sweet after one week at Launceston, but after a month of waiting for the arrival of the circuit judges and for the assizes to begin, the comfort had begun to feel a thin shield against the horrors of the jail.

Tom had sent money with Hilde, enough to try to better her circumstances in the jail, but as much as the guards were willing to take the coin, there was little they could actually do to help. The jail was so overcrowded that even heavy bribery could not secure a private cell, and there was besides an institutional belief in the corrective power of misery. The jail had no well, and therefore no water to spare for washing. The money had managed to purchase a little extra food, but her cellmates had in their own unique way insisted upon sharing.

She was not the only one there on a charge of theft. One unfortunate girl had been incarcerated for stealing a single linen handkerchief. Others were guilty of highway robbery, having lurked in the bushes in groups and set upon vulnerable travelers. One silent woman had taken powders to rid herself of an unwanted pregnancy, and had died in the night of the lingering aftereffects. Two of the highway robbers had divested the poor creature of her clothing before the guard was called to haul away the body.

Hilde had visited twice a week, which was all the guards would allow. Her expression had told Konstanze that she was not faring as well as she had hoped in prison. Better than a mirror, her maid's growing concern spoke of her loss of weight, her dirt and lice and fleas, and the possibility of illness. Typhus was rampant at Launceston, and she had a sickening fear in her belly that she would succumb.

And succumb she did. She had a headache that would not leave, and when there had been light enough to check she had peered down her bodice and seen the telltale speckling of the red typhus rash. She was burning with fever when the guard came again to the door to call her name. This time when she stepped out into the courtyard it was Tom who was there waiting for her, looking thin and pale and none too strong himself. He turned when he heard the door open, his face showing his shock when she stepped out into the light.

"Your wound!" she said, before he had even a chance to come toward her. She little cared how sorry she must look, her concern all for him. "Have you recovered? Are you well?"

"Well enough," he said, and closed the distance between them, reaching for her. The shock on his face had changed to something different, something softer and infinitely sad.

She didn't want him to risk catching her illness, and stepped back, but he followed and pulled her into his arms, holding her close despite her dirt and disease, rocking her in his arms as he whispered soothing, meaningless words in her ear. She didn't know if the soothing was meant more for her or to calm himself, as she could feel the strain of intense emotion in his muscles as he held her. The warmth of another body was not welcome in her feverish state, but she clung to him anyway, closing her eyes and disappearing into a world where he was all that existed.

After a while he began to tell her about his trip to London to meet with acquaintances who, in turn, had connections with the judges who rode the western circuit. She listened with only half an ear, the vibrations of his voice much more important to her than the words he spoke. These friends of friends, he said, would plead her case in private, asking for clemency. He had hired the best barrister money could buy, to defend her. And then he said something that took her completely unaware.

"I want to go see Bugg."

She pulled back, not believing what she had just heard.

"Bugg II's evidence against you is solid, Konstanze, but with a word from your husband the charges would be nothing. I swore to you once that I would not contact him for any reason. Release me from that now."

"No. Never." The very thought made her feel ill.

"Konstanze . . . If they convict you, you will hang."

"If they release me, Bugg will have me. I'd rather die than go back to him." Anything was better than returning to Bugg. Launceston Jail was a friendlier home than Bugg House had ever been.

"I won't let him have you. The moment you are free I'll take you away. He'll never know where you've gone."

"No." It was unreasoning, this fear and hatred she had of her husband, but it was also overwhelming. How could she agree to any contact?

"His son has likely told him already where you are."

She shook her head. "No, he won't tell him until I'm dead. He won't risk having me freed."

"Trust me, Konstanze. Let me contact him. Trust me."

She met his eyes, and saw the desperation there, and the love that he did not himself recognize. How could she deny him another way in which to fight for her freedom and her life?

"Don't let him have me," she said softly.

He held her tight, and she tried to hold tight to her belief in him. He would not let Bugg have her; he would not. She had to believe that, even more than she had to believe that he would not let her hang.

*Hamoaze Waterway, near Plymouth*

It had been six weeks now since Bugg II had come and torn her life apart.

The five women to whom Konstanze was shackled looked no better than she herself felt, their clothes so filthy and worn that the original colors were indistinguishable, their hair lank with grease, their faces gaunt and pale and sheened with the sweat of fever. They were all six sitting in the bow of a small boat, being rowed out to the prison hulk *Dunkirk*, where they were to remain until the next ship scheduled to carry women set sail for Australia. She was to be transported.

A week after Tom's visit to Launceston the assizes had begun, and her trial. She hadn't been able to speak privately again with Tom, but had seen him white-faced in the courtroom gallery, having just arrived back from London. Through her barrister she learned what Tom had discovered in London: her husband was dead. He had suffered a series of heart attacks, the first of which had come soon after she left him. All this time she had feared him, and he had been lying helpless in his bed.

She supposed she should feel some bit of sorrow or pity for the man, but it was relief she had felt more than anything else, even though his death meant that he was unable to withdraw the charges against her.

The relief had lasted three quarters of an hour, which was how long her trial had lasted, Bugg II taking up more than his fair share of the time testifying against her. Despite Tom's petitions on her behalf, despite the evident loathing with which the judges and jury regarded Bugg II, the verdict had come down against her. The judge had placed the black cap upon his wig and solemnly intoned that she was to be "hanged by the neck until you are dead."

The meaning of that sentence had not come home to her until she was back in the noxious jail, back in the dark and the filthy straw, with a rat nibbling on her shoe until she kicked it away. The truth did not affect her as she had expected it would. She had thought she would weep, or shriek, or lose her senses completely. Instead, a weird calm had descended upon her. She would die, or some miracle would save her. She had no control over which would be her fate. There was nothing to do but wait. Either way, it would all be over in the space of a few days.

She had been wrong about that. At the end of the assizes the judges had gone over their lists of the convicted and had chosen her as one of the "lucky" ones who would have her sentence commuted from hanging to transportation. She was convinced it was because of Tom's efforts that they had done so, and hope had taken new life within her. The next day she and the women to whom she was chained were put in a cart and hauled down to the coast, to the hulk *Dunkirk*.

The hulk drifted almost imperceptibly on its anchor chains, the gray early morning light doing nothing to illuminate its black sides. Ramshackle huts had been built on deck, and between the stumps of the former masts stretched a line of laundry, hanging damp and lifeless. The hatches facing shore had been boarded shut—she'd heard because local residents had complained of the stench that blew to them on the wind. She could believe it. Even from fifty yards away the hulk smelled like an open sewer at the height of summer. She'd thought that nothing could be as bad as Launceston Jail, but perhaps she had thought too soon. The *Dunkirk* had been serving as a floating prison for seven years, and would likely remain here, polluting the waters of the Hamoaze Waterway, until its timbers rotted and it sank to the muddy bottom with its chained occupants gasping for their last desperate breaths of air.

The boat at last reached the hulk, and Konstanze heard the hideous sounds coming from within the floating prison. Even through the shut hatches and gunports the groans and cries of the suffering prisoners could be heard, their misery infecting the air as surely as did the stench of their bodies and waste.

A pair of marines waited for them at the foot of a stairway built onto the side of the hulk, and after the boat had been tied off they helped the prisoners disembark. None of the women tried to make a dive for the water. Not only were they chained together, but they were too weak to do more than try to stand. Looking up at the creaking mass of timber and rot, Konstanze almost thought a watery death would be preferable to spending the next one, two, maybe even three months on board.

The marines directed the chained prisoners up the steep gangway and onto the deck, their hungry eyes inspecting faces and bodies for reasons Konstanze could too easily guess. The deck of the hulk was even more forbidding up close than it had been from a distance, looking like nothing so much as the back alley of a Paris slum, and smelling three times as bad. The force of the stench up close had the women gagging, the air thick as porridge as it filled nose and throat.

The chains joining them together were removed, although the irons on ankles and waist remained. Only half the hulk was for women, and as they were herded in the direction of that hatch the clouds above thinned, and an illumination of pale sunlight painted the prisoners. Konstanze squinted up at the clouds, then across the water to the green slopes of Cornwall.

Tom would come for her. Somehow he would save her. She didn't know how he would manage it, but she had to believe that it was so.

# Chapter Twenty-one

*Penperro*

He didn't know how to save her.

He had tried everything he could think of, and had called in every favor, had pulled every string. Even the commutation of her sentence had been due to factors other than his own influence: it was understood that female prisoners were needed in Botany Bay to relieve the "needs" of the many men.

He kicked his desk, then again and again, putting dents in the rich polished wood of its front. The pain in his foot was nothing to the pain tearing him apart inside.

"Tom!"

Hands pulled him away, and he turned to see Matt, who had come into the house without his even noticing. "You won't help her by breaking your foot."

365

"I can't help her at all!"

"She won't go to Botany Bay. You'll think of something. You've been going at it too hard, is all. You haven't rested, you haven't eaten—it's a wonder you have a single lucid thought in your head."

"I don't know where to go from here," Tom said, the words a plea.

"Eat first. Then we'll talk. She won't like getting free only to find you've turned into a raving lunatic. She'll pitch you over for someone else. And look at yourself—you're not a sight for anyone's sore eyes. You're too thin, and have a ghastly color. It's a miracle you've healed as well as you have—you look ready for the grave. I wouldn't want to take you to my bed if I were her, that's for sure," Matt said, leading him to the dining room. Mrs. Toley had already set out the china and silver, and dashed out of the room as they appeared, presumably in a hurry to bring the food before her master could change his mind.

"Is this how you minister to the suffering?" Tom asked.

"Only to asses like you."

Strangely, that made him feel better. Only a friend would call him an ass in that tone, and it finally occured to him that he was not alone in this: Matt would help, however he could. "Thank you."

"Shut up and eat."

As usual, Mrs. Toley had prepared far too much. He was too sick with worry to have an appetite, but Matt was right. He would be no use to anyone if he didn't take care of himself, and he had yet to regain his strength after being shot. The food made him feel queasy, especially when he thought of how little Konstanze had had to eat, and how frail she had felt in his arms at Launceston, frail and hot and speckled with the rash that told him that if the hangman didn't kill her, typhus might. He forced himself to swallow, a bite at a time.

"Hilde is in as bad a shape as you," Matt eventually said, his own plate of food already half consumed. Hilde had returned with Tom to Penperro after Konstanze was removed to the prison hulk, as if she did not know where else to go. After a day in the empty Penrose cottage she had shown up on Matt's doorstep, and had been staying with him for the three nights since.

"I'm not surprised. She watched over Konstanze like a mother bear," Tom said.

"I think she'd like to actually be a bear, if only to have the chance to rip the bellies out of everyone responsible for taking away her cub."

Tom knew the long list of people to whom Matt referred, starting with the mayor of Penperro, who had acted as magistrate. Although he had been told by several concerned townsfolk that Konstanze had been of help to them—he himself profited now and then from smuggling—he had been more concerned about his own neck than hers. He didn't want to draw suspicion on himself by displaying leniency for Konstanze when there was such clear evidence of a crime as the tickets from the pawnshop. He'd agreed that Konstanze's fate should be decided at the Launceston summer assizes, and had chalked Tom's wound up to an accident incurred during a struggle.

## Lisa Cach

Tom would dearly love to leave the man alone in a room with Hilde and see what was left of him when an hour was up. Himself, he would like to throw the man facedown in the harbor mud and stand on his head until the tide came in. Bugg II he would bury in a pile of rotten, oily fish heads—his face bore some resemblance to a bass, seen from the front—and then he'd set the mound alight.

He couldn't hold anything against Foweather, though, for all that without him Konstanze would still be free. The Preventive man had been subdued ever since that night, hardly speaking to anyone. Tom had heard rumors that he often went to the rocks and gazed out at the sea, as if not quite believing his mermaid had not been real.

As far as anyone knew, Foweather had no idea that the mermaid and the smuggling were connected, and instead thought only that an elaborate prank had been played upon him by the man he had thought his friend, and by the "woman" to whom he had lost his heart. He was perhaps too simple a man to ponder why they would do so, feeling only the hurt of being the butt of their supposed joke.

Even Bugg II hadn't bothered to delve into the question of why Konstanze had been pretending to be a mermaid, so happy had he been to see her arrested.

Dinner was cleared away, and Mrs. Toley served them dishes of spotted dick with hot custard. Tom poked at the spongy cake with his spoon, digging out the raisins, then gave up. He'd forced himself to eat as much as he could. Matt raised an eyebrow at him, and he pushed his dessert dish over to his friend.

"I've eaten, but I don't feel any great solutions coming over me," Tom said. "I still don't know what to do. All legal routes have led nowhere, and all I'm left with is contemplation of somehow breaking her free."

Matt spooned up a bite soaked in liquid custard sauce. "So break her free."

"From a prison hulk guarded by marines?"

Matt shrugged, finishing his dessert and starting on Tom's. "Or you could have one of your privateering acquaintances attack the ship that takes her to Botany Bay."

Tom frowned, thinking of the painting above his desk with cannons blasting and splintered wood flying. "There's got to be a better way. How many guards do you suppose are actually aboard the ship at any one time?"

"I have no idea. Not more than six or eight, I would think, and I imagine they give more attention to the half of the hulk that holds the male inmates. No one expects trouble from women, even when they're convicted felons. I've heard that the marines even sleep with the women, in exchange for washwater or food. Not that Konstanze would do that," he added quickly.

Tom had heard the same thing. It was no surprise that women in terrible circumstances would do what they must to better their situation. He could not believe that Konstanze would be one of them, and hated to think that she might almost be desperate enough to do it. If she did, he had no one but himself to blame for not freeing her sooner.

"You don't suppose they sleep with them amidst all the others, do you?" Tom wondered aloud. "They'd bring them up on deck, wouldn't they, or to their own quarters on board? They'd take their irons off, as well."

"And let them bathe, I warrant. What are you thinking?"

"I'm not certain. But if there was some way to get Konstanze above decks . . . It occurs to me that the hulk is surrounded by water, and, mermaid or no, that is very much her element."

"It's the element of the marines, as well. You don't think they'll have a boat right there waiting for such an attempt? And I doubt Konstanze will have the strength to swim either far or fast. And if she does manage to escape, where will she go? She'll be a hunted woman. She won't be able to sleep easy anywhere in England."

Tom nibbled a hangnail, slouching down with one foot up on the edge of the table in his favorite thinking position, his mind beginning to tick. He had the pieces of a plan before him, but did not yet know how to thread them together into a workable plot to free Konstanze.

Konstanze. He remembered her telling him the origin of her name and the ridiculous plot of *The Abduction from the Seraglio*. In the final, improbable scene the pasha reversed himself, and released Konstanze and her lover to go live happily ever after.

The connecting thread began to appear.

# Chapter Twenty-two

*Kent*

Bugg II was whistling a bawdy tune as he got out of the cab in front of his father's home. The driver unloaded his box of things while Bugg II stretched and held his arms out wide, surveying the large brick house with an eye toward improvements. It was as good as his now, as soon as the old man gave up the ghost.

He paid the driver and swung open the front gate, the cab's rattling sounds of horse and carriage fading as he came up the short walk. The garden looked a trifle weedy, he noted. He'd have to flay someone's hide for that.

A cheerful explanation for the unkemptness hit him. Perhaps dear Father was dead already, and the staff were loafing in absence of a master's presence.

If he wasn't dead, then hearing that his beloved wife had been hanged as a thief would surely kill him off.

*Father, I did all I could to save her,* Bugg II would say, weeping. *It was terrible, terrible! Her eyes bulged, her tongue stuck out, getting more purple by the second. She thrashed and thrashed, but her arms were tied behind her and there was nothing to be done.*

It would be one of his greatest regrets that he had not stayed in Launceston for Konstanze's execution. The moment her sentence was read, he had lit out of town. The fury on the face of Tom Trewella had warned him that his life was in jeopardy if he stayed. He contented himself with the knowledge that he had finally won, and seeing Konstanze in such sorry shape had been balm to his soul. She had looked as if she'd been dragged through the back streets of London, then dunked in the Thames for good measure. He'd hardly even recognized her in court.

He put his hand on the front doorknob and tried to turn it, but it would not budge. He gave the wood a few sharp raps.

Throughout his long search for Konstanze he had sent periodic mocking letters to Quarles, letting him know of his progress, but as he had never been certain in which direction he was headed it had been impossible to give an address for a reply. His blood fairly bubbled with excitement, waiting for Deekes to appear at the door and tell him if his father still lived.

A minute passed, and no Deekes.

He rapped again, harder this time, and longer. He stepped into the flower beds and pressed his face to the nearest window, cupping his hands around his eyes. It was a sitting room into which he looked, and it appeared even bleaker and more bare than he remembered. That seemed a good sign.

The door opened.

"Deekes! It's bloody well—" he started, then stopped in surprise. It was Quarles standing there.

"Mr. Quarles! Where's Deekes?"

"Mr. Bugg. What a pleasure to see you at long last."

Bugg II stepped out of the flowers and back up onto the porch, then shoved his way past Quarles into the house. "Why didn't Deekes answer the door?"

"Mr. Deekes is no longer employed here."

Bugg II looked at him in some surprise. "No Deekes? I thought he'd never leave. Father must have booted him out for letting Konstanze leave, eh?"

"I'm afraid your father didn't get the chance."

"Eh?" Bugg II asked, feeling a grin pull at the edges of his mouth. "Didn't get the chance?"

"Your father passed away shortly after you left for Exeter."

"Damn me!" Bugg II exclaimed. "Did he? Bloody hell. What a damned shame."

"Mmm. Yes, it is, really. I expect you shall be in mourning for quite some time."

"He was a good man. Best father a boy could hope for," Bugg II said, enjoying himself. "I'm sorry I couldn't have been here, but I was only doing as he begged me."

"Oh, yes, you were quite the dutiful son," Quarles said, sounding a bit as if he found the entire situation amusing.

Bugg II didn't quite like the sound of that. The solicitor tended to be amused only when someone else was about to get a nasty surprise.

"I found Konstanze," Bugg II said. "She—"

"Was arrested as a thief."

Bugg II gaped at the man. "How did you know that?"

"Her, er . . . friend, Mr. Trewella, contacted me, in a bid to have the charges dropped. Of course, there was nothing I could do to help, as your father was already dead."

"Quite right. A shame for Konstanze, wasn't it?"

"Indeed. And I received word a few days ago that she was convicted of her crime."

"And hanged for it!" Bugg II said happily.

"Not precisely."

"Eh?"

"Shall we go into the office? I have a fire going in there. It's a much more comfortable place to talk."

Bugg II obediently followed the lawyer. "Why hasn't anyone come to take my things inside?" he asked.

"The staff . . . is no longer present," Quarles said. "But about your stepmother, Konstanze—"

"What did you mean by saying she was not hanged?" Bugg II asked, taking a seat. He liked to think he was in a far stronger position now than when he had left on his quest, but Quarles's little smirk was bringing to life a worm of anxiety in his chest.

"Her sentence was commuted to transportation to Botany Bay for a term of seven years."

"What?"

"Yes, your stepmother still lives."

"But—" he started, his mind trying to wrap around this news. "So does that mean she gets the money?"

"No."

Bugg II released a breath and relaxed. "You had me frightened for a moment."

"Perhaps you should still be frightened." Again Quarles had that self-satisfied smirk upon his face. "You do recall that I said your father died shortly after you set off for Exeter?"

"Yes," Bugg II said, the worm of anxiety growing into a veritable snake now, its jaws opening wide to swallow his heart.

"And you do remember what I said about his will, that all but ten pounds a year was to go to Konstanze?"

"Yes; but if she died first I was supposed to get it all. If she doesn't get it, then who does? Not you, I warrant! I'll see you in the courts if that's what you're trying to pull!" Bugg II exclaimed, jumping to his feet.

"No, not I. There is one other player in this pretty drama."

"What? Who?"

"The Crown."

Bugg II's eyes went wide. "You don't mean—"

"Your father died. His estate went to Konstanze. Konstanze was then convicted of a felony, and at that moment all her wealth was forfeit to the Crown. I am only here today to complete the inventory of the house. The contents will be auctioned off this Saturday."

"Bloody hell . . ." Bugg II moaned, his world going black around him, the snake swallowing his heart and then squirming down to sup on liver and intestines for good measure. "It can't be."

"Take heart, old boy," Quarles said, slapping him on his back. "You've still got the ten pounds a year."

# Chapter Twenty-three

*The prison hulk* Dunkirk

Slivers of orange sunset peeped through the dark blue-gray clouds, the only hint of color in the chiaroscuro scene outside the barred port. Konstanze knew it had been a cannon that had once sat where she did now, peering out into the falling night. The *Dunkirk* had once been a warship.

She'd been locked inside its hull for ten days now. Two of the women with whom she had boarded had since died of typhus, and of the thirty or so surviving inmates at least two-thirds were infected. She didn't know if she was worsening or if it was only the lack of proper food and clean air that had her so weak it was all she could do to sit up.

Where was Tom? When would he come?

The trick of losing herself in fantasy had helped

Lisa Cach

keep her sane in Launceston Jail and here in the hulk. She knew that if she'd had to live in the full awareness that the others endured she would have gone raving mad weeks ago.

Sometimes she came to her senses enough to watch the other women, and see how some of them almost seemed to thrive in the hulk. They made whispered arrangements with the guards, and disappeared for a few hours, only to reappear looking cleaner and rather smug. They jockeyed for position in the pathetic hierarchy of prisoners, taking for themselves the best places to sleep—if any place could be called better than another—and serving themselves first from the bucket of soup or gruel that was given at noon. They never took a turn at cleaning out the waste buckets.

Konstanze stayed as far away from them all as she could. After a time the others seemed to accept her as part of the furniture, so to speak, and left her alone. She retreated inward, and in her private world she lived in both the past and the future, but never the present. Every moment with Tom was lived again in her mind, up until they finished their midnight supper and began to leave the kitchen of his house. From there her mind skipped forward, past meeting Bugg II on the street, past the jail and the trial. In her future imaginings Tom came striding into this cell and swept her up into his arms, carrying her out of the death and disease and into a life of sunshine and green hills.

It was an image to which she clung fiercely, elaborating it in her mind, adding details like the smell of the fresh air and the sounds of birds, making the fantasy more specific and realistic. The scene grew so true in her mind that every time footsteps heralded an arrival outside the door she perked up, expecting it to be Tom come to take her away.

Sometimes, when the door opened and it was only a marine who stood there, she wondered if her attempt to save her sanity had itself pushed her over the edge. When she had such a thought she would gaze about her at the bare room, with the straw that was never changed and the crusted filth, and she would decide it was better to be crazy and safe within her own mind than crazy and completely aware in this cell.

Tom would come. He had to come. She had staked her soul upon it.

It was full dark now, and the other women had settled down to sleep. Konstanze realized it must have been hours that she had been sitting near the open port, lost in her own imaginings. Heavy, booted footsteps approached down the passageway, then stopped outside the door. A key turned in the lock, and Konstanze stared toward the sound, and the faint yellow lantern light that came through the small barred window of the door.

The door swung open to reveal a marine, not Tom, holding high his lantern and stepping just inside the cell. She looked away.

"Constance Bugg!" the marine barked. "Which of you is Constance?"

For a moment she didn't think he meant her, but then his words sank into her brain and she understood. "I am," she said, her voice weak, but the cell was quiet enough that he could still hear her.

The marine raised his lantern higher, peering toward her. "Who said that?"

"I did," Konstanze said, raising one hand slightly. "I am Konstanze Bugg."

The marine looked her over and gave a grunt of disgust. "Get off your arse, Constance. There's someone here who's paid a lot to see you."

Hope fluttered up inside her chest, lending her the strength to push herself up to her feet. With chains dragging she slowly made her way to the door.

"Hurry up now!"

She gave him no answer, all her concentration on staying upright. When she finally made it to the marine he grabbed her arm and pulled her from the cell.

"God knows he's going to be sorry when he sees what he's paid for," the marine said. "Come on, we can at least clean you up a bit."

The marine hauled her down the passageway to the foot of a ladder. "Hold still," he directed, and as she held on to the side of the ladder he took out a ring of keys and unlocked the irons from her ankles and waist. "Now clean yourself up," he said, pointing her to a bucket of water and a rag.

She took the two steps over to it, her feet feeling strangely light without the irons, as if they might float away on their own. Her arms were still heavy, though, and when she put her hands in the bucket of cool water she wanted to leave them there.

"Move it!" the marine ordered.

She obeyed, bending down to wash her face, and realized as the water touched her lips that it was fresh, not salt. The pleasure of that coupled with the thought that Tom was waiting for her above gave her another burst of energy, and she scrubbed at her hands and face.

"Good enough," the marine said, and pulled her away, prodding her then to go up the ladder, to where another marine was looking down, waiting. Both of them had to help her up, but at last she was out in the night air. It smelled considerably better above decks than below, although the stench was still enough to knock down a horse.

She was led toward the stern of the ship, where there was a clear portion of deck walled off from sight of the rest of the boat by the makeshift cabins and sheds around it. A figure waited for her there, and she hurried her step, leaving the marines behind.

"Tom . . ." she whispered, coming toward him, and then he stepped out of the shadows and grabbed her by the shoulders, and she saw that it was not Tom at all. It was Foweather.

He stared at her in something akin to horror, his hands holding her in place as much as they held her away from him, and then his expression collapsed into one of incredible sadness. "What have they done to you?" he asked.

She was too stunned to reply, still trying to accept that Tom had not come for her after all.

"Your hair, your lovely hair," Foweather said, looking at what she knew were greasy and snarled locks. "Your face. You have wasted away to nothing. He was right: this would be the death of you."

"Who was right?" Konstanze asked hoarsely.

He met her eyes. "You truly are the mermaid, aren't you?"

She didn't know how to answer that, didn't know what stories might have been poured into his ears, so she said nothing.

"Tom explained it to me. I knew what I had seen was real! I knew it!"

"What did he tell you?" Konstanze asked.

"The truth. I should have seen it for myself. Isn't the world full of stories of mermaids who live amongst us for years, looking as human as anyone else? I know you were trying to go back to your life in the sea, but were torn by your love of humanity, by your love of men."

She was?

"Tom told me that you would die if left aboard the hulk, or transported to Australia. It is too long a time for a mermaid to be out of the water, and I see for myself the truth of that. You are dying."

"Yes, I am," she said. She could agree to that much. "Can you take me from here? Will they let you?"

"I cannot take you, but I can free you," he said, and swept her up in his arms.

Her eyes went wide, her hands clinging to his coat as dizziness hit her. "What are you doing?"

"Tell me one thing," he said, then paused, looking away for a moment. "Did you ever love me?" he asked, looking back at her.

There was such pleading in his eyes, she knew what she had to say. She cupped his soft cheek in one hand. "You are a gentle, noble man. Of course I loved you," she said, and leaning upward she gave him a soft, chaste kiss.

"Then God go with you," he said, and in two strides was at the rail, and with a great heave he tossed her overboard. "Swim!" she heard him call as she fell, "Swim away!"

*He still thinks I'm a mermaid*, Konstanze thought in stunned amazement, and then she hit the water, her back slapping hard against the surface before it swallowed her.

Instinct took over and she struggled for the surface, her weak limbs fighting the water. As she broke up into the air a hand grabbed her out of the dark, and she shrieked and tried to bat it away.

"Shh! It's I, Tom!"

She stilled, then tried to latch on to him, in her joy forgetting that they were in the water at the very side of her prison.

"Konstanze, stop!" Tom ordered, as voices were raised up on deck. "Hang on to this," he said, shoving a buoyant piece of wood into her arms.

"You got her?" a male voice asked from a couple feet away.

"Yes. Do you have your lines?"

"Ready," another voice responded.

Shouts were coming from up on deck now, and arguing.

"I can't swim far," Konstanze said to Tom. "You're going to have to help me."

"Just hang on to the wood, darling."

She obeyed, her legs tired already from treading water.

"Go!" Tom ordered.

The piece of wood was almost torn from her arms, and she clung tighter, pulling herself up so the top of her body was resting on it. She felt where three lines were tied on to the leading edge of it. She was being towed through the water at a weirdly fast pace.

More shouts from behind, and then shots were being fired, plunking into the water several feet away.

"Don't shoot her!" she heard Foweather yelling. "Can't you see, she's a mermaid!"

The angry argument on deck turned to shouts of surprise as the moon came out from behind the clouds, silvering the water. Konstanze saw that three men—Tom one of them—were swimming at the ends of the lines tied to her board, around which a frothy wake was forming as she plowed through the water.

"She's being borne away by seals," Foweather cried. "They have come for her!"

The clouds once again covered the moon, throwing the water into darkness. In a strange silence they moved through the water, no splashing but the soft sound of the wake around the board. The shouts aboard the hulk slowly faded away, the last voice she heard that of Foweather, calling into the night, "Remember me, my mermaid. Remember me. . . ."

Long minutes passed, and then they came up to a small fishing lugger. Men on board reached down and plucked them all from the water, and when Konstanze saw Tom and the others clearly she understood the reason for their unusual speed: they were all three wearing fins like those Hilde had made for her. She started to laugh.

"Hush," Tom said, gathering her up into his arms, both of them dripping wet. Someone tossed a blanket over them, and Tom pulled her out of the way as the men raised a dark sail. "Hush now. You're safe."

Her laughter turned to tears as she lay against his chest. "I knew you would come," she said. And then she lost consciousness.

She awoke in a narrow bunk, the white cabin filled with diffuse sunlight from a porthole and from the heavy glass prisms set in the deck overhead. The room swayed with the rhythmic motion of a ship under sail. She felt weak but cool, her body clothed only in a nightgown that still held the scents of a recent washing. There was something on her forehead, and she lifted her hand to touch a damp cloth.

"You're finally awake," Hilde said in German, taking away the cloth and rinsing it in a basin.

Konstanze turned her head, seeing the familiar, beloved face of her maid. "Hilde."

Hilde wrung out the cloth and put it back on her forehead. "Your fever is almost gone. You will be a lucky one and live, I think."

"Where are we?"

"A ship. Mr. Trewella calls it a privateer. After he got you onto that little fishing boat, you were brought here and transferred."

"Where is Tom?"

"Pacing, I think. We tell him to sleep, but he does not. I sent him away a few minutes ago, telling him to go eat. He was annoying me."

Konstanze smiled.

385

The door opened, and Hilde gave a fierce frown, but Konstanze's smile only grew wider. "Tom!"

Seeing her awake he came quickly to her side, taking her hand. "How are you feeling?"

"Clean."

"I gave you a good bath," Hilde said.

"Would you excuse us for a bit?" Tom asked Hilde. "You need to get something to eat, yourself."

Hilde narrowed her eyes at him, then straightened the sheet covering Konstanze before leaving the cabin.

Konstanze felt as if she could lie where she was, staring at Tom, for the rest of her life. "You are well? Your wound has healed completely?" she asked, wanting him to come lie beside her, to hold her.

"Nearly as good as new," he said, patting his side. "I was lucky."

"I wouldn't have survived, if you had not," Konstanze said.

The comment seemed to pain him. "Don't say that."

"It's true. You were all that kept me alive. I knew that you would come for me."

"I could never have left you there."

"How did you get Foweather to help? What did you tell him? He said some strange things to me."

Tom grimaced. "May God forgive me for being such a liar. I wouldn't have even asked for his help except I knew that those marines would never have let me aboard. But a Preventive man—they would trust him. I only hope he was not punished for throwing you overboard.

"But to answer your question: I told Foweather that you were a mermaid who had been living as a human

386

for several years, but that your husband had discovered your secret, so you fled. Mermaids, selkies, fairies, they all do that in the stories. I said that you were indeed the daughter of Penperro's first mermaid, and that you wanted to find a new husband before you returned to the sea, and that you had been having a hard time deciding. I told him I had fallen in love with you and managed to turn your affections from him, and then I begged for his forgiveness and his help. I let him know that he would be the true hero of the story if he could do as I asked and free you, despite the hurt he had suffered."

"And he believed you?"

"I think he preferred to believe me. It hurt less to be betrayed by a lovesick friend than to have been made the butt of a colossal joke. He's a hero now, in his own mind and in the minds and hearts of the people of Penperro. They have a new ending to their mermaid tale."

They were both silent then, just being in each other's presence enough for the moment. Tom stroked her cheek with his fingertips. "There is something I should have said to you long ago," Tom finally said. "And something I should have asked you."

"Yes?"

He looked down at the hand he still held, and she felt him gently rubbing her knuckles. Then he met her eyes. "I love you, Konstanze. With all my heart. It took nearly losing you for me to see what should have been obvious. Everything in which I once took joy turned to dust when you were taken away. Nothing was worthwhile. Nothing had any meaning, not even work. There was nothing to which to look forward."

A smile curved her lips. For all that she had told herself she could live content without hearing those words from Tom, they were sweet balm to her soul, giving her a sense of warm security that even this ship or his arms could not.

"Konstanze, will you marry me?"

"Yes, Tom. I will."

He embraced her then, pulling her up into his arms and holding her gently, as if afraid of her fragility. She pressed her face into his neck, feeling his kisses at the side of her face. Then a thought hit her, and she pulled back.

"But Tom—I'm a fugitive now."

"A fugitive in England, perhaps, but not in America."

"America?"

"Tomorrow we will meet up with the *Swallow,* a ship bound for America. It will take us to Boston."

"But your business, the smuggling, your house—"

He smoothed her hair back from her face. "It meant nothing without you. I've liquidated what I could, and Matt will oversee selling off the rest. Some of the shipping contracts I will be able to retain. We have enough to make a new start for ourselves in a new world."

"I thought you never wanted love to overrule work. Why did you sell everything for which you've worked so hard?"

He held her face between his hands and kissed her firmly on the mouth before replying. "There's no point to working for wealth if I have no one upon whom to spend it." He grinned. "And besides, I hear there are all manner of opportunities for enterprising men in America."

"Will you promise me one thing?"

"Anything."

"No more mermaids."

He laughed. "I promise. No more mermaids." He eased her back down and picked up the damp rag, rinsing it again in the basin before replacing it on her forehead. "Do you suppose they have banshees in America? You could do that wailing quite well. Perhaps—"

She flung the damp cloth at him.

He caught the cloth and gave an exaggerated sigh. "So it's honest citizens we're to be?"

"To our dying day."

"For you, I can do anything. Even that."

# *Epilogue*

*Penperro*

The midsummer fair was in full swing, the streets crowded with visitors. It had been nearly fifteen years since Hilde had first seen the fair, and at long last the associations she had with it had begun to weigh more heavily on the positive side than on the negative.

"I want a good seat," she said in German to Matt, to whose arm she clung. He had grown stockier in the time she'd known him, and his hair had gotten wilder. He was a good husband, and she did not regret her decision to let Konstanze go to America without her. There was a time when you had to let your ducklings swim off into the world on their own. Konstanze was singing on the stage now in America, with Tom providing financial support for her preferred productions.

"You've seen this play a dozen times," Matt complained in English. Their conversations were always held this way, with each speaking their native tongue.

"Don't play the sour-faced old man. You want to see it as much as I do."

"Woman, when have I ever been sour-faced?"

"When are you not?"

He grunted, and she smiled. She liked his grumpiness, and sometimes suspected he played it up to please her. He was the type of man children liked to pretend to be afraid of, but they followed him around like stray dogs after a bone.

She needn't have worried about the seats. The same as every year, there were two places in the front row of the temporary outdoor theater reserved for her and Matt. They were the living link between the present and a past that had become a fairy tale, even to those who had been adults when the mermaid had come to Penperro.

"I wish Foweather could have seen this," Matt said. He would repeat the sentiment when the final curtain came down on *The Mermaid and Her Lovers*. It was part of their tradition.

Foweather had died eight years ago, during the heroic rescue of a foundering fishing vessel during a storm. A bronze plaque in the harbor wall commemorated his bravery, as well as his part in the now much-altered mermaid story. He had become the tragic figure in a legendary love triangle, his character in the play sighed over by young girls.

"I think he watches," Hilde said. "He's immortal now."

# Bewitching The Baron

## Lisa Cach

Valerian has always known before that she will never marry. While the townsfolk of her Yorkshire village are grateful for her abilities, the price of her gift is solitude. But it never bothered her until now. Nathaniel Warrington is the new baron of Ravenall, and he has never wanted anything the way he desires his people's enigmatic healer. Her exotic beauty fans flames in him that feel unnaturally fierce. Their first kiss flares hotter still. Opposed by those who seek to destroy her, compelled by a love that will never die, Nathaniel fights to earn the lone beauty's trust. And Valerian will learn the only thing more dangerous—or heavenly—than bewitching a baron, is being bewitched by one.

___52368-X                                    $5.50 US/$6.50 CAN

# The CHANGELING BRIDE

## LISA CACH

In order to procure the cash necessary to rebuild his estate, the Earl of Allsbrook decides to barter his title and his future: He will marry the willful daughter of a wealthy merchant. True, she is pleasing in form and face, and she has an eye for fashion. Still, deep in his heart, Henry wishes for a happy marriage. Wilhelmina March is leery of the importance her brother puts upon marriage, and she certainly never dreams of being wed to an earl in Georgian England—or of the fairy debt that gives her just such an opportunity. But suddenly, with one sweet kiss in a long-ago time and a faraway place, Elle wonders if the much ado is about something after all.

___52342-6                              $4.99 US/$5.99 CAN

# *Aphrodite's Kiss*

## *Julie Kenner*

Crazy as it sounds, on her twenty-fifth birthday Zoe has the chance to become a superhero. But x-ray vision and the ability to fly are only two things to consider. There is also her newfound heightened sensitivity. If she can hardly eat a chocolate bar without convulsing in ecstasy, how is she to give herself the birthday gift she's really set her heart on— George Taylor? The handsome P.I.'s dark exterior hides a truly sweet center, and Zoe feels certain that his mere touch will send her spiraling into oblivion. But the man is looking for an average Jane no matter what he claims. He can never love a superhero-to-be—can he? Zoe has to know. With her super powers, she can only see through his clothing; to strip bare the workings of his heart, she'll have to rely on something a little more potent.

___52438-4                                          $5.99 US/$6.99 CAN

# A Passionate Magic
## Flora Speer

Sent as an offering of peace between two feuding families, Lady Emma is prepared to perform her wifely duties. But when she first lifts her gaze to the turquoise eyes of her lord, she senses that he is the man she has seen in her most intimate visions. Dain of Penruan has lived an austere life in his Cornish castle on the cliffs, and he doesn't intend to cease doing so, regardless of this arranged marriage to the daughter of his father's hated rival. But though he attempts to disdain Lady Emma, the lusty lord can not ignore her lush curves, or the strange amethyst light sparkling from the depths of her chestnut eyes. Perched upon the precipice of a feeling as mysterious and poignant as silvery moonlight on the sea, Lady and Lord plunge into a love that can only have been conjured by . . . a passionate magic.

___52439-2                                                          $5.50 US/$6.50 CAN

# Alicia's Song

## Susan Plunkett

For Alicia James, something is missing. Her childhood romance hadn't ended the way she dreamed, and she is wary of trying again. Still, she finds solace in her sisters and in the fact that her career is inspiring. And together with those sisters, Alicia finds a magic in song that seems almost able to carry away her woes.

In fact, singing carries Alicia away—from her home in modern-day Wyoming to Alaska, a century before her own. There she finds a sexy, dark-haired gentleman with an angelic child just crying out for guidance. And Alicia is everything this pair desperately needs. Suddenly it seems as if life is reaching out and giving Alicia the chance to create a beautiful music she's never been able to make with her sisters—all she needs is the courage to sing her part.

\_\_\_52434-1                                        $4.99 US/$5.99 CAN

*. . . and coming*
*May 2001*
*from . . .*

# Moonshadow

# PENELOPE NERI

"Lillies-of-the-valley," he murmurs, "the sweet scent of innocence." Yet his kisses are anything but innocent as he feeds her deepest desires while honeysuckle and wild roses perfume the languid air.

"Steyning Hall. It is a cold place. And melancholy," he warns, "almost as if it is . . .waiting for someone. Perhaps your coming will change all that."

Wedded mere hours, Madeleine gazes up at the windows of the mansion, stained the color of blood by the dying sun. In the shifting moonshadows she hears voices calling, an infant wailing, and knows not whether to flee for her life or offer up her heart.

___52416-3                                    $5.99 US/$6.99 CAN